Natural Mage

Also by K.F. Breene

DDVN WORLD:

FIRE AND ICE TRILOGY
Born in Fire
Raised in Fire
Fused in Fire

MAGICAL MAYHEM SERIES
Natural Witch
Natural Mage
Natural Dual-Mage

FINDING PARADISE SERIES
Fate of Perfection
Fate of Devotion

DARKNESS SERIES
Into the Darkness, Novella 1
Braving the Elements, Novella 2
On a Razor's Edge, Novella 3
Demons, Novella 4
The Council, Novella 5
Shadow Watcher, Novella 6
Jonas, Novella 7
Charles, Novella 8
Jameson, Novella 9
Darkness Series Boxed Set, Books 1-4

WARRIOR CHRONICLES
Chosen, Book 1
Hunted, Book 2
Shadow Lands, Book 3
Invasion, Book 4
Siege, Book 5
Overtaken, Book 6

Natural Mage

K.F. Breene

Contact info:
www.kfbreene.com
books@kfbreene.com

CHAPTER 1

"PENNY, HURRY UP and come down. Half of them are already here."

I froze in front of the full-length mirror on my walk-in closet door, listening to see if my new landlord, Callie Banks, would yell up any more instructions.

"Penny?"

Not instructions, then...a warning posed as a question.

"Be right down," I called, because otherwise she'd come up, grab me by the hair, and drag me.

I'd exchanged an overbearing mother for an overbearing trainer. My decision-making skills still needed improvement.

Taking a deep breath, I smoothed the faux-silk lilac dress down my stomach and breathed in deeply, trying to ignore the nervous tremors.

Tonight Callie and her husband Dizzy were formally introducing me to their large and influential magical circle. I was a real mage now, with a couple months of training under my belt and power enough to rival the best of the best. Or so they told me.

Truth was, power alone wasn't enough, something I'd learned firsthand from working closely with Emery, the natural mage who'd gone rogue from the magical community. *He* was the best of the best…no, *together* we were the best of the best. With his power, experience, and know-how, and my…well, power and temperamental intuition, we'd pulled off the impossible—an attack on the Mages' Guild's stronghold in Seattle. Without him, I felt like a novice with a lot to learn.

My heart ached whenever I thought of the handsome natural mage who had woken me up in so many ways. We'd spent hardly any time together, but it felt like we'd known each other for a lifetime, and with him gone, a piece of me was gone with him. My mother thought I was foolish, and the Bankses thought I was naive, but it didn't matter. The sound of his name, the memory of being ensnared in his magic and his arms, still affected me.

I'd let him walk away in Seattle, and at the time, everything in my person had thought he'd come right back. That he wouldn't be gone a week. Couldn't be, not after what we'd shared.

That was six months ago.

I needed to stop thinking about him. At this point, I looked every bit the fool my mother thought I was. But that didn't change the fact that he was a benchmark for what I could be—what I *should* be, as a natural—and that I had a lot to learn…with no time in which to learn it.

The Mages' Guild had rebounded from the break-in faster than anybody could've guessed. They'd changed their wards, repaired their buildings, and expanded their influence within Seattle and surrounding areas. They were creating a solid foundation with which to go after the naturals who'd escaped them.

Emery and me.

I had no doubt they'd move in as soon as they locked down their targets.

It was only a matter of time. Which meant I needed as many friends as I could get.

So tonight I'd slapped on a dress, curled my hair, and dabbed on some makeup, all in a play to make nice with the New Orleans magical community. I needed them to accept me. To stand by my side when the Guild came for me.

They'll never be enough.

I gritted my teeth against my inner dialogue, trying to pretend I didn't feel the truth in that statement. Because they would have to be enough. They were all I had.

"Penny?" Callie called up, and this time it wasn't a warning. It was a threat.

"Yup. Coming!"

I wondered how long it would take me to out myself as a socially awkward and seriously weird person…

My phone clattered against my desk on the other side of the room. I gritted my teeth, knowing exactly who it was. A quick jaunt over showed I'd been right.

My mother.

She'd stayed behind to both give me my space (proof that miracles did happen) and to monitor the mood and tone of Seattle, all from the safety of a couple towns away. No one would admit it, but I suspected Darius, the vampire with his influence all over my life at the moment, wanted her out of the way so I could get training without a peanut gallery.

I had no complaints.

Her text read, "*Don't be fooled, the proof is in the pudding.*"

I stared at it for a second. What the heck did that mean?

Not like I'd text back and ask. She'd turn it into a half-hour conversation about all the things I wasn't doing that I should be, like flossing. And studying harder.

"Hey." My bestie, Veronica, peeked her head into the room. She'd decided to make the move to New Orleans with me. Originally, she'd intended to get her own place, but Callie had taken control of the situation.

She'd offered Veronica to stay at the house with us for cheap. She even got a break on rent when she straightened up Dizzy's constant messes, which, being an organizational freak, Veronica was all too happy to do (much to Dizzy's dismay).

At least I had one ally, even if a non-magical one.

"Wow, you look great," I said. She was dressed in a form-fitting black dress that accentuated her curves and gave the viewer an eyeful of her bust. Would I fit into a dress like that? Maybe she'd be willing to trade.

"You better get going," she said, looking me up and down. Her brow furrowed. "Why'd you pick such a hideous dress?"

Maybe not…

"What?" I plucked at the fabric, putting the phone back. "What's wrong with it?"

She tilted her head. "It's just… It doesn't suit you. You look like a flat stick that would break in a slight breeze. And the color…"

I smoothed the fabric down my legs. "What's wrong with pastel purple?"

"It just…makes you look sickly. Like you have a brain tumor."

"That's specific." This was a classic example of her inability to gently break bad news. "Also…a flat stick?"

"Flat-chested. You know what I mean."

"And you're an editor?"

"Give me a break. I fix this stuff, not make it up from scratch."

"Penny Bristol, if I have to come up there—"

Veronica's eyes widened. "Dude, you gotta go!" She hurried forward and grabbed my arm, leading me from the room. "She's super stressed. She spent the morning yelling at Dizzy and the caterers. All the hiccups you've been having in training have put her on edge."

"I wouldn't say *all* the hiccups…" A heavy weight settled over my shoulders and my stomach flipped in anxiety.

I'd stayed in Seattle for a while after Emery had left, helping my mother get set up and waiting for Callie and Dizzy to be ready for me. A couple of months later, I finally made the trek, only to be knocked completely out of my comfort zone.

The dual-mages didn't work with me the way Emery had. He and I had hung out in my magical bubble, a place of balance that made working magic easier, collectively weaving the spells from the materials we felt in our surroundings. My studies with Callie and Dizzy were so much more clinical. Standing at a distance, they would give me the recipe for the spell, I'd memorize it, and then I'd perform it like a trained monkey.

At first the change in technique had badly jammed me up, making me useless for a couple days straight. Finally I'd stopped for a moment, closing my eyes and tuning in to nature. Callie had thought I was cracked, but it was a compromise that seemed to work. After I got the hang of it, I could replicate the spells just fine, fast and effortlessly.

The problem happened when they threw something unexpected at me and wanted me to randomly choose a spell I'd learned and fire it back. Half the time, my mind shorted out and went blank. I stood there like an idiot, grasping at air. Eventually I could come up with something, but my reaction time was slow.

They said it would take practice, but I felt like I'd accidentally stomped on the brakes and couldn't figure out how to shift my foot to the gas. I should've been further along by now, especially with the Mages' Guild out for vengeance.

Something was missing…or maybe someone.

"Come on, hurry," Veronica said, giving me a little tug, shaking me out of my nervous reverie. "You do not want to get on her bad list right now."

"I'm on her bad list at least three times a day."

"Trust me, that's a different bad list. Dizzy usually yells back at her when she's being a bully, but not this time. He went and hid in his shed."

Yikes. That *was* bad.

"Ah. There you are." Callie stood at the bottom of the stairs with her hand on the banister. Her long black dress had a frilly neckline that plunged down her chest.

A sparkly red something or other under it kept the situation from being a peep show. "The guests are anxious to meet you."

Butterflies swarmed my belly. If I'd learned anything during this short trip into the magical world, it was that I was the least mage-like person possible.

"What do you have on…" Callie's voice trailed away as she dropped her hand. She sighed and shook her head. "It doesn't matter. You're pretty despite that dress. Next time, though, pick something a little less…"

"Dreadful," Veronica said. Callie nodded.

"It wasn't as awful as the one on the rack next to it," I muttered, reaching up to tuck a strand of hair behind my ear.

Veronica slapped my hand away. "Don't ruin your hair."

"Then next time, pick a better store." Callie motioned me down. "Hurry up. John is here. I'm going to parade you around to everyone else before introducing you to him. I want to see if he cuts the line." A wry grin twisted her lips.

"John is…?" I asked, climbing down the stairs reluctantly, hearing the murmuring from the next room. Veronica trailed after me.

"A high-powered mage," she said. "He may be more powerful than I was before I formed a dual-mage partnership with Dizzy. He'd be a good match for you,

Penny. He'd complement you nicely." When I got on her level, she shrugged. "Worst case, he'd be a good rebound. Maybe you'd stop sulking about that Rogue Natural leaving. His loss. You need to move on."

I blew out a breath to calm the sudden churning of my stomach. I did need to move on, but…

"Oh, there you are." Dizzy hurried toward us as I reached the landing. My mouth dropped open in shock at the sight of a crisp suit without one stain or burn mark on it. "The guests are wondering where the star of the show is." His kind smile loosened my shoulders a little, but didn't do a thing to calm down the butterflies. "You look beautiful. The belle of the ball. Just don't let on that you're hiding tiger claws behind your pretty face."

"Because I'll seem less ladylike?" I asked in confusion.

"Goodness, no." Dizzy laughed and squeezed between Callie and me before bending an arm around my back and leading me forward. "What an absurd thought. No, you shouldn't show that side of yourself because right now you're giving an illusion of daintiness. Many will take that for weakness. You look soft and willowy and in need of guidance. Let them think that's your sum total. They'll let down their guard and reveal their secrets. We don't fear people we perceive to be weaker than ourselves, so we aren't as worried about our vulnerabilities in their presence. See what I'm saying?"

"Yes."

"There's a good girl." He patted my shoulder jovially.

"I was just telling her about John," Callie said from behind us in a low murmur.

"Oh yes. He has a lot of power and the ladies seem to like him. He'd be one to chat with, for sure. That would be a good match."

"He's a little shy on power for her, but she can't expect to find another natural," Callie said.

"Yes, that's true," Dizzy said. "Here we are."

A crowd of people stood within the large living room. Off to the side, a bartender in a black uniform mixed a drink at the mobile bar for one of the women waiting at the counter. Most of the furniture had been removed and little tables dotted the ample space. Larger tables topped with food, plates, and utensils lined the back wall.

A few people carrying crystal goblets sauntered in from the formal dining room around the back corner. If Callie had pulled out all the stops, which she surely had, her china would be out and crystal glittering. She wasn't usually a show-off, but clearly these events warranted a reminder to the community of all that she and Dizzy had accomplished.

"Penny, let me introduce you to Mary Bell." Dizzy stopped us in front of a petite woman losing the fight to gravity. Her skin hung from her hunched frame and her braless lovelies dangled just above her waistline within her loose shirt.

With a smile, she reached forward a hand. "Pleased to meet you, Penny. Welcome."

Her grip nearly crunched my bones. "Charmed," I wheezed out.

"Yes." She braced her hands on the ball of her cane, her serene smile belied by the fierce glint in her eyes. "You are a lovely little creature. So late to the magical life. How will you adjust?"

"Badly, probably," I said honestly.

Her smile grew. "Yes. Probably. But it is not what happens to us that matters the most—it is how we respond to it. Don't let anyone put you in a place you don't wish to be."

"Mary Bell is a powerful mage," Dizzy said as Callie strutted toward the food table, where an older woman hovered indecisively over a plate of shrimp. "She has done some truly great spell work in the years we've known her."

Mary Bell's eyes sparkled as she surveyed me. "You don't care for any of that, do you, child?"

I jerked straighter, wondering what my face was showing. "I do, of course! I really do!" I needed to tone down my forced enthusiasm.

The older woman chuckled softly. "I have never met a powerful mage that wasn't also ambitious. They always want to know how they can better their position. The amount of knowledge I can offer you has exponentially increased."

Dizzy and I both shifted, in opposite directions, and I could tell we were equally confused.

Mary Bell picked up on it. "You see, I thought you'd want to talk about unique spells, ancient relics, and whatever else you might pry out of my dementia-ridden grasp."

"Good grief," I whispered, fidgeting with the neck of my dress.

"I didn't realize you had dementia," Dizzy said conversationally, and somehow, when he said it, it didn't sound quite so socially awkward. I needed to learn that trick.

"I don't have dementia," Mary Bell said brusquely, and an edge crept into her voice that had my small hairs rising. "But most younger people like Penny don't realize that. They see an old woman with a stoop and a smile and assume she is two seagulls shy of a flock."

"Seagulls…right…" Dizzy drew out the words.

"But were they to stop talking and *listen*, they would learn that I possess a wealth of knowledge from being a dual-mage near the top of my discipline, from traveling the world and battling the wicked. They might stop their reductive thinking that magic itself is good or evil." She raised a gnarled finger. "When it comes to magic, the perceived nature of the spell itself is not what matters—it is the intent with which the mage *uses* the spell. There is no inherent right and wrong. No light and dark. There is just magic, and how we manipulate it to serve our own ends. After all, sometimes one must commit darker deeds to ensure the greater good."

"The view on magic is true enough, but the darker deeds issue…" Dizzy waggled his hand and moved his head from side to side, as though debating the legitimacy of her statement.

I, however, was in rapture. It sounded exactly like something Emery would say. I liked the image of a fat, gray, fuzzy line cutting through the light and dark of magic. Nature would exist there in the middle, harsh and brutal, serene and bountiful. Life ending in death. Death creating life.

"Yes." Mary Bell's stare held mine. "Penny is not the mage I expected to meet tonight. How refreshing. I myself was a headstrong, entitled youth…I only wish I had started the journey as unburdened by hubris as she is. It wasn't until everything was stripped from me—my love, my youth, my strength—that I learned what was truly important."

"Hm." Dizzy nodded, but I could see he was probably back to thinking of dementia. He smiled and stepped away, holding out his arm so that I might join him. "Thank you, Mary Bell, for coming."

"She battled wicked people?" I asked in a hush as we made our way to a group of men and women sitting around one of the tables.

"I didn't actually know her then. I did hear that she and her dual-mage partner were always described as a wild pair. They got into lots of trouble. Dabbled in the dark arts once or twice." He slowed and turned a little before we reached the table. "She is on the straight and narrow now, but be careful what you take away from speaking with her." He met my eyes and held them. "There is a side to magic that can corrupt the soul."

CHAPTER 2

A COUPLE HOURS into what had become the longest, most name-riddled night of my life, I was standing with Callie as she trundled through the same conversation we'd had over and over since the beginning of the evening.

"We're just going over the basics right now," Callie said to Aileen, a pudgy, middle-aged woman with a perma-smile. Even when her brow furrowed, she still smiled. It was the strangest thing. "She didn't even know that vampires existed a year ago, let alone how to create a spell." They laughed as though that was the most absurd thing either one of them had ever heard. "But we'll get there."

"What spells and lessons are you starting with?" Aileen asked, and I clenched my jaw so I didn't mouth Callie's response, which I knew would be exactly the same as the last five times I'd heard it.

But before she could recite the tediously familiar words, a man's voice sounded from behind us.

"Callie Banks, long time, no see."

Callie stiffened and a delighted grin crept up her face. She didn't glance back, and her tightening fingers on my arm said I shouldn't either.

An imposing presence moved up along my side, a hair too close for comfort.

"John. How lovely of you to make it." Callie turned slowly, a move that spoke of having the upper hand. In what, I didn't know.

John, standing with a slightly puffed-out chest, showered us with a charming smile. His teeth glittered, so white that I nearly squinted.

"Hello, ladies," he said. "Great to see you again." He smiled down at Aileen, who giggled dramatically.

Confused by Aileen's girly reaction, I couldn't help but frown as I studied him. With a broad nose to match his wide face, a chin that was trying to hide from the world, and a hairline that was running from the chin, he wasn't anything special. But even Callie had sparkles in her eyes, relishing his presence. Others in the room, girls and guys alike, were glancing his way fervently, like he was some sort of celebrity.

What was I missing? Did mages truly value power this much?

"And you must be Penelope Bristol," John said, his smile just a little sly.

"Yes. Hello." I stuck out my hand, and he took it gently, his palm smooth and soft, the opposite of

Emery's.

I gritted my teeth and glanced away, pushing the thought from my head. I couldn't very well get over him if I kept mentally bringing him up. I spied Veronica in the corner talking to some older man with long white hair encircling a shiny bald spot on the top of his head. She glanced over and saw me before raising her eyebrows, asking if I needed saving.

Hold that thought, Veronica.

"You're a natural, did I hear that right?" John asked, bending a little to recapture my gaze.

"That's what they tell me." I shrugged. "I'm new to all this."

"So you don't really know if you have enough power to be a natural?"

"She doesn't, but I do," Callie said, stepping closer. "She kept pace with the Rogue Natural. *He* was the one who first declared her a natural. He would know."

"Or maybe he was just telling a beautiful woman what she wanted to hear." John's smile was kind, but his tone made me want to punch him.

"I'm not interested in defining my power level," I said, ready to scooch away. "I just want to learn how my magic works, then get better at it."

"A mage who doesn't want to reap the rewards of being the best in the business?" John rolled back onto his heels and looked around the room incredulously.

Everyone within earshot chuckled, sharing the joke. Callie's face reddened, and I couldn't tell if it was out of embarrassment for me, or anger at his joke.

As usual tonight, I'd missed the punch line.

"I assume you don't mean rewards as in being able to do more advanced spells," I said, "since my outlook would have no bearing on that. So what type of rewards would I get just by being a natural?"

He looked around the room again (his audience) like I was daft. "You'd be the best in the room, for one." He lifted his eyebrows at Aileen, who giggled like a schoolgirl while nodding knowingly. "You're new to all this, but eventually you'll come to realize the importance of respect. Position. Authority."

"I guess that's why I haven't seen you before," I said without thinking, connecting the dots. "You can't be the best in the room when Callie and Dizzy are present."

Shocked silence fell over the room. John's eyes narrowed and his face flushed, anger brewing below the surface. I'd stripped away his varnish.

This was the wrong way to make allies. I *knew* I'd be terrible at this.

I opened my mouth to apologize, but he was already talking.

"That problem will be solved when I find someone worthy to be my dual-mage partner," he said in a low tone, the challenge to Callie clear.

She bristled and squared off with him. Prickles of anticipation rolled across my skin. The room held its breath.

I looked for magic to rise around us, weaving into a spell. I waited for the intent of the spell to give its purpose away.

That failing, I looked for a capsule dug out of a pocket. *Something.*

The two mages stared at each other. Soft jazz played in the background.

And then it occurred to me.

They couldn't do a danged thing. Neither had a satchel (no one did—there must've been a rule against it at a gathering), and I was sure neither could fight physically. For one, Callie was too old. But also, John's hands were too thin and his body too gangly. He probably hadn't so much as slapped a younger sibling. They weren't naturals, so they couldn't weave spells from the elements around them like Emery and I could. They were at a standstill, which meant the two powerful mages had to be content with a hard-faced stare-down.

Laughter bubbled up at the absurdity of it all. Of the swagger and wealth on display tonight. Of the ladies' fawning over the frankly unimpressive John simply because he was powerful…under the right circumstances.

We could hardly hope the circumstances would be

"right" when the Mages' Guild rolled through with their army of trained and attack-ready mages. We'd all be sitting ducks, completely vulnerable.

Tears came to my eyes, and I couldn't be sure if I was crying from fear or from the ludicrousness of the situation. Veronica was by my side in a moment, her hand on my arm.

"Here, look." I shook out of Veronica's grasp and pulled elements—as Emery had always called them—from around the room. Magic rose from the dirt in the potted plant, the cotton in Aileen's pants, the wool in the rug, and dozens of other sources. Colors and patterns streamed toward me before I organized them in a mass just above my head.

I picked and chose what I needed and wove the strands together in a hasty, somewhat messy sort of weave. It was my version of a spell the Bankses had recently taught me, intended to dazzle or surprise.

"What am I looking at?" John said, his charming facade back in place and his smile light and easy. The humor hadn't returned to his eyes.

"That's just it, isn't it?" I pulled the weave taut. "You can't see what I'm doing. You can't see the collection of elements hovering three feet in front of your face."

The last string pulled into place and I let the spell go. It spun and blossomed before ballooning out. An umbrella of flashing colors suddenly covered the room.

Everyone *oohed* and *ahhed*, looking up with wide or blinking eyes. After going through colors of the rainbow three times, the umbrella winked out.

Pop!

The sound was jarring. Women screamed. Men jerked. John bent and threw his hands up over his head, dousing himself in his drink.

"Magic should be marveled at and respected," I said loudly, intending the whole room to hear. No doubt I was making things super awkward again. But I couldn't help it. These mages, who'd been lucky enough to grow up with magic, were so ensnared in one-upmanship that they'd lost sight of what made magic great. "It's natural, it's beautiful, and it exists all around us. It should be revered." I let the elements I'd collected dissipate back into the environment. "It shouldn't be used for some sort of ego boost. If you aren't good enough without magic, then you will never be good enough with it."

Mary Bell rapped her cane on the ground. "Hear, hear!" she shouted.

"I don't have as much exuberance as that woman, but I agree," Veronica said, nodding. Eyebrows rose, and people looked back and forth between Callie and Veronica. John watched her closely as he straightened up.

"Oh…" She pointed at herself. "I'm a nobody. My magic is in my pen. I'm just here for moral support and to make sure my friend doesn't do anything hasty."

I turned toward John, but spoke loudly enough for the others to hear me. "I'm not sure what sort of proof you were looking for. Admittedly, Emery doesn't care about pecking orders. Or sticking around—not that it's given me a complex or anything. I could very well be less powerful than he said. But I don't care about being the best. What I do care about is learning as much as possible. If I don't, the Guild is going to capture me, probably punish me for ruining their compound, and then chain me to their organization. I'm just here to learn. Everything else is a sideshow act."

I paused for effect, but Veronica gave me a small shake before I could continue to spew word salad.

"You should probably stop while you're ahead," she whispered, pulling me away.

She had a fair point, though "ahead" was up for debate.

"I don't think I belong here," I murmured as she led me to the kitchen. "I'm clearly not like these people. They all think I'm nuts."

"Callie and Dizzy don't think you're nuts—"

"They think I'm naive, which is bad enough. Even if it's still mostly true."

"—and that girl Reagan that broke you out of the broom closet in that old church doesn't think you're nuts—"

"That's because she's insane."

"—so I really think you're overreacting. Look." She sat me down at the kitchen island and moved to the cabinet before taking out a bottle of tequila. It was a whiskey house, but I hadn't developed a taste for it. I was just fine with hanging out in Margaritaville. "Had you been trained in all of this from an early age, you'd probably think exactly like they do. It is a learned social structure, and it feels good to be at the top of it. But because you've never fit into *any* social structure…at least not near the top, or in the middle…or kind of even at the bottom—"

"What if I don't want to fit in?"

"Then I can stop lying, because as much as I hope you'll fit in, I'm not sure I actually believe it."

I blew out a breath as she pulled out a bottle of fresh-squeezed lime juice and a shaker. Callie didn't believe in pre-made margarita mixers.

"Emery and I fit together." I put my elbow on the counter and leaned my cheek against my fist. "He thought my quirks made me a better mage. Callie and Dizzy are trying to iron them out."

Veronica grimaced. "Yeah, I don't know what to say about that. I mean, your mom tried to iron out your quirks throughout your life. She's the biggest steamroller in the world, and it didn't work."

"She wasn't trying to teach me magic, though."

"No, she was trying to teach you to fit in."

"Yeah, well, consider the source."

Veronica burst out laughing. "This is true. She is a bit on the eccentric side."

"She's a looney. Clearly that's where I got it from." I massaged my eyes with the heels of my hands. "Was this the right choice? Moving here, being a part of mage society, getting trained by Callie and Dizzy—"

"Yes. And do you know how I know that?"

"How?"

"Your mother stayed in Seattle to passively spy on the Guild, and she left you in their care." Veronica poured the margarita into a glass. "There is no way she would've done that if this wasn't the absolute best thing for you. Maybe the only thing for you."

"True." I sipped my drink and my face instantly contorted, my eye squeezing shut. "You didn't get that drink quite right."

"No?" She tasted it and jerked back. "Definitely not, no. Man, I thought I was better at making these." She dumped the contents back into the shaker. "Anyway, you don't have to fit in, but you should make friends. Acquaintances, at the very least."

"True." I slumped. "Which means I should go back out there and apologize."

"Yeah, probably. Though that guy had it coming. I mean, what sort of douche planet did he come from?

Oh, and he wants to be—"

"Knock, knock."

Veronica froze mid-rant with wide eyes and an open mouth. We both snapped our faces toward the archway to the kitchen, where John stood with his charming, toothpaste-commercial smile. "Penny, got a minute?"

Veronica shot me a *what should I do?* glance.

"It's okay," I said softly, clasping my fingers in front of me.

"Right." Veronica set the mixer on the counter next to my drink. "I'm probably needed out there, anyway. For some reason."

"I just wanted to apologize," John said after she stalked from the room with a straight back. "It sounds silly, but you get caught up in all the politics when it comes to this stuff, you know?"

I didn't, so I chanced a smile.

"You get into the upper levels of magic, and people start expecting certain things from you." He peered into the shaker. "Oh. Here."

"No, it's—" But he was already pouring the still-unsweetened contents into my glass. I chanced another smile. "Great. Thanks."

"Your perspective is fresh." He paused for a beat, and it seemed like he was chancing his own smile that he clearly didn't feel. "I like it." He pushed the glass forward. "Anyway, I get where you're coming from. And I believe you. I mean, I saw it with my own eyes, right? You made magic without having any ingredients in your hands. Unless you were holding a casing I couldn't see..." His voice drifted away and his eyes delved into mine, searching. A moment later, he laughed. "Just kidding." He stuck out his hand. "Friends?"

Veronica was right, this guy was definitely from a douche planet of some sort, but I still needed to make friends and somehow immerse myself into the magical world. He had power and knowledge—he could learn to fight. And would have to, because I'd plop him down on the front line when the Guild charged me.

I put my hand in his. "Friends."

CHAPTER 3

THE NEXT MORNING, I awoke from a *bang!*

"Farmer John's Sausages!" I threw off the covers, waved my hand through the air, and sprang from my bed—all in one harried, dizzied moment. I hit the ground with a solid thunk, echoing the door hitting the wall and rattling off its hinges. A heavy boot landed on the hard wooden floor, and I popped up as streams of magic swirled through the air.

Before my spell was fully realized, the magic dissolved like cotton candy in the rain. Absolutely nothing remained in its absence—no intent, emotion, or residue.

Crap.

Reagan was back in town.

"White flag, white flag," I yelled, waving my hands above my head.

"Your mom really has you trained not to swear, huh?" Reagan stood with her hands at her sides, decked out in head-to-toe leather and thick-soled black army boots. Dirty blond hair was pulled back into a tight ponytail and no eyebrows adorned her expressionless face.

I'd always thought she'd be a real beauty if she weren't so jaw-clenchingly frightening. The no-eyebrows thing only made that worse.

"I mean, you weren't even totally awake, someone barged in, and you yelled about some guy's sausages..." Her bare brows pinched together, which was a very strange sight. "Ah. I get it. Sausages. Okay then, that makes it marginally better."

I decided not to ruin my almost-cool factor by mentioning that I hadn't been thinking of *that* kind of sausage.

"First things first—that was some shoddy spell work." She shifted and I flinched. I couldn't help it. She was one of the most unpredictable people I'd ever met in my life. "Were you even trying on that ward covering the door? It took no time at all to get through it."

"I just learned that ward last week," I said in a slightly higher pitch than I'd intended. "It is the most advanced ward I've ever seen. Callie and Dizzy can't break it."

"I'm not Callie and Dizzy."

"Yeah but...you're not anybody. There is no logical magical explanation for half the stuff you do." Something I had learned firsthand when I was helping her with a situation in Seattle a few months before. I'd helped them take down a couple of mages who were protecting a summoning circle, and also helped dissipate that circle.

She held out a finger, and I readied myself for a blast of fire or something else surprising and horrible.

"That you know of," she said. "You just started learning magic. How could you possibly have explanations for everything?"

"Okay, but..." I narrowed my eyes at her. "Following that logic, you shouldn't be mad at me for putting together the best ward I could. I've just started learning magic."

"Anyone can read a spell out of a book. With power like yours, that's easy. And guess what else is easy? A counter-spell." She leaned against the doorframe, a problem-solving stance, which meant she was less likely to attack me (at the moment). "What you need to do is get creative. You need to use your power in ways people don't expect." She crossed her arms. "I had a lengthy talk with Darius. He thinks you don't go about magic like normal mages. That Rogue Natural mage you know—"

"Emery," I said with a pained release of breath. It would be easier on me if his name would stop coming up.

"—said something to Darius about it. He seemed to think you were more like a witch than a mage, but with a crap-load of power." Reagan tapped her chin.

"I just don't understand how witches and mages are different," I admitted. "Everyone acts like they're so different, but when you drill down to the root, the only real difference is power quantity." I paused, suddenly unsure of myself. Reagan was an encyclopedia of spells and magic. She could read, if not speak, multiple languages. I was confident this was something she'd know about. "Right?"

Reagan's finger stilled. "Yeah. Well, and training. Mages get formal training, and witches work together in circles and kind of learn in a community."

"Formal training like…school? Because my training isn't formal."

"Say that to Callie, I dare you."

I pressed my lips together. No, I would not.

"Mages can visit the Realm, too," she said, "whereas witches can't."

"That's still just power quantity."

"And with vampires, it's just age." She shrugged. "It's a big enough distinction to create two separate groups. Anyway, you're different. You shouldn't just memorize a spell and then plaster it up on your door. That's for Guild members. They're drones. No, you should learn the spell, alter it in your weird way, and *then* string it up. That's how you'll be the best. Because here's the thing…" She straightened up. "Before you came on scene, Darius thought the Rogue Natural was the most talented mage in the world—"

"Emery."

"—but Darius doesn't think so anymore. He thinks you'll surpass the guy."

"I doubt it. Emery is unbelievably adaptable. Everything I came up with, he could alter and enhance on the fly. He is worlds ahead of me and excellent at survival. I don't even have the tools to be better than him."

Reagan's focus homed in on me, and the room stilled for a moment…before she made a sudden movement.

I jerked as though slapped. Magic ballooned in front of me, my reaction speed significantly faster after the last few months of study, but nowhere near as fast as hers. If she wanted to attack me, I'd have to jump from the window to escape. And she was so unhinged, she'd surely jump after me with a manic cackle. She had absolutely no fear.

Reagan finished scratching her chin—*oops*—and then waved her hand through the air. My magic fizzled away with little sparks and spits.

"How do you *do* that?" I muttered, not able to see the magic she used to counter my weave, and not able to get a whiff of intent when she did it. I was flying blind when it came to her. When I didn't get an answer, though, I left it alone. The dual-mages could be prickly about my continuing to ask questions they weren't ready to answer. Reagan was the last person I wanted to piss off.

But I wondered if Emery would know more about her abilities, since he'd traveled far and wide.

I wondered if he would ever come back.

I wondered if I'd stop thinking of him if I started punching myself in the face every time his name popped up.

Reagan crossed her arms and tapped her finger against her chin again. "I think Darius is trying to wind me up."

"Wind you up?" I asked, reaching for my robe while keeping a wary eye on her movements.

"Irritate me. Get me agitated—sorry, I was in London and Ireland for a while. They talk funny." Which she'd probably told them to their faces…and started a bar fight because of it. "He knows that if there's a chance you could be pushed into becoming the best, I'll make sure you reach your full potential. I mean, what else have I got to do with my time, right? I'm supposed to lie low. A hobby would be good for me, and you'd be a worthwhile hobby. But if Darius is just saying you're the unrealized best because he wants me to push you, which will also push the Rogue Natural to be *his* best—"

"Emery."

"—then Darius would be manipulating me to get

what he wants. Which I do not take kindly to. If I find out he's manipulating me, I'll walk from this game. No questions asked. But then, maybe he thinks I'll have a vested interest in you by the time I figure out he's manipulating me, which would make it harder for me to walk." She bit her lip. "Hmm."

I rubbed my temples. "Sorry…*what?*"

Reagan fanned the air like she was trying to rid it of a bad smell, shook her head, and took a step back. "Vampires twist my brain up. It was so much easier when the most confusing part of my day was which pair of leather pants were cleanest. Bottom line, I hate getting involved in vampire politics. Helping you is cool. Helping him is not."

"But…" I just could not get a grip on this conversation. "You and he are an item. You're bonded, and Callie says that's forever. Or until she kills him."

"Yeah. I'm an idiot, aren't I?" She rolled her eyes.

"Reagan, hello," Dizzy said from just outside the door. "Oops, it seems you've misplaced your eyebrows again. I thought you'd moved on from those days?"

"My neighbor surprised me with a blowtorch," she answered. "I got my hair covered in time, but my eyebrows didn't make it."

He *tsk*ed, and I didn't know if that was because of Reagan's slow reaction speed, or her neighbor thinking it acceptable to blast someone in the face with a blowtorch.

I knew she had a strange relationship with fire from when I helped her that time in Seattle, but I'd never gotten to delve further into it. Clearly, this wouldn't be that time, either, because Dizzy had edged into my line of sight, his gaze taking in the damaged door. "Reagan, I thought you weren't supposed to kick in doors in this house."

"Oh yeah." She grimaced.

Dizzy scratched the wispy gray hair on the top of his head. His red shirt was burned and torn in places, and his pants looked like he'd stolen them from a homeless painter. "Callie likes order and intact doors, you know that."

"I do. That was my bad."

"It's not a strange rule, if you think about it," Dizzy continued, still studying the door. "Kicked-in doors are very dramatic. You should only do that when the situation calls for it. Like busting in on the bad guys, or breaking and entering."

"Well…" Reagan gestured at my room at large. "Technically I *was* breaking and entering. She had a ward up and everything. I didn't knock or seek permission to enter. I just busted in. So at least that part of things lines up."

He nodded. "That's true. Okay, then." He trudged past.

Reagan grinned at me, delighted with herself.

"Callie won't be pleased she has to repair my door again," I said.

The smile drifted off Reagan's face. Score one for me!

"You have a package downstairs," she said. "Callie thought you'd want to know."

A shock of adrenaline coursed through me. I tried to bat it down. "Is it from my mother?"

Her eyes started to sparkle and a little grin wrestled her lips. "Nope. Anonymous. Postmark is from Ethiopia. It was delivered by carrier a half-hour ago."

My heart hammered against my ribs. I was running before I could attempt any sort of decorum.

Only one person sent packages like that.

CHAPTER 4

CALLIE WAS AT the stove on the other side of the enormous kitchen, tending something in a pan. The fan wafted the smell of bacon through the air, immediately making me salivate.

On the island sat a small box wrapped in plain brown paper and tied with scratchy brown string. Colorful stamps adorned the top and sides, marring the handwritten address.

I let my hands linger on the counter while analyzing the graceful, tightly knit magic coating the surface of the package. I would have recognized Emery's deft touch anywhere.

I'd received a total of five power stones, nearly one a month since I'd said goodbye to him. He knew how much power stones meant to me, and that I collected them, after a fashion. He also knew where I was staying. He'd not only remembered and was okay with my idiosyncrasies with the power stones (most people laughed when I mentioned that the stones had personalities), but he'd clearly checked up on me to see where I was. The packages never came with a written note—his only signature was his magic, the feel of which only made me miss him more—but at least he hadn't forgotten about me completely.

"I was wondering—" I started.

"Hey!" Callie half spun to look behind her, her brown eyes wide. She had on a bright orange velvet sweat suit with "Queen Bee" written across the backside. "What did I tell you about sneaking around?"

"She all but sprinted in here." Reagan filled the archway of the kitchen. "If you weren't deaf, you would've heard her."

"My hearing is just fine, thank you very much. It's these accursed fans." Callie turned back to the stove.

"Humor…longing…" The words spilled out of my mouth as I studied the nature of the spell, but I didn't want to say the next word out loud. *Lonely.* He wasn't happy. I could feel that hidden in the depths of the weave. He wasn't willing to stay in one place for me, but he missed me, too.

"This is from the Rogue Natural, then?" Reagan asked, sauntering over. "Mr. Impressive Mage the magical world is talking about. He was always on Darius's radar, but now it seems like everyone is talking about him." She ran her hand through the air over the package, her way of feeling out the spell.

"Yes." I chewed my lip and closed my eyes, balancing the magic around me.

"Figures." Callie huffed. "No one ever remembers the woman that helps the hero take down the enemy."

"The woman hasn't been on the run for years, suddenly came back on the grid, then disappeared again. Mysterious is more interesting. Penny has to work on her marketing." Reagan studied the package, ignoring Callie when the older mage told her to quit talking nonsense. "This spell is…wild. Unruly," Reagan said, and I opened my eyes to see the smile curling her lips. Her eyes flashed. "It is fantastically complex. He's got…what, three layers in here? The simplest one is obviously meant to shock any would-be thieves. The others seem…playful. Hmm." Her brow furrowed. "I don't even know the root of these spells. He must've made them up, which is exactly what I told you to do, Penny."

She paused, and her eyes took on a keen light as she cursed softly. "See? Darius was playing me. Do you see how sneaky elder vampires are? Well I'm not so stupid as to fall into his plans, willy-nilly."

"You bonded him, didn't you?" Callie muttered from the stove.

"That was different," Reagan said, her hands still over the box. "My blackened heart was involved in that one." She surveyed me with intense eyes. "The Rogue Natural—"

"Emery."

"Does he subscribe to your improvisational approach to magic?"

"What's that?" Callie asked, moving two strips of bacon to a paper-towel-covered plate.

I closed my eyes, feeling the different layers of the spell that Reagan had sussed out. "He was willing to go along with it."

"But that wasn't his chosen approach?" Reagan asked.

"What are you girls talking about?" Callie demanded. "Reagan, do you want breakfast?"

"I always want breakfast," Reagan said, waiting for my answer.

"You're wanting for some lessons in etiquette," Callie grumbled.

"His magic was wilder," I said. "But he usually did follow spells. I was the one that created things out of the blue."

"Well that was only because you didn't know any spells." Callie transferred more bacon before tucking the plate into the oven to keep it warm. She grabbed more bacon from the fridge. It was widely known that Reagan had the appetite of an NFL linebacker. How she didn't gain any weight was beyond me. "Now that you do, Penny, you'll be much better equipped."

Reagan dropped her hands, a troubled look on her

eyebrow-less face. "I told you, I don't think that's the right way to go. Even if we had all the time in the world, it seems like such a waste to turn her into a drone like everyone else. She's different. She should celebrate that."

"Do you think I'm a drone?" Callie half turned.

"Tricky question, that..." Reagan comically grimaced.

Callie huffed. "What's your point?"

"The marks who are predictable are easy. I can gag 'em and bag 'em in my sleep. It's the brainy ones that keep me guessing, that are incredibly risky to take down."

"Penny doesn't need to keep people guessing. She has power in spades," Callie said.

"Compared to you." Reagan held up a finger. "But she is not the most powerful magical creature in the Brink, and certainly not in the Realm. Going up against someone like Darius will get her killed if she relies on cookie-cutter spells. He'd outthink her in a heartbeat and break her neck in the next."

"I hate these talks," I muttered, weaving magic together.

"Even in the Brink—"

"That's where we are now," Callie cut in.

"I remember," I said, coating my counter-spell over Emery's first spell. I held it there for a moment, feeling the soft intent of his magic. Remembering his teasing, and the yield of his lips. Letting myself feel the connection to him.

"Even in the Brink," Reagan started again, "you have naturals. Not many, no, but the Guild has a couple, last I heard. Those naturals have just as much power as Penny. And they have more books from which to pull spells, and more experience hurtling them at an enemy. If all she does is learn the way everyone else has learned, she'll be outgunned. No, her power is in her uniqueness."

"That's basically what Emery always said." I broke the spell apart, leaving the other two, which were woven tightly together.

"Who's Emery?" Reagan asked.

"Do you have a block for a head?" Callie scowled at Reagan. "Emery is the Rogue Natural."

"Oh right. Right, right." Reagan nodded like that had rung a bell. Given her newly enhanced memory from bonding a vampire, she'd clearly been tuning me out earlier. "With the Guild bouncing back so incredibly quickly, it's clear Penny doesn't have much time. It would've been better had she come here directly after the Seattle skirmish."

"She couldn't," Callie said in a strangely thick tone. "Not with…what was going on."

"My trip down to… Yeah, right."

"Where?" I asked, perking up. This was as close as they'd come to talking about their activities a few months ago. I'd been all set to come to New Orleans when an unforeseen problem had postponed my move. But no one had filled me in on the details. I'd only been told that Reagan and Darius were out of town traveling.

"It's complicated," Reagan said. "Anyway, with the Guild's directive to bring in Penny and the Rogue Natural—"

"I don't understand why you can't remember his name," I said.

"I can, but taunting you is great fun." She grinned at me. I scowled back.

A manic light started glimmering in her eyes.

I tore my gaze away. It wasn't worth an altercation.

Her sigh said I'd made the right decision.

"Marie has been monitoring Penny's situation for Darius," Reagan said. Marie was a middle-tiered vampire that I'd fought with when we'd broken into the Mages' Guild compound in Seattle. Given that I hadn't seen one hair on her beautiful head since I'd set foot in New Orleans to get trained, I had no idea how she'd been keeping tabs on me. "She's worried enough to call Darius back into town. They have word that Guild scouts are already here, and in enough numbers to make him nervous," she said. "But they're in a watchful capacity at the moment. Red said he's seen them hanging around. They don't engage with anyone, but they're on the ground."

Red was a shifter that primarily hung out in the French Quarter. He'd contacted me in my first weeks, saying he was Reagan's acquaintance and welcoming me to the city. He'd instructed me to contact him should I need anything, which I'd thought was really nice of him.

Shivers crawled up my spine. Knowing the Guild was coming was different than hearing they were already here. It felt like the door to my house had been flung open, inviting burglars inside.

"It is only a matter of time before they have more numbers than this town can handle," Reagan went on, moving away to lean against the archway again. "The Magical Law Enforcement office has seen increased calls about magic gone wrong. Darker magic. When they show up to investigate, they can't find any relevant evidence leading them to the perpetrator. Whoever is practicing these spells obviously knows how to skirt around the system."

"The MLE office is filled with a bunch of desk jockeys." Callie shook her head. "If they hired you to sort it out, you'd have the mages caught in no time."

Reagan's jaw clenched and her eyes flashed. "I'm supposed to lie low. You know that."

I didn't, but I had a hunch I wasn't supposed to ask.

Everything to do with Reagan seemed a secret, and I was met with hostility when I asked more into it.

"I'm just saying that the MLE office isn't the be-all-end-all when it comes to assessing magic and finding the people responsible."

Reagan shifted and crossed her arms, exuding pent-up aggression. "Even so. We know for a fact the Guild is here. Among us. They're sticking to the shadows and watching, for now. Reporting back. But that won't last forever, especially if they see an easy grab. We need to get Penny trained up so she can protect herself, and the fastest way to do that is to enable her to think on her feet."

"She can already protect herself," Callie said, moving another batch of bacon to the plate. "No matter what the ladies of the Rum Social threw at her the other day, she handled it beautifully." She cocked her head. "Except for those few times when she froze, but Penny worked it out eventually. Like she was born to magic."

"She *was* born to magic."

Callie huffed and batted her spatula at the air. "You know what I mean. Born to fighting. Born to this life. Just look at what happened in Seattle at the rail yard. She was a pro."

"Except for that bit where I had to implode her spell before she killed everyone."

"Well sure, except for that. But, as I said, we all

make mistakes."

Reagan was talking about the demon situation I'd helped her and Darius and the dual-mages with in Seattle, something I was forbidden to tell anyone about.

Reagan drummed her fingers against her arm. "But Darius seemed to think she was far more outstanding when fighting the Mages' Guild than when fighting in the rail yard…"

"The rail yard wasn't really a war zone," I said, thinking back. I'd had plenty of backup and people to hold my hand. "Fighting the Mages' Guild, on the other hand…"

"Fighting the Mages' Guild was a clusterfuck, right?" Reagan asked.

I infused Emery's last two spells with my own magic, feeling the same intense longing that I'd sensed in the first layer. Light and color exploded upward, sparkling and simmering through the air. The energy around me electrified and I closed my eyes with the feeling, my magical bubble stabilizing naturally for a moment. A soft feeling of joy drifted down with the filaments before the spell dissolved away.

"A little touchy-feely for my taste," Reagan muttered, her hands out, feeling the dissipating spell.

"A punch in the mouth is a little touchy-feely for your taste," Callie said, cracking an egg.

"She's not wrong." Reagan pursed her lips in

agreement.

I pulled away the string and tore open the paper, finding a pink box underneath.

"Ew," Reagan said. "Why not red? I'd much prefer a deep crimson."

"Who is that package for, her or you?" Callie said, glancing back before cracking another egg.

"Just saying." Reagan moved so she could watch me pull the top off the box. "Pink is highly overrated. As is yellow. I hate yellow. I don't need a color telling me to be happy any more than I need one telling me to be soft."

"You have problems," Callie said.

"Again, not wrong."

I peered in the box and my heart squished. A single power stone, about the size of my hand, lay on a bed of pastel tissue paper. Stripes of vibrant color sliced through its brown surface, turning an ordinary stone extraordinary. The stone couldn't wait to get out of the box and be shown around its new home, very happy-go-lucky for a power stone.

"I know what would help with your wards," Reagan said, sitting at the island in anticipation of Callie getting her plate ready. "A night sleeping at Darius's French Quarter house. That would scare the bejeezus out of you. Oh!" she snapped. "And what about trips to the bad parts of town? You need to get more street-wise.

Maybe it would also help if I exposed you to some serious spells to get the juices of creativity flowing. I have a couple books you're probably nearly ready for."

"She is not ready for those books, Reagan Somerset," Callie said. "It hasn't even been a year since she turned all those witches into zombies. Not that I'm blaming you, dear." Callie gave me a grimace that was probably supposed to be a smile. Years of scowling had clearly frozen her face. "Any idiot that would make a potion without knowing what it does, while letting a complete novice with more power than sense lead, deserves what they get."

"Wow. Don't hold back for her sake," Reagan said with a laugh.

"If you gave her that book, she'd end up accidentally killing someone," Callie said, turning with a plate heaped with food. She set it in front of Reagan. "Honestly, she has come a long way, even in the last couple of weeks. Just you wait and see."

"We need to fast-track her training. And if there is one thing I know all about, it's fast-tracking training." Reagan eyed me. "I hear she's great at creating spells when she fears for her life. Let's put that to the test."

CHAPTER 5

THE NEXT NIGHT, I stood trembling at one end of Reagan's large warehouse. The warehouse, where she could practice her powers in peace, had been Darius's idea of a present. My utility belt encircled my waist, filled with herbs and grasses and other elements I thought would be useful. My power stones were precisely positioned in various places around the floor, and would hopefully help me when things got dire.

So…in about five minutes.

Callie and Dizzy stood at the other end, each with an open satchel, wearing padded catcher's vests and helmets. On their right side waited six of the mages from the party the other night, John being one of them. Currently he was leading the others in snickering at the Bankses' choice of headgear.

They wouldn't be snickering for long.

Reagan stood in the far corner draped in dark leather and shadow, her head slightly turned, studying me. I didn't need to see her eyes to know the violence that lurked there. She was in battle mode.

Four vampires, one of whom seemed jittery compared to the rest, drifted out to line up on the other side of the room. All of them were completely nude, their clothes neatly folded and stacked on a chair.

"That new vampire is a true danger, Darius," I heard Callie call out. "He's blood-lusting—look at him. He won't be able to come back from the brink."

"I inherited him," Darius said in a cool voice. "This is his trial. If he disappoints me, I will kill him."

"Preferably before he kills Penny," Dizzy said in a strained tone. That wasn't usual for Dizzy—he was legitimately worried that the vampire could kill me before anyone could stop it.

As if I needed more anxiety to fuel my rising blood pressure.

"Would it be too dramatic if I said I hated my life?" I mumbled.

"Not at the moment, no," Reagan said. She had vampire-like super hearing. "You're surrounded by a bunch of annoying mages without a clue, a couple of annoyed vampires, and a newbie vampire on scene that is going to lose himself to bloodlust and try and drain you dry. I doubt your strange fascination with rocks will help, so I'll have to step in to protect you. Everyone will see things they can't, and then Darius will have to kill all of these powerful mages. Someone is terrible at planning."

"That someone would be you," Callie called out. "And for the record, this situation is taking the fun out of my being right."

"That's only fun for you, hon," I barely heard Dizzy say.

"The child will be monitored," Darius said in a voice that effectively ended the discussion.

"Am I the child?" I asked softly. I needed to know where I stood—not that it would help anything.

"No. I was speaking of the vampire," Darius answered. "You are in no danger."

Easy for him to say. He wasn't the focus of a bunch of people who intended to do him harm.

Starting with Darius, the vampires shifted into their monster forms. Their skin color turned pasty or swampy, depending on age, and their bearing bent and bowed. Claws extended from their fingertips, black filled their eyes, and fangs filled their mouths. Dark, stringy hair took the place of cut and styled locks.

The mages shuffled closer together, even John. He might be powerful among mages, but against an elder vampire, he was child's play. Even against a middle-tiered vampire like Marie, he would be hard-pressed to make it out alive.

And here I stood, a know-nothing mage with witch tendencies, standing on my own, facing off against two columns of power and a pair of dual-mages in sports gear. While being watched by an immensely powerful supernatural of unknown origins.

"It is definitely not too dramatic to mention that I hate my life."

Without warning, the new vampire rushed forward.

"Oh crap." I pulled down elements as spells ran through my head, confused and blurry. A spell sped toward me from the dual-mages, powerful but simple. I barely countered it before another came from the other side.

"Crap. Oh crap. Crap." I blinked as the new vampire ran, his speed faster than thought. My thoughts, at least.

I barely got off my bug zapper spell—the first one I'd created on the fly—making him change course, before a spell came at me from the side, weak and reddish.

I ran forward so it wouldn't hit me, not bothering to waste precious time countering it. Another spell zoomed toward me before ballooning. Hives or a rash or flaking skin or something. Callie had obviously done that one. She knew how I hated to itch. She was as blunt and direct in her magic as she was in everyday life.

Unfortunately, she was also powerful, and it took me a moment to tear down her spell. But I didn't have a moment. The newbie was back, dashing in with his swampy green and black mouth spread open much larger than should've been natural, fangs glinting in the overhead light.

"Stop thinking, Penny," Reagan yelled. "Stop flicking through your mental spell Rolodex and react."

"Soon the spells will be second nature," Callie said, palming her helmet out of her face. "Until then, she has to remember her teachings."

They were telling me opposite things. What was I supposed to do?

The vampire jerked to a stop again, this time fifteen feet from me. His magic rolled over me, putrid and vile. Sharp, stinging, desperately hungry. Whatever was going on with him, he was losing the fight.

Sweat dripped into my eye. Callie's spell brushed my arm. I jerked away as I unraveled it.

A swampy white monster sped toward me, movements so fast I could barely see it.

I screamed, because that was what one did in this situation, and feinted to the side as though we were playing capture the flag.

"You don't need a Rolodex, Penny," Reagan yelled. "Don't listen to Callie."

"Get it away!" I ran right, screeching when the monster easily turned and reached out for me. "No—"

His clawed hand grabbed my upper arm. He threw me aside as if I weighed nothing.

A spell zipped by, thankfully missing me. Another sailed overhead. These mages clearly needed more practice with moving targets.

I hit the ground and my head thunked against the hardwood floor. My limbs slapped the surface and I skidded to a stop.

"Survive!" Reagan shouted.

White flared around me, creating a wall that accepted two different spells intent on teaching me some sort of lesson. My survival magic enveloped the spells and spun, growing as I fed it energy.

"Don't think, just do," Reagan yelled. "React like you did in the Mages' Guild. Create. Feel."

I tried to send the spells back to the casters, but my survival magic sputtered out. From the mass of organized elements that unconsciously gathered when in a pressurized situation, I pulled ingredients for an attack spell. The weave twisted through my fingers before forming a shaky sort of goo that quickly dissolved into nothing.

"I can't—" Tears of frustration blinded me. The monster I recognized as Marie rushed in then. I knew she'd try to scare a spell from me, but when her claws slashed across my arm, opening up four bloody gashes, another half-formed spell fizzled out.

My power stones pulsed around the room, offering aid, but I couldn't draw on them. I couldn't get my head above water.

CHAPTER 6

MOIST AIR SLID against Emery's skin as he stood behind a great boulder, feeling the sharp edges catch his badly worn clothes. The cold day bit deeply into his bones, sapping his energy as a chill shook his limbs. Dark clouds rolled overhead, the rain never far away in the Emerald Isle.

A human shape hugged the end of a rock wall some hundred yards away. A few more crouched ahead of him, hidden poorly within the crumbling ruins atop the green bluff overlooking the tumultuous ocean. Still more waited farther down the meadow, having ducked behind a different wall. His pursuers had plenty of choice in this part of the country, where low rock walls lined the countryside.

He turned and looked back the way he'd come.

A narrow road led down to this sorrowful strip of lonely land. A worn-in bicycle leaned on its kickstand, waiting for him.

He'd come to Ireland for the beauty. For the sweeping views and fields of green. For the pints, the laughter, and the merriment. He'd come to forget the grave he couldn't bring himself to visit, and the woman he'd left behind.

Instead, he'd found himself wandering away from the tourists and the pubs to this bit of untamed land. The rain battered him and the chill soaked through him, but his thoughts weren't dark. No, he found himself thinking of the jokes and laughter he'd shared with his brother before their lives had fallen apart. Penny's warm embraces, and how she'd grabbed hold of his heart.

How it had felt when the two of them worked together in her magic bubble.

All the while, he'd been followed by mages with seemingly one task—watch and report.

The spies were tenacious. The first time he'd noticed them, at a magical street fair in France, there'd only been two. He'd given them the slip easily.

They'd found him again at a bar in Brussels, and that time, it had been harder to get away without notice.

But here they were again. More this time. The Guild was getting serious. They'd make a move soon. He needed to get back to the Realm, where his magic was the strongest and there were better places to hide.

First, though…

He peered around the large boulder to the reason he'd stopped his bike.

Amidst a circle of smallish, plain gray stones throbbed a deep pulse of power. Raw and wild, the stone promised reserves of power for the weary magic user. It was exactly the kind of thing Penny would fawn over, with some sort of personality only she'd be able to read. It was like the others he'd gathered for her.

He clenched his jaw.

The problem was its proximity to the mages' crumbling hideout. They'd clearly stationed themselves there in anticipation of his riding past on his bicycle. They'd probably had no idea he would stop near such a desolate, ravaged, old structure with no tourism merits.

Unless their previous directive of "watch and report" had changed to "take him down at all costs," and this was a good location to wait until he was close before springing into action.

Though…given that he *was* close, and they hadn't sprung…

No, they must've thought he would ride by. They probably had a car on the other side and intended to inconspicuously follow him. Like they had inconspicuously followed him all those other times, sticking out like sore thumbs.

The Mages' Guild employed idiots.

What to do…

If he ran at the stone in an attempt to snatch it on the fly, they'd probably assume it was an attack and reciprocate.

A battle would ensue.

But if he nonchalantly wandered that direction, his hands in his pockets and whistling, like anyone out for a stroll through the wet fields on a cold, miserable day, they might assume he was vulnerable and attack.

A battle would ensue.

The alternative was to turn around, get on his bike, and go back to the mindless pedaling. They'd continue to watch, and he'd continue to mind his own business until he could get out of here and do a better job of losing them this time. He didn't need that power stone—Penny had plenty, was surely over him, and likely wanted him to leave her the hell alone—and he didn't need to further blacken his already corrupted heart by going on a killing spree.

Leaving was the smart thing.

He slapped the rock he stood behind in frustration. Smart or not, he couldn't bring himself to do it.

The feel of that stone was special. It called to him. Whispered to him of the woman who plagued his dreams. Begged him to grab it, package it up, and send it to her.

He blew out a breath, the memory of her sweet smile drifting through his thoughts.

It was probably harassment at this point, but he had to send her one more. Just one more to let her know he was thinking of her. That he'd never forget her. After that, he'd leave her alone and let her move on.

Boy, would this whole scheme crumble if the source of power wasn't actually a stone, but some item that couldn't be removed.

"So what do I do?" he whispered softly. "Run at it, or meander toward it?"

A cold wind swept along the ground, scraping his cheeks with icy claws.

Whatever he did, he needed to do it soon, or he'd turn into a magical popsicle.

"Meander. Meandering is the safest approach." He stepped out from behind the boulder, his head pointed toward the ocean beyond, and his eyes cut to the various figures hunkered around the stone like ill-fitting goobers.

As expected, most of them jolted. Then shifted. Two heads came together in an impromptu meeting.

"Nothing to see here, folks," he murmured without moving his lips. Little translucent tags waved from the various elements around him, offering themselves up for use in his quick-fire spells. "Mind your business."

The soggy earth squished beneath his feet. A light drizzle shifted down, layering his skin. Still, the frigid air scraped across his face.

The shapes within the ruins stilled as he came within a hundred feet of the circle of stones. Those near the end of the rock wall crouched, their focus acute.

Did they think they were hiding? They couldn't. Which meant they were more confident than the last pursuers he'd encountered. And why wouldn't they be? They had more magical workers fanned out around the area. If they worked together even the slightest bit, they'd easily elevate their might and pose a real threat to him.

But they weren't natural witches like Penny. They wouldn't give him any surprises. They'd been brainlessly trained in the same lessons he'd learned: learn your spells, guard your secrets, and, above all, power is king.

In the world of mages, he was a king.

As he came closer, he could feel the hard thrum of power from within that plain circle of rocks. It pulsed in time with his heart before quickening just a bit, infusing him with energy. Closer still and his adrenaline surged higher. Energy spread through his limbs and tingled in his fingertips and toes.

An arm moved sideways by the end of the rock wall, and magic rose around him, rolling and boiling, shifting and spinning, practically churning in anticipation.

Ready to kill.

It was what he excelled at. What he could do with barely a thought.

It was why he'd walked away from Penny, lest his blackness of character corrupt her goodness.

A sad smile graced his lips as the magic around him darkened, his survival magic infusing it.

The person by the rock wall stilled again, probably bracing for his attack.

One footfall at a time, Emery made his way more carefully toward the circle, weaving together the first spell as slowly as he possibly could. His hands were low, his waggling fingers hopefully blending in with the darkness of his pants. The mages were still too far away to see clear detail.

Ten feet to the circle and the power throb ramped up again. Blackness crowded his vision for a second and an image of him standing with his back to a blast of magic took over his sight. It disappeared the next second.

He dove to the ground and rolled, finishing the weave and seeing two mages behind him with their hands full of ingredients. If not for his ability to foresee mortal danger to himself, he would've been dead ten times over.

Their spell was already airborne, rushing at him in a sloppy, loose weave that wouldn't do much more than stun him.

They were trying to capture him. What fools.

As soon as he zipped off his spell, he immediately worked on another one. He sent it off to the people at the ruined castle as he called up yet another one.

A blast of magic sped toward him from the group of mages gathered at the end of the rock wall. He caught it with a shield built of his survival magic, which encompassed the spell and then ate through it.

He hopped up and weaved familiar spells together as he jogged toward that circle of rocks. He sent another spell at the ruins, one at the rock wall, and then turned to hit two mages behind him, standing much too closely together.

“Thanks for making my job easy,” he said. He’d reached the rock circle now and glanced down to the middle.

His heart fell.

It was a stone, all right. A gray, ordinary stone that blended in with the other mundane, easy-to-look-past stones around it. There was nothing exciting or unique about it. Nothing that drew and kept the eye, making a person want to look at it for hours on end.

Basically, it was more like him than her. He should probably just leave it there and make the last stone he sent to her something truly exceptional.

He fired off one more spell into the ruins. A scream rose before cutting off. Someone stood up from behind the rock wall forty feet in front of him. A jet of blue raced toward him.

He rolled, annoyed that he was nearly soaked now, and felt a surge from the power stone. If he were a betting man, he'd say the stone was desperate to be used.

Is this what Penny feels when she's around the stones?

Pulling on it, he amped up the spell he was weaving, adding a touch more energy to the effort and spicing it up with a little extra nastiness. There was that lack of moral character he was talking about. Let Penny try to tell him he wasn't evil now.

The spell plunged through the mage's chest, then ballooned out, ripping his body apart. He barely had time to scream.

"I really should just leave you here," Emery said to the power stone, still using the extra boost to form a spear to send through the air at the last mage he could see. She took a big step forward and shoved her hands in front of her, trying to use her body for an extra push or something. Emery hadn't seen it done before. Maybe it worked, but it sure looked stupid.

He added an acidic component to his spell and sent it off before she could fire hers. Rather than watch the spell's trajectory, he snatched the power stone off the ground in all its humdrum, dull glory, and turned in a circle, seeing if anyone else planned to pop up like a jack-in-the-box.

The mage near the ruins was working on something else, but she didn't get a chance to fire it off. Emery's spell had torn her initial spell apart without dissipating, and was carrying on toward her.

Smarter than the average bear, the mage turned to run. But too late.

Emery's spell smacked into her back. The scream sailed across the green fields before ending in a ragged gurgle.

Back at his bike, Emery tucked his stone away, still looking for anyone hiding among the rocks. No one had made a move.

"I should've gone for a truck or something," Emery said to the stone, then laughed. He was talking to rocks now. Penny had turned him into a weirdo like her.

His thoughts drifted back to her. He hadn't had any communication with Darius for weeks. Last he'd heard, Penny was safe and sound, living and training with the Bankses, a mostly calm dual-mage pair with decades of experience.

She had the life she deserved. Balanced, just like she was.

CHAPTER 7

"Mother trucker. Holy fudge sticks…butter frack…nickel *turdswallop*!" Sweat poured down my face. My hair clung to my cheeks. I'd been on the defense for about twenty minutes and couldn't get out from under my attackers.

"Butter frack?" Reagan called out. "What are you even saying?"

She'd been taunting me the entire time. It was as bad as the newbie vampire continually dashing at me, only to jerk to a stop twenty feet away and stiffly back off.

I tore down the next spell, one I recognized, but when I went to retaliate…nothing. My mind went completely blank again. I just stood there, daft and blinking, waiting for whatever came next.

"Stop." Reagan pushed forward from the wall. She looked as frustrated as I felt.

The mages stationed around the room lowered their hands, most of them hardly taxed. Callie palmed her helmet, and her bulldog expression said she had an *I told you so* headed Reagan's way on my behalf. Dizzy gave me a supportive thumbs-up, and for some reason, that was the worst of all.

Last but certainly not least, the green monster dashed forward again.

I staggered backward. Darius flinched.

Time slowed down.

The mages hadn't so much as reacted, but the vampires had already braced themselves to move. Their muscles flexed. They were two heartbeats away from surging forward to grab the newbie.

They would never make it in time.

As that thought ran through my head, I saw Reagan's eyes widen. Her shoulders turned, as though she were about to fling out a hand.

I didn't have time to look around in wonder.

The green vampire bore down on me, its magic vile and intense and boiling.

Its intentions were clear: *Nourishment. Destruction.*

It intended to kill me, and no one would get there in time to stop it.

The Mr. Happy-Go-Lucky stone pulsed out a shock wave of power. It hit me dead center, slicing through the film of the vampire's acidic, rotting magic, giving me a boost and a push at the same time.

I needed to act.

Another heartbeat and the vampire was ten feet

from me and launching into the air. His fangs dripped saliva. His claws clicked before spreading.

My temperamental third eye—my souped-up intuition—took over.

Survive.

I closed my eyes, feeling the currents around me. Bending the vampire's magic into my own. Using the resources in my belt, yanking on the power in the stones littered across the floor, and stealing from the mages' satchels.

Kill it or it will kill you, I thought, time running out. *Kill it or it will kill you.* The newbie seemed to hang suspended in the air, bearing down. The second his monster form landed on my body, I would be done.

Rage pushed at me from one of the stones, giving me another boost. Ice and fire rolled through my blood, carrying Reagan's signature flare, and I felt a wave of primal protectiveness from one of the vampires—Darius. Energy flared around me and I sucked it all in.

My fingers danced to the beat of my will, pulling the various strands of magic together faster than I could think. Responding to the need of the moment. Using every resource and type of magic available to me.

The newbie was mere feet away.

Instinctively, I pulled back and slapped my palms together. My eyes blinked open.

Blaring white light exploded from my hands. It

burst into an array of colors and then hardened into a shiny wall. The vampire's face, one foot from my own, smashed into hard, colorful air. Bone cracked. Its body hit next, like smacking a force field.

The wall wrapped around the falling body, covering it from head to toe. It condensed, and bones popped like fireworks.

"Oh, ew." I didn't have time to retch.

Without warning, an unseen hand slapped me to the side and sent me sprawling. Swampy green limbs scooped me up and ripped me away as a flash of pasty white took up a post between me and what was left of my attacker.

"Gross, gross, *gross*. Marie, put me down." I held my hands away from her strangely clammy skin.

She didn't comment, instead dropping me by the wall and standing in front of me. I peered around her knobby knee.

Reagan stood with a transformed and naked Darius. The squeezed and definitely dead vampire lay mangled at their feet, oozing a black sort of goo.

"Gross," I breathed, fire climbing up my esophagus. I was not cut out for all the death and mayhem of this new magical life. I'd had no time to gear up for the nasty things I now saw regularly.

Reagan and Darius's gazes pointed in different directions, not landing on any one thing, as though they were trying to play it cool. Between their flat expressions and the mages' antsy shifting, fear crept into me. Doing a spell like that in the Mages' Guild, where I'd been surrounded by enemies, was one thing. Doing it in practice was entirely another. But then again, that vampire would've killed me.

Right?

My rocks started to release a pounding beat of magic, reacting to my anxiety. Magic drifted up and collected above my head, roiling in a cloud only visible to me.

Which meant I was the only one who knew I was not completely in control and, based on my current feelings, was quite possibly dangerous.

"You should probably hold my hands down," I said to Marie.

Darius's head snapped up and his eyes immediately found mine. His head ticked a fraction, and without his having said a word, Reagan came striding toward me, her expression still flat.

"I got her, Marie," she said when she approached. "We'll just go for a little walk."

Marie, still in her ugly form, stepped aside.

"What, ah…" Reagan stopped short. She glanced upward before lifting her hands to feel my cloud. "What have you got brewing up there?" Her head tilted to the side. "That's…" A smile spread across her face. "That is the stuff, right there. I mean, it's terrifying, don't get me wrong. Marie, you might want to run. But that is some interesting and complex spell working. Is it…" She squinted and looked up and to the left. "Is it actually a spell? I'm having a hard time figuring out…"

"I don't know what it is. It is a mass of magic and a lot of anxiety."

"Well, okay. Let's walk it off, shall we?" Reagan jerked her head for me to walk with her.

I fell in step. "Am I going to get in trouble?"

"Where are you taking her, wannabe?" John stepped forward with a pale face and a jerky sort of swagger. "Because she had no choice but to kill the vamp. That thing shouldn't have been allowed in the Brink. None of 'em should be. I should phone Roger."

Reagan laughed. "Like you know Roger, sure."

I'd heard Roger's name a few times. He was clearly someone powerful.

"John, leave it be. Reagan doesn't mean Penny any harm," Callie called out, starting forward.

"Everyone knows she's the lap dog of these vamps." John tilted his chin up. "What's to say she isn't just separating Penny from the group so they can get their revenge?"

"That's not what Reagan is doing." Callie pulled off the helmet and stopped in our makeshift circle. "The newbie vampire succumbed to bloodlust, and Darius was rushing in to stop it. *Too late*, I might add. He put Penny in grave danger. Not to mention all of you."

"I could've handled it," John said with obviously false bravado. His trembling voice gave him away.

"The newbie, sure." Callie fluffed her hair. "The elder? Not even remotely. Just do yourself a favor and thank Penny and Reagan for your lives."

"Not me," Reagan said. "The job was done by the time I showed up. Figuratively speaking, obviously. Bottom line, it's all over, the practice is done, and only a few very perplexing questions remain."

"You didn't create the…" Callie stared hard at Reagan.

"That perfectly executed invisible wall that shouldn't be possible for an ordinary mage's magic, regardless of whether they're a natural?" Reagan grabbed my sleeve. "No, I did not." She went to start forward, but John didn't move, staring down at her with an obstinate expression.

She smiled, showing even, white teeth, a terrible sign. The small hairs stood up along my arms.

"I didn't finish that question for a reason," Callie said into the stare-off, completely oblivious to the danger that was brewing. There it was again—the unspoken thing between Reagan and the Bankses.

"Like these hacks will get the relevance," Reagan replied in a bored voice, another terrible sign. "John, do you plan to move?"

"No. You need to—"

Faster than thought, she reached out and shoved him to the side. The angle was awkward, and while John was thin, almost skinny, he was tall and had to be somewhat heavy.

None of that mattered.

His body flew. Not expecting the shove, or the incredible strength clearly behind it, he didn't react fast enough. He hit the floor on his arm and thigh and slid five feet.

Reagan gave all the other mages a fierce gaze, and the rest of the small hairs on my body joined the ones on my arms. "Anyone else want to try and throw their weight around? Attempt to prove that power and stupidity somehow trumps my ability to kick your ass?"

Laughter bubbled up my middle and a smile spread across my face, all completely unintentional, because I was scared on their behalf. She wasn't kidding—she could definitely kick their asses without her magic, and their power didn't trump hers on her worst day. I didn't understand her magic, but I knew she was packing an awful lot of it.

Intelligently, the rest of the mages shook their heads and backed up in frightened, jerky movements.

"John, we should've warned you about her temper," Dizzy said, still in his helmet, as Reagan motioned me forward. “She’s not one for talking things out.”

“How could you talk things out with that numbskull?” Reagan said. “Honestly, why would they want to set you up with him?”

“What questions do you have?” I finally asked as we left the warehouse. The night was windy yet quiet, peaceful compared to the last half-hour.

“Well, for one…” She held the door for a moment, glancing back. Darius stood next to the dead vampire’s body, his gaze holding hers for a moment. After she closed the door, she asked, “First question: how did you make the air condense into a wall?”

I thought back, trying to remember my head space before it happened. All I could properly recall, though, was blind panic. “I’m not sure.”

“Two, how did you make that wall suddenly come alive and squeeze the vamp’s body to death?”

I grimaced. That had been seriously gross. I definitely blamed Darius for making me do it. Which fit, because I kind of blamed Darius for everything horrible I’d done since meeting him. It was easy, particularly since he usually owned the questionable achievements with pride.

“I’m not really sure,” I said.

“And three, what did you do to keep the vampire from healing? The head is still attached and the heart appears to be intact, but he’s definitely dead.”

"Oh. Huh. Is that how you kill a vampire? An old-fashioned staking or beheading?"

"I can see you have no idea how you did the third one. That'll make Darius relieved, wary, and extremely nervous." She nodded with a smile. "Want to be my best friend?"

"No," I said without meaning to.

She nudged me with her shoulder. "You'll change your mind. I'm really fun."

"No," I repeated, my politeness filter missing in action.

She laughed, and I was glad her feelings were almost impossible to hurt.

"We have a lot to unpack from this one failed practice session," she said, leading me to Darius's car and leaning back against it.

I swallowed. Yes, we did. And when in doubt, shove it onto the *ignore* list and carry on with your day. "Can't I go back to working with Callie and Dizzy?"

"Not on your life. You're a special sort of mage, and we need to figure out a special sort of training. Well...Darius does. It sounds like the Rogue Natural would've been your best bet, but he's gone off-grid again." She shook her head. "That Rogue Natural is wily. Anyone that can hide from Darius should get a medal. I want to meet him."

"Great," I said dryly. Would no one let it go?

"Anyway, I'm way out of my league with you. And a little weirded out, to be honest. It felt like we were connected for a moment. Like Darius and me, but without certain…intimate aspects."

"Ew." My filter was still on hiatus.

"No, I think tomorrow your training will go in an entirely new direction."

"Which direction is that?"

"From what I know of Darius? The one you're least expecting."

CHAPTER 8

THE NEXT EVENING, I stared down at the little cream card pinched between my dirt-stained fingers. A loud *bang* issued from Dizzy's rebuilt shed a few feet away. The new shed had been extremely expensive because he'd insisted on using reclaimed wood so it would look old and decrepit. To get him out of her clean house, Callie hadn't even batted an eye at the cost.

I brought up the envelope, which looked fancy enough to hold a wedding invitation. White chalk had transferred from my hand to the clean paper.

A little table stood in front of me, round and of a similar appearance to Dizzy's shed. Just under the lip of the tabletop was a small drawer with a key sticking out of a keyhole.

I'd walked this way ten minutes ago. The table and the note had appeared out of nowhere.

Confused, I looked around the closed-off yard, the high wooden fence cutting off the views of the neighbors. Tree branches waved in the breeze and plants swayed. The two-person swing on the back porch drifted lazily from side to side. Nothing else moved.

"Reagan—I mean, Penny, did you get the flower for the spell?" Dizzy poked his head out of the shed. "Oh. What have you got there?"

I held up the card and envelope for his inspection, then looked down at the little table, directly on the route Dizzy always used to get to the house through the flowerbed. It had been placed in that location on purpose. The person (vampire?) who'd left it clearly knew Dizzy's habits, and wanted him to find it quickly.

He took the card. "You are cordially invited to…" His voice trailed away, but his lips kept moving as he read the artfully scripted cursive.

His brow furrowed and he flipped the envelope over, showing my name. "Well…he has always done things the civilized way. No denying that."

"Who?" I asked, taking back the card. "It's not signed."

"Darius, of course. That's his address. One of them, at any rate."

After last night's botched practice session, the Bankses had grudgingly agreed with Reagan that their version of training didn't work with my strange brand of natural—they'd even said *strange*, as if I didn't already have a complex. Without any other options, they'd agreed that Darius would find a suitable replacement.

"Oh, look. A drawer. With an old-fashioned key!" Dizzy beamed and bent, pulling out the little drawer tucked under the lip of the table top. He extracted a similar card to the one I held. "'Dear Mr. Banks'"—Dizzy leaned toward me—"he's always so polite and formal." He straightened back up. "'Please accept this table as a small token of my gratitude. It can't be easy to hand over a pupil as bright and with as much potential as Miss Bristol. I am honored you think I will manage her aptly. Sincerely, Darius Durant. PS.'" Dizzy chuckled. "How did he know I love PSs in letters? They're like secret messages pinned to the bottom. It's such a shame the practice is falling by the wayside. 'PS This table was made of reclaimed wood from the *Satisfaction*, the flagship of Henry Morgan, circa 1670.'"

Dizzy blew out a breath and took a step back. "Wow." He bent to the card again, read it a second time, and leaned back with another sigh. "Henry Morgan! The famous pirate! This is really fantastic, Reagan—I mean, Penny. The stories that must be captured in this wood."

The pounding of feet signaled Callie was stalking our way. She appeared on the back deck across the lawn, her hands on her hips with a little card sticking out. "What is that vampire up to?" she hollered. She held out the card. "He's trying to buy us."

"What did you get?" Dizzy replied, delight on his

face. “I got a table made from—”

“Don’t fall into his hands.” Callie stomped down the deck toward the stairs and around the covered patio set to reach us. I had to give it to Dizzy—despite the harm to the flowers, tramping across the yard to the house was much faster. “He knows very well this is a short-term situation.” She came to stand in front of his table. “We’re not handing her over for good. And she’ll still live here. I already lost one to their devious ways, I will not lose another.”

“Now, hon,” Dizzy said, “Darius merely means to train her up. Then he said he’d let her go off on her own.”

“You can never trust a vampire. Everyone knows that.”

Dizzy’s face fell, because he’d said the same thing a few times over. “But Darius isn’t like normal vampires,” he said in a weak voice.

“When it comes to something as rare and important to the magical world as Penny, or her Rogue Natural—”

“He’s not mine,” I mumbled.

“—you better believe he’ll try to get his hooks in any way he can.”

After a beat, Dizzy quietly asked, “What’d you get?” almost as though he couldn’t help it.

“Never mind what I got. It’s going back. As is your God-awful table. If we accept his gifts, we might as well hand over our souls. He's trying to buy our silence."

"But… Well, those aren't even the same things."

"Don't split hairs." She eyed the card in my hand and her eyes narrowed. "What did you get, Penelope Bristol?"

I wasted no time in handing it over. "A dinner invite."

"Ah ha!" She waved my card at Dizzy. "See? The seduction has already been scheduled."

"I very much doubt he will try to seduce Penny. Reagan would never go for it."

She paused, staring at him as if he'd sprouted a second set of legs. "I didn't mean sexually, you donkey! He'll charm her and offer her riches and lavish accommodations. He'll fly her around the world, wine and dine her, all the while hooking her into his billion-dollar enterprise."

"That doesn't sound so bad," I said just as Dizzy said, "I don't think he has *that* much money, does he?"

An incredulous expression crossed Callie's face. "She'll be another asset for him to exploit! Of course that sounds so bad, and how should I know how much money he has? He has a lot of it. He makes more every day. And do you know why?"

"He's really old and got into the stock market early?" Dizzy ventured.

"He's good at business?" I tried.

Callie jabbed her finger at me. "He is good at business. He is good at maneuvering people and products."

Dizzy deflated and looked longingly at his table. "I love pirates."

"You wouldn't love them right after they robbed you and killed all your crewmen." Callie held out her hand for the card.

"Does this mean I'm not going to the dinner?" I asked hopefully. Because a ride in a private jet was one thing, but dinner with a cultivated elder vampire sounded stressful. He'd probably have a bunch of forks and spoons set up, with a whole bunch of glasses and courses, and I wouldn't know the right way to go about any of it.

Callie stared at me with determination. "Yes, you're going to that dinner."

"She gets to go, but we can't keep the presents?" Dizzy whined.

"Honestly," Callie said, "when did you become such a big baby?"

Dizzy flung his hand toward the table, straightening up. "Do you have any idea how rare that is? I don't even know how he got it. It's from a newly found pirate ship. A pirate ship!"

I edged away. They were very good at working things out, either with civilized conversations, or full-out yelling at each other. It was best to steer clear and leave them to it.

Callie shifted until her body squared off with his. She lowered her arms to her sides and leaned forward a little.

I edged a little farther away.

"He is managing her training," she said with deliberate slowness. "He'll need to speak with her to do that. His version of communicating often revolves around social norms. With humans, that usually means eating or drinking. We know this."

"Yes, but..." He went back to hunching and looking longingly at the table.

Having won that (very short) battle, Callie turned her attention to me. "This is what you need to understand." She held up a finger. "You are business partners. He has a lot of power in the vampire hierarchy, in business, in the Brink... You name it, he's acquired power in it." Her head tilted to the side and her finger stayed raised. "Except magic and spells." She took down her hand. "He relies on high-powered mages and Reagan for magical know-how, spell research, and practical application. He has donated a lot of time and effort to acquiring knowledge about magic, yes, but that is because it is something he cannot properly master on his own. Do you see what I'm saying?"

I bit my lip, thinking through all the possible things she could be saying. Dizzy's blank stare wasn't helping.

"Not…really."

"In magic," she went on with a patience I seldom saw in her. It meant this was important. "*You* are the one with the power. Even now, not knowing how to use your magic, you are still the one with the power. You can accidentally kill a vampire with nothing more than fear and two seconds of your time. If you start to feel bullied, or charmed, or things are going too easily or not easily enough, just remember that at the end of the day, *you* call the shots. His job is to help *you*. His purpose is to make *you* happy. You don't owe him squat, and you don't have to bend one bit if you don't want to. Now do you get what I'm saying?"

Dizzy smiled and nodded at me. He did, at any rate.

"I'm not sure what you've noticed," I said meekly, "but I'm not great with standing up for myself. I'm so used to being bullied that it doesn't bother me half the time."

Callie shifted her weight and a frown creased her brow. "You're too easygoing for your own good. But do you know what?"

Dizzy's face fell again. He didn't know what, either.

"Being easygoing and being a pushover are not the same things," Callie said, and Dizzy nodded. "The Rogue Natural didn't push you around, did he?"

"Even now, when there is no real relevance, he's brought up—"

"When you took over, he stepped out of the way." Callie nodded and resumed resting her fists on her hips. It was her default stance. "You're easy to get along with, but you aren't easy to push to the side."

I sucked in a breath to speak, because I was often pushed to the side, sometimes bodily. Emery had only stepped to the side because of mutual trust and respect. But I held my tongue. The last thing I felt like doing was arguing over a guy who thought a couple rocks every now and then would ease the sting of his abandonment.

Great. I was officially a woman scorned. Perfect.

"So when you sit at that vampire's table tonight, you look him straight in the eye," Callie said. She held her pointer finger between her eyes, and I ended up looking at her nose. "You discuss what comes next, and you remember that if he doesn't work out as a *business partner*—because that's what this is, a *business* relationship—you can get a different business partner. Got it?"

Dizzy and I nodded together.

"Now." Callie glanced at the table before looking at the house. "Penny, Dizzy and I need your help constructing a better ward. One of those sneaky devils came into the house to leave my gift. No one picks my locks, magically or otherwise, without getting one hell of a shock for their efforts."

CHAPTER 9

AT MIDNIGHT, I stood in front of a massive house in the French Quarter, which all the ghost tours claimed, accurately, had once been owned by a vampire. It sat on a corner lot in a mostly quiet area, if any part of the French Quarter could be called quiet, and rose three stories into the sky.

I smoothed my lilac dress down my stomach and contemplated walking away.

As the power holder, that was in my power, right? I could turn around (hopefully not as stiffly as I was standing there) and trudge back the way I'd come.

But that ultimately wouldn't solve my problem of freezing up in battle. Whether I liked it or not, I needed someone other than the Bankses to teach me, and at the moment, everyone thought Darius had the answer. He was all I had.

I took a deep breath and stepped forward to knock as a strange awareness washed over me. Goosebumps coated my body, hinting of a presence lurking close by. Not long after, an itch between my shoulder blades flared to life, my body's way of telling me someone was watching.

I spun, half expecting to find a vampire on the other side of the street, watching to see that I actually approached the house. Dark shadows coated the walls of the houses and spilled onto the sidewalk. The leaves of the few small trees rustled in the cool night air.

The itch grew stronger and I took a step backward, toward the door. The soft scuff of a shoe on cement interrupted the still night. Another footfall, someone slowly sneaking my way from the other side of the street, obscured by the corner.

Heart in my throat, my failure the night before rode heavy in my thoughts. Was a vampire about to attack me? Had the Mages' Guild finally stepped up their game?

I turned quickly to knock, but the creator of the footfalls staggered into view before my fist could land.

All the breath left my lungs as the man noticed me.

"What's up, pretty lady?" the trendy guy in his mid-twenties slurred from across the street. He held up a tall plastic cup, half-full, with a long bendy straw sticking out of it. Noticing that I didn't immediately turn away, he staggered to a stop, his body tilted to the side.

We stared at each other for a moment.

He straightened, bent in an arc the other way, and leaned in the opposite direction again, fighting gravity.

"It's not a great idea to pass out on the street in this area," I said. Delivering a fair warning seemed the neighborly thing to do. "Or…any area, I guess, but especially this one."

His lean came around to the front before he started—or burped, I couldn't really tell. "You care about me?" He'd barely formed the words before bringing up the drink hand to tap himself in the chest. He snorted and bent backward, at odds with gravity no matter what position he was in, and staggered back. His head hit the wall of the house behind him and he ducked like the sky was falling.

"What was that?" he muttered, looking upward at a very strange angle. A moment later, he finally lost the battle for balance. He staggered forward, but his feet couldn't catch up with his increasing momentum and he fell, face first, onto the sidewalk. His hands caught up a moment later, and he scraped the edge of his cup against the cement.

"Ugh," I heard in a long moan, his cup dramatically tilted but not spilling. "Noooo," he groaned, looking like a guy after a bad hit-and-run accident. "Didn't spill."

Small miracles.

I turned back to the door, finding a black maw in place of the wood. A shape loomed in the darkness, tall and wide and full of muscle.

"Hah!" I flung out my hand, and a shot of red zapped from my palm. The ol' zapper never let me down. Except when I was trying to kill rodents. Those buggers were fast.

The shape in the doorway dove to the side.

"I will save you," came a collection of grunts from across the street. The man was fighting gravity again.

As I backed up, knowing the reflex attack was almost certainly my bad, Darius's assistant, Moss, who I'd briefly met in Seattle and had been one of the vampires at the training the night before, reappeared in the doorway with a surly expression, a ruined suit jacket, and a burned arm beneath. How bad the wound was, I couldn't say because of the shadows draping him, but it was more than a skim.

"Miss Bristol," he said in a less-than-enthusiastic voice. "How good of you to come. Please, come in."

The man across the street was braced on his forearms, staring my way. "Isn't that place haunted?" he asked, apparently to himself.

Inside, gorgeous furniture graced the well-appointed and spacious rooms. Fresh flowers sweetened the air and oil paintings hung on freshly painted walls.

"Wow," I said, taking it all in. Callie and Dizzy's house was really nice, but this took luxury to a whole new level.

Moss led the way up a winding staircase with strings

of flowers draping down from the banister.

"Are those flowers magic, or…?"

Moss didn't so much as glance to the side. "We are not in the Realm."

"Is that a no, or…?"

"Those are real flowers."

"Right." I nodded, breathing in their fragrance. "Is it to mask the smell of death in here, or…?"

This time he did glance back at me. With a frown.

"I mean, you know"—I waved my finger at him and then around—"vampires. You smell good with cologne, but in your other form… Does that form smell as swampy as it looks, by the way? I'm usually too caught up in the moment to notice."

At the second-story landing, Moss paused and turned to me, his face expressionless in the low light.

"Is this a taboo subject?" I asked, suddenly unsure. "It probably is, isn't it? Sorry."

"This way."

I wasn't sure I'd ever seen a vampire stiffen, despite the whole "being dead" mythos, but Moss came awfully close.

"Do you get the flowers delivered fresh every day?" I couldn't let go of the flower situation. Why Darius, or whoever arranged it, wanted them draped on the banisters, I didn't know. Vases would do just fine for overall appeal, and the flowers wouldn't die nearly as fast. What a waste of money and plant life. "Oh!" I snapped, the light bulb clicking on. "The flowers lost their lives, just like you, but they're still beautiful. It's symbolic, right?"

Without a word, Moss stopped in front of a pair of double doors. He stared down at me with a clenched jaw and his magic, seething, pulsed around us.

"Get in," he said, not moving in any way to indicate the door beside us.

"Sure. Yup." Hunching reflexively under that hard, dangerous stare, I scurried into a formal dining room.

A huge table occupied the middle of the room, surrounded by four chairs, one at the head of the table, and the others close by down the sides. Each place setting held my worst nightmare: multiple fine china plates stacked on top of each other ending in a bowl, forks and spoons for days, two knives, and three crystal glasses in front. A crystal chandelier hung in the middle of the table, bedecked with electric candles. Big, draped curtains closed off the windows, blocking out all light, and a large cream rug stretched beneath all of this.

"What a nightmare," I murmured.

Heavy footsteps sounded just outside the door, like someone was standing in one place and stomping their feet rhythmically. After a short pause, Moss followed me into the room, his body tense. His suit coat had been changed and his injured arm hung down by his side, the hand clenched.

"Miss Bristol," he said. "Please. Shall we sit?"

"Um, yup. Sure." I stepped backward, and he paused, eyeing me. I kept my hands down to ease his mind. "There's no magic around me. I mean, I haven't collected any of it…at present. There's magic around us all the time. You, for example, count as magic." His blank stare was off-putting. "What I mean is, I won't accidentally zap you." I figured I should cover my bases so I didn't turn into a liar. "At present."

"Yes. Fine." He held out his hand, gesturing toward the table. "Would you like to sit down?"

"Sure, yup." I took another step back to allow him plenty of room to cross in front of me—he didn't seem nervous *per se*, but he didn't seem at ease, either—and waited patiently.

His brow furrowed.

"Sorry, am I supposed to be doing something?" I asked.

"Pardon me. I wondered why you were backing away. Would you prefer drinks in the lounge, first?"

"You have a lounge? No, this is fine. I don't even really know what a lounge is, to be honest. Where, uh…do you want me?"

"Oh. Of course." He pulled out the chair at the head of the table.

"Right." I unslung my small handbag from over my

shoulder and briefly thought about looping it over the back of the chair. Realizing it would look gauche in this fine establishment, I quickly dropped it by my feet so no one would notice it. I considered taking the napkin off the table and draping it in my lap, but that seemed a little premature, given there was no one else at the table.

Moss took the seat to my left, one of the two chairs on that side. Darius and Marie entered a moment later, each looking beautiful and glamorous and dressed to the nines.

I smoothed my dress over my lap, wishing I could sink back into my chair. I really should've bought a new dress. Or even borrowed one of Veronica's.

"Miss Bristol," Darius said with an earth-shattering smile. The man was a looker, no two ways about it. When he was in this form, of course. The other form would crack glass. "How has your evening been?"

"Great. Going well." I bobbed my head and crossed my ankles, as if that would somehow bring me on par with these gorgeous folks.

Moss stood as the others approached, moving a seat farther away from me. He was probably all too happy to do so.

"You remember Miss Beauchene, of course." Darius held out the newly vacated chair for Marie.

"Of course, yes. Hi." I gave her a little wave.

"It seems Mr. LaRay startled you earlier." Darius

took the empty seat on my other side.

Another silent cue must've gone out—as if by bat sonar—because a lovely woman wearing a black wraparound dress and carrying a bottle of wine entered the room with a smooth glide. A faint tickle of her magic crawled across my skin like a cloud of insects, hinting of hunger and hunting, now a familiar warning.

I stiffened, watching her closely. After the failed training session, Reagan had given me some markers on how to tell a vampire's age, going over the level of danger for each. Newbies, like the one I had killed, were totally unpredictable and wild. They'd lose themselves to bloodlust at the drop of a hat, and even though they weren't incredibly strong or fast for vampires, they were plenty stronger and faster than me. But while the young ones were unpredictable, the elders—calculated, strategic, and wickedly strong and fast—were more dangerous in the long term. The other vamps ranked in the middle somewhere on a sliding scale according to age.

This woman's gait, though smooth, had little hiccups that wouldn't seem out of place for a human, something I'd never noticed with the other three vampires in the room. Her jaw clenched and unclenched, and her nostrils flared more than once. Her hand shook just a bit when she poured my wine, and her fingers bent in a flexed sort of way, like they were ready to spring claws.

Given that she did retain some level of smoothness, it was clear the struggle wasn't too difficult for her. New, but not incredibly so.

I relaxed silently, only then realizing the rest of the vampires were watching me placidly. Probably waiting for me to answer a question I'd been too distracted to hear.

"Sorry, what?" I said.

"Not at all," Darius answered politely, his posture all ease. "Please, take your time."

"Oh, I was just… Um." Would it be rude to say I was sussing out the danger? Probably. Although everything I did would probably be deemed rude in this highbrow setup.

"You were just taking in your surroundings." Darius smiled in a disarming sort of way. It didn't disarm anything. "On that topic, I noted your reaction to Mr. LaRay earlier this evening."

"Right, yes. Yeah, sorry about that. He startled me."

"Yes, so I gathered. And you reacted quickly and immediately. As you did with Clyde in the Edgewater."

The Edgewater was a plush hotel in Seattle owned by Darius's child—someone he'd made into a vampire. Someone I'd zapped a couple of times on impulse. I'd stayed there a few nights with some guy I didn't want to keep thinking about.

"Yes." I leaned back so the waitress could drape my napkin into my lap.

"You struggled to react to the various bombardments last night. Why is that, do you think?"

I barely stopped myself from nervously dabbing my forehead with the napkin. "If I knew the answer to that, I probably wouldn't be sitting at this huge table with vampires."

Speaking of the huge table…

"Where are all the other chairs?"

"I had them removed," Darius said, not at all impatient or cross that I had changed the subject instead of answering his question. "Reagan doesn't enjoy extra chairs around the table. You two are so similar, I thought you might have a similar issue."

"Us? Similar?" I frowned at him. "We're complete opposites."

"I think Darius is confusing life with battle," Marie said. "You and Reagan are similar in battle. Which is why we are perplexed that the training session didn't go well. You froze up. Why?"

It seemed I wouldn't be wiggling out of that topic of conversation.

I sipped my wine, thinking back to the night before. "My mind just went blank. I was trying to remember all the spells I've learned, and nothing would come."

"Yet, when you are not thinking at all, spells come

easily, as Mr. LaRay can attest," Darius said.

The waitress and a couple of helpers wheeled in a tray before visiting each place setting and moving the plates around. My small plate received a piece of bread and my bowl was filled with soup. She paused next to Darius and the helpers waited by their tray.

"Would it make you more comfortable if we ate?" Darius asked me as if it were a normal question. Why else would someone invite guests over for a midnight dinner if not to actually eat dinner?

"I don't mind," I said, locating the large soup spoon and picking it up gingerly.

"She feels awkward. We would do best to eat," Marie said.

"I agree." Darius gave a little wave, and the helpers sprang into action, arranging the rest of the plates like they had mine.

"Do vampires not generally eat?" I asked. There were plenty of other things to do besides sharing a meal in close quarters. Like sitting idly with a cup of tea. In public.

"Not generally, no." Darius took up his soup spoon. "It makes us hungry for our true sustenance, which is not always on hand."

I wrinkled my nose, knowing he meant blood. His comment about hunger made the memory of the newbie flash through my mind. Almost immediately, a wave of goosebumps covered my body and magic rose around me, ready for action.

Marie lifted the spoon to her lips, and without warning, the magic started to churn, wild and feral.

CHAPTER 10

"DON'T EAT," I said, my voice rough and my control wobbly. Their magic was swirling around me. If their bloodlust rose, I didn't trust myself not to reach for my magic cloud on impulse.

All three vampires paused and, almost as one, slowly lowered their spoons. The helpers drifted back in and whisked the bowls away.

I sat back, my appetite gone and the magic still churning around me. I locked my fingers together so I wouldn't do anything crazy.

A flick of Darius's eyes and my bowl was cleared too, followed by my place setting. The man could read people better than anyone else I'd ever met. Secrets would not be easy to keep around this crew.

"You have no control, is that it?" Darius asked, studying me.

"Absolutely none, no. Not when I'm in the thick of things. I don't think about what I'm doing at all, I just *do*."

"Yet in the training session, you could not *do* at all."

"She countered the spells with ease," Moss said. "Her defense wasn't lacking—it was her offense."

Darius sat back. "Yes, of course." He crossed his arms over his chest and tapped a finger against his chin. "Interesting."

"For the most part, she didn't attack first in the Guild compound either," Marie said. "She retaliated."

"Watch her hands," Moss murmured. They were clasped tightly on the table, the better for me to avoid accidentally killing someone.

Darius dropped his own hands to his lap. "I am sorely tempted to rush you and see what would happen."

A thrill of fear ran through me; I knew how fast he could move and how long his claws could get. My hands shook.

"But I must be honest: I am somewhat worried about what you would do." He continued to study me, and strangely, the others weren't looking at me at all. "You have a fantastic imagination when it comes to spell work."

"I don't know about fantastic, but it's certainly overactive." I swallowed past the lump in my throat and resisted the urge to wipe away the moisture beading on my forehead. I couldn't give my hands the opportunity to work magic without my permission.

"Reagan says that we should focus on that. On your

creativity. Based on what I have seen, I would agree, but you have to learn some sort of control. As you are, you are dangerous."

My temperamental third eye was screaming at me to get up, nice and slow, and get my butt out of that house as fast as possible. The pressure in the room seemed to be increasing. Rough and putrid magic brushed against me. The feeling of insatiable hunger scraped along my spine. Twisted in my gut.

"That's been the case since I first showed up at that church and met Reagan and the Bankses," I said, and licked my lips nervously. "Say, by the way, how often do you guys feed?"

"The older a vampire gets, the less he must feed," Darius said, as calm as a summer's breeze. He was probably lucky he couldn't see the turbulent magic rolling and shifting above him. "I am perfectly satisfied, I can assure you. Everyone in this room is. I ensured that would be the case before arranging this meeting with you."

Everyone *in this room* was perfectly satisfied.

Why had he needed to clarify the location?

"I would like to get you doing as many spells as possible in Reagan's warehouse," Darius said, and a soft scrape sounded from outside the room. "Over and over. I want them in your muscle memory. That will take the thinking out of the equation. I also want you exposed to dangerous or uncomfortable situations as much as possible. You need to spend some time living in fear to get used to what it does to you. Only when you understand your reactions can you begin to control them. Lastly, you need a teacher that understands you. That knows how to work with you."

A strange sort of panting invaded the tranquility of the dining room. It sounded like a dog was sitting in the hot summer sun just outside the door.

"You need me alive, right?" I said, having a hard time focusing on what he was saying. My mind went back to Emery telling me about vampires when we were in Seattle. *You should always keep your wits when dealing with a vampire. They are smart and cunning. If a vampire can get one over on you, or use you, or…something you probably wouldn't even think of, they will. Without hesitation. They have no loyalty.*

"Yes, about what happened last night," Darius started. "I had not intended to put you at such risk—"

I held my hand up to stop him. Callie had told me I held the power, and it was time to exert it. "Answer my question."

Something sparked in his eyes. His pause was slight, but enough to give away his pivot. "I do need you alive, yes. But I will not allow the enemy to use you."

The air thickened and my temperamental third eye started doing a jig, trying to get me moving. "You need me alive as long as I'm not a threat to you."

"Just so."

Which meant he'd kill me if the Guild successfully captured me.

I exhaled slowly, trying to calm my rapidly beating heart.

With everything I had, I wished Emery were with me. He would know how to navigate this situation.

"Then I guess we know where we stand." My throat clearing didn't cover the sound of a soft scratch outside of the door, as though a claw had gently slid down the wall.

Darius's words came back to me.

You need to spend some time living in fear to get used to what it does to you…

"What is outside that door?" I asked, my knuckles white from gripping my hands together.

"That took much too long," Marie murmured, and Darius and Moss both slightly nodded.

"I think it wise for you to leave the safety of the Bankses' house," Darius said, ignoring my question. "You are welcome to stay here, if you would like. Reagan has opened her home as well. Or, if you'd prefer—"

I held my hand up. "What is outside that door?"

"—I can rent something for you in the area. I would advise your friend to stay put. A non-magical person has no business in your life at the moment. It would likely be incredibly dangerous for her, and she has been through enough magical drama."

Light footfalls passed the room, like something was running. Another set of footfalls, this time with nails softly clattering on the wood floor, shifted closer to the door.

"You need to be pushed, Miss Bristol," Darius said. "Known Guild members have been seen in this area. My people are keeping an eye out. The shifters are on alert, as are the local mages and witches. But the Guild is notorious for their covert tactics. I expect to see some of the local mages shift their allegiance. That will lead to spying. People who have acted as friends may help trap you. You must be ready before that." He paused for a moment. "To answer your question, you have finally clued in to the five brand-new vampires waiting outside of this room. I will not let them kill you, but I will let them try. Your training has begun."

I stared at him with a slack jaw.

Five?

That one new vampire had nearly taken me down yesterday. Darius thought I could handle *five*?

"Kill as many as you like," he continued. "They should never have been turned, and their creator has since been destroyed. If you don't destroy them, I have no doubt the shifters will."

"But…they're people," I said, aghast.

"Prisoners convicted of heinous acts to their fellow man. The vampire that illegally turned them thought their past would enhance their maliciousness. She was right. They are a danger to both the magical world and the human world."

"They're like the vampire you brought with you last night? The one that almost killed me because you didn't properly guard him?"

Darius's lips thinned, the only indication that what I'd said cut him. "That vampire was the best of the lot and from a previous turning. His inclusion was a test…which he failed. Have no fear; he would not have reached you. Had you not reacted, another would have."

Something—a vampire, I now knew—snorted near the door. The sound was inhuman. They were all likely in their swamp thing forms.

I wanted to ask just who Darius thought would've helped me from across the room, but I didn't have the luxury of talking back. I had other things on my mind right now. Like the five hungry and out-of-control vampires waiting outside of this room, blocking my exit.

"Why aren't they coming in?" My voice was high and tight. "Are you going to let them bite me?"

"I am their master now. They will listen to me until

provoked beyond their limit. They will not enter this room while we sit idly at this table." He put his hands on the table, palms down. "They won't bite at this age. They will tear into your skin. I will not let them do that around a vital nerve, but otherwise..."

He let the sentence linger. It was probably better that way.

I blew out a breath, good and slow, trying to still the tremors racking my body. It didn't do much.

"Why the hell did Reagan bond you?" I asked. "You are, quite possibly, the worst person alive."

"I am not alive."

"That just makes it worse!"

"He has your best interests at heart," Marie said, finally looking at me. I saw a burning hunger in her eyes. She was reacting to my fear. Her hunger was rising, and her desire with it. I could feel them both. "He is being more lenient than I would've been. We fought side by side. I felt your greatness. These parlor tricks are beneath you. And so is that hideous dress."

"Nope. They sure aren't. Neither of them are. I think you are greatly overestimating my prowess, here. And my bank account."

Darius pushed back his chair and stood. "It is time you started your training, Miss Bristol. And please remember, you are welcome to stay here, should you wish—"

"You're out of your mind."

"—or stay with Reagan—"

"How am I going to get out?"

"—but please respect my wishes and stay out of the Bankses' home. While it is as safe as can be at the moment, soon it will be a target. The Bankses would never shift their allegiance, I am certain, but they would be in the way of those who did. Not to mention they'd find themselves in the crossfire."

"Fine, fine. But that won't be a problem if I'm bleeding from a dozen fang marks, will it? This isn't the right way to train, Darius." I pushed back from the table, my shaking body giving away my utter terror. "I am in control here." I struck a finger toward the ground. "*I* hold the power. And I say that I do not want to be trained by you. I do not. This ends now. Get rid of those vampires and let me out of here."

His expression didn't shift at all.

"No," he said, neither firmly nor angrily. He was completely unaffected by this whole scene.

"What do you mean, no?" I hollered. The time for decorum had long since ended. "I don't want to train with you. I have the power to choose. So end this."

"Only you have the power to end this."

I gaped at him for a moment. The other two vampires stared up at me calmly from their seats at the table.

"That is completely untrue." I lifted my hands and felt the magic slide through my fingers, ready to be used. "You know that you are in control of this situation."

"Yes, I do."

"And you also know I can kill you." I hadn't known that string of words was waiting to be said, but I didn't want to take it back. He was needlessly putting me in extreme danger. A threat or two was hardly amiss.

"I doubt *you* know you can kill me. Which is why we must start at the beginning." His gaze flicked to the door. "But I would advise against attacking anyone in this room before dealing with the vampires waiting behind it. You'll need your energy."

I clenched and unclenched my fingers. Then clenched and unclenched my jaw. Callie had been dead wrong. Darius held all the power in this situation. And he'd continue to hold all the power until I mastered my craft enough to put him in his place.

Which I would absolutely do.

"That's how it's going to be, is it?" I asked, my voice hard and rough and reminding me of my mother. For once, that wasn't a bad thing. "You're going to put me in your enemy corner?"

"If that is how you choose to view it, then yes."

"Fine. Fuck you."

His lips tweaked upward just a little and his eyes

glittered. "Those words have much more weight when they are seldom used."

"When she finally lets out her fire, it always scorches," Marie said in approval.

I nearly swung my finger at her and delivered the same threat, because she'd put herself squarely in my enemy corner as well. But I resisted the urge and turned away. They weren't my problem right now.

Still, it would be so gratifying when I finally got to punch them right in the kissers.

"Good luck, Miss Bristol," Darius said as Moss walked through the door of the dining room without turning his back.

"Wait…" I could feel all the blood drain from my face as Marie followed, connecting eyes with me for a moment before she disappeared. "You're leaving?"

"Of course. I must strip away all your safety nets. You'll do fine." He offered me a slight bow before gracefully striding toward the door. Almost there, he paused and half turned back. "I will keep them at bay for a few moments to let you get your bearings. After that…"

I'd never snarled in my life, but there was a first time for everything. Unfortunately, it didn't sound quite as forbidding as I would've liked.

"You will regret this," I ground out, anger flaring deep inside of me.

His smile was as slight as his bow. “I surely hope not.”

And he was gone, leaving me in an empty room blocked off by new, bloodthirsty vampires.

CHAPTER 11

"I'VE BEEN IN worse situations," I muttered, retreating toward the wall. For the moment, anyway, I was sheltered from visibility by the inwardly opened door. My breath caught in my throat, my panic working to override any pretense of thinking. "You've been in much worse situations. You've broken into a compound full of highly skilled magical people. You took them out in groups larger than five." My breath exited my mouth shakily. "But how?"

The answer rose, unbidden.

By running at the enemy and letting nature guide my hand.

I zipped my gaze to the far corner of the room where a leafy potted plant sat idle. I remembered the flowers I'd noticed on the way in—sitting on the shelves and draped down the banister. What I'd seen indicated there were plants in each room.

This house ruled by death was a haven for the natural.

Had Darius planned that?

I didn't know or care. I had to bust out of here, and that wouldn't happen if I wallowed in a puddle of fear. I needed to seize the moment.

"Okay. I can do this." I shook out my arms and welcomed the pump of adrenaline through my body.

I closed my eyes again, taking a moment to feel the energy of that plant, of the wind softly whistling through the window. Magic throbbed around me, alive and vibrant. It collected just above me in a cloud, my organized mass of the elements I could pull from this room.

Without thinking and before I could stop myself, I pushed off from the wall. I'd need to blast my way out, that was certain.

I stalked out from behind the door. As I rounded it, I caught sight of what I faced.

Forest green and ever so swampy, the group of vampires in their monster forms crowded at the doorway, staring in at me with hungry eyes and gaping, fang-filled mouths. Matted black hair fell down the sides of their gaunt faces, and their bowed legs and stringy arms ended in a set of vicious claws.

"The worst part about you is the way you look, did you know that?" I said through my teeth, my courage waning. "Oh holy crap, I'm not up for this. I'm not made for this kind of thing."

The magic pulsed above me as if to argue. The sweet

song of nature drifted from that lonely plant in the corner.

I balled my fists at my sides.

"Yes, I am," I said. Arguing with yourself was a sure sign of insanity, wasn't it?

Maybe insanity would help. It sure seemed to give Reagan a leg up.

"Yes, I *am* made out for this kind of thing!"

I started the weave without thinking, creating a spell reminiscent of the time I'd mixed glue, sage, and honey together as a kid and somehow made it explode. That jerk Billy Timmons had put gum in my hair, and Veronica and I had played at making a potion to blot him off the earth. Stupid Billy Timmons hadn't been hurt in the ensuing explosion, but I had blown a divot into the table, burned my hair, and succeeded in getting grounded for a week.

If I mixed in an explosives spell Callie had taught me, ballooning the power, it would surely do more than cut a small divot into those vamps.

It would blow out some walls.

Eat ants, Darius. I'm about to tear up your house.

I weaved the spell tightly, infusing it with my desire to do damage to both the monsters and the house. After I finished, a strange sensation kept me from throwing the spell.

Five.

Four.

A ticking clock, counting down.

Three.

Two.

I pushed the spell forward and braced myself, dropping a layer of survival magic in front of me in case there was backlash.

A stream of murky yellow zoomed at the collection of monsters shifting side to side in the doorway. Two of them pushed back to get away from the magic streaming at them. They were clearly the thinkers of the group.

The spell hit one of the other vampires center mass, plastering onto its chest.

It grunted and wiped at itself, first like a human might do after spilling coffee down his front, then more harried and intense. Its claws ran deep scratches through its flesh. From its agonized squeals, it seemed like the spell was burning away its skin.

"That's not what I was going for," I said under my breath, struggling to cobble together a different spell.

Without warning, my original spell exploded, the concussion hitting my wall of survival magic and pushing it back at me. The force took me off my feet and threw me at the wall five feet behind me.

The breath gushed out of my lungs as I hit the hard surface. I slid to the ground, my vision swimming. Wood groaned and something heavy crashed down not far from me.

I shook my head and shakily got to my feet, my ears ringing.

A vampire lay on the ground in the middle of the doorway, its chest torn open and black goo seeping out.

Bile rose in my throat at the carnage, but I pushed it down and sprinted forward. This was life and death. I didn't have time to throw up.

Another vampire was on the ground beyond the door, an arm blown off but its head and chest fine. It would heal.

I had to remember that. I couldn't just hit them with a spell and expect to be on my way. They'd get up and chase me with whatever limbs still worked while their bodies stitched back together.

It wasn't a fair fight.

Unless I purposely stopped their magical ability to heal.

But how?

The vampire on the ground was barely moving, so I leapt over it, planning to bolt for the stairs. Before I could get another foot down, though, a vampire rose in my way. Black burn marks covered half of its body and a flap of skin and tissue hung from a chunk in its thigh.

"Oh, that is freaking gross." I needed to work on my weak stomach.

Another vampire rose, shaky but with two feet and

two arms, all still adorned with razor-sharp claws. Desperate, hungry magic slammed into me, prickling my skin and scraping down my spine.

The closest vampire surged forward, faster than any human, claws and fangs out and ready to tear into me.

"Flipping Frisbees!" I zapped it, following up with a stream of white survival magic, all while back-pedaling.

I'd forgotten about the vampire on the ground.

My heel struck swampy flesh and I tipped, falling backward with a terrified scream. An arm came around me and claws dug into my side, changing the trajectory of my fall. My back hit bony ribs and my top half was yanked toward the fallen vampire's head. The thing—and right now these newbies did seem like things, not people or former people—hissed like a predator. Then the vampire's arm constricted, holding me still while its head bent to my neck.

Pure, primal fear woke up every sensory receptor in my entire body. I pulled the organized mass of magic above me down into the fiber of my being. I gave myself over to it completely, and then—

Fangs scraped my neck.

I let go.

A pure sheen of white rolled over my skin and attached to anything foreign touching my body. It latched on to the vampire's arm and sizzled acid along its claws. The hard bone under me softened, and the vampire started to wail…then to scream.

Magical spears dug into the vampire as I rolled off it, keeping the monster put while eating it alive. It convulsed and spasmed as a huge hole ripped through its middle. Black goo rose in the cavity, but my magic didn't let up.

Movement made me yank up my head. The surviving vampires were standing in a cluster on the opposite side of their fallen friend. Behind my magic. That stomach-twisting hunger was still very much pulsing from them, but it was interwoven with a new, unexpected strand. The intention was clear enough: *command us.*

Yeah, sure. Command you as you are reaching for my neck to cure that hunger. Nice try.

I couldn't go through them, and something told me they couldn't cross over to me until the white spell fizzled out. My legs felt shaky, and I knew it was because of the spell I'd just unleashed. If I tried to blast them now, the outcome would be weak and they'd easily take me down. I needed to stall our next confrontation until I got my second wind.

That, or I needed to find another way out.

I turned and sprinted deeper into the house. If I worked around to the other side, I'd hopefully find some servant stairs to the kitchen. Or something. In a house of this size and age, it was definitely a possibility.

The next large room I came to had a path through the center to a large archway, which then led to a hallway. I dashed in before immediately slowing down, my hands held out in anticipation. A quick look told me the room was probably empty. Couches, chairs, coffee table, a large Oriental rug, and a fireplace.

A strange pressure settled on my shoulders and a swish of movement in my peripheral vision had me spinning around.

Silence greeted me in the still room. The shadows seemed to laugh at me.

Warning butterflies stirred in my stomach and that same strange pressure bore down on my chest. I felt the itch of watchful eyes between my shoulder blades.

I was being watched.

But the onlooker wasn't advancing, and he or she was far enough away that I didn't feel any foreign magic.

Best not to count my blessings.

Quickening my pace, scanning constantly, I finished crossing the room, emerging into a round area with two hallways leading away, one off to the right, and the other mostly straight ahead, both cloaked in shadow. A painting of a boat hung next to a closed doorway on my left, and a short column supporting a vase of flowers stood just inside the hallway to the right.

I licked my lips, knowing time was limited.

If I stayed straight, I would be heading deeper into the house, toward the side that (I was pretty sure) pushed up against the neighbor's house. My only chance for escape would be the possibility of servants' stairs.

The hallway leading right would eventually take me to a wall with windows that led to the outside world. Of course, I was on the second floor, and jumping to my death was not on my agenda.

The only other option was back the way I had come.

I looked behind me.

In the middle of the room I'd just crossed stood a single newbie vampire, a line of spit hanging from its mouth. Its gnarly claws clicked off each other, glistening in the low light.

"Butterballs." I couldn't go back.

I had to choose. Two options, and the wrong one might get me killed.

CHAPTER 12

EMERY STOOD AT the top of a cliff in the Realm, watching magical creatures of all kinds zip past him on the fast-track paths. The elves had set up the system of paths, which magically sped up travel from point A to B, allowing magical creatures to travel through the Realm at high speeds.

Emery sank to the ground and tucked his legs under him, content to watch all the species sail past.

A faerie giggled as she or he—it was hard to tell the fair folk apart from a distance—drifted past. Purple magical dust sparkled and swirled behind her or him, washing into the eyes of a sylph, a species of notoriously ill-tempered air sprites about half the height of humans. The sylph waved his hand in front of him in annoyance, trying to wash away the magical dust before sliding to the side.

Emery let his gaze drift up to take in the other flying creatures, but a cloud of black mist rushed in to disrupt the scene. He went on edge immediately, ready for the premonition that would tell him from which direction the danger would come.

Penny's beautiful face came into view. Her luminous blue eyes held blind terror and sweat beaded her forehead. She stood at the mouth of a darkened corridor in what looked like a well-appointed house. An oil painting of a small boat in turbulent sunset seas hung on a wall to the left, and a small column to the right held a large vase full of flowers.

If she went down that corridor, she would die. He felt it as clearly as he did the dirt under his suddenly clawed fingertips.

Throat constricting in panic, he scrambled to his feet. But what could he do? He was worlds away, literally. If he took the absolute fastest route back, it would still take him a week or more. That, and the fastest route through the Brink would put him on display. Considering how easily the Guild had tracked him so far, they'd catch sight of him in no time, and he'd essentially lead a hostile army to Penny's door.

A sick feeling twisted his gut.

He'd told himself he had to leave, that she'd be better off without him, but he'd walked away and left her in danger. He'd all but put her on display for the Guild, then abandoned her.

He shoved away the guilt, trying to think rationally. Trying to use logic.

She was extremely valuable. The Guild wouldn't kill

her. Neither would Darius. They would protect her and try to use her to further their own ends.

So why had his foresight kicked in?

Because trying to control Penny was like trying to keep a candle flame lit when running in the wind. Getting into trouble was as natural for her as breathing, no matter how much the people around her wanted to keep her safe. The best thing to do was stick by her side and run with her through the middle of chaos. Try to be on her team, letting her lead as often as she followed, and hold on for dear life.

He'd barely had any time with her, but he'd learned that much. And using that method, they'd made it through impossible odds.

He paced, waiting for another premonition. Wondering if he would somehow feel it if something happened to her.

His head said not to go to her right then. It said to stay apart from her and force the Guild to split their resources. Logic dictated that one of the most strategic, powerful, and ruthless vampires alive would not let one of his prized assets fall into irreparable harm. If Emery had to trust one vampire, it would be Darius. In all of their dealings, he'd learned that Darius's strict code kept him largely predicable and trustworthy…for a vampire.

Emery bit his lip.

It was that last part that threatened to unravel that

line of thinking.

For a vampire.

That wasn't saying a whole helluva lot.

The black mist drifted in again.

CHAPTER 13

HEART HAMMERING, KNOWING I should turn and fight rather than run, I jogged toward the hallway on the right and peered down it. The old-fashioned electric candles bracketed to the wall were turned down low, and dark shadows lined the walls and pooled along the ground. There were doors on either side, probably bedrooms. The sweet smell of flowers from the column on my right tickled my nose, helping to calm the magic gathered above me. Even so, the picture up on my left felt like a perfect representation of my mood. A small boat rolling amidst crashing waves, its passengers wondering if this was the end.

It won't be the end.

It couldn't be. I couldn't die before I got to slap Emery in the face for failing to meet my expectations. I didn't even care if it wasn't his fault; he'd still get a slap.

And Darius needed that punch in the kisser.

But as I stood in the archway of that hallway, the hard clicks of nails on wooden floor of my newbie pursuer getting ever nearer, joined now by other clicks from other pursuers, I couldn't seem to will myself forward. Vampire magic hung heavy in the air like a fog, hot and sticky. The vampire lurked in these walls somewhere. Not Darius and not a newbie.

A soft hiss invaded my decision-making. The clicks stopped, so damn close.

A glance back and I started.

The newbie vampire stood in the archway behind me, braced and ready to attack, claws out.

"Fickle blanket weavers." Adrenaline dumped into my body.

I spun and launched forward, readying a spell to toss behind me as I went. Movement registered in my peripheral vision before I could even gasp. Strong fingers wrapped around my forearm and yanked me back.

"No," I heard, low and urgent.

Magic swirled through my fingertips as I came to a stop, facing Mr. Devilishly Handsome Vampire.

Electricity surged around me, charging my skin before pumping into Darius's hand and arm. A bug zapper sound preceded him flinching away, and I jumped to the side, my hands already up and weaving a spell. The act strangely felt like knitting, and a stray thought curled away—I wondered if that was why my mother had taken up knitting (before failing at it and stabbing the couch in frustration).

Darius stood in front of me, his hair standing on end and his hands fisted at his side. He looked like he'd just stuck his finger in a light socket.

His hard hazel eyes beat into my head. "No," he said, and despite his hair issue, his voice came out calm and unaffected. "Do not go that way."

I glanced down the dark hallway before looking back at the room from which I'd come. The green monster stood frozen in place, looking at me with bunched muscles and thick cords of drool falling from its mouth.

"Why should I trust you?" I whispered.

"I am training you, not trying to kill you," he said, unconcerned about the newbie vampire panting in the doorway behind him.

"You didn't do a lot when that other one had its fangs on my neck."

"I was about to step in when you handled the situation beautifully. I would love to leave you alone and see what new surprises you have in store, but you are exuding a lot of magic right now. Strong, powerful magic. Helpful in keeping weaker creatures at bay, yes, but I worry it might awaken aggressive urges in the elder residing down that hall. I am not sure I could defeat her should she decide to engage, so I would rather not take the chance."

There was a lot to unpack in that speech, like his

belief that my magic would keep weaker creatures at bay when they were still clearly chasing me through the house. Or how my anger toward him softened just a bit from knowing he'd kept an eye on me this whole time. Or the absolute terror of imagining a vampire capable of intimidating him.

Hard clicks sounded, and I tore my focus away from Darius and shifted it to the newbie vamp edging closer. A strange sort of growl preceded a glob of drool dropping from its mouth.

"That must destroy the rugs," I mumbled.

Another vampire waited behind the first, impatiently shifting.

Darius barely moved, his head turning just slightly, and a wave of his spicy magic filled the space. The closest vampire stopped where it was, but the one behind it scooted up so they were clustered again. Their bloodlust was rising; I could feel it in the dizzied magic mingling with mine. With Darius's.

My mind whirled, back to wondering if I could trust him, or if he'd purposely stopped me from escaping.

"Why would you let such a powerful creature hang out in your house?" I asked, watching his face for signs of lying. "Especially when you invited me over?"

"I did not foresee you would use your magic this way. I've never experienced it before. I wonder if Emery knows of it."

I pointed up at the organized mass above my head. "That, you mean? Because lately, I always have that brewing, and it doesn't seem to bother anyone else."

Darius's brow wrinkled as he followed my point. "I don't know what you are pointing at, but what is happening with your magic is a recent development, and it is not standard."

"That's a nice way of calling me weird." I gritted my teeth as the clicking resumed, those hungry buggers edging toward me again.

Darius glanced over his shoulder. But instead of warning them back, he offered me a slight bow and then stepped away. "I'll leave you to it."

As if on cue, the closest vampire broke from the pack and lunged for me.

Eat. Kill. Devour.

Fangs, claws, and sinewy muscle stretched across its bones.

That was all I could see. All that registered.

My body locked in deep, paralyzing fear. Energy pulsed and throbbed around me. Spells rolled through my head, one by one, but the only ones I could latch on to were mostly steeped in feelings. Random thoughts. An image of a sunny day, a magnifying glass, and an anthill.

"How is that helping?" I whispered, watching the creature cross the small patch of hallway between us, intent on reaching me and ripping me open.

I knew I needed to move. To do something other than stand around like a fool. Very recently, I had been better than this. I had reacted.

Why was I locking up again?

The creature's claw came up to slash. Darius twitched, and I thought he would step in. I thought he would grab the hand.

He stepped back.

"Help," I begged, a sad, feeble little cry that would do nobody any favors.

The vampire grinned, of all things, and the claw swung at my neck.

CHAPTER 14

A SHOCK OF power ripped out of my middle, yanking on my ribcage and spilling heat down through my core. Heat turned to fire and filled me to bursting, tingling in my fingers, my toes, and all the way up to my hair follicles. White blasted out from my body, a blanket of white-hot power that punched through the vampire's middle, creating a hole as big as two of my fists.

The creature didn't have time to howl. It jerked once, its limbs thrown wide, before it fell to the ground in a pile that quickly turned into oozing black sludge.

My survival magic didn't stop. It rocketed out again, aiming for the first one's buddy. Its eyes widened a moment before my magic pierced its middle, the hole smaller but just as deadly.

It howled and clutched at its chest before its legs buckled.

A metallic click sounded down the hall at my back. The soft creak of hinges announced a door opening. A magical presence filled the hallway. *Fight. Tear. WAR.*

"Go!" Darius shoved me behind him. "Marie! Moss!"

A woman wearing a beautiful crimson evening gown glided into the space. Small and slight, she held her hands up near her chest, worrying one of her nails. Her shoulders were straight, but her bowed head put me in mind of a timid housewife from a 1950s TV show.

Kill. Kill. Kill.

No matter what she looked like, there was no denying the rush of intent filling the hallway.

Marie was by my side in a moment, her hands bracing my shoulders and her gaze rooted to the woman. Moss zoomed in next, taking up a position beside and a little behind Darius.

An ancient sort of power filled the hallway, long dormant and just waking up, like a mummy throwing off the lid of its sarcophagus and slowly sitting up. It was the magic I'd sensed before Darius's arrival, only stronger. Active.

"I have badly underestimated what it means to be an untrained natural in a pressurized situation. Marie, get her out of here," Darius said, his usually calm demeanor tense and voice tight. "Hurry! Moss, we must keep Ja confined to this house until she regains sense."

"What's—"

Marie lifted me and threw me over her shoulder

before I could get another word out.

"And Marie," Darius said, and she stopped to turn. "Bring back blood offerings."

I could just see the woman's hands separate and move to her sides as claws grew from her fingertips. Very little about her posture had changed, but a primal fear I could barely understand crawled through my insides. Moss braced for an attack and Darius stripped down, even now worried about preserving his expensive suit.

Logic fled. Trying to do the right spell wasn't even a concern. Like I'd done in the warehouse and in the Guild's compound, I instinctively wove Marie's magic into my own. The pattern came naturally, my focus on *protection* and *repulsion* both. My goal was simply to keep the vampire away, but if push came to shove, I would unleash hell.

Marie's body tightened under me. More of her magic pumped out, primal, aggressive, and thrilling. I wrapped it into the spell I was weaving, going with the flow.

"Get the natural out of here," Darius yelled, startling Marie into action.

She spun, but not before I loosed the spell. It tumbled down the hallway, barely missing Darius before expanding.

Ja hissed. Her clothes ripped, and milky-white skin

burst through them as she changed into her monster form.

"Oh crap," I said, her image jiggling as Marie ran. "That one is really old."

My magic flowered right before it got to the vampire, flashing brightly colored light, but I didn't get to see anything more than that. Marie turned the corner into the room I'd walked through earlier, finding one last new vampire, huddled near a couch. Even upside down and bouncing around on her shoulder, I could tell it was shaking like a frightened animal.

"That old vampire is intense if she's making the new one cower," I said, trying to keep my breath with her shoulder cutting into my gut.

"The young one is afraid of you." She gracefully sped down a hall and to the mouth of the stairs, so much faster than a human.

"Feel free to take these slow—" A shock wave rumbled through the house. The walls and ceiling groaned with the flux. The floor shook.

Marie put on a burst of speed, taking two stairs at a time. I felt weightless, then slammed down on her shoulder. Weightless, slammed down.

"Slower," I tried to get out between the grunts, struggling to find a way to stop the pain.

She leapt three-quarters of the way down, holding my legs with one hand and holding the other out for balance.

"Nooooo—"

She landed, something snapped, and she guided my body to land on her shoulder again, all in one graceful, ice-skater-like movement.

I wasn't so graceful.

The impact knocked the air from my lungs. I gasped and shoved at her, trying to get free. Trying to straighten up, or curl over, or something that might help me get more air.

She staggered to the side, and I realized it was her shoe heel that had snapped. The dip helped me escape, and I rolled off, hitting the ground painfully.

Kill. Kill. Kill.

I looked up as the corrosive magic slammed into me, trying to drag me under its hypnotic spell. Marie's body ripped through her beautiful dress as she shifted to her monster form, taking two fast steps before crouching in front of me with her claws out, hissing.

"Go." The scratchy, badly articulated word came from Marie's vampire form, something I hadn't realized was possible. "Go!"

A white, black, and red form walked in jerky steps to the top of the stairs, one of its legs crunching with each step from a wonky knee, causing the lower leg to angle off in the wrong direction. Once it reached the top of the stairs, I could make out the intense burn marks scoring its front, some of them dribbling blood. Other areas, not burned, had gaping wounds, some showing bone and others dripping blood like a faucet. One arm was out of the socket, and two fingers were missing off the other hand.

That vampire should be dead. My spell had obviously blasted through it. Charred it. Cut it. Darius and Moss, the backups, had clearly smashed and ripped at it. Had stood in its way and fought tooth and nail.

"Oh my God." I breathed softly as realization dawned. My lower lip trembled. "Did that thing kill Darius and Moss?"

Something else occurred to me, and it squeezed my chest painfully until I could barely breathe. Darius and Moss might have died to give me a fighting chance to escape. Marie stood in front of me, crouching and hissing, ready to fight for me too.

They were putting themselves in harm's way to protect me.

I'd always heard vampires weren't loyal. That they couldn't be trusted. But Darius had tried to save me twice tonight, and his people had backed him up. Even now, Marie could easily stand aside. If that thing up there had killed her boss, she could walk away without looking back.

Yet there she stood, her body trembling and her fangs and claws out, ready to fight a much more powerful vampire.

What type of person would walk away from this? Would whisper a thanks and saunter out the door?

"No more hiding in closets," I whispered. That was the promise I'd made to myself after Emery had left. That I would learn magic, excel at it, and never hide again.

Well, here I was. Challenge accepted.

I flexed my fingers and squared my shoulders. I didn't know what the heck I was doing, but I was going to do it *big*.

CHAPTER 15

THE VAMPIRE STARED down at us, ready to descend.

Pushing away the fear, ignoring the list of spells running through my head that only seemed to throw me off, I centered myself by focusing on the nature drifting around me. The fragrant smell of the flowers. The air drifting along my skin.

The magic leveled out, balanced. My knees shook.

Another footfall hit the stairs. The old vampire's magic tried to swirl within mine. She was gaining power. Healing.

Gotta go quick.

Shut up, that's not helping.

What do you want to do, Penny? What do you want to do?

"Go!" Marie said, getting ready to fight. "Penelope, run!"

I want to protect Marie.

I took stock of the knowledge that she believed in me, that she was willing to risk her life for me, and grimaced a little at how awkward it was that a grown woman who looked just a bit older than me often carried me around like I was some deranged doll. I began to weave the magic between my hands, delighting in the feel until I latched on to the older vampire's magic and snaked it through the weave.

Sometimes, the hardest person to fight was ourselves.

I hoped that was as true of vampires as it was of humans.

"Move, child," I heard, and peeled an eye open.

The older vampire was halfway down the stairs, noticeably less messed up. Its arm was now back in business, and its leg was almost there. It had been taking its time to heal the big issues so it could fight.

Marie had surely known that, but she still hadn't charged it.

"I got you, Marie," I said, taking a few steps back because I couldn't help myself. Despite the older vampire's smaller stature, its mere presence was enough to pull out my old fears and wrap them around my face like a suffocating scarf. Something about it said *death.*

"My fight is not with you," the older vampire said to Marie, and a chill settled into my bones. I shook with it, wondering if I'd ever be able to get warm again.

"I will go through you," the elder vampire warned her.

I thought of Emery slinging spells at my side. He

wouldn't have given the vampire a chance to heal.

A spark flared deep inside of me. A new feeling emerged.

Joy. Laughter. Love.

The weave came easier, now, almost done. It zinged between my fingers, complex and beautiful, and I couldn't believe I was creating it.

Look away or you might mess it up.

I closed my eyes again, focusing on the feelings. Giving it the time it needed. Knowing that even this wouldn't help in a real battle. Not if I was on the front line. This vampire was moving at turtle speeds, and still I wove.

"Run, Penelope," Marie shouted. "Run, you stupid human!"

The older vampire launched forward. Marie surged up the stairs.

I jolted and accidentally released my spell a little early. "Oh, blooming bollocks!"

Trying to save it, I followed it with a hasty re-creation of the exploding weave from earlier, pushing them both forward. I staggered with fatigue, only now realizing how much energy I had used.

Five.

Four.

Dizzy but hanging in there, I grabbed for the edge of the entryway table. It shook and a vase of flowers tumbled to the floor. "Run, Marie, it's going to explo—"

She spun on a dime and rushed back my way. I screamed and nearly zapped her out of surprise. She grabbed me around the middle and threw me up over her shoulder.

"Ow. No. I can run." She ripped the door open.

Two.

Ja quickened her pace but fumbled on the steps as she looked down at her torso in surprise. The burn from the spell must've started. Thankfully, it slowed her down.

Marie ran me across the street and to the opposite corner.

Boom!

The door burst from the hinges and tumbled end over end. Parts of the frame followed it. They all skidded to a stop in the middle of the dark, deserted street.

A surge of backdraft magic (a term I'd just made up) reached us, blowing back our hair before dissolving into nothing. Lights clicked on across the street.

Marie put me down and her body transformed back into a beautiful woman…who was now standing naked on the street corner.

"What was that spell?" she asked, out of breath. I wondered if changing was the same kind of energy suck for vampires that it was for shifters.

"Honestly...I'm not sure. The end was actually happiness, so I'm not sure how it worked."

She looked at me, ignoring the car that dramatically slowed as it passed.

"You stayed behind to help me," she said.

"*You* stayed behind to help *me*," I replied.

"I typically have no use for humans. They are a daft, weak, stupid sort of species that acts as a virus to the Brink." I grimaced, not sure if I wanted to hear what came next. "But you are different, Penelope. I am glad you won't be training like other mages. It would reduce you."

"That's another lovely way of calling me weird."

"Yes." She grabbed my shoulder, turned me, and gave me a shove that sent me staggering away. I was unreally weak after that spell. "Go now. I need to see about Darius."

"Do you need help? My spell obviously worked in one way, but it might not have taken that vampire down completely."

"Ja was not after him. She should've been happy with disabling him."

Her voice didn't waver, but I remembered that Darius's seldom did, either—except when Ja had come at him. Then I'd heard his panic.

"Now go." She waved me away. "Your magic is the reason Ja came out of her stupor. Your power is sensational, as I said, but not always in the best ways."

"That was a backhanded compliment if ever I heard one," I muttered as she strode away, stepping out in front of a coming car without any concern for her nudity or her safety. "I sure wish I had that confidence."

I stared after her for a second, wanting to follow. Wanting to see Darius and Moss for myself, wanting to help. They'd set me up in a bad way, but it wasn't in me to hold a grudge. In the end, they'd stepped up to protect me. I couldn't argue with that.

But Marie was right. For some reason, something in my magic had set off that really old vampire, and if she had survived, I would just set her off again.

I sighed and slouched, bone-tired, before starting off down the street, no direction in mind. I needed to call Callie and Dizzy. I shouldn't stay with them long term, maybe, but one more night wouldn't kill me.

A lump formed in my throat. I should also probably call Reagan and tell her what had happened. She'd want to know.

I brushed my side and a sickening realization dawned. I'd left my handbag in the house, which meant I didn't have my phone or money for a cab.

I stopped up short. I was in the French Quarter, where all manner of things went on, looking like I'd just walked out of Thunderdome, without a car, a place to go, or money. Most importantly, like Reagan had pointed out the other day, without any street smarts.

"Shhhii—" I ducked my head, cutting the swear short. Karma had clearly gotten me into this mess somehow, and I didn't want to make it worse by defying my mother. Sounded stupid, but there was no denying she'd kept me safe for twenty-four years.

Then again, she'd rarely allowed me to leave the house.

"Okay, Penny, think." I bit my lip and looked back toward Darius's house. A few more lights from surrounding houses had clicked on.

There was probably no way I could just pop back over, tiptoe around the mess, and grab my forgotten handbag…

I turned in the opposite direction, racking my brain for a way out of this mess. If any of the mages from the party the other night lived in the area, I didn't remember. The only other species I knew that hung out here that might be friendly were…the shifters.

That guy Red had called me when I'd first come, after all. He'd said to call if I needed anything.

He hung out in the bars up near the river. That was where I needed to head.

Fifteen or so minutes later, I was hurrying through the mostly quiet streets, my cheap shoes squeaking dramatically. Before I reached the stretch of bars, the street opened up, the lane splitting around a grassy island area that housed a few groups of loiterers, still awake despite the hour and chatting on makeshift chairs or the ground.

I clutched my sweater a little tighter over my chest, looking straight ahead so as not to make eye contact with someone who might think I was open for business. Granted, ladies of the night probably wore nicer-looking, or certainly more revealing, apparel, but these guys probably fell in the "beggars can't be choosers" camp.

"Hey, pretty lady," someone called from across the street. A few hoarse chuckles followed.

I grimaced, looking sideways at a flare of light. A man cupped a lighter to his glass pipe. The flame was sucked through the barrel of the pipe, illuminating his unibrow and dirty forehead.

"I'm just minding my own business," I said softly, picking up the pace. My shoes protested.

"Hey," some guy shouted, his voice ringing across the quiet early morning. "I said *hey!*"

The someone's-watching-me itch from earlier flared to life with a vengeance, so furious that I stutter-stepped to a stop and couldn't help looking. A couple guys in the grassy island glanced over, without any real interest. Across the street, in a weed-choked area beneath a large, leafy tree, movement flickered, catching my eye. The shape stilled almost immediately, covered in heavy shadow, but I could just make out the form of a stocky character looking my way, watching me. The way his body was braced against the tree, sitting but not at rest, rose my hackles.

He wasn't like the others in this area, lounging with a bottle or his drug of choice—he was here for a purpose.

Was that purpose me?

Butterflies of anticipation filled my stomach, and the pressure of danger pressed on my chest.

Gritting my teeth, I turned away and started to walk—no, swagger. Predators liked to chase. They liked to hunt. If I acted nonchalant, maybe the watcher would have second thoughts.

Sensitive to the sounds around me, I put distance between myself and the collection of people behind me.

Breathing got a little easier with every step, and I slowed as I approached the bar where Red usually hung out. I just hoped he was there. Based on the mostly quiet street, the odds weren't entirely favorable. The bars were clearly closed.

I drifted close to the wall and into the shadows, hunching to make myself smaller. I peeked around the corner like a creep, listening hard. Shifters kept late hours. The bar was closed, but maybe the partygoers hadn't all gone home. The two big guys loitering outside would support that theory. If they *were* shifters, they'd likely know Red and let me inside. Or they'd call him.

If not, I needed to come up with another plan. And quick. The itch between my shoulder blades had diminished, but if the Guild was in this area, they'd be roaming around. Any one of them might seize the chance to try and grab me. Given how weak I felt after the display at Darius's house, that could be disastrous.

Straining, I pointed my ear in their direction, but it was soon apparent that they were either quiet or mute. I couldn't hear a single word.

Blowing out a breath, I racked my brain for a fix to the problem, and almost immediately (albeit belatedly) remembered the concealment spell I'd created in the Guild compound.

I rolled my eyes at myself. My mother would slap me upside the head for that memory slip.

Chalk it up to experience, Penny.

I summoned as much energy as I could muster and closed my eyes while sorting through the elements that would make the spell. The familiar weave came naturally. I had it draped over myself in no time, and the light shimmer around me said I'd done it right.

Taking a deep breath, I slipped around the corner, continuing to hug the wall and stick to the shadows. In the event the spell faltered, it was better to be safe than sorry. Or as my mother would say, "Penny, don't be an idiot."

Fifteen feet from the men, I could hear their soft murmurs. A little closer and I could make out their faces in the flare of their cigarettes. One was a broad-faced guy in his mid-thirties with a big block of a body, and the other had jutting teeth and an expression like something smelled bad. Neither was Red (thank you, random selfie in the email—it turned out it hadn't been as odd as it had seemed at the time). Still, they could be shifters.

The broad-faced guy's shoulders stiffened, and he held up a hand to the other, his face pointed my way.

I froze, staring at him with wide eyes, wondering if my spell hadn't worked like I'd thought.

"What is it?" Smells-a-Stink asked in a hush.

Broad Face sniffed and scanned the street. "You smell that?" he murmured.

The other guy stepped into the gutter, keeping one foot on the street. He looked upward and then away before facing my direction. "Yeah. Don't see nothin', though."

Fabulous. *I* was the stink.

"Filthy vampires, is it?" the first asked.

"Nah, they ain't invisible. They don't smell as good, neither."

"Too bad. Tearing one of them apart would get us noticed in the pack. They're hard to kill, I hear."

"What about one of those mages wandering around

the city?" Smells-a-Stink said, taking a step in my direction.

It finally occurred to me that these were magical folk who could smell exceptionally well, hanging out near a shifter bar, and had mentioned the word *pack*. My mother's voice sounded in my head: *Penny, stop being slow.*

Shifters.

My concealment spell fit around me like a bubble, deadening sound to some degree, but I hadn't thought at all about smell.

Since these guys were shifters, I could just show myself to them…only they clearly weren't so hot on vampires or mages. Given that I was a mage and my new trainer was a vampire (I had not resigned myself to the possibility he might not have made it through), I was not on their "awesome" list.

And now they knew I was here.

CHAPTER 16

I COULD NOT remember if shifters had enhanced hearing, but it seemed like a strong possibility, given that animals did. Which meant a sound-suppressing spell wouldn't work as well with them, especially if they were already onto me.

Careful with my footfalls, I took a step away. Then another, putting distance between us. Unfortunately, Broad Face took one step toward me with a much larger stride. Smells-a-Stink matched him.

I held my breath and picked up the pace, trying to choose each step carefully.

My overburdened shoe groaned with the effort. I froze with my other foot off the ground.

"There's something there," Broad Face said, pausing with me. "A female."

How could he possibly know that? I was certainly sweating as much as any man.

"A mage, then," the other murmured, the words almost unintelligible. He was trying to keep me from hearing. Clearly he didn't know I was all of seven feet away.

"Rush her," Broad Face whispered.

"I don't know where she is," the other murmured, this time without moving his lips.

"That way somewhere." Broad Face jerked his chin in my direction. "If we just run at her, eventually we'll run *into* her."

"We should *change*, or we'll run right into a spell."

"Not if we surprise her."

It wasn't clear why these two had been given the duty of guarding the door. Or any duties at all.

"You go at it, and I'll circle around," Broad Face said out of the side of his mouth. He used the same volume.

This was about to get interesting. If they weren't rushing me together, it would be similar to dodge ball, which I'd always been surprisingly great at. I'd just have to step aside when they barreled past. Of course, red balls didn't have long, grasping arms.

"Ready?" Smells-a-Stink asked, his volume increasing with his excitement.

"Yeah," the other whispered.

A door squealed somewhere behind them and a tall man stepped out. "What are you guys doing?" Light spilled across his familiar face.

"Red," I said in relief, stepping forward.

"There!" Broad Face swung a finger toward me, but

not right at me. He squinted at nothingness. "Did you hear that?"

"I heard that!" Smells-a-Stink backed into the street between two parked cars. "I definitely heard that. You sure that is a mage and not a ghost?"

"Mages can do tricks like that," Broad Face said, putting out his hands. "I'm pretty sure."

"Red," I said again, unraveling the spell as Broad Face moved somewhat in my direction with his arms waving in front of him.

"There!" Smells-a-Stink pointed at me. "It was a female, all right."

Broad Face jerked and took a quick step away before getting his bearings and hop-stepping back into position. He looked me up and down with his shoulders back, squinting at me. "Didn't think I'd catch you, did you? Well, I did. You filthy mages can't get nothing past me. I knew you were there the whole time."

"So did I," Smells-a-Stink said, nodding adamantly.

"Sorry. I just wanted to talk with Red." I pointed lamely, doing nothing to straighten out of my hunch. Invisibility had its perks.

Broad Face stepped between Red and me. "What business do you have here?"

"She's a rat," Smells-a-Stink said in disgust.

"Yeah." Broad Face adjusted his belt. "A rat, and a filthy black magic mage. Ain't that right? I heard all about what's going down in Seattle. Well, let me tell you something..." He paused for effect.

"We're not having it," Smells-a-Stink said.

Broad Face's jaw clenched as he tilted his head in irritation. Smells-a-Stink had clearly stolen his thunder.

I pulled my cardigan tighter and stepped to the side so I could see past him. "Red, please, I need help."

A slim hand appeared on Broad Face's arm. Red looked around him, his eyes roaming my hair and face.

"I know her," Red said, stepping closer. The two other shifters calmed down marginally, but didn't drop their tough-guy stances. "You're staying with that mage couple in the Garden District?"

"Yes. Please." I stepped closer to him. "I need to contact Reagan Somerset. You know her, right? Something happened at Darius Durant's house, and—"

The two shifters stiffened and Red licked his lips nervously.

"What's this, Red?" Broad Face asked. "You in league with the vampires now?"

Red shuffled closer before protectively (and awkwardly) slinging his arm around my shoulders. It didn't seem like he was used to bodily contact, but I was grateful for the show of support.

"She doesn't know anything about all that," Red said, turning me toward the bar door.

Broad Face stepped into our path. "Now wait a minute. I got a few questions first."

"Would you get out of the way?" Red waved him off. "Roger has an interest in this young lady. I'd hate to tell the Alpha of the North American Pack that you guys gave her a hard time when she came to us for help."

Broad Face gave me a hard look before finally stepping aside. "Fine. But you better mind your manners, little mage, is that clear?"

Red shook his head in exasperation and ushered me toward the door, releasing my shoulders so he could open it for me.

"I'll be watching," Broad Face said as I stepped through.

"From where, outside the door?" Red mumbled to himself, filing in behind me.

Dim light greeted me, splashing across the bar and highlighting two guys at the far end having a drink. Another group was tucked behind a divider at the other side of the door. Soft music played in the background, weaving in and out of the murmuring of conversation. My hunch had held water—legally the bar was closed, but drinks were still being poured for magic people who were quiet.

Red tried to usher me to a seat at the bar, but I hesitated. "I just wondered if I could use your phone. I left mine behind. And maybe borrow a few dollars for a cab?"

"Yeah, sure. Do you want a drink?" Red offered, scooting in front of me. "It's safe in here. I meant what I said about Roger. He knows you're not part of the Guild. No one in their right mind would lay a finger on you in here."

The murmuring died down as we approached the bar. The two guys sitting at the end of the wood counter turned my way. They looked to be in their forties, each of them nursing a bottle of beer. I could see the table behind the divider now, three guys and a couple of girls.

"What's this, Red?" The bartender sauntered over and the light glinted off the ring in her nose. Tattoos ran down her arms and across her breastplate, dipping into her low V-neck shirt.

"That mage snuck up on us." Broad Face had opened the door and stood dramatically in the frame. "She was invisible. Said she came from that elder vampire's house."

All murmuring stopped and a tense hostility clouded the air. Great.

"She was teamed with the Rogue Natural in Seattle," Red said. "If you're worried about it, call Roger. I'm sure he has nothing better to do than corroborate my story."

"*She* was with the Rogue Natural?" one of the guys at the bar said, turning in his seat so he could see better.

"I've heard all about the Rogue Natural. There's no way she could keep up with him. Look at her."

"This was literally the last place I would've thought he'd be mentioned," I mumbled. "The last place."

"She didn't say nothing about the Rogue Natural," Broad Face said, taking a step back.

"I hear that guy is the best there is." Smells-a-Stink stepped into the doorway to replace his buddy. "He works alone, though. Everyone knows that."

"Wait, was she the chick involved in that huge Guild takedown in Seattle?" someone from the table in the corner asked. "Because there *was* a chick in all that. The vampires own her…"

I was too mystified for a rebuttal.

Smells-a-Stink pushed in farther so he could look around the divider. "I don't know about a chick, but I know about the Rogue Natural. He's a real cowboy. A renegade. But he works alone. He's stronger that way. I mean, *rogue*? What does that mean to you? Works well in groups?" He huffed incredulously.

"Honestly, I just need a phone," I said. "A phone and cab money."

"I thought about going rogue," Smells-a-Stink continued, and I wasn't sure who he was talking to at that point. "No bosses, no one bothering you—"

"Here." The bartended handed over a cordless phone. "By the time anything gets through their thick heads, you'll be frozen to death." She pointed at the back of the bar. "The bathroom's back there if you want to freshen up." She eyed Red. "Or some alone time."

"I'm just trying to help her out," Red said, taking a step back and raising his hands. "She doesn't know anything about this life. She grew up human. She's out here getting trained by the dual-mage pair in the Garden District, but something went wrong with last night's training and she's been handed over to the vamps. Now look at her. Clearly something went wrong again."

I blinked at him for a few seconds. He certainly knew a lot about my life. And if he did, the Guild certainly would.

Time to go.

I reached for my hip and my phone, but grasped empty air for the second time that night.

The numbers were in my phone. Which meant I didn't have them. The only person whose number I knew by heart was my mother, and I wasn't desperate enough to call her. Yet.

"What do you mean, they handed her over to the vamps?" one of the guys at the table said, bristling. "What kind of shit is that?" He shot up and headed for the bar, although I wasn't sure what, exactly, he planned to do. The guy was dressed like some sort of hipster lumberjack—carefully groomed beard, plaid shirt, and seriously tight jeans.

"She's too powerful for anyone else to train," Red said.

"What about that Rogue Natural?" one of the girls at the table asked, standing to get a better view of me. "She can't be more powerful than him. I saw him, once. I'd take training with him any day."

"Not cool, Gail," the guy next to her said.

"What?" she shot back. "You don't think I see you looking at other chicks? I see you looking. What's good for the goose, as they say."

"Please, can you give me Reagan's number, Red?" I asked through clenched teeth.

"Reagan?" one of the guys at the end of the bar murmured. "Did she say Reagan?"

"I knew she was bad news." Smells-a-Stink huffed and backed out.

"Just perfect," I said to myself. These people practically deified Emery.

"Listen, honey," Hipster Lumberjack said, "you gotta stay away from that vamp-banger. Anyone that messes with those filthy creatures has got a screw loose."

My smile was tight. "Red, the number, please. *Now*."

"Red," the bartender barked, leaning over the bar. "Get her that number. This is getting ridiculous."

The others kept piping up, offering to train me

themselves, telling stories about Emery, but I blanked it all out.

"What'd they do to you?" Hipster Lumberjack leaned toward me, resting his elbow on the bar. "We can protect you. I'm sure Roger can find training for you somewhere else. We got plenty of mages on the payroll. Let us handle it."

"That's a neat trick." The bartender nodded at me. "That soft and vulnerable look really suits you. Don't let them know what you really are until it's too late."

It felt like I'd walked into a circus and was currently stuck on a rotating stile. What in God's goosebumps was she talking about?

"Look at her," Hipster Lumberjack said, straightening and scowling at the bartender. "Clearly she's had a rough night. She wouldn't be asking for help if she could help herself."

The bartender threw up her hands and took a step back. "Just saying. There's more to her than you think." She winked at me and sauntered down the bar.

"Here. You can use my phone. Her number is pulled up." Red handed it over. The number on the screen was labeled "She-Devil."

"That's not very nice," I said, taking the phone.

"You're a lovely girl, don't get me wrong, Penny," Red said. "But you would change your tune if Reagan were the one beating up on you."

"I'd rather her than vampires."

Before I could call, someone shouted, "Hey!" outside.

Broad Face spun around. He had time to brace himself, bringing up his hands, before two arms came into view, grabbed his shirt, and yanked him through the door.

"Whoa," we heard, and the door started to swing shut behind him.

The whole bar jumped to their feet. A loud bang had me flinching. The door swung open wildly and slapped the edge of the frame. The top hinge tore loose and the whole thing teetered.

"Oh no," Red groaned, and tried to slink away.

She-Devil had arrived.

CHAPTER 17

THE STREET LAMP behind Reagan outlined the curve of her hips, interrupted by the bulge of her fanny pack. Leather covered her legs, leading down into thick-soled boots. Only a tank top covered her upper body, but she didn't hug her arms against the chill.

I'd never been so glad to see someone.

"Red, where are you running off to? Aren't you glad to see me?" she asked, watching him skitter to the back.

Her gaze swung to the two guys at the end of the bar, both larger than her, and both ready for battle.

She didn't even flinch. "What are you two lug nuts looking at? Sit down before you hurt yourselves. Hey, have any of you—Oh, Penny. There you are." She sauntered in like she belonged, when she most certainly, without even a question, did not.

Hipster Lumberjack stepped in front of me like we were besties. "We know the vampires did something to her," he said, refusing to move. "The last thing she needs is help from your kind."

"Oh yeah?" Reagan said as Broad Face filled the

doorway behind her. He wiped blood off his chin, but didn't advance. He probably didn't want to be thrown again. "And. What. Kind. Is. That?" Each word was its own threat.

"Blood junkie."

The bartender reached under the bar for something.

"Trixie, no need to jump to conclusions. I'm just here to pick up my friend," Reagan said, giving a thumbs-up to the bartender.

"I'm not tryin' to hate on you, Reagan, but I gotta do my job," Trixie said. "We both know you have a reputation for ruining bars."

"That was one time, and it wasn't even my fault. A Mages' Guild wannabe started it." Reagan didn't elaborate as she turned back to Hipster Lumberjack. "Blood junkie is a derogatory term for a vampire, actually. I'm not the one after the blood, so therefore, I am not a junkie."

"Trixie, do you need someone to take out the trash?" one of the guys from the corner asked.

"He means me, Trix." Reagan raised her hand. "*I* am the trash in this scenario."

"You've got five minutes to settle down, Reagan, and then I gotta throw you out," Trixie said, shaking her head with a small smile still on her lips.

Reagan nodded. "Sounds good to me. Like I said, I'm just here to pick up my friend. And hopefully have a little libation as I do so."

"We know the vampires did something to her," Hipster Lumberjack said, refusing to back off.

"Five minutes, you said?" Reagan asked Trixie.

"Four, now," Trixie answered.

"Right." Reagan leveled her gaze at Hipster Lumberjack. "You know what the vampires did to *her*, do you?"

"Yeah. Look at her."

"Yes, look at her. Look at the untrained mage who killed four newbie vampires, scared the fifth so badly it cowered from her, and protected a mid-level vamp from one of the oldest vampires who walks the earth. A vampire so old and powerful that she very nearly killed my boyfriend—who *is* a blood junkie, by the way—and the higher mid-level vampire fighting by his side. If I hadn't given him my blood just now—which is legal, since I'm magical and also willing—he would've perished, I would've gone crazy, and you'd all likely be dead. All because no one has ever documented what happens when you force an untrained natural into a life-or-death situation."

"If she did all that," Broad Face said, his hands on his hips and his expression sour, "then how come she is in here looking for help?"

"I said she was extremely talented and powerful." Reagan stepped closer to Hipster Lumberjack, their faces now a foot apart and neither one backing down. "I didn't say anything about her intelligence level. I mean, seriously. Who runs for their lives in this day and age without at least taking their phone? Wallet-schmallet, you can steal what you need. But a phone? Yeah. You need that. Or, at the very least, a good set of running shoes. Penny, you fail that test, I don't mind telling you."

"You got one minute left," Trixie warned her, pulling out her shotgun.

"I just called Roger," Red said, emerging from the back. He stayed on that side of the bar. "He's not too far away. He's thinking about paying us a visit."

Reagan stiffened and turned her head, her focus no longer on Hipster Lumberjack. She narrowed her eyes at Red, who flinched before lifting his phone up like a shield.

"I can't tell if he's bluffing," Reagan said softly.

Trixie lowered the gun to the bar, her eyes on Red, too.

Reagan noticed and took a step back. "Come on, Penny, let's get moving."

"Afraid of a little muscle, are ya?" someone from the corner table said.

Another one of them snickered. "That's right, run away, little vamp maggot."

Reagan swung her gaze in that direction and the taunting cut off.

"Tell Roger that Darius took a beating to keep Penny alive," Reagan said, and it was clear she was talking to Red. "He's in this all the way. I'll be taking over Penny's training for now, but that means I can't keep my eye on the city. The Guild is already slipping in. If we don't start hunting them down soon, we'll be overrun. The *blood junkies* have the nights mostly covered, but we could sure use some help during the day."

"Roger won't help some vamp lover," Hipster Lumberjack said with a sneer.

"Congratulations," Reagan replied. "You're as dumb as you look."

"Wait just a minute—"

Hipster Lumberjack didn't get time to finish his sentence. Reagan spun and grabbed him so fast that even my flinch was delayed. She threw him like an empty trash can, ramming him into Broad Face. The two of them tumbled out of the bar.

"I didn't see what happened. I was putting the shotgun away," Trixie said, straightening up.

"I did. She—"

"Awesome," Trixie said over Red. "Reagan, you'd best be leaving."

"Ten-four." Reagan gave her a salute and stalked from the bar.

I stared after her for a beat before starting. All eyes

were glued on me.

"Sorry. She's…" I had no excuses. She just *was*, and they likely knew it. "I'll just…" I hurried after her. "Thank you," I yelled over my shoulder.

"Don't lose that trick, Penny," Trixie called after me. "That is the best weapon in your arsenal."

"What trick?" Reagan asked as we turned down the sidewalk. Hipster Lumberjack was fighting Broad Face's limbs to stand on his own. "What'd you do?"

"She thinks my looking forlorn and vulnerable is a trick of some sort."

"Oh. Yeah, it totally is. Not to mention your whole Snow White vibe with that pretty face and those batting eyelashes. You had that hipster dude ready to change his whole world to fit you in it. You need to use that whenever it suits you. Catching an enemy off guard is the easiest way to defeat him."

"I'm out of my element," I admitted, feeling the sting of failure from my time in this city.

"You've been extremely sheltered all your life. And now you're in the thick of things in the wildest magical city in the nation. It would be weird if you *weren't* in culture shock, to be honest. But we'll get there." She nudged me with her shoulder in camaraderie.

I took a shaky breath and let slip a smile, feeling the heavy weight on my shoulders lighten a little. She couldn't have known how much I needed to hear those words.

She turned left suddenly, and I hurried to catch up.

"Where are we going?" I asked, glancing behind us, thankful I didn't feel the furious itch between my shoulder blades anymore.

"This is going to cause a massive fight, but Darius and I agree that you shouldn't stay with the Bankses. They're jamming you up." She stared into my eyes as if she was looking for something. "The only time mages usually pair up is if they form a dual-mage pair. But you want to work with everyone willy-nilly. You don't even care if it's someone from the same magical species. You're so desperate for team sports that when you can't pair up with anyone humanish, you give personalities to rocks and work with them. You leeched off my power in the warehouse, without asking, and used me to help you do that spell. That power is unheard of, as far as I know. And it is massive. You're the sneakiest type of thief. I'm not even mad about it. I'm too jealous to be mad."

She turned right at the next corner.

"So where are we going?" I asked again.

"To get my car. I had to get to Darius in a hurry, so I took the fast one that I borrowed without asking the other day."

"Did he really almost die?"

"No. I was being dramatic. But he was in a bad way. She broke his back, then each limb, and tossed him to the side. She wasn't trying to kill him, just get him out of the way. Which she did. With quick economy."

Agony welled up inside of me. "I'm so sorry."

"It wasn't your fault. He's the ape that challenged you while he had a very old vampire hanging out in his house. Granted, no one could've known how your magic would affect her, but for a guy who is a master at overthinking the smallest detail, this is definitely his fault. Moss is still blaming you, though. He'll always blame you. Unless there is even a remote possibility that he can blame me."

"Is he okay?"

"He has a lot of broken bones from getting his ass kicked, but he'll mend."

"So you got there in time?"

"I was already on the way. I can feel when Darius is in pain and…various other things through the bond. That guy is very rarely worked up. I know when shenanigans are going down. Here we are."

A shiny midnight-blue Lamborghini sat around the corner from Darius's house. Red and blue flashing lights from police cars lit up our surroundings.

"You stole his Lamborghini?" I asked with awe.

"Can't you hear? I said I borrowed it."

"Yeah. Without asking. That means *stole*. He's going to be pissed."

"Probably, but he's in the doghouse for keeping secrets lately, so I don't really care."

I took a deep breath and shrugged it off. I had my own problems…I didn't need to jump in the middle of theirs.

"I didn't think magical people used human cops for magical issues," I said, pausing by the Lamborghini, almost afraid to touch it lest I mess it up somehow.

"You set off a great many explosions and ruined quite a bit of his house. Not to mention blew the door off. Hats off for that, by the way. My kinda girl. Get in."

The car beeped and the lights flashed, unlocking it.

Red and blue played across the leaves of a bush at the corner. There had to be a lot of cops over there.

"How is Darius dealing with all of this while…mending?"

"Darius, Moss, and Ja are all tucked away in the vampire chambers on the third floor. The doorways are hidden. Marie is dealing with the human element."

"Wait—"

"You'll want your seatbelt." Reagan looked pointedly at my lap while starting up the car.

She pulled away from the curb, and I stretched the belt across my body.

"Ja isn't dead?" I asked as she meekly drove the car out of the area.

"No. Well…Marie couldn't tell. You did a number on that ol' broad. She probably rues the day she accepted Darius's invitation to visit his lodgings in the Brink. That thing was sliced, diced, and fried."

"Could you tell what the spell did?"

Reagan glanced at me as she got onto the freeway. "You don't know what spell you used?"

"No. I made it up. The idea was to protect Marie."

"Well, you certainly did. From what I could tell, Ja was blackened by an explosion, strangled by something resembling a flower, and she also had razor slashes, and missing fingers—that broad was torn up."

"The last spell didn't do all that. She went through quite a lot." I stared out the window as Reagan shifted gears and stomped on the gas. The car shot forward.

"She did go through a lot. A *lot*." Reagan sounded troubled, and I looked over in time to see an anxious expression cross her face. In a moment, it was gone.

CHAPTER 18

I COULDN'T REMEMBER ever seeing her anxious. "What?"

"Well…" Reagan drummed her fingers on the steering wheel. "That old broad went through some sort of 'washing machine fluffy razor' spell of yours, as Darius described it—he was delirious at that point—before going through the two of them."

"My spell must've been weak for a vampire to get through it."

"Has no one told you that vampires can cut through magic if they're in their monster form?"

"It's actually called a monster form?"

She frowned at me. "That's what you took away from that question?"

"Well, I mean…" I shrugged, clasping my hands in my lap. "They do actually look like monsters, but I didn't think they'd actually call themselves monsters. They seem much too vain."

Reagan huffed. "You're a nut. No, they probably don't call it that, but I have no idea what they do call it.

Because I don't care. 'Monster form' is a good description. I suggest you use it. To their faces. Especially when they're angry. You'll appreciate the fireworks in their eyeballs."

"No, thanks," I said, somehow not at all concerned that she was weaving in and out of cars at over a hundred miles an hour. Clearly my brain had shut off at this point. I'd been through too much. "No, no one told me that. I killed that one last night, so I just assumed…"

"Well, here's the thing. It depends on the age of the vampire and the power of the mage. The older the vampire, the stronger their ability to cut through magic. So Darius *might* be able to cut through one of your spells, but I doubt Moss could. Moss *might* be able to cut through a Callie and Dizzy spell, but Marie couldn't. Get it?"

"Yes," I said. "Are shifters the same?"

"In a way. They don't cut through spells, but they can withstand them. Shrug them off, is how I'd describe it. It's weird."

"That stands to reason. It seems like it's basically all about where you are on the power grid."

"Yeah, basically."

"And where are you, Reagan? No one will tell me anything about your powers."

"It's a secret."

I stared at her for a count of three, realized she

wasn't going to crack, and looked away. With fatigue pulling at me, dragging me down, I didn't have the energy to get it out of her. And honestly, I probably wouldn't be able to, anyway. "Cool."

Reagan exited the freeway, barely slowing down to do so. Hopefully, this thing had great brakes.

"Before Marie ran you out," she said, thankfully downshifting quickly and slowing the car, "Darius instructed her to organize blood for Ja. It was a precaution in case your spell was nasty, and in case he and Moss had to finish subduing her. Darius clearly had no idea how powerful a riled-up, old-as-sin vampire could be. *No idea.*"

"Is there a point in there somewhere, or are you uncomfortable with silences?"

She turned and smiled at me, her eyes glimmering in the red dash lights. "Aren't you fun when you're at your wit's end?"

"I don't feel very fun."

Reagan crawled through a run-down neighborhood. The car wouldn't have fit in even if it was missing both bumpers, its tires, and was peppered with dents. "You're a hoot, trust me."

"Are you taking me somewhere to kill me?"

"Possibly. We're going to my house, where you'll get to crack open some very advanced books and take a few spells for a test drive. I'll be running interference so you don't kill yourself or the whole neighborhood. I can't wait to start. Anyway, I did have a point buried in there somewhere. Marie got the blood and locked Ja into a vampire chamber with two guys that really should evaluate their life choices."

"But you said Marie didn't know if Ja was alive."

"Right. There was none of that black sludge they usually exude when they die, but Ja is in really bad shape. So, she might die, which will, in essence, be Darius's fault. Ja has mostly removed herself from all vampire politics, but she is still an elder vampire. The other elders won't like it."

"Then I guess we should hope she lives…and suffers from amnesia."

Reagan turned down a street with houses on one side, all small, broken-down hovels with chipping paint and weeds struggling through walkways. A large concrete wall lined the sidewalk on the other side. After passing an opening in the wall, I saw that it was a graveyard. The large gravestones rose in rows, a couple lightly showered by a weak street lamp, the rest stewing in the darkness. The vast space felt like an enormous black hole, pulling at lost souls with the intent to trap them within its confines forever.

That, or my imagination was going haywire again. I really needed to get some sleep.

"The thing is…" That troubled expression crossed

Reagan's face again as she turned left, keeping the graveyard on our left side. She parked in front of a little house with fresh paint, flowers blooming in a box in front of the raised porch, and two unbroken chairs facing the graveyard entrance across the street.

"What a dismal view," I muttered, seeing the same pool of darkness at this opening. The light from the street lamp didn't reach far before dissipating into murky oppressiveness.

"What?" Reagan followed my gaze before shooting me an incredulous look. "*Dismal?*" She shook her head and pushed open the door. "That is a great view. You'll see. Anyway…" She came around my side and stood next to the door as though waiting to see if I needed help out. After realizing I didn't, she trudged up the nearby porch steps to the door.

"Shouldn't you lock the car?"

She pulled open the screen door before pushing open the interior one, then waited in the doorway for me. "I don't want some idiot to break a window out of some misguided hope they'll find something of value. This way, they can have a look, take anything I was stupid enough to leave behind, and go on their way. No hassle."

"But…what if they steal the car?"

Her lips curled ruefully. "Anyone in this neighborhood knows better than to steal a car, nice or otherwise, parked outside of this house. Any outsiders that try to boost cars from these streets will find a world of hurt waiting for them on the other side of theft. A world of hurt, and not just from me. My neighbor does not like people invading his territory."

"Right…" My body was starting to shake again, a sign that I was still horribly outside of my comfort bubble. "And we're positive I can't stay with Callie and Dizzy?"

"You'll be fine. Promise. C'mon." Reagan gestured me in. "As I was saying, it makes me nervous that Darius was blindsided by Ja's power. Hell, it makes me nervous that a vampire can be that powerful. An elder is no joke. Ja is clearly far beyond that."

Her entryway opened up into a small living room with plush furniture, a giant TV on the wall, an expensive rug, and paint and decorations that perfectly accented the space. It was cozy and comfortable while still trendy and top of the line.

"Want a drink?" She disappeared through an archway into a kitchen that had received the same treatment as the living room. The various gadgets would be at home in a rich person's kitchen. Even Callie and Dizzy would've been envious of all the state-of-the-art appliances, though probably not of the tiny quarters into which they were all systematically crammed.

"Water, please." I sat at a small, round table in the

corner, with artfully aged wood, each strip a slightly different color than the other, but all blending into a really neat piece. "Did you decorate?"

She laughed as she pulled down a bottle of whiskey. "Yeah, right. No, Marie came through and did all this up after my house was burned out by a ridiculous mage hopped up on—" She stiffened before continuing, "Painkillers. Never mind."

I sagged into the chair as she got to work on our drinks. A suspiciously short time later, she delivered a glass with a lime floating among the ice cubes.

"That's my version of a margarita. You'll love it." She sat opposite me with a darker liquid that was almost certainly whiskey, her version of water.

I ignored the glass in front of me. "I don't understand how I made Ja react like that. Darius said my magic was doing it, but…" I shook my head, at a loss.

Reagan set down her glass and leaned forward. "Marie said your magic acted as a catalyst. It pumped out a sort of aggression that said, in essence, get lost or I'll kill you." She leaned back again and took a sip of her drink. "Elder vampires use a similar approach with newbies, I guess. They exude a sort of…mood or something that gives them control. I don't totally get it, but you must've shoplifted the ability without knowing it. The problem is, elders are the scary ones, not the ones who are scared. Darius thinks Ja felt your intention, and it stripped away all the layers of dust collected on her personality. You, in essence, woke up the beast."

Shivers ran through me as I remembered that red, white, and black thing jerkily walking toward the top of the stairs. She'd been through hell, and refused to sit down for a rest. "Will she go back to sleep, or whatever?"

Reagan stared into her whiskey. "That's what has me concerned. If she lives, and she *doesn't* slip back into a dormant state—which is basically a vampire's version of a vacation from life and intense introspection—there's no telling what it'll mean. We might be introducing another, very intense, player into the supernatural game of politics."

I took a sip of my drink, then sputtered and shook, immediately putting it back down again. "That's straight tequila."

"No! It has a lime and a little sugar. I said it was *my version* of a margarita."

I pushed the glass away. "So what will Darius do if Ja wants to get back to life?"

Reagan shrugged. "That's the real question, isn't it? What will *Darius* do. Because honestly, it has nothing to do with me. Unless that she-bitch tries to kill him to steal his interests. Then it very much has to do with me, and I'll get to see how hard it is to kill an ancient vampire. Otherwise, it's Darius's problem. Tomorrow we're going to hit the books. You have the power to be great. I'm going to help you blindly stumble into actually being great. It's a foolproof plan."

"Certainly seems so." I stood and went to the cabinet.

"Oh good, you're already used to waiting on yourself. We're gonna get along fine. Bottom line: we're in unknown territory, and if anything makes vampires itchy, it is unknown territory. So we'll avoid them for now, especially the old one you drove crazy, hole up here, and do some magic. Easy."

If there were any certainties in life, one was that Reagan's and my versions of *easy* were vastly different.

CHAPTER 19

EMERY TURNED OFF the fast-track path in the Realm. Ever-blooming flowers lined the side of the cobblestone track, giving the slight breeze a floral fragrance. A green meadow stretched away, dotted by small huts with grass roofs in the distance.

He'd picked the fastest possible route to the gateway into the Brink, on pins and needles the whole time.

After that first foretelling about Penny's possible demise, he'd received two more of the black mist visions in quick succession. He couldn't totally make out the situation based on the fits and starts of the scenes, but in the end, it seemed like she was battling vampires in a very nice house.

He'd rarely seen vampires engage in open battle in the Brink unless defending themselves from the shifters, and one of those vampires had looked very old, which was even rarer, yet—if he had made sense of the images—that was exactly what had happened. In that very nice house.

Trust Penny to engage in something that made very

little sense.

There had been a pause after that, long enough to lodge his heart in his throat. Had all of those close calls eventually ended in her death?

But then he'd had one more.

A dark area outside. A leafy tree leaning over a weed-choked patch. And a shape sitting within the shadows, its identity obscured.

There had been no movement, and no sense of urgency. Just an open letter of warning.

He'd never experienced that type of foretelling before. Usually the situation was immediate, and if he didn't react, he was done. But this…

He didn't know what was happening, but it was unfolding on a large scale, and it involved Penny.

He'd been walking before he knew it. She needed help, and he would offer what help he could give.

It had only belatedly occurred to him that she might not want his help. He'd left her in the lurch, after all. He'd walked away with a "Good luck, I traded my monetary freedom to an elder vampire so he'd watch over you, which will probably shackle you to him for life. Bye-bye, you're welcome!"

By now she either hated him or wished he'd just leave her alone already.

But he couldn't. That was the bottom line. He couldn't, not only because she was in danger, but also because he couldn't stop thinking about her.

On the walk through the Realm, trying to get to the Brink gateway closest to her whereabouts, he'd made a compromise with himself. He'd just check on her. That was all. She didn't even have to know he was in the area. He'd get a glimpse of her beautiful face (possibly from a distance, like a true creep), maybe talk to the Bankses, and calmly assess the situation.

If he wasn't needed, fine. But at least he would know she was safe and happy. He couldn't offer her a single thing, but he could ensure things were going well for her. That, at least, was in his power.

A white, fuzzy line jagged through the air up ahead, indicating a gateway into the Brink. To the side was a bench with an old-fashioned street light next to it. On the bench sat an old and slightly deformed creature. The elves had designed all of the gates to be especially beautiful—an ego thing—and this being's ugly appearance and stunted growth made it an eyesore. Based on its characteristics, Emery guessed it was some form of goblin, which was odd.

Goblins almost always crossed to the Brink in darkened places, like mines or deep forests. Though some could take the form of a human, most could not, and if they went into more populated areas, they'd be noticed immediately. A big no-no in the magical community. So for this one to be hanging out here, by the gate that let out closest to New Orleans, meant something was amiss.

Emery slowed, on his guard.

The goblin, whose head had been nodding like it was asleep, jerked up and blinked its knobby eyes. It looked around and smacked its slobbery lips, only then noticing Emery's presence.

"Oh." It shifted in its seat and stretched out its legs. "Oh." It bent one leg, then the other. "Forgive, master. Forgive." It stood up stiffly, as though it'd been sitting on that bench for days. "I must've dozed off within such a lovely area. Forgive me."

The creature stomped through the row of flowers separating itself from Emery, who narrowed his eyes. Goblins, as a whole, did not cherish flowers, meadows, and soft breezes. They'd prefer dark, dank little caverns filled with unsuspecting humans carrying valuable trinkets ripe for the stealing.

Clearly this goblin assumed Emery knew very little about the creatures of the Realm. Something that got many a Realm creature killed.

At the end of a newly created dirt trail, the creature stopped and looked up at Emery.

"You are the Rogue Natural, are you not?" it asked.

Emery started slowly weaving an attack spell he knew worked particularly well on goblins and the like. "Who's asking?"

It nodded, as though that was answer enough. "I've been posted here to stop the Rogue Natural from using this crossing. My great master believes this crossing is too near New Orleans. A crossing at this point will likely have devastating consequences, since mages are continually setting up spells on the other side. The Rogue Natural should, therefore, choose a crossing in another part of the country. One of the coasts would be ideal—the busier the better. Should the Rogue Natural agree to follow these precautions, intended to keep the Rogue Natural and the creature Penny safe, the Rogue Natural may call my great master from whatever location it uses to enter the Brink, and my great master will send its jet to collect the Rogue Natural."

Emery shifted, putting a little more space between himself and the goblin. The spell he'd spun unraveled because of the time lapse, and Emery started it again, intending to be ready at a moment's notice in case this was a trap.

Though he doubted the Guild would use a goblin to carry out their bidding. They wouldn't want to be connected with such a vile, mischievous little creature, but he had a notion of someone who wouldn't particularly mind…

"Your master is Durant, then?" Emery asked.

The goblin hissed. "One does not use names in places where little ears are known to hide just out of sight."

"You used my nickname."

"You are not my great master."

"Fabulous." Emery glanced at the fuzzy line separating the worlds. He'd known it would be dicey entering so close to New Orleans if the Guild was already set up there, but without a car, proper ID, or any of the other items required to purchase travel in the Brink, he hadn't had much choice. Until now, he'd been hoping in and out of the Realm.

He ran his fingers through his hair. The logic checked out on what the creature was saying. If he did land somewhere else, Darius would definitely collect him. The vampire liked to keep tabs on all of his assets, and after asking him for a favor, Emery was definitely in his pocket.

If only that was the least of his problems.

"Fine." Emery stepped away. "Get word to your master that I will oblige."

"Of course, master."

Emery barely kept from swearing as he headed back to the fast-track magical path. The Mages' Guild had attacked him, the last black mist vision had implied they'd also attacked Penny—or were toying with the idea—and now they were covering the crossings. They were already organized and their plans were well underway. Time was winding down, and he'd just increased his travel time by *days.* And that was *if* Darius was quick to send a jet.

If Penny was in danger and on her own, days could make the difference between her freedom and magical enslavement.

CHAPTER 20

REAGAN STOPPED NEAR the archway leading into the kitchen, dressed in a new set of leathers. She pointed at me. "Don't go anywhere."

I wasn't sure where she thought I would go. I didn't have a car, was mostly afraid of the extremely rough neighborhood in which she lived, and was utterly exhausted from the intensive spell work and physical training (a.k.a. getting beaten up) we'd just finished.

It had been this way for the last three days. We made spells, discussed the feelings of the spells, talked about when it would be best to use the spells, and then engaged in physical combat, after which I limped to the couch and collapsed in exhaustion.

Oh yeah, and there were daily, or sometimes twice-daily, calls from Callie, who kept checking in to make sure I was still alive. That was what she said, anyway. Since each call devolved into a rant about my being stripped from her house without any notice, I had a feeling she was just venting.

Regardless of her anger, she never asked for me to

come back. Instead, she asked to be passed on to Reagan to get a rundown of what we'd done that day. She was monitoring me from afar.

I could read the writing on the wall: she agreed with the others. No matter how much she blustered and blew about it, she thought I was better off with Reagan. Whether that was because of the training, my safety, or the giant mess that had unfolded at Darius's house, I couldn't say, but she was worried about the magical climate to trust the vampire's decree.

For better or worse, I was stuck with Reagan.

And actually, despite the pounding I got every day, it was working out surprisingly well. She never told me something was right or wrong. She didn't even point out how someone else might have done it.

In spell work and fighting, I was really coming along. In just three days, I had progressed much further than in all that time with Callie and Dizzy. But that was in terms of reading spells and duplicating them. When it came to making them up on the fly—in a controlled, precise manner—or pairing a spell with a situation, I was still freezing up.

At this rate, when the Guild came calling, I didn't have any faith I'd be able to beat them back.

I sighed heavily and fell into the couch, immediately regretting it. My butt hurt from the multiples times I'd fallen on it in the last hour. "Where are you going again?"

"I have a friend who knows a guy who said the Magical Law Enforcement office might need some help bringing in a banshee. With Darius preoccupied, it's the perfect time for me to do a little contract work." She waved her hand nonchalantly, a gesture she often used to make light of doing something very wrong. "It'll be a super-easy case. Nothing to worry about. I'll just help out real quick and that's it. No reason to mention it at all." She paused and lowered her voice. "Do you hear what I'm saying?"

"That you'll beat me bloody if I go telling anyone, yeah." I glanced at the clock. "It's two in the morning. Who is working now? Not that I'm complaining about my practice session being over."

"The magical community keeps different hours. Don't worry; you'll get used to it. But this isn't the actual job, just a little information gathering. I want to know exactly what's going on before I make the captain hire me. There's no way I want Darius on my case about doing something stupid. And that's the problem with boyfriends—they're always on your ass about jeopardizing your future and committing yourself to an eternity of servitude."

"Uh-huh." Now that I was temporarily living with her, I'd decided it was in my best interest to ignore her crazy life. I rubbed my eyes. "Well, he can't really talk, can he? What with the ongoing Ja situation and all."

Ja was going to live, though we didn't yet know if that was good or bad. Darius had started hitting the books really hard to determine how badly he'd messed up by making me entice her back into vampire politics (I totally blamed him for the whole debacle). Until he knew more, we were in the dark.

Not that it mattered. Reagan assured me that it was a vampire problem, and it was best to let them duke it out themselves. With Ja thinking rationally again, I was in no danger.

Or so they said. I planned to stay as far away from her as possible, just in case.

Reagan put up a fist. "I knew you'd see it my way."

Before I could bail myself out of that sinking ship, she was striding through the front door.

"Right." I stared after her in the sudden silence.

I was alone, really alone, for the first time in what was probably a very long time.

Wasn't that something? I hadn't been alone much in my life. My mother had always been hanging around, peering over my shoulder. After moving, Callie and Dizzy had always been home, not peering over my shoulder so much as wanting my company. And Veronica—

Veronica!

I'd talked to her as much as Callie since the night at

Darius's house, but I hadn't been able to see her. It was starting to wear on me. And truth be told, I was a little worried about her. The last time I'd moved locations in order to hide from the Guild, she'd been taken hostage. I didn't want something like that to happen again.

After painfully hefting myself off the couch, I waddled my sore butt to my room and grabbed my phone. One missed call from Callie. No 9-1-1 text, though, so she probably just wanted another crack at the day's rant.

"Hello?" Veronica answered in a sleepy voice.

"Oh my—I am so sorry, Ronnie! I completely forgot normal people are asleep right now. Forget I called. I'll talk to you tomorrow."

"No, it's fine." I heard her shifting. "What's up? What are you doing?"

"Are you sure? It's nothing important."

"No, it's fine. What are you up to? Did you do your training and everything?"

I told her about a breakthrough on a recent spell, and also about how much my punch was improving. I could even, almost, occasionally deflect Reagan's punch or kick. Sometimes.

"That's great. But how are you supposed to fight when you're using your hands to do magic?"

"Right. I've asked that so many times it isn't funny. But Reagan is convinced that knowing my body, and feeling less physically helpless, will improve my confidence."

"Oh. Well that's true enough."

"Yeah," I said miserably, finding the couch again. "That's the conclusion I came to, too. Unfortunately."

"So now what are you doing?"

"Sitting on the couch. Reagan went out for something. I've got the rest of the night off."

"She…went out?" Alarm crept into Veronica's voice. "Where did she go? Did she go far?"

"Why? What's wrong?"

More shifting, and the rest of the tiredness seeped out of Veronica's voice. "Callie and Dizzy are a bit on edge these last couple days. First they were pissed that you weren't headed back to their house, especially after what went down at Darius's, but yesterday John was hanging around, asking about you. We all know he's smitten, right?"

"He just wants a powerful dual-mage partner."

"Well, right. For him, that counts as smitten. He's a douche. Anyway, he was hanging around, and then Mary Bell came over out of the blue. She wondered where you were, too, and spent the rest of the time giving John the side-eye."

Tingles crawled up my spine. "Dizzy told me Mary Bell has had a somewhat foggy past."

"I know," Veronica said in a heavy voice. "Callie filled me in. She was doing human sacrifices at one point!"

I curled up and hugged my knees to my chest. I had liked the old mage's approach to magic…theoretically…but murder was categorically wrong.

"They wanted to try and sacrifice a vampire, so her and her dual-mage guy tried to capture one. Well, her dual-mage guy got killed. That was when she changed her ways. Callie said it was the heartbreak that did it, not a return to morality."

"Goodness," I breathed out. "And yet Callie has this chick hanging around?"

"She's powerful. Callie is keeping an eye on her, or so she says. I really think they all like to keep tabs on one another. I wouldn't say they're friends."

"Well with a past like that…"

"Right. And then…" She let her words trail away, and I knew she was conflicted about telling me something.

"What?" I prodded.

"Well…Dizzy says it was nothing, but you know how he is? Everything is nothing until he's knee deep in blood."

"That's not…" I blinked, trying to match up our different takes on his personality. Maybe I'd just spent too much time around blood lately.

"But I don't know. Lately there's been more people around this neighborhood than normal. And, I mean, no, they don't seem particularly suspicious, but I get the feeling they are watching me. Like, when I go around fixing the grammar on signs, I always feel eyes on me, you know?"

I nodded, forgetting we weren't speaking face to face and she couldn't see my silent cues.

"And then last night," she went on, "I glanced out my window because I thought I heard something bang, and I could *swear* a person slipped into Dizzy's shed. I could *swear* it, Penny. Dizzy says he has a good warden or something on it, and that the warden or whatever was fine in the morning, but…" She sighed forcefully. "I don't know. Maybe magically it doesn't make sense, but I know what I saw."

"I could probably take down a ward, then put the same ward back up." I chewed my lip. "But there aren't a lot of people with enough power to do that to one of the dual-mages' spells, I don't think."

"Right. That's what he said. But…"

"Well, keep your eyes out. If you saw one, you'll probably see more. Information can be just as important as spell work." Reagan had said that to me once, and it seemed to fit my life pretty well lately.

"Yeah," Veronica said, letting go of the thread of the conversation. "Well, anyway, Callie and Dizzy are certain you're in the safest place. Especially because they said you put some sort of warning or something on

Reagan's house."

"Ward. The same thing Dizzy had on the shed."

"Ah."

"I have to physically bring people into Reagan's house, or they can give a blood offering."

"Gross. Really? Isn't that dark magic stuff?"

"It's like giving a DNA offering, basically. A way of getting foolproof ID."

"Oh. Okay, then. So yeah, you should stay there."

"Does anyone know where I am?"

"No. Callie and Dizzy won't say—she gets hostile about people asking—and I try to make myself scarce when they come around. Which has been more frequently lately. They were impressed by the warehouse thing. Word has spread that you are a bona fide natural."

"The failed practice session, you mean?"

She started laughing. "The ones with all the power know you can do better, and the ones without it think you're fabulous. I don't know heads or tails about magic, but I'm getting a pretty good idea about the mage social structure at this point. Because here I am, stuck in the middle, breaking the magical rules because I'm a normal human who is privy to this stuff."

"So Dizzy and Callie have been filling you in?"

"Yeah. I think I am actually getting your lessons. They really did want to teach someone. You know what's funny?" She shifted again. "I'm editing this paranormal book right now that is depicting vampires completely inaccurately. I want to do up notes about each point that's incorrect, but the author thinks she's writing fiction. So I can't say anything. She'd think I was crazy." She paused and then mumbled, probably to herself, "I think I have to stop editing that genre. It'll drive me bonkers."

A knock sounded at the door.

I hopped up, then regretted it the moment my body screamed in protest. "Oh, that's the nightly maid crew. I gotta go."

"You are *so* lucky," she said before we said our farewells.

I was so lucky, that was true. Somewhere along the line, Darius had paid people to "plague" Reagan, as she called it. They looked after her place, stocked her fridge, cooked food, and cleaned up. Now that I was living here, I got the same benefits.

She was worried about an intrusion of privacy. I thought she was crazy. Having people look after us was awesome. As far as I was concerned, if they wanted to do my chores, they could snoop as much as they wanted.

"Come in," I called, staying where I was for the moment.

The door swung open and a head slowly came into

view. His eyes darted around the house, probably looking for Reagan, who would try to torment him in some way, before landing on me. And there they stayed, wary.

His body slowly followed his head. Hair styled *just so* and a face beautiful enough to make angels sing, the maid was surely a vampire. His graceful movements only confirmed it. And based on his nervousness, he'd clearly heard about the other night.

"You're good." I threw up my hands in surrender, and his eyes blink-flinched. Had I thrown magic, I totally would've had him. "Oh, sorry. I just meant that I won't do any magic. You can come in. Worry-free."

And this was what working with Reagan had done to me—think about every situation as a possible life-ending event. Yesterday's vamp had been greeted by my bug zapper. What would happen when someone went to hug me? Would I sucker-punch them?

The vampire nodded and scooted to the kitchen with his bag of groceries. He didn't even want to be in the same room as me.

There went my hope of having vampire friends. If I'd ever had one.

I thought about texting my mother, just to check in, but I'd probably wake her up. That would guarantee me a call and a serious tongue lashing. Best to wait until tomorrow and claim forgetfulness for not doing it today.

I stopped near the edge of the living room, deciding which way to go. My room was obviously the no-brainer choice, but if I did that, I'd end up falling asleep. As good as that sounded, I'd wake up early (by Reagan's standards), and tomorrow would be a *long* day.

So it was either sit in the backyard with the dummy I'd tried to kill on multiple occasions, or on a porch chair looking over a sea of remembered loss.

The vampire glanced over his shoulder at me, his eyes tight and body language nervous. It occurred to me that I was standing in the middle of open space, staring off in the distance—in his direction. He probably thought I was staring directly at him, with crazy eyes and an unhinged personality. The poor guy was clearly wondering if he would make it out of the house un-dead.

"Thanks for ironing, by the way," I said to lighten things up. "I mean...if you were the one who did it."

"Of course." His formal bow turned into another wary stare. When I didn't say anything further, he scooted into the pantry, where I couldn't see him.

Grimacing, because that hadn't gone well, I let myself out the front door and took one of the chairs facing the cemetery across the street. I glanced up at the light, considering whether I should flick it on. It would look creepy sitting here in the dark. I was still within the bounds of the ward, which covered the whole house and backyard, so I was safe even in the light.

Then again, I was looking over a cemetery. Creepy fit in.

The moist chill covered me like a blanket, the neighborhood quiet and subdued, which made sense, given the late hour.

I thought over what Veronica had said. Callie and Dizzy were nervous, which was more telling than all of the visitors who'd come bearing questions. They didn't rely on their intuition much, from what I could tell, but it was still there, working away below the surface. Their subconscious minds would be processing body language, tone changes, and anything out of the ordinary, feeding the information to their brains on the sly.

They thought something was amiss. And I'd learned to pay attention to that sort of thing.

Movement caught my eye. A grizzled-looking older man clad in black drifted out of the cemetery entrance across the street. Dark clothes hung off his bony frame. He stared at me as he peeled off to the side and stood in front of the wall.

A thrill ran through me as I wondered who he could be. A drug dealer sounded about right, with his rough look and the hours he kept.

Then again, would Reagan put up with that kind of thing across from her house?

I doubted it.

So then what? A thief, maybe? A guy casing houses?

Whatever he was, I knew what he was *not*. He was certainly not a mage. He didn't have the satchel, for one, or the pompous strut that said he was *somebody*. Even Callie and Dizzy, lovely people, had a certain lift to their shoulders and height to their chins.

This character stooped, and not because he was trying to be sneaky, but because he didn't want to be noticed.

I knew that posture well.

I watched him…watching me.

The scene should've been awkward, yet as I stared, and he stared back, I didn't want to look away. I wanted to see if he did something fantastical that identified him as a magical person of some kind.

And strangely…it seemed like he was waiting for the same thing.

A car rolled by at the end of the street, the engine clunking badly.

The man's head turned slightly, catching the motion, but it immediately snapped back, like he expected to catch me sprinting away.

That was when I felt something drift toward me along the air currents. It felt…welcoming, almost. A come-hither sort of invitation.

Wisps of colorful magic wafted up over the walls of

the cemetery, curling into the air. Light and playful. They fizzled out at a certain distance before more, stronger streams of magic blossomed.

The man near the cemetery didn't turn around. He didn't so much as glance up at the sky. If I didn't know better, and I really didn't, I would say he couldn't feel the magic going on behind him.

Unable to help myself, I leaned forward and pointed. "Do you feel that?"

He didn't start, or jerk, or do any of the things I would have expected from a stranger with whom I'd engaged in an impromptu stare-off. He merely shifted one shoulder toward the cemetery.

"No," he said. "Is it bad or good?"

I frowned at him. I'd expected him to say "yes," or ask "what?" Instead, he'd asked about the danger level of something he could neither see nor feel. That spoke of a magical creature. Or…maybe just the sketchiness of the neighborhood.

"It's good, I think. Done by people." I braced my elbows on my knees. "Am I allowed to ask what you are?"

"Yes. Am I allowed to ask what you are?"

"Um…that depends."

Joy and light and radiance flowered in my middle as I continued to watch the colorful display in the cemetery. Nature danced and sang and asked to be pulled into spells. I closed my eyes so I could savor the delightful feeling of it.

This—this was what I loved about magic.

"I'm human," he said. "But…" He looked around before slowly crossing the street at an angle, heading for the neighbor's house on my right. Once outside, he turned to face the street again. "I know what goes on in that house. Mostly."

"Which house? This house?"

"Yes. Reagan and I are friendly. I know her…friends."

The way he said *friends* left no doubt he knew they were vampires, or at least not human. It seemed the rule of not allowing humans to know about the magical world wasn't followed as closely as I'd been led to believe.

"I watch over things," the man said, his gruff voice low as he scanned the street. "I make sure all is calm in the neighborhood. You're new here. Reagan hasn't mentioned you."

"Oh." Magic drifted into the organized mass above me and my fingers longed to weave spells to add to the glory of whatever was happening in the cemetery. "I'm kind of…"

I stopped myself.

Great, Penny, nearly tell a creepy stranger that you're hiding out.

He nodded like he'd heard my thought. "You're in a good place," he said. "A safe place. She has things pretty well tied down."

"Right, yeah." I frowned at him again, wondering how much he knew about Reagan. And if he'd be willing to fill me in.

"Are you…of her kind?" he asked.

"I don't even know what her kind is, honestly," I said without thinking, feeling a strong pull toward the cemetery. Almost like, if I didn't show up, I'd miss out on a truly startling awakening. "I am of a magical kind, though you're not supposed to know that."

"I hear you loud and clear." He touched a gnarled finger to his nose. "What did you say you felt over there?"

I stood, impatient, and rapped on the banister softly. "Wholeness. Unity. Nature. Everything that is good and right with the world. It's really hard to explain—"

"That must be the Ladies of the Light. They're the nice witches. We've got some bad ones that come through here, trying to call Satan and what not. I don't mess with them. Reagan or No Good Mikey always chase them out. But if it's the Ladies of the Light, they won't hurt anything. They come here every so often to call the corners. They don't get too loud or anything." The man's head turned toward the left and he looked down the sidewalk.

When he didn't look away, I followed his gaze. A large, slope-shouldered man, thick from head to toe, ambled down the street looking at his phone. I straightened and stepped closer to the house, not trusting the sheer size of the guy. He looked like he could do some damage.

"Don't worry about him, he's a resident," the creepy guy said. "Keep your mouth shut about what you are, though. He doesn't know about any of that."

A human…warning me not to talk about magic…to another human. What a strange neighborhood. Then again, Reagan chose to live here—of course it was strange.

"Hey, Smokey," the newcomer said as he got close. Seeing me, he startled, his body jerking, and his phone sailed out of his hands. He grabbed for it, hitting it with a finger and then the back of his hand. It struck the ground with a hard plastic *cack*.

This man had no problem with swearing.

Phone back in his possession, he looked over the screen to make sure there were no cracks before finally straightening up and looking at me a second time. He exhaled in relief, one foot on the street and one foot on the sidewalk, leaning away from the house. "Oh, thank God. You don't look like no serial killer."

"She's Reagan's friend," Smokey said.

"She's on Reagan's front porch. They better be

friends, or this lady here would find herself in a bad situation." The newcomer slipped his phone into his pocket. "Who're you?" he asked me.

"I said, she's—"

"I know she's Reagan's friend," the newcomer said, palming his chest. "I heard that. What I'm asking is, what's her *name*?"

"You should make yourself clearer," Smokey said.

"You should mind your business," the newcomer shot back. He raised his eyebrows at me. "What's your name?"

"Penny," I said before I could stop myself. I wasn't used to hiding my identity in normal—well, normal-ish—settings. "But don't blab that around."

The man took a step back, all the way into the street now, and showed me his palms. He looked incredulous. "Do I look crazy to you? I'm not about to go talkin' about Reagan's business. I got enough problems."

Smokey nodded in approval.

"I'm Jerome, but people call me Mince," phone guy said. He crossed the threshold of the property and stepped onto the lawn, clearly coming forward to shake my hand.

"No, no, you—" I said as Smokey stuck out a hand in warning.

Mince's fingertips hit the invisible barrier at the edge of the porch, far enough back that a regular Joe wouldn't reach it unless he was trespassing. A flare of light preceded a loud zinging noise. Mince's body rocketed backward, hitting the sidewalk before rolling into the street.

"Oh my God, are you okay?" I asked, coming around the banister of the porch and stopping at the top of the steps. I didn't want to break the barrier in case he was pissed.

"Huuuuuugh." Mince shook like he'd just been fried with electricity. Which, magically speaking, he had been. "Huuuuughnga."

"I can't… I don't know what you're saying," I said apologetically.

"Hung nafunga. Uuuuugh." He convulsed to his side and then rolled over onto his stomach before lying there for a moment.

"Should you help him up?" I asked Smokey.

"Reagan told everyone to stay off her lawn. He shoulda known better," Smokey said without remorse.

"I mean…" I looked down at the little manicured patch of grass, the only one on the block. "Grass is made to be walked on."

"When it comes to Reagan, you do what she says, or you get an awful surprise. Mince just got an awful surprise. He should've known better."

Mince stiffly pushed up to his hands and knees, groaning. "She…looks…innocent. Uuuugh."

"The most dangerous ones always do." Smokey glanced in the other direction as the sound of a car going too fast barreled down the street. "The best assassins are the sexy, manicured ones, aren't they? You shouldn't let appearances deceive you."

Mince looked over his shoulder at Smokey, his face a mask of anger. "Ain't no…ass-ass-ins 'round…here." A tremor shook him.

"How do you know? Do you know everyone?" Smokey asked.

Head shaking, Mince painfully got to his feet. He gave me a glance from beneath lowered brows.

"Sorry," I said.

His body convulsed before he stiffly strode away, muttering to himself.

"I really was going to warn you," I called after him.

"Don't worry about him," Smokey said, still nonplussed. "He forgot himself for a moment. That was his fault, not yours. He knows better."

"Maybe this wa—Um. This…security device is a little too strong."

"Forgive me for saying, but you don't seem like the type to hang around here. And Reagan doesn't seem like the type to have roommates. So if you're here, there's a reason for it. And that probably means you need strong protection. Don't go second-guessing yourself."

"Yeah, well…" I couldn't really argue with that.

I blew out a breath, still feeling that tug of magic calling to me from the cemetery. Promising me something I'd been missing.

"How bad of an idea would it be just to run over there really quick, do you think?" I asked.

"I wouldn't do that, Miss Penny. Not if you're in need of protection." Smokey moved to the edge of the steps. "You have no idea what has been seen in that cemetery. Human and magical both. There are bad people that roam through there."

"But you said the Ladies of the Light—"

"They aren't bad, no, but they might be set upon at any moment by a swarm of birds that turn into hideous monsters. Or a black magic coven that kills small animals. Or a thug wanting a cheap fix or some dough. You never know."

I paused at the end of the steps, debating. He was certainly right. It was a cemetery, for criminy sakes. Anyone who was up to no good would head to a cemetery. That was true of any city in any town across the world. This one, smack in the middle of Reagan's weird neighborhood, in particular. Smokey was right: there could be any number of really nasty things hanging around.

And then there was the most obvious threat, the Mages' Guild, lying in wait for me to cross the threshold keeping me safe.

I turned back and looked at the house, a sanctuary if ever there was one. All the while, my temperamental third eye buzzed, begging me to walk across that street and see what was there.

My temperamental third eye had gotten me into a lot of trouble in the past.

But it hadn't always been wrong…

I was walking before I could talk myself out of it.

CHAPTER 21

"WAIT. PENNY. MISS Penny." Smokey caught up with me. "Can I just call you Penny? What do your people call you?"

"Naive, mostly." I made it to the other side of the street and stalled at the entrance to the cemetery. Strange feelings washed over me. Dense and thick, they seeped into my middle and took up residence. Not magic, or at least not any kind of magic I'd encountered.

"Are ghosts real?" I asked softly, starting forward again, albeit much slower.

"I'm inclined to think so, based on all the other things that are real."

"Good point." I blew out a breath, a creepy-crawly sensation taking over my body.

"They won't hurt you, though. Of the things that might be in this—"

"I got it, I got it. That doesn't change my terrible decision-making process. Where are these witches?"

He hesitated a moment, clearly not sure if he should

help me.

"It'll make things faster if I know where I'm going," I whispered, moving down the concrete path, large gravestones to either side.

"Take a left when you're able."

I could've taken a left after each gravestone, but I figured he was talking about an actual path. When I came upon one, the same size as the one we were on, I did as he said and kept going. Soon he had me take a right, and my final instruction was to go straight back until I hit the wall.

"Will we walk right into them?" I asked, stooped now and half crouched, like a burglar.

"No. We'll skirt beside them, go beyond them, cut in, and then sneak back toward them in the shadows."

"My mother would batter me senseless if she knew I was getting tips from a person who lurks around in the shadows."

"I like to know what's going on without being seen."

"Yes. I caught that."

"Keep your voice down. They'll be right up here off to the right. Drift this way." He moved toward the left, and I followed, thankful he hadn't put his hand on my shoulder in silent communication. The magic felt lovely and calming, but I was still traipsing around a weird-feeling cemetery in the dark after being blitzed with warnings about bad things. I wasn't positive I'd be able to refrain from zapping him, or worse.

A few steps later, I could see candlelight flickering through a row of gravestones. A slim form moved in a languid sort of way, hands raised toward the sky. Another form, this one clearly a woman, had her hands raised in exactly the same way. I saw a couple more, all of them in the same pose, most wearing rings of flowers around their heads, some swaying in place to silent music. The one whose face I could see had a serene smile.

The most inclusive magic I'd ever experienced swirled around me, bringing joy to my middle and a grin to my lips. I contemplated joining them, partaking in the joy I was feeling. But it wasn't my circle, and I didn't want to disturb them. I said as much to Smokey, ready to retreat.

"You sure you don't want a closer look? We won't disturb them at all. We'll just spy from the shadows."

He really did the creepy thing well.

"Maybe just a look," I said softly, curiosity getting the better of me. "Not spying, just looking."

He was nice enough not to mention that it was essentially the same thing.

Smokey took the lead, drifting to the other side of the aisle and then around the corner. The view was much better from here. The group—they looked to be all women—sat in a circle surrounded by glowing candles. A plethora of items littered the ground in the middle. They chanted softly, either looking toward the sky or the ground.

Magic rose from the items between them, called to life by the words they were saying in harmony. The source of the beautiful magical light I'd seen. They were using their emotions for this chant, and using one another for more power.

"You see?" I said softly, hunching down next to Smokey in the shadow of a gravestone. "They're coming together as a unit and speaking the spell. They are using one another for power boosts. Why can't mages do that?"

"Mages…is that like…guy witches?"

"No. They're witches with more power."

"Ahh." He nodded.

"Mages are usually super solo when it comes to magic," I whispered. "They kind of shut everyone else away."

"Many hands make light work," he said.

"Yeah, right? I'm not crazy for thinking this way is better, am I?"

"No you are not. Working together usually gets the job done faster. Even salesmen do better in a unit."

I squinted in confusion, not knowing what salesmen had to do with anything.

A scent wafted our way, earthy and dense. Incense,

if I had to guess, though I couldn't place the fragrance. A few words sporadically reached my ears, but the intentions of the magic were coming through loud and clear.

Comforting. Love. Healing.

"What do you think—"

"*Shhh!*" I waved away his words.

"May she be peaceful and joyous," the group murmured softly.

I closed my eyes as paper crinkled. A new smell hit me, like something burning.

"Now, I don't approve of that at all," Smokey said, stiffening. "Starting fires is a no-no. Fire can get dangerous. Occasionally these witch—or mage—people accidentally create fireballs. Big fireballs that puff up into the air. That kind of practice is going a bit far."

I didn't have the heart to tell him that the fireballs were probably Reagan's way of messing with him. She had an odd view of jokes.

"May we bask in the light, blessed is this night."

Protect. Heal. Safety.

They were doing an utterly simple protective spell intended to keep one of the members safe. Narrowing in on their magic, on their connection, I got a more complicated read on what was happening.

It seemed one of the lovely ladies was having issues with abuse.

As the magical currents ran through me, fire kindled deep inside my gut, forcing out ideas of what I would do to someone who was physically or emotionally abusing me. Amazingly, they weren't all magic spells. Not at all. The first, out of the blue, was a head butt.

No one would expect a random head butt.

Well, except for me. I'd learned the hard way.

I'd dug into their efforts before I could stop myself, weaving a rich, complex spell within and around theirs, mindful of the necessary elements for healing and recovery.

"They seem confused," Smokey whispered, looking over my shoulder. "Are you participating with them or something?"

Magic wove in and out of my fingers, and I wanted to laugh with the joy of it. I felt buoyant, strong, beautiful, sexy, and powerful. I felt how glorious it was to have my finger on the pulse of nature.

This was what I had been missing. Emery had been right those many months ago. He'd said I was more like a witch. A deep connection with others and the world around me was necessary to my magic working. I did think like a witch. The joy and love of this community buffeted me. It made me long for deep roots of my own.

But something was missing from the Ladies of the Light: the male half. Nature existed in both. Kooky though she was, Mary Bell was right about one thing:

nature was the light *and* the dark, and everything in between. The magical world was rough. Wild. The calm *and* the storm. It required balance. These ladies did themselves a disservice by calling only to the feminine. And only to the light.

I missed Emery. I missed the balance we had found together. It had been so natural with him. So light and easy. We belonged together, whether he was ready to admit it or not.

I shook it off and shoved the spell toward the group, watching it swirl around until it sank into one of the ladies, a short-haired girl with black glasses and a pug nose.

May you kick his ass, lady.

"The witches are good people," Smokey said. "Just wait until you meet one of the foul creatures that inhabit this world. That'll ruin anyone's mood."

"I've already met plenty."

Smokey's laugh was low and rough. "You're probably talking about vampires, right? Since you're hanging out with Reagan. Maybe a shifter or two? All nice folk compared to some of the other things that exist out there, believe you me. I've thought about leaving this place a million times. Going out to Florida and retiring. But there is one thing this place has that Florida doesn't."

"What's that?"

"Reagan."

"Right." I'd heard something like that a time or two.

I headed back, passing him. He wasn't long in following.

"You'll follow her lead, if you know what's good for you," he whispered.

I wasn't sure if that was true, but these days, I wasn't sure about much of anything. Except that if you placated someone, they were likely to go away.

"Got it," I said.

"She has her finger on the magical pulse of this town. Of any town."

"Totally. I sensed that."

"You'll see. If you get in a bind, she'll help you out of it."

I turned back toward the house, slowing when I saw a man standing in the entrance of the cemetery. Thick shoulders reduced down, making his upper body a V. He dominated the space by virtue of both size and presence, seething a sort of malice that had me plucking ingredients out of my magical cloud for a painful sort of cocktail.

He took a step forward, and the weave easily rolled through my hands, similar to a spell from one of Reagan's books. I found myself incorporating strands and strings of the bright, sweet feeling I'd been reintroduced to through the witches, much like I'd pulled happy thoughts into my spell in Darius's house right before slamming it into Ja.

"*Ohhhh!*" I shifted as an explosion of understanding hit me. The happier strands added balance, which actually made the spells stronger.

During my blast of awareness, the spell I'd been weaving fizzled out and I was left standing unprotected in a darkened cemetery with a creep and a possible thug.

"Blooming bollocks," I muttered, starting the weave again.

"What's she doing out of the house?" the man asked, his stance wide and arms pushed just slightly away from his body. The posture screamed, "Flee before I bust your head."

I nearly tap-danced backward, having no problem with following unspoken orders. This wasn't a confidence issue, it was a keeping-the-peace issue.

"I couldn't stop her," Smokey said, tensing. "I tried to talk reason, but she was hellbent on coming in here. She wanted to see the"—he lowered his voice to a whisper—"witches."

The newcomer's exhale was loud. "Did you chase them out?"

"No, these are the quiet ones. They're not hurting anyone," Smokey replied, and I relaxed a little, realizing they knew each other. Given Smokey's fierce loyalty to

Reagan, I figured I was in the clear.

"I don't care if they're the mute ones. I don't need no quacks rolling up in my neighborhood, messing with things they don't understand."

"In fairness…" I raised my hand like a kid in a classroom. Silence descended and I flinched a little, knowing I had the big guy's undivided attention—something I'd bet most people tried to avoid. "They were totally harmless. They didn't have enough power to do much, and even if they did, they only have light and love in their hearts."

The man shifted. The silence stretched.

I got the feeling he wasn't pleased with my answer.

"But I support keeping all witch and mage folk out of this cemetery," I went on quickly, half to keep the peace, and half because it was a good idea. "At least until I'm gone."

"A mage has more power than a witch," Smokey said.

"I don't care." That was what the man said, but what he clearly meant was: "Do not mention anything magical to me again. Ever. *Or else.*"

"Reagan said you had trouble following you around," the man said, jerking his head and turning toward Reagan's house. Smokey and I hurried after him. "I ain't seen nothing out of the ordinary."

"The people who are after me will likely be carrying

satchels." I mimed the outline of a satchel across my side even though I was behind him. "Or maybe a belt with compartments. That's how you'll know they're dangerous."

"Guns aren't so easy to spot," the man said, looking both ways before crossing the street.

"I don't think they use guns. I've never seen them use guns, at least. Or even knives. In the past, they've relied solely on their ma—" I abruptly stopped when he turned to scowl at me.

"I've got my eye out," Smokey said, drifting to the side and stopping in front of Reagan's house. The newcomer stopped just off to the side, in the area between Reagan's house and the neighbor's place.

"I saw one strange face, but that was when Reagan's new car was parked here." Smokey crossed his arms over his chest. "You need to talk to her about that, Mikey. She can't keep parking that thing here. It draws all kinds of notice. Cops think it belongs to a drug dealer or is stolen, drug dealers want to steal it, preppy tourists want to cross over for a gawk—dent or no dent, it is a fine piece of machinery, and everyone is stopping what they're doing to take notice."

The man—Mikey—nodded slowly and turned so he was looking out onto the street. "Yeah, I hear ya. She said it was temporary. I'll talk to her."

"Or…and this is just spitballing." Tingles of fire

scuttled up my spine, though I had no idea why. "Let's steal it and teach her a lesson. I can get the keys, easy."

Mikey turned slowly and looked at me, his expression blank. In precise movements, he raised his arm until it was perpendicular to the ground and then pulled up his sleeve. His gaze shifted from me to his arm before landing back on me as he dropped his arm back to his side.

Smokey edged away slightly. I backed up until my heels touched the stairs, not sure what was happening, but ready to run just in case.

"Keep that shit to yourself," Mikey growled.

"Oh, we wouldn't really be stealing it. I'd get the keys, we'd move it—I mean, I would do it on my own, but I don't know how to drive a stick—and then I'd put the keys back," I babbled. "She wouldn't kill us, promise. And I'm pretty good at anticipating when she's going to throw a punch. I very rarely get it right to the face anymore. So I can just warn you. Then we can tell her what we did and laugh and laugh."

"I don't mean that shit," Mikey said, his voice rising. "I mean the supernatural shit. I don't want none of that. I've told Reagan before and I'll tell you now. Keep that shit away from me. I got a simple life and I'm not trying to mess it up with the likes of you fuckers."

"Wow." I grimaced and looked at my feet. "If you're friends with Reagan, I can certainly see why the absence of swearing seems abnormal to her."

"Reagan said she was untrained," Smokey murmured. "And Penny mentioned that she was largely naive—"

"I said people *call* me naive, not that I actually was—"

"—so she might not know what it is she's doing," Smokey finished.

"Oh, I'm not doing anything." I gestured at the magic-less air around us. "There's nothing going on here. This is all above board."

"Fucking hell." Mikey spat on the street, shook his head, and turned. In a moment, he was walking up the stairs of the neighboring porch, his steps much quieter than I would've thought for a man of his size.

"It's nice to meet a neighbor—" The door shut behind Mikey without him acknowledging my attempt at further conversation, and I was left staring with my mouth open.

"They call him No Good Mikey for a reason," Smokey said, back to watching the street. "He's rough by nature. Don't let it get to you."

"Oh." I shrugged. "It's fine. He's more normal than the other people I've met these past few months."

Smokey glanced at me. "Pardon me for saying so, Penny, but that tells me you should really meet some new friends." With that, he was drifting across the street, slightly hunched, before slipping back into the cemetery.

CHAPTER 22

BOOM!

The door burst open and swung inward, slamming against the wall. I always left it cracked for just this reason.

I startled, but I'd gotten accustomed to Reagan's theatrics. She wouldn't really hurt me.

Not until later.

"Rise and shine, buttercup. Time to get cracking!" Reagan sauntered in wearing her usual getup of leather pants and a tank top.

I rolled over and pulled the comforter over my head.

"Come on." She shoved me with something hard. It felt like a boot. "We have to get going. I've got things to do."

"My life is the worst." I groaned and curled up a little tighter. I hated getting up. I didn't care what time of the day or night—I did not like leaving the warm, snuggly comfort of my bed.

"Your life *is* the worst, yes. Blame your mom. Come

on."

The covers were ripped away, exposing me to the chilled air. "Why?" I whined.

"Sexy nightie. Who are you hoping to see?" She laughed and crossed to my dresser. "Get your leathers on. I want to play with fire today." She opened my drawer and pulled out clothes. Strangely, it didn't bother me as much as it had when my mother used to do it.

I pulled myself to sitting and swung my legs over the edge of the bed. My green silk negligee didn't do much to keep out the cold, so I wrapped my arms around my body while Reagan pulled out stuff for me to wear. "Marie bought this nightie, like everything else in there."

Based on the "hideous" dress I'd worn to Darius's house the night of the…um, incident, Marie had decided I needed a fashion overhaul. She'd taken it upon herself to supply it. I'd politely tried to refuse, but she'd just shoved me out of the way and put everything away herself.

"And before you ask," I went on, shivering but hating the idea of getting the day started, "I wear it because it's silky and soft against my skin—"

"Hey, I get it." Reagan dumped a leather vest onto the leather pants on the edge of the bed. "When she decided I needed better clothes, she bought me a bunch of them, too. That was before I was banging Darius, but I still wore them. C'mon, let's go. I got a date with the MLE office later."

She stalked out of the room.

Once dressed in material much less comfortable than the jeans I was used to, I trudged to the kitchen for coffee. As I was taking my first sip, I heard, "I know your secret!"

I jumped. Hot coffee splashed over my mouth and dripped down my cheeks.

"Hot, hot." I banged the cup down and snatched up the nearest towel, folded neatly near the microwave.

Reagan's shining eyes watched me from beside the kitchen entrance and her finger made circles in the air. "I know all about it."

I wiped my face. "Know all about what?"

"Your trip into the cemetery to spy on a group of witches. The Ladies of the Light, right? They're harmless. I never chase them out."

I thought about picking up my coffee cup again, but while I was decidedly less jumpy than when I'd first arrived in New Orleans—even than a couple days ago—I clearly wasn't ready to drink a hot beverage within the confines of a kitchen with Reagan. I grabbed some water instead.

"That wasn't a secret," I said, then stopped myself. "Should that have been a secret?"

Her expression fell and she stopped circling the air with her finger. "You are much too honest, do you know that? No wonder your mother was able to keep you in line." She crossed her arms and leaned against the archway. "And yes, that should've been a secret. Leaving the protection of the ward for a wide-open, dark, deserted cemetery was an incredibly stupid thing to do. It was basically an attacker's wet dream."

I eyed the coffee again. Water wasn't doing the trick. "Smokey said as much, but…" I shrugged. "Their magic called to me."

"Hey"—she held up her hands—"I live in a glass house. I'm not trying to throw stones. Tonight I'll be doing something fairly stupid myself. I'm not judging. Did you get your rocks off?"

I sidled over to my cup of coffee and filled it back up. There were some things I just couldn't do without. And unlike Reagan, whiskey wasn't one of them.

"You're right. You and Darius…and Emery. I've been trying to acclimate to the mages' way of doing things," I said after taking a much-needed sip, "but it's closed me off. When I came across the witches doing magic, it felt so natural. I remembered how to find balance."

"Ordinarily, I'd ask you not to tell him because it would inflate his already massive ego, but after the other night, I think we're good on that score. Hurry up. Let's get to burning some shit. Maybe your new balance will make you less terrible at it."

It didn't. While my reinstated balance made it easier for me to put together spells—including setting fire to my poor, defenseless practice dummy and creating mini explosions—Reagan's ability to control fire was still beyond me. Probably always would be.

"Are you an elemental?" I asked at one point, panting with my hands braced on my knees. "They can do fire, right? Because the weather one can do weather. I'd imagine there's a fire one."

"From what I've heard, some of them can do fire. One of them really well, I think. I don't know any more than that."

"So you're not an elemental?"

"No."

"Would you tell me if you were?"

"Probably not, since I'd probably be a rogue elemental on the run from my family's crushing pressure to become what they want me to be."

I blinked and shook my head. "Uh-huh. So what are you?"

"An asshole, remember? Come on, one more spell, and then I got to go."

An hour later, we were both in the kitchen, me tired but not drained—I thought that was an improvement—and her bright as a spring day.

"What is it you're doing again?" I asked between gulps of water.

"I'm going to take a contract with the Magical Law Enforcement office." She bent to wipe off the thighs of her leather pants before twisting so she could see the backs. "These are fine, aren't they? Not too dirty?"

A few scuffs and a couple smudges of dirt marred the surface. "They're a little dirty."

"But, like...*too* dirty?"

I paused. "I don't know what your definition of *too* dirty is."

"Too dirty to wear in public to a job where I want to show how awesome I am?"

"Oh." I chewed my lip, wondering how to be tactful. "I mean..." I cocked my head. "They're a bit dirty."

"A bit." She squinted at me. "I hear what you're saying." She stalked out of the room, only to return wearing the same dirty leather pants. She clipped her fanny pack onto her hips. "Okay. Ready for action."

A wave of anxiety washed over me and my body tingled, my temperamental third eye telling me of danger ahead.

"Wait..." I put down my water and stepped forward. The danger didn't feel like mine. It...strangely felt like hers. "Aren't you supposed to lie low...or something?"

She waved the thought away. "Not for this. This'll

be fine."

Butterflies filled my stomach and I stepped forward again, not sure what this feeling was. "Um…"

She cupped her breasts. "I should get a sports bra. I'll probably need to run." She left the room again.

Grateful for the break from her keen gaze, I closed my eyes and opened up, letting my intuition feelers guide me. A strong sense that something was coming hit me first, tickling my premonition centers, as vague as ever. I was nothing like my mother when it came to that particular talent. It felt good, whatever it was, like I would enjoy it.

Mail, probably. This was the sort of thing that had always spooked our old mail lady.

That had nothing to do with Reagan leaving, though (I didn't think), so I tried to home in on this particular situation. Her walking out the door to go into some sort of battle—

The desire to jump at her, wrap my arms around her legs, and stop her accosted me. But why? Was she in danger?

I should call my mother.

"All ri—What are you doing, sleeping standing up?"

I peeled my eyes opened, seeing her standing in the archway with her leather pants and tank top, her fanny pack, and her hair in a ponytail. Her stern face and kickass vibe.

"I want to go with you," I blurted.

Wariness crossed her features. "I'm going to go into the thick of things. The MLE office hasn't been able to bring this thing down. It's a surly one. This is no place for a newbie."

Pressure made it hard to breathe. "I know. I get that. And I'm a fu—I'm an idiot for trying."

A grin twisted her lips. "You're trying to swear your way into my heart, aren't you."

I totally was. "But you and Darius and the Bankses brought me into the thing in Seattle for a reason," I went on, talking quickly now. "You called me to help. And I did. I pulled through. In the Guild compound, I pulled through. I can see my way out of a pinch, I know I can."

She shifted, her eyes clouding over, and I could tell she wanted to say no.

I rushed on before she could get the words out. "I feel like I'm finally in the right headspace. Now I just need experience. *Real* experience, not torturing a put-upon rubber dummy in a magically closed-off backyard."

Her grin was back, but her brows were still pinched tight.

"Look, worst case, I can run," I said, *knowing* I needed to go with her. Somehow, it felt like she was in danger. Maybe it was my imagination, but… "I am extremely good at knowing when to run. I've been practicing that my whole life. Or I can fight. I'm not great, but I can pack a mean kick."

"Yes, you can. Your kick is fantastic. I have three intense bruises from it."

"And I won't tell Darius…and you won't tell Callie and Dizzy. We'll keep each other's secrets."

"I love the attempt at blackmail, but it'll be a hard secret to keep if you die."

"I won't die."

"How do I know?"

"Because…I won't, that's how." Of all the weak arguments…but I doubted she'd believe me if I told her she was the one I was worried about.

"Look." She spread her hands, and my heart sank. She had a fast car and I had none. If she planned to leave me behind, there was nothing I could do about it. "It's not my place to tell you how to live."

I opened my mouth for a hotheaded and extremely swear-y rebuttal, but paused when her words finally registered. "Huh?" I managed.

"We're working side by side. I'm learning as much as you are. You're making me stronger at understanding spell work and unraveling it. As far as I'm concerned, you're a peer. I have no more power over you than you have over me. Beyond that, I'm the absolute last person on this green earth who's in a position to tell *anyone* the best approach for sticking to a low-key life. But you need to understand what you're getting into. I'll be working with other mages. Well"—she waggled her hand back and forth in a so-so gesture—"I'm supposed to work with them. They usually just slow me down. But they'll be there. And we'll be combating an extremely dangerous magical creature that you don't know the first thing about. There are worse things than vampires and shifters that go bump in the night."

"Smokey said as much."

She nodded. "He should know. He nearly got his soul stolen by a doozie of a creature."

I squeezed the edges of the counter to keep from grimacing.

"You're also going to leave yourself wide open for the Guild," she continued. "I'll be busy. So will the other mages. You will be completely on your own. If they spot you, you'll be ripe for the plucking."

I blew out a breath. Even one of these risk factors should've been enough to keep me home. I turned my head to the side and closed my eyes on the sly, listening to my intuition.

"God, you're weird," I heard her say.

Not so sly, then.

Her boot scraped against the ground, shifting. She was probably anxious to get to the door. To leave.

"Let me get my stuff," I said, hurrying to my bedroom.

"This is probably a terrible idea," Reagan muttered as I passed.

I had to agree, but I was doing it anyway. Hopefully, this wasn't one of the times my temperamental third eye led me into troubled waters.

CHAPTER 23

"LET A VAMP suck on your neck and get paid like a painted lady, is that it?" A pointy-faced man with a huge Adam's apple and receding hairline stood off to the side as Reagan got out of the dented, recently scratched Lamborghini. She'd tried to slide across the hood like in a cop movie, without remembering the buckle on her fanny pack and her lack of finesse. She'd ended up scratching the car then tumbling onto her head.

Reagan shut the door, exuding a rough-and-tumble malevolence that had my stomach fluttering. She was smack dab in her element.

We were at an old-timey plantation, about an hour outside of New Orleans. From what little Reagan had heard (she apparently wasn't overly concerned about details), a banshee gone rogue was plaguing the tourist attraction, making people drop dead with very little warning. So far, four people had suffered an untimely fate at the plantation, starting a rumor that the place was cursed, since humans didn't believe in banshees, and hadn't been told about this one.

"Painted lady…that's a whore of some sort, isn't it?" she asked, not at all bothered. "My, my, Garret, your insecurity is showing. Or are you speaking from a place of experience?"

His beady gaze shifted to me as I got out of the car. "Who's this?"

"My work associate."

He centered his weight, using a wide stance that spoke of authority. "Your work associate?"

"Yes, Garret, I know words are hard. I'll give you a second to think through that sentence."

She stalked straight past him, moving toward a group of five people gathered around a huge tree with sprawling branches that seemed to weep from it. A great house crouched in the distance, with large pillars all the way around. Manicured grass, mostly dark at this time of evening, stretched across the property with more of the large trees dotting the way.

Garret, unfortunately, caught up. "She doesn't have associates, except for that vampire she sold herself to," he said, eyeing me.

I pulled my sweater—some fashionably bright red affair that Marie had bought for me—tighter across my chest and hurried after Reagan. I might have more confidence now, but I'd never been the type for hostility among perfect strangers. Besides, this guy reminded me of my nemesis, stupid Billy Timmons. I didn't intend to find a new bully in New Orleans.

Reagan stopped just outside of the circle of hard-faced men and women. One of the men, a dark-skinned man sporting a decent-sized belly, stopped what he was saying and turned toward Reagan.

"Sorry I'm late," she said as the circle shifted, creating a hole for her to step into if she so chose. She didn't. "My plus one decided to come."

The potbellied man frowned before looking at me. "I didn't authorize that. Only you are on the contract."

"It's fine, captain." Reagan waved the thought away. "She knows she won't get paid."

"But what happens when she's killed on the job?" Garret said, joining the circle.

"Melodramatic much?" Reagan asked. The captain shifted and put his hands to his hips, ready to object. "She'll be fine. I vouch for her."

"How do we know she won't be in the way?" Garret asked.

"Because I just vouched for her. Also because she's twice the man you are, without having a pair of dangling balls. Chew on that. You know, it really does suck to be you, Garret. I can't think of anyone I would less like to be."

"Big words from someone who'd be dead if it weren't for me." Garret gave her a smug look.

I assumed Reagan would quickly retort that such a thing was impossible. Instead, her face closed down into anger, and even in the darkness of the evening, I could see her cheeks turn red.

"What did he save you from?" I murmured, unable to help it. The guy seemed like a boob. I couldn't imagine him saving anyone from anything, and Reagan seemed basically immortal.

"He saved me from the glory of being the best in the office. But we'll see what's up tonight." Reagan adjusted her fanny pack.

"We already saw *what's up*," Garret said. "You just don't want to admit you were a damsel in distress. Nice fanny pack, by the way. Did your new undead boyfriend buy you that?"

"For the last time, *it is a pouch*! Why can't you people get names right?" Reagan said.

"Enough," the captain said, still eyeing me. "What's the nature of her magic?"

Reagan, clearly still mad at Garret, half turned so that the captain could see me better. I hunched under the full blast of his assessing gaze.

Silence drifted over us, and I realized that Reagan hadn't planned to answer for me.

"She doesn't even know her own magic—how could she possibly help us kill a banshee?" Garret asked, too loudly.

"It is a wonder you are standing so close to me, Garret," Reagan said in a low tone. "It's almost as if you are daring me to punch you."

Garret's teeth clicked shut. A moment later, he slowly edged sideways. To avoid being stuck between the two of them, the frizzy-haired woman on his other side edged away as well.

"What is your name?" the captain asked me.

"Penny," I said quietly, still clutching my sweater. "And I'm a mage. Kind of."

"She's untrained. Mostly," Reagan added.

"A kind of mage? What is that, a witch?" Garret asked.

"Keep it up, Garret. Keep it up." Reagan rolled her neck, and a shock of intense, sharp magic rolled over me. I'd never seen someone get her dander up like this. Usually she laughed or shrugged off any sort of aggression or tomfoolery, but each of Garret's jabs seemed to hit home.

"I operate more like a witch, yes," I squeaked out, wishing I could embody the confidence I'd thought I'd gained.

"You operate—"

"Garret, enough." The captain held up his hand with a whip crack of command. "I'm not sure what you mean. You are a mage, but you operate like a witch?"

"Look, you're probably going to figure it out sooner

or later, so I'll just tell you." Reagan hooked a thumb at me. "She's the natural the Guild is trying to get its hands on. She has a unique magical style because she wasn't trained from a young age. Or ever. I'm training her, in a way. Her style works very well for her. She's not someone to underestimate, trust me. She looks all trembly and vulnerable, but if that banshee tries to throw magic her way, Penny will react in ways that will suck your balls back into your body, I kid you not."

"Graphic," one of the circle members, a guy in his forties with wispy hair, said.

I dropped my hands and clenched my fists. I most certainly was not all "trembly." I was (almost) ready for action.

"So…she's not even trained?" The captain shook his head. "Reagan, you've had a lot of bad ideas in your day, but this might take the cake. We can't have an untrained mage on our team."

"She's not on your team. She's on my team. You all can chill here as far as I'm concerned." Reagan dug through her fanny pack. As much as I wanted to call it a pouch just to oppose Garret, he was right. It was most definitely a fanny pack. She was fooling herself. "Right, let's get to it. When was she last seen, and what form was she in?"

"Captain, you're not seriously considering going along with this, are you?" Garret pointed at me. "Look at her. I could break her in half. Call her whatever you want, but she's not cut out for this line of work."

"She's a natural, you nitwit," Reagan spat. "You could only wish you had her power. She's perfectly cut out for this role."

"How do we know?" Garret said. The captain was not great at keeping order where it concerned those two. "She could be your hairdresser, for all we know. We've seen no proof."

"Penny, prove it so we can get the show on the road," Reagan said. She didn't look Garret's way, but she didn't have to. I knew she was telling me to make an example out of him.

Gladly.

I pulled magic from around me, elements I'd used for the explosions in Darius's house, but much more subdued, because I didn't want to maim him. Through that, I braided in the intent to push him back a few steps, along with the feeling of a sweet summer's night to balance out the spell's intentions. I still didn't have much experience with that kind of technique, but my intuition told me it was a building block to better outcomes.

All of that took about two seconds, the fastest spell creation yet. Proud of myself, I grinned a little as I shoved it into the world, drifting toward Garret at a turtle's pace.

"Wow." Reagan grinned. "You don't pull any punches, huh? I like it."

"Wait, what?" I said, and worry bled through me.

Too late.

The spell hit his chest and exploded. Instead of knocking him back a few steps, it launched him into the air, throwing him ten feet.

He fell with a loud grunt and a belated yelp before rolling through the dew-soaked grass. The scent of burned hair drifted toward me, and I realized I'd accidentally woven a thread of fire through it. Thank God my fire was still weak.

"Oops," I said, shifting back and forth, ready to run if someone came at me in retaliation. "Balancing the spell really amps the power. I need to practice that a little more."

"A *little* more?" Reagan said, a lopsided grin on her face as she watched Garret jerkily get to his feet. "If that was supposed to be a tiny, weak spell, yes, I'd say you need more practice. Just a little more." Her sarcasm rang through.

"Did she say the incantation?" a slight woman with a dagger belted on her side, opposite her satchel, asked.

"She didn't use any herbs," the frizzy-haired woman said. The others in the circle shifted and looked at my belt, which I hadn't reached for once.

"Yeah. Natural. Keep up, people." Reagan clapped.

Three of the five circle members jumped. "And it should be noted that if any of you are friendly with the Guild, and I find out you flapped your gums, she or I will kill you. I mean..." She shrugged. "That should be a given, but with this crew, I feel like I need to call it out."

"All right, that's enough," the captain said, his eyes on me. "I am not giving my permission for her to tag along."

"Cool," Reagan said, not bothered.

"But—"

Reagan held up her hand to stop me. "You're not supposed to be here. You're loitering. And now we know where we stand. Though this situation poses extreme danger to you, there is no liability for the MLE office. That's fair. Now, what have we got?"

CHAPTER 24

WARY BUT FRESHENED up, anxious and a little fearful, Emery stepped out of a Lincoln Town Car down the street from the Bankses' house in the Garden District. He'd jogged through the Realm to a gate that would dump him out on the West Coast near Los Angeles, a place with mild weather where he'd experience no flying delays.

At the nearest coffee shop he'd charged his phone and called Darius, somewhat surprised that the vampire had used a lower-level assistant (not even Moss) to deal with the travel arrangements. Usually Darius treated Emery like an honored guest, or one of his prized assets. This break from normality was unsettling.

Not for the first time, Emery wondered if the situation with the Guild had already ramped up into a fever pitch. Something was surely going on, and if not that, Emery couldn't begin to guess.

He smoothed his freshly pressed pants before slapping the roof of the car twice. The driver pulled away from the curb and continued down the street, leaving

Emery behind.

Nervousness turned his stomach.

He'd originally planned to meet her face to face to assess the situation. That was what he owed her. But as he stood there, so close to the house where she was staying, he couldn't stop thinking of what Darius's assistant had mentioned in passing. Penny was heralded as a catch, and she'd caught the eye of a higher-level mage that had been hanging around her trainer's house. Darius was subtle. He was probably warning Emery against any romantic expectations.

A surge of white-hot jealousy came out of nowhere from imagining her with someone else. His stomach curdled, and he didn't know if he'd be able to handle it. He'd had no experience with this. No other woman had ever tickled his possessive side. Had ever made him want to turn around and take off with the fear she'd chosen someone else.

He ran his fingers through his hair.

Could he blame her? He'd told her to move on. He'd left her for good. A goddess like her, gorgeous and talented and kindhearted, would have no trouble getting any guy she wanted.

Of course she'd moved on.

He clenched and unclenched his fists.

He had to keep his head. Above all, he wanted her to be safe and happy. So no matter how much it twisted his heart, he would bear the situation with a smile. But maybe he needed a little longer to prepare…

He felt the tingle of watchful eyes dig into his back. Having recently been actively hunted, he knew better than to slow down or look around. He didn't let on that he felt the presences tucked into the shadows, watching his progress.

The Bankses' house was under surveillance, and he didn't think it was by friendly forces.

His heart sped up and he barely kept himself from quickening his pace.

He hoped the Bankses knew the score and had taken the necessary precautions on Penny's behalf. He also hoped Darius had started gearing up for a Guild strike. Knowing the high-level vampire, Emery imagined he was walking into a well-oiled machine.

A pink sign taped to a street light caught his eye, the yellow-orange light falling across it. Someone had come through with a red pen and marked out all of the grammar and spelling errors, of which there were quite a few.

He committed it to memory. It wasn't a subtle way of leaving hidden messages, but the Mages' Guild wasn't exactly a subtle organization. He'd think on the sign later, when he wasn't so preoccupied. See if he could ferret out any form of code.

A rustling to the left caught his ear, and he noticed a

few sprigs of a bush in the neighbor's side yard waving out of the corner of his eye, as though someone had quickly dashed by.

He continued on his way. Going by the address, the Bankses' house was right there on the right, white, huge, and with a well-manicured front yard. When he reached the neighbor's place, he saw magic glittering in the air above the Bankses' side fence leading into their backyard. The spell reeked of experience and economy, with no flourishes or anything to prove. It was strong, sturdy, and did the job it was supposed to.

A higher-powered mage with a thorough mental catalogue of spells would be able to crack it open without much of a problem. But then, that was true of most spells. He had to be thankful there weren't too many mages with the power to achieve it.

The scuff of a shoe caught his attention up the way. A dark shape zipped in behind a house, the figure's slight frame dressed in black.

This place was teeming with surveillance, more so than he'd originally thought.

Cold washed through his middle. Penny needed to be taken out of here. *Now.*

Also, his cover was already blown. He hadn't been thinking, approaching it so overtly.

"Damn," he swore softly, at the edge of the Bankses' property. With the anxiety of meeting her troubling his thoughts, he'd completely lost his senses, missing some very basic survival precautions.

Another weave glimmered near the Bankses' front door, overlaying the wood. Without getting closer, he couldn't tell what it was for, but he imagined it was a beefed-up ward, meant to do harm to anyone trying to break through as well as alert the casters to unwanted visitors. Though he couldn't see any weaves, he would bet the windows had something similar.

Cars lined the street in front of the Bankses' house and filled the long driveway. Their lower windows were almost all lit, and a couple glowed on the upper floor. They seemed to be hosting a party or a meeting, possibly introducing Penny around the New Orleans magical community.

Maybe that was the reason for all the posted surveillance. The Guild could pick off a few magical people as they came and went, maybe turn them into Guild spies. It wouldn't be the first time. Or maybe they'd already found spies.

There were too many "shoulds" and "maybes" on the table. No more stalling. Emery had to face this, for Penny's sake.

Palms sweating, warning tingles from watchful eyes running his length, he started down the walkway toward the front door. It took everything he had not to turn around and try to catch whoever was watching him.

His heart sped up and his breathing became laborious. Even his legs were trembling, of all things. There was a great deal on the line, but all he could think about was seeing her. Her beautiful blue eyes. That giant, glittering smile.

How much it would fucking hurt if she yanked out his heart and kicked it to the curb.

"Steady on, Emery," he said, stopping in front of the door.

With gritted teeth, he gave three hard raps on the door. The next moment, he turned and quickly scanned the street. As expected, two shapes ducked for cover—one directly across the street, the other a little down the way.

Once he was sure Penny was secured, he'd clean up this street. From now on, if any Guild spies got close enough to be seen, he'd snuff them out. The battle was about to begin in earnest.

Turning back to face the door, he rapped again, analyzing the weave layering the wood. As with the spell on the side of the house, it was straight to the point and packed a good amount of power. It would take a few run-of-the-mill Guild workers a few days to get through it, or a knowledgeable power player. The Bankses knew what they guarded, and they were doing their best to hold up their end of the bargain.

It wasn't enough.

The door swung open and light blasted into him, making him squint. Warmth and the homey smell of cookies wafted toward him as a barrel of a woman filled the doorway, her fist on her hip. Covered in a light blue faux-velvet sweat suit, she slammed him with her bold gaze.

"Yes?" she asked, her eyes traveling his frame and sticking a little on his hip, where others might wear a satchel.

"Hello, ma'am." He slipped his hands into his pockets so he seemed less of a threat. "I've come to inquire after Penny Bristol."

Her eyes narrowed and her body stiffened. "Who are you, and where do you get off calling me ma'am? Do I look like my mother to you?"

He couldn't help a lopsided smile. That wasn't exactly the answer he'd expected. "Um…" he said, confusion and nerves creating a potent cocktail of stupid. He cleared his throat. "I'm Emery Westbrook, and I've never seen your mother, so I'm afraid I can't say, but I would assume, based on your comments, that it is doubtful. I'm sure you're much younger and more—"

"Never mind," she said, waving him to silence. She squinted this time as she looked him over. "Emery. *The* Emery? The Rogue Natural?"

"Yes, ma'—Yes."

She shook her head as someone called, "Who is it, hon?"

A man about her age showed up at her side, wearing a stained shirt and a pleasant expression. Keen eyes looked out from over half-moon reading glasses, and something told Emery this man wasn't nearly as jovial as he looked at first glance.

"Do you think I was born yesterday?" the woman asked, looking suspicious. "That's not even possible, and it's an even worse attempt than the one you made yesterday. We aren't going to invite you through this ward, so you can just stop trying. You better get off my property, or you'll meet the same fate as that poorly dressed vacuum salesman."

"What's not possible?" the man asked.

"This idiot claims he's the Rogue Natural," the woman said. "The Mages' Guild clearly thinks we are as empty-headed as they are."

"Oh." The man shoved in a little closer, his eyes now scrutinizing, and his gaze touched the same empty patch on Emery's hip. "He is handsome enough."

"What does that prove? A bunch of guys are handsome enough," the woman said.

"He's the right age."

"So they went to a modeling agency."

"I hadn't heard he was so large." The man made a

movement like he was flexing.

"I can prove it, if you wish," Emery said quietly, feeling the pressure of the eyes on him.

The woman crossed her arms over her chest. "If you are who you say you are, you'd know what you've been sending Penny."

"Power stones that pulled at me more than typical power stones, or ones that were particularly beautiful. She can feel their personalities, and I wondered what she'd feel in the ones I sent her."

The man made a duck bill with his mouth. "Well, that seems right enough—"

"*Shh.*" She elbowed him. "That doesn't prove anything."

"Yes, it does," the man said in a flash of anger. "The spells protecting those packages weren't tampered with."

"Everyone knows the Guild is keeping eyes on the Rogue Natural"—she leaned forward, her gaze boring into Emery's—"who is on the other side of the world right now."

"Well, yes, I suppose that information could've been obtained another way," the man conceded.

Emery spread his hands. "How can I prove it?"

"Do some magic," the woman said.

He looked harder at the spell covering her door, blocking access to her house. He pulled magic from the elements around him—the dew on the grass, the rubber from his boot, the chemicals from his hair care products—and quickly constructed a countering weave.

"You might want to stand back," he said. "It will spark."

Both of them took a step back as he laid his spell over theirs. Multicolored fizzing filled the doorway. Their eyes widened, and suddenly the woman was hurrying away and the man filled the door, as though he planned to fight Emery off should he tear down the spell.

"You have no need to worry," Emery said, putting his hands back in his pockets when the spell was done. "I'll put up a new spell, one that very few mages will be able to take down."

The spell in the doorway unraveled, its energy dissipating back into the natural world, from whence it came. Or so Penny would say.

"How is she?" Emery asked quietly, unable to help it. "Is she happy?"

The woman showed up with a satchel draped over her shoulder and held another out for the man. "Here," she said, gathering a handful of basil and sage.

"Wait." The man took the satchel.

"You've studied that spell, have you?" the woman asked, taking a capsule out of her bag. "Well, that crossed the line. We don't—"

"Would you wait?" the man said, his anger flaring again. It seemed to be his way of counteracting the woman's badgering. It was clearly the way they balanced as a dual-mage pair.

"He's tearing down our spell! We can't wait," she said.

"It's gone," Emery said. "I do not treat the act of tearing down a ward as an invitation to come inside. The Guild and I differ in that, somewhat."

"He asked if Penny was happy," the man said, lowering the satchel.

"So?" the woman said.

"I know how a man acts if he actually cares about a woman. This man didn't ask about her magic, or her fighting prowess, or where exactly she is—he asked if she was happy. Which means he actually cares about her."

She lowered her hands, the wheels turning.

"That wouldn't be a question the Guild would think to ask," the man went on. "If they were pretending to care, they'd ask if she was safe or something."

"I can tell you about our breaking into the Guild, or my experiences with her mother, or our first meeting," Emery said. "Or you can just take a picture with your phone and have Penny verify. Whatever you choose, please hurry. I do not like standing out here, flaunting myself to the Guild. They might get antsy and come for me. They're all around us."

The woman stepped forward while tucking her herbs back into her satchel. "So you're Emery." She nodded slowly. "Even more handsome than I'd heard. Penny has good taste. Hi." She put out her hand to shake. "I'm Callie Banks." He shook it before she stepped back and nudged the man next to her. "This is Desmond."

"Dizzy." The man put out his hand. "People call me Dizzy. We thought you were in the wilds."

"Did the vampire send for you when he proclaimed us unfit?" Callie asked.

Anxiety bled through Emery again. "He declared you unfit?"

"See? There." Dizzy pointed at Emery's face. "Concern. He is worried about Penny. Yes, this is our guy. I'm certain. Come in, come in."

"We were already certain." Callie waved him in before turning. The word "Savage" was etched into the seat of her pants in pink sparkles. Emery couldn't argue with it.

"We tried to train her how we'd been trained, you know?" Dizzy stared out for a minute, his eyes tightening, before he shut the door a little harder than was necessary.

"Did you want me to put up another ward really quick?" Emery asked, hesitating.

Dizzy hesitated as well, wariness crossing his features as his gaze returned to the door. "It can wait for a moment. Adding you, we have a lot of power in this house right now. They won't come in. I don't think they have the resources. Not yet." Dizzy's smile didn't reach his eyes. "Anyway, we tried to train her the usual way. We walked her through the theory of the spells, gave her the ingredients, as Penny called them—"

"Ingredients and recipes," Callie said, leading them through a large foyer. "And she made each spell as easily as she could make spaghetti, let me tell you. All she needed was the recipe."

"But they didn't stick," Dizzy said. "The spells."

"They stuck, all right," Callie said, turning into a living room filled with people sitting at tables and talking quietly. They looked up when Callie came into the room. "But whenever she needed to use them in a practice battle, she drew a blank. She was left standing defenseless. Well, until she reacted in blind terror."

"Oh yes. Best to steer clear of her whenever she reaches the stage of blind terror," Dizzy said with a smile. "She is a force unto herself, but horribly unpredictable."

All eyes in the room stuck to Emery, the mages' expressions assessing.

He increased his swagger, owning the room and everyone in it. These mages might be necessary allies at some point, so it was best to place himself at the top of their hierarchy. His brother had drilled that necessity into him, harping on about how much time and effort it would save.

Thinking on what Dizzy was saying, he frowned. That didn't sound right. Penny had excellent recall, and was a force to be reckoned with in real battles. She should've been in her element. He said as much.

"That's what we thought. But no, she choked. Big time." Callie stopped in the center of the room. "Everyone, meet Emery Westbrook, the Rogue Natural."

Gasps replaced the soft murmurs. Eyes widened and mouths dropped open. A woman with a red face and delighted smile fanned herself, her eyes taking on a gleam Emery knew would eventually turn into a handsy sort of invitation. He'd need to steer clear of her.

"He's resurfaced for our Penny," Dizzy said joyfully.

"I just came to check on her," Emery said quickly, noticing the glower of a gangly man with slicked-back hair. He didn't want to step on any toes before he fully understood the situation.

"She froze up, and it wasn't until a newbie vampire charged her that she came out of her shell." Callie started through the tables. "Dizzy, get this meeting wrapped up and get them out of here. We need to have a powwow with our new friend."

"We should put up the wards first, hon," Dizzy replied.

She hesitated and worry filled her expression, making Emery's stomach flip over. The Bankses were not comfortable with what was going on around them. It seemed like they were trying to barricade themselves in. But surely they had to know that such a strategy would only work until the Guild came after them.

And the Guild *would* come in after them.

"Fine," Callie said. "Give them some liquor until we can get everything into place."

"Hi." A woman stood up quickly from a table as Emery passed it. "Hi, I'm—"

"He doesn't care who you are, Cheryl, hack that you are." Callie yanked Emery along behind her.

"Is Penny here?" Emery asked as Cheryl called out, "She's just bitter that she doesn't also have *Seer* abilities, like I do. We'll chat later."

"If you had *Seer* abilities, you'd already know you're going home alone to your twelve cats," Callie yelled back.

More people stood up, their expressions eager and hands outstretched.

"We're so privileged you would visit," a woman said.

"Penny is one lucky girl," another said.

"So great to meet you," a man said.

"Let him through," Callie roared. "He has important

business here. Do you not remember the meeting we *just* had?"

No one seemed to hear her. Instead, they fawned over Emery like he was a celebrity. Had his brother felt like this all the time when working with other mages?

"Don't worry about all of them." Callie led him through a dining room where an older man was filling a plate. She hooked a thumb over her shoulder at Emery. "This is the Rogue Natural."

"The..." The man's eyes rounded and his mouth dropped open.

"Yeah, I know. Dizzy and I have become the hub for two of the most powerful mages in the world. So..." Callie shrugged and led the way out.

"Big on status in this neck of the woods, huh?" Emery asked, finally reaching a large kitchen that was, blissfully, empty.

"You're a mage; you know how it works. You need to constantly prove your place in the power and prestige pyramid."

"I've never really taken an active role in that. I left that to my brother."

Her face fell and she nodded sadly, but didn't comment. That small gesture endeared her to him. Made him connect with her on a more human level. He was thankful for that.

"So, the bad news is that Penny is no longer under

our care," she said, each word angrier than the last. The world stilled for a moment. So many questions blasted through Emery's mind that he couldn't focus on just one.

"We hoped to break down her bad habits and build them anew," Callie said, "but the vampire didn't think it was the best strategy for her. If only he wasn't right, I would've done it anyway. He thinks he has a better way of training her."

His mouth dried up and his heart pounded, terror squeezing his throat. If he hadn't already acknowledged the hold she had on him, he'd be severely wigged out by his own dramatic reaction. As it was, he couldn't shake the fear that Penny was exposed. That she lacked protection as the Guild slithered into the city in ever-larger numbers.

The black mist of warning that had clouded his vision had promised some sort of demise for her…

"And she is in his care?" he said with a suddenly dry mouth.

Pride flashed across Callie's expression before unease settled in. "No. As part of his training method, he tried to force her into survival mode. Well, he succeeded, all right. And she nearly blew his house apart." She proceeded to tell him about Penny killing four new vampires, somehow scaring a fifth (he hadn't realized that was possible) and awakening an extremely old vampire that had been in a sort of stupor.

She finished, "Darius was not expecting that dinner to go as it did."

A grin worked through his concern. That was the thing about Penny: no one could ever predict the outcome of a situation when she was stuck in the middle of it. He loved that about her. The innocent volatility. The excitement and challenge that she created over the normal course of her day.

His heart ached. He missed her something rotten. Which would make it extremely awkward when he had to see her with someone else. Extremely awkward.

"Her power is unlike anything I've ever witnessed," he said as she took down a bottle of whiskey. "I can see how she wouldn't respond to the normal training. Though her choking in a mock battle is…"

"Alarming." Callie nodded. "I know. It has made me wonder. Her survival magic hasn't failed her yet, but she has absolutely no control over what she does with it."

"And she was…unhurt after that dinner, I assume?" he asked tentatively, afraid of the answer. Afraid of how much he cared about the answer.

Callie paused in pouring drinks, her gaze roaming his face before resting on his eyes. "You really do care for her. Dizzy was right."

"Yes, and I don't want to see her come to harm."

She went back to pouring drinks. "Other than a few

blisters on her feet from those God-awful cheap shoes I told her to return, she was unhurt, yes. Though she did need to ask a bunch of derelict shifter barflies for help."

He gripped the edge of the countertop. "What's this now?"

"Don't worry." She patted his forearm. "Reagan came to the rescue. That's whose house she is in now. No safer place, trust me. She probably should've gone there first."

"Who is Reagan?"

"A friend of mine. She has very powerful magic and is bonded to Darius."

"She's—" He felt his eyes widen in surprise. "Darius bonded someone? I wouldn't think he'd stoop to binding himself to a human, magical or otherwise."

"She's not just any magical human, and yeah, she bonded him. It was necessary at the time, and she says she'd do it again, but I think she's a damn fool."

"I'd have to agree."

"So now Penny is training with Reagan, and it seems to be going really well. Or so Reagan says. If it couldn't be me, at least it's her and not some conniving, egotistical, selfish vampire."

Emery ignored the smack talk about vampires. Darius had his uses, but Emery generally thought along the same lines. Most people who weren't vampires did. "Reagan is a mage?"

"No. More of a…mutt."

He was losing his patience for this conversation, hating these non-answers. "Does she know how big of a disaster Penny can be?"

"Trust me, Penny is nothing compared to Reagan."

"And yet you think the setup is a good one?"

Callie's eyebrows lowered. "There's a difference between *caring about* someone and being overbearing. You'd do best to remember that. And yes, I do. Because Reagan can handle herself, and she can handle anything Penny might throw at her, including intense spells. That woman is a walking spell encyclopedia. Like I said, Penny is in good hands."

"But what if Penny is out in the world and freezes up again?"

Callie took a sip of her whiskey. "Impossible. Penny is stuck working her butt off within an extremely powerful ward. So far as we know, the Guild hasn't locked on her location yet. And before you ask how we could know that, just trust me. Reagan's neighborhood watch is particularly vigilant. If Penny freezes up, it'll be in the safety of Reagan's house."

"And if Penny leaves?"

"If you knew her at all, you'd know she's a rule follower. She won't leave."

His knuckles turned white where they gripped the countertop. He did know her, and yes, she was a rule follower…up to a certain point. But if what she called her temperamental third eye convinced her to get into mischief, she'd run at it full steam. She wouldn't stay put for long.

If she was freezing up, it meant something was blocking her use of her considerable power. Probably the integration of a different way of working magic, one that didn't feel natural to her. Until that issue was completely worked out, she'd have times when the spells just wouldn't come. He knew that from experience.

And if the Guild was there to cash in on just one of those occasions, she'd be a sitting duck, easy prey.

"Call her. Call them both. I need to speak to them. *Now.*"

CHAPTER 25

REAGAN'S PHONE VIBRATED in her pocket. She fished it out and glanced at the screen. "Callie calling. She needs her daily rant before she goes to bed." Reagan silenced it and put it back in her pocket. "We'll call her back when this is done. You might want to silence your phone, too. Or turn it off. If it goes off when we're sneaking around, that could become a very bad situation."

I tapped my pockets as I tiptoed through the grass behind her, completely exposed. "I left it in the car."

"Not married to your phone, huh? I'm jealous."

"Shouldn't we have a plan? The others stayed behind to come up with a plan. I feel like a plan, even something totally basic, like what we're doing right now, would serve us well."

"Plans get you killed."

I chewed my lip and avoided a reaching shadow from one of the enormous trees off to the right. "I feel like you're mistaken on that one."

"In situations involving wily creatures who excel at

improvisation, the last thing you want to do is stay married to a plan. You'll end up trapped. Trust me on that. This isn't my first rodeo. What you have to do is know your opponent, and act accordingly."

"Right, sure." We angled to the left corner of the massive house in front of us, its front entrance still and silent. "Except I don't know a poo-tossing monkey's hindquarters about my opponent."

Reagan glanced back. "A what? Never mind. Look, check it out." She hooked a thumb over her shoulder, pointing back the way we'd come. "First, their plans haven't worked yet. This is their third attempt, and they are down peacekeepers—the people who are supposed to go after bad guys—because the banshee injured a few. They're out of their league. The captain knows this. Usually at this point he'd hire me for the job and leave his people at home, but he probably suspects I can't do it alone."

"Then why did he send you in here alone?"

"He didn't. He sent me with you."

"I'm not sure I'll be much help."

"I was kidding. No, you probably won't be much help, but at least you'll get a little experience, amiright?" We reached the corner of the house and she slowed down, walking more quietly now. "He sent me alone and kept them back to 'plan' to give me a second to scout this on my own. He'll see if I can handle it alone, and if not, he'll rush in to save the day. That's why he gave me the ear piece." She touched her left ear.

"It would've been nice to get one of those," I muttered.

"Nah. I doubt I'll have it long. They're annoying. So. About the opponent." She dropped to a whisper as she slowly worked her way along the side of the house, keeping as close to the house as the shrubbery would allow. "Do you know what a banshee is?"

"Something that wails. And has to do with death."

"In essence, it's the red-headed stepchild of the fairies. Do you know what they are?"

"Like Tinker Bell?"

"Right…" She drew the word out, not agreeing with me so much as bemoaning my lack of magical knowledge.

"I'm new to all this," I said apologetically.

"Clearly. Right, so *usually* a banshee isn't a bad thing. Annoying as all get-out, with their loud, obnoxious wailing at all hours of the night, but *usually* they don't do any killing. Their cries are basically a forewarning someone's about to die. Think of them as *Seers.* When the person dies, the banshee helps them into Death's chariot, or so the myths say—I've never seen this fabled chariot—and wishes them farewell. So that's pretty nice.

"Banshees can also use their power to help ease the

transition from life to death. This might happen, say, if someone is very sick, won't ever get better, and is suffering. The banshee will cradle them into the afterlife and onto the chariot. She's a rather nice lady in times of strife, with a fiercely bad, and mostly undeserved, reputation as a bringer of death. Welcome to being a woman—always blamed for shit going wrong whether it's our fault or not."

"So banshees aren't actually harmful."

"Usually, no. Once the person dies, the banshee moves on."

"But this one hasn't."

"Look at you, noticing the extreme obvious."

I opened my mouth, willing a witty comeback, but came up dry.

"Banshees, like anything, can go bad," Reagan whispered, slowing to a stop as she neared the rear corner of the house. She crouched and waited for me to crouch with her. "They have the power to kill. They can force someone into the afterlife. They don't even have to put the poor sod on the chariot—they can let the soul they've released wander aimlessly. So, she can be a lovely lady, or serious asshole."

"How does she kill?"

"There you go. Now you're asking intelligent questions." Reagan looked out across the grounds. Most of it was wide open, but beyond the back corner of the house, various bushes, trees, and shrubs cut into our visibility. “The easiest way is to don the form of a young woman and lure men to her side. That’s quite easy, as I’m sure you can guess. Once they’re within striking distance, she embraces them, and wrestles them across the line between living and dead.”

“So don’t let her hug you.”

“Yes, obviously. You’re not a hugger anyway, right?”

“I’m socially awkward.”

“Excellent. See? You were made for this gig.”

I got the feeling she was making fun of me, but she was so deadpan that I couldn’t really say.

“She has a couple forms, and she has her wail. The wail cannot hurt you. The creature cannot hurt you from a distance. But she is a glider. A fast glider. Not as fast as a vampire, but faster than you. She’ll launch herself at you, wrap her hands around your head, and muscle you out of this life.”

A shiver skittered across my skin before punching cold through my middle. “What other forms does she take?”

“Young woman, stately middle-aged woman, and an old crone. She’ll be in a lovely dress, twisted sheets that have no place in this century, or some sort of robe. Oh, and occasionally she poses as a washerwoman trying to get stains out of bloody clothes.”

"Uh-huh." Adrenaline pumped through me. "How do we kill it?"

"How do *you* kill it? I have no idea. Magic, is my guess. As for me, I will stab my sword through its middle. Or yank its head off and set it on magical fire. Or maybe crush it. I haven't tried to use my other form of magic on one of these, so that might be fun. I'm anxious to try it out. But worst case, my sword. Ol' trusty."

She fell into silence, clearly thinking about the battle to come. I blinked at her.

"So." She slapped my knee and I jumped. "Ready?"

"But…"

Reagan was up and walking again. "She apparently likes to hang out around the fountain back here. If she's in the world of the living, she will be visible. But she can cross over, so be prepared for her to wink out. Oh, and keep moving around. I don't think the crossing is a quick, easy affair, but just in case, you don't want her disappearing from one spot and popping up right next to you. That's a sure way to die."

Adrenaline soaked my body and set my heart to beating at unnatural speeds. Sweat covered my forehead and upper lip, giving me a chill in the nighttime air. Tremors and tingles and all manner of fear-induced issues racked my body.

"Why did you let me come?" I asked with numb

lips.

Reagan was a badass powerhouse who'd lived this life for a very long time. I was a goober who bumped around blindly, swimming in the deep end when I wasn't prepared.

What had possessed me to think I could hang out on the same playing field? To think I could actually help her if we came face to face with danger?

"Don't worry, it'll be fine," she said, blasé. "I've dealt with ten times worse. Remind me to tell you about the *aswang* one day."

We finally reached the rear corner of the house and got a view of the large, circular fountain, currently turned off. Little patches of trees and shrubs marked the corners of the larger concert area, surrounded by a series of smaller trees and bushes. Beyond those lay the wilder grounds. No other houses or establishments existed for miles.

"Come out, come out, wherever you are," Reagan said quietly, pulling out her sword.

I collected magic and half wished I had a sword of my own. If nothing else, it would be a great prop to let the creature know I meant business.

"Don't think about which spell you'll use," she said quietly, walking to the center of the concrete area. The back door was behind us, the fountain directly in front of us.

My mental Rolodex stopped spinning.

"Do that balance thing," she said. "You know, the witch thing."

My legs trembled and my chest felt strange, heavy and anxious but also desperate to expand. It was like waiting in line to enter a horror house on Halloween, only the horror house had real haunts.

"Training exists to commit spells and combat into your muscle memory," she said, even now training. How did she have the mental capacity?

Leaves rustling to the right stopped our forward movement.

Reagan didn't brace herself like I expected she would. Like I had. Her body stayed loose and at ease, holding her sword a little drooped. She didn't even clench her teeth in anticipation of an attack.

I pried my jaw open.

Silence lay over the scene like a heavy film, suspending us in time, keeping us put while the banshee circled her prey, licking her chops and clicking her claws.

My imagination was in overdrive again. Nothing had happened but a little rustling.

I took a shaky breath as Reagan started forward, each step soft and strategic. Her knees bent. Her eyes darting this way and that. Totally calm.

Next to her, my feet scraped the concrete. My legs moved in jerky fits and surges and my nails were picked to nubs.

The oppressive darkness pressed on us, crushing us to the ground. Pushing against us.

A soft sound, like a footfall, had Reagan stopping again.

"Are you doing that balance thing?" she asked softly, her hand drifting through the air toward me.

I collected my ingredients, stuffing them in the air around me. That part was extremely easy. I did it constantly, often without intending to. But the soft feeling of the world around me was interrupted by my heightened senses, screaming at me that something was here. Watching our progress from the shadows. Her eyes itched the skin between my shoulder blades, and I imagined her poking my temple with a long, pointed claw.

Was that my intuition or my imagination? In times like this, I could never tell.

"Are you doing the balance thing?" Reagan asked again, her tone like a spring day near a tranquil pond.

"It pisses me off that you are so damn calm."

"Yikes. So that's a no. Listen, getting worked up isn't going to help anything. In fact, it'll slow you down in the long run. It'll lead you to bad decisions. You need to relax and take in the night. Open up that intuition that I know you have in spades and *listen* to it."

My breath came too fast, and trying to slow it down

only reminded me of how much I was shaking.

"I've never been a fan of the unknown," I said.

"Yeah. This waiting bullshit is the pits. I hate it." She looked to the left, then swept her gaze in front of us as we reached the edge of the fountain. With a firm hand, she pushed me to the right while she drifted left.

"No, no, no," I whispered furiously, not moving any farther. "What are you doing?"

"It's too quiet, don't you think?" She kept going. "No animals skittering about, no angry bird calls, no insects."

"Yes, I do think. I definitely do think. So we should stay together."

"We are together. You're right there. Now pay attention in case something darts out at you from that side."

CHAPTER 26

I SPUN IN that direction, squinting through the darkness.

"Dang it," Reagan muttered.

"What? What is it?"

"We don't see anything yet. Give us a little more time."

"What?" I chanced a look over at her. She was dropping her hand from her ear, having advised the others to hang back. "Won't more people be merrier?"

"Not those clowns. The captain is all right, but he's seen his day. He usually hangs back, and then Garret gets all up in my business."

I hurried along the periphery of the fountain, slowing down at the halfway point to be level with her. The sooner we met up, the better. In the meantime, I eyed the murky water separating us. If I had to, I'd sprint across that without a problem. I wouldn't be fazed in the least.

A twig cracked, startling me, and movement caught my eye. A woman with an hourglass figure and long, flowing hair moved through a gap in the foliage beyond the cement enclosure. Colorful streams of magic flowed around her, wispy but bright. Gleeful intent that should have been paired with cackling beckoned us near, drawing us in.

"She wants us to follow her," I said, cold flowing over my skin. My impulse was to run back the way I'd come, refusing the magic's invitation.

"What? Where?" Reagan hopped up on the lip of the fountain.

"There." I pointed. "Just through there. I saw her meander by."

"Meander, huh." Reagan gracefully jogged along the lip, not at all concerned about losing her balance on the half-foot-wide surface and falling into the dirty pond. "She thinks she has nothing to fear, does she?"

I picked up the pace and met Reagan as she hopped off the fountain at the far end. "How do you know?"

She shook her head. "Where did you see her, exactly? And in what form?"

"Lady form. I couldn't tell if she was young, but she wasn't old. Right through there." I pointed. "But she was moving that way."

"Time to rock." And Reagan was off at a fast jog, heading in the opposite direction of the banshee.

"This is where we need a plan," I said, not knowing what else to do other than run after her. I certainly wasn't going in the direction the thing was going. I might get tucked into the chariot of death before Reagan could save me.

"Never do what they want you to do. We don't follow the rules." Reagan did a circle in the air with her finger. "Circle around."

"That doesn't mean anything to me," I said desperately, crashing through the bushes into a small opening with a bench off to one side and a small path running through it. Leafy trees and bushes blocked off my visibility beyond the opening, making me a prime target for a banshee ambush.

Reagan was already ten feet in front of me, with the distance growing.

I launched forward, trying to open myself to the world around me, and instead noticed all the little pockets of darkness dotting the way. Anything could jump out of those pockets. Sure, the size was off for a person-sized ghoul, but if she could change form, maybe she could change size.

Various banshee forms rolled through my head, effectively eliminating my ability to summon spells. I couldn't tell if that was better or worse.

The path forked—I could either go straight ahead or turn left through the trees. I hadn't seen which way Reagan had ducked. The leaves on the right shivered. It wasn't until I had turned left and was jogging past another bench that I noticed all the leaves were shivering and the branches ahead, where the path dumped into empty space, shook.

It was just the wind.

I released a heavy breath.

"Reagan?" I called as loudly as I dared, slowing on the path. Dried leaves rubbing together filled the silence, like an audience laughing and cheering at my vaudeville act of bounty hunting.

"Reagan?" I called again, a little louder.

A soft song drifted over and around the bushes flanking the path. Sweet yet sad, the music was intended to bring tears to my eyes. Wisps of magic rode the breeze, trying to pull me to the left side of the path.

There wasn't a specific spell being aimed at me. More of a feeling. A deep longing to feel the warm embrace of a loved one, safe and secure. It didn't even claw at me, though the underlying intent seemed to hint that it would, but it stroked my face and cupped my cheek.

"Hells to the no." I took off, running faster than Reagan had and aiming for an open area up the way. I needed to see this thing coming.

The soft song turned into an intense wail, loud and long. It pulled back the fuzzy blanket and exposed a set of iron fangs, chomping through the air right on my tail.

I chanced a look back. My eyes didn't see anything, but my imagination was really going wild on this one, and it was severely messing me up.

A body burst out of the bushes in front of me. Magic swirled around it, whipping and lashing. An old woman reached for me, welcoming me into her arms.

"Cluster-sucking wally twat!" Reagan had taught me some new Euro-slang that Americans (namely my mother) might not realize were swear words.

My mind buzzed, no spells at the ready, so I reacted how I did when Reagan was after me and I had nothing magical with which to beat her back.

I pulled my fisted hands to my chest, jumped into the air, and struck out with my foot, the execution perfect.

My shoe hit the banshee's face. I pulled my leg in, landed on balanced, evenly spaced feet, jabbed with my left hand and, seeing the old woman reeling, stepped forward and delivered a strong right hook.

Without slowing down, I pivoted and took off running. I was no freaking hero.

I dove through the bushes, followed by a scream-wail like nails on chalkboard. Once on the other side, I heaved a sigh, seeing a stretch of grass to the right. I just had to make it—

A body crashed through the bushes on my left.

I screeched and spun, punching out. A hard forearm swiped through the air, knocking my fist away. Only then did I see who it was.

"Where is it?" Reagan asked, completely cool.

"Sorry…" I jogged farther away from the bushes. "There." I pointed back the way I'd come.

She was gone in an instant, crashing through like a rampaging elephant.

"Crazy," I said between pants. "She's…crazy."

But she was also my partner, and I couldn't leave her to chase that thing on her own, regardless of how excited she was by the prospect.

"Bollocks." I jumped in after her, finding her on the other side, crouched, her sword in hand. She shoved me behind her when I staggered into her side, and put her finger to her lips.

I put my hands out like claws, because without a sword, I had to do *something* scary, and let the night roll over me. The dense smell of foliage greeted my senses and the moisture of the night layered my skin. Stars blinked down at us from overhead and the breeze ruffled my hair.

Everything stabilized. My fear drifted into the background and my brain stopped buzzing. Nature reached out her comforting hand for me, and I took it. Within one of my compartments, I felt a power stone beg to be taken out.

It was the rock Emery had sent me from Ethiopia,

Mr. Happy-Go-Lucky. I was now pretty sure it was most pleased when around danger. Like Emery when certain moods struck him.

"There you go," Reagan said, rising enough to step forward slowly. "There's the power. Now, use me. Connect with me the way you did with those witches. And for the love of God, turn around so you can watch our six."

Of course she hadn't shoved me behind her so she could protect me. She was looking at me as an equal, not a damsel in distress.

I felt a little sheepish, and a lot empowered, as I about-faced.

I felt Reagan's magic pulsing near me, a riptide of power, ready to suck me in and overcome me. The woman was packing large, and it still impressed and disconcerted me. I pulled it into the bubble I'd formed from my magic and Mr. Happy-Go-Lucky's, letting her intense, spicy magic bolster ours.

"Did you do it?" she asked, taking another step forward.

"Yes. Can't you feel it?"

"No. I don't have that kind of magic. Okay, here's the situation. She's good at hide-and-seek, and we can't just go crashing into her or she wins. Quite tricky, this one. A worthy adversary." Reagan looked behind. "The ol' broad is hiding from me, but she went after you. She clearly senses that vulnerable thing you do and wants easy prey. So we're going to dangle the bait."

My stomach twisted. "I'm the bait, aren't I?"

"Yes." Reagan took another step forward. "So. Off you go. And hurry. Those clowns are headed our way, trying to help trap her. They honestly have no clue. It's embarrassing."

"Aren't you using me to trap her?"

"No. I'm using you to entice her out of her hiding place. It's a game of cat-cat-mouse."

"There are too many cats in that game."

"Probably. Off you go. Oh yes, that hunching thing—do more of that."

The hunching was a natural reaction to the fear and stress of the situation, and I didn't need to be told to do more of it. That was a given.

My bubble wobbled, but my power stone got twice as excited, so I focused on that. Overtaking Reagan, I walked toward where the path dumped into the clearing, hoping I could reach that before the creature came after me. A quick glance behind showed Reagan drifting into the bushes, hiding from sight.

I wasn't on my own, though. She was on scene. She'd be watching.

Steeling my courage, holding the power stone in a white-knuckled grip, I inched my way up the path and dunked back into the liquid, unnatural silence that had preceded the creature's wails. Dark gaps laughed at me as I passed, possibly hiding evil within their depths. A cloud wafted across the moon overhead, seeping what little color there was from the world around me.

At the end of the path, nothing had happened. No sound had reached my ear. If she was waiting for me to be alone, she clearly wasn't satisfied yet. She had to know Reagan waited just out of sight.

Fine. You want me by myself, let's do this.

I started up a jog, past the bushes and out to the grass beyond, blessed space opening up around me. One of the massive trees stood sentry a hundred feet out, and I headed for that, stopping near its huge trunk. Branches bowed around me, some swooping low enough to kiss the grass.

Shouts and calls sounded in the distance, and I figured that was probably the other team getting into a position.

With a freaking plan.

After scanning the bushes back the way I'd come, I shifted my gaze all the way around me, stopping at the edge of the house. Nothing moved or even shook. All was quiet. Waiting.

Knowing that whatever vulnerability I exuded, magically or otherwise, was tied to my fear, I let the tremors come. The uncertainty. I was out here, on my own, without a magic sword, any experience, or the slightest clue of how to kill a banshee.

My bubble wavered and the buzz of terror crept back into my brain.

Before I could try and call back the bubble, I heard it. The soft song on the breeze. The longing for a comforting embrace.

The banshee was taking the bait, but I was no longer ready for it.

CHAPTER 27

REAGAN HAD SAID that if the banshee was in the world of the living, it would be in a solid form. But as the song grew louder, the pull of it tugging at my middle, I knew she'd been mistaken.

Magical wisps curled into the air in the center of the grass, nothing rooting them to the ground. A moment later, they were gone, disappearing into the night.

I blinked a few times, then opened my eyes wider, making sure my eyes weren't playing tricks.

The song turned into a moan, winding toward me on a sweet-smelling gust of wind. Near my face, streams of magic twirled into the air, bright colored with busy patterns.

Comfort. Distract.

"Why is that?" I asked softly, stepping away from the tree and turning in a circle. "Why are you trying to distract me? To sneak up on me?"

A new thought struck me. Maybe it could cast its magic, like I did spells. It could be throwing distraction spells to keep me looking in another direction while it snuck up on me. And here I was, falling for it hook, line, and sinker.

"No, thank you, scary lady." I wandered out a little farther, trying to look all around me at once. It essentially meant I turned in constant circles and my head swiveled in all directions.

But it wasn't working. I wasn't focusing long enough on any one thing to pick the banshee out of the darkness. If she wore a dark dress, robe, or bunch of sheets, she'd be all but invisible. And that was assuming she wasn't invisible already!

I hefted my power stone and closed my eyes for a moment, feeling the push of nature. The throb of life. Lo and behold, there—woven into the song of life was one of death, weaving in and around in perfect harmony. Balance.

A new intent smacked into me. The feeling of forever. Of being sucked into the void and then carried forth to eternity. Death.

Coming for me.

Right now!

"Wally Wanker's twinkle toes!" I snapped my eyes open and spun around, bringing up my claws for a bit of scare. A shape came at me in the night. Flowing and graceful, with a robe fluttering out behind it like a great silk cape, it didn't sprint so much as glide very quickly. Very, very quickly.

I should've run at it, throwing my magic.

I should've stood my ground, throwing my magic.

I about-faced and sprinted, not at all graceful, but at least not standing still.

The banshee's wail tore across the grass, ear-splitting and bone-chilling. It spoke of death, decay, and ever-lasting rest. She was forewarning a death, one that she planned to create herself.

"No you won't, she-bitch." Tall words for someone running away like a coward.

I ran past a tree, thought better of running in a straight line, given that I wasn't the fastest person in the race, and turned quickly. I looped around the tree and caught sight of the old crone moving so fast that it was a wonder both hips didn't give out and go skittering to the side.

Reagan's magic had pulled away from my bubble when I'd left her, but that didn't matter, because I could feel the pulsing power of the banshee. Dull and peaceful but throbbing, it didn't at all speak of a villainous woman trying to steal someone's life. It was calm and comforting and—

"Oh no you don't! I'm onto you!" I took off running again—no idea why, just knowing it was too fast for me to stand still. Also, while my magic was urgently waiting for me to sculpt it, my brain buzzed with that freaking old woman tearing through the grass toward me, her face a mask of horror and her claw-like hands braced in the air.

"I knew clawed hands were scary," I said as I pumped my arms as fast as I could, running toward a line of trees. "Very scary."

Wait, why I was going *away* from Reagan? Salvation was toward her.

I cut right, throwing off the banshee, thankfully. She was a fast glider, but a slow turner. I'd wait a moment and cut right again, heading back toward Reagan's last hiding place.

The banshee's wailing dug into my core and gnawed on my bones. Its magic blanketed out from it, soft and pleasant and deadly. It would be a lovely song to hear on one's deathbed, and that was what scared me most—part of me *wanted* to let her carry me out of my body and this world.

I was in serious danger.

Defend yourself, you flugging moron!

I stopped randomly, no longer totally in control, and turned. The thing was forty feet from me and closing the distance between us fast. I wouldn't have made it to Reagan, if she was even in the same area. I dropped the stone, and the weave flowered in my fingers before I even properly willed it, springing to life and spiraling out. A wall to stop the thing. A cage to contain it. A lullaby to still it and, above all, forgiveness.

I didn't know why that last bit was so crucial, but I felt it. I knew it. It would root both the spell and the beast.

After that, I'd wait for someone to do whatever they would with it. I didn't want to be responsible for its demise. That felt wrong, to me. Unnatural.

The irony didn't fail to register, but the notion was too firm to shake.

Twenty feet and bearing down. Fifteen.

I unleashed my spell, pushing my hands forward to help throw it. Tighter than any weave I'd yet done, and sparkling like a disco ball, it smacked into the creature. Tight, sparkling bands wrapped around it, stopping its progress. Caging it.

Look at me with the bedazzled spells.

The creature howled and dodged right, but my magic was there, barring the way. Another wall went up, then another. The cage shrank, smaller and smaller until the creature was shaking, fighting my magic.

Pounding feet came up behind me. "Hurry," Reagan said, but her words were drowned out as jets of magic fired from my left and right. Weak spells, poorly constructed, they had a weird, stale quality that made me wrinkle my nose.

A moment later, I saw why. The small group we'd left behind had darted in, cracking casings as they approached. These were bought spells, used on the fly.

"They need a better distributor," I murmured, catching a few of the intents but not all, as the magic covered the banshee. It wasn't good news for the creature.

She shrieked and wailed, held in place and now writhing. Death's chariot would be awaiting her on the other side, and I knew she wouldn't come back. That was the price a magical person paid for breaking the rules.

"Got her!" Garret ran in, cracking one more spell to seal the deal.

The creature shrieked one last time before sizzling out before our eyes. A dark fuzz accompanied my dissipating spell.

"We did it." Garret smiled from ear to ear, his walk becoming a strut. "I knew we could do it. Mine was the killing spell. That goes in the books."

"You didn't do squat, you weasel," Reagan yelled, stalking forward. Her cool from dealing with the banshee was completely gone. "That was all Penny. She lured that thing, trapped it, and was just about to disband it when you morons tramped through. She didn't need you."

"It was chasing her all over the grass!" Garret said as the captain stalked into the area. "We saw it."

"I wasn't going to kill it," I said, fatigue washing over me. I'd poured too much power into the spell.

Then again, maybe it had been needed. "It felt wrong."

"See?" Garret pointed at me.

"That didn't mean she needed you, moron," Reagan said. "She could've kept it there all night."

"It was chasing her!" Garret jabbed a finger at me again in renewed intensity.

"Until she trapped it. I know you're dumb, Garret, but at least *try* to communicate with smarter beings."

"I didn't see any spell." Garret crossed his arms over his chest. The other peacekeepers, as Reagan had called them, gathered around to watch the spectacle, most of them out of breath from running in. Even the captain stood by placidly, watching. I got the distinct impression that this wasn't the first showdown between Garret and Reagan.

"She's a natural. You can't see what she does. But did you see that thing stop in midair, didn't you?"

All the peacekeepers looked around at each other. The captain said, "We were running in, readying our spells. Last I saw, it was chasing her. Then my people showed up with their spells."

Reagan's movements slowed down and she braced her hands on her hips. My small hairs stood on end and I edged away. This was a bad sign. It meant heads were about to be kicked in.

"Captain, why do you think I was hanging out back there?" She gestured behind her.

"Because you're a coward," Garret said.

"Shut up, Garret, or you'll walk away with another broken nose," the captain said.

"Because she had it. She was in the zone. She's new, so sure, she needed to run off the jitters, but when she did, she locked it down. I mean"—Reagan threw out her hand at the spot where the banshee had been—"since when do banshees stand idle, *waiting* for mages to throw spells at them?"

The captain shifted and looked around at his crew. "Is that true?"

"Why does it matter?" I asked, ready to go home. "I trapped it; they killed it. Justice served."

"Your role remains to be proved," Garret said.

"Well?" the captain pushed.

The woman with fuzzy hair and the man in his forties both shrugged. The others shifted and looked at their feet. With all the commotion, adrenaline and (I guessed) no small amount of fear, their brains had been in overdrive. No one had noticed.

"It's fine, let's—"

"It's hers," Reagan said, cutting me off. "It's hers."

The captain started nodding until Garret said, "No way. She's not even a legit part of this operation."

The captain stilled before nodding again. "He's right. This goes down as a group win."

"What?" Reagan said, incredulously. "You couldn't

get it done *either* time you tried before, but *suddenly* it went easy on you, and you don't think it had anything to do with Penny?"

The captain shrugged, looking at the place the banshee had stood. "You were hired. She was not, something I made clear before we started out. Had you bagged it, you would've gotten the tag. As it is, it was a group win. Sorry, Penny. Next time, get on the books."

"I got the kill shot," Garret said, wiggling his pointer finger like the captain had a book out and was writing in it. "Did you hear me, captain?"

"Explode him, Penny. He's earned it," Reagan said, shaking her head and turning toward the cars.

Garret flinched and jogged backward, his wide eyes on me.

The guy was extremely annoying, no doubt about it, but my dog wasn't in this fight.

I turned and hurried up to Reagan. "You intentionally didn't engage? When that thing was chasing me?"

"Well, I would've engaged at first, but you ran away from me. I figured that meant you wanted a little more time. So I gave you a little more time. Then I thought it would overtake you, but I would have needed to get closer to use my magic. By then, you were running away from me again. Honestly, if you need help, running away from your partner isn't the best idea."

"Hindsight."

She scoffed. "Well, anyway, by the time I was thinking about helping again, you were facing it. Great work, by the way. Why didn't you kill it, though? That would've been easier than trapping it. And we wouldn't have had to deal with this nonsense."

"It didn't feel right."

"Then why not just banish it and let the other side of the veil sort it out?"

"What?"

She turned to me with a confused expression before a look of understanding crossed her face. "Ah. Right. You didn't know that bit. My bad."

CHAPTER 28

"IS THIS WHY you don't have partners? Because you only give them enough information to get themselves killed?" I asked, amazingly calm in the car on the ride back to Reagan's house.

Reagan hadn't even waited to give the others a proper farewell. She'd walked straight to the car, gotten in, and taken off.

"I usually don't have partners because they are ineffective, and I need to do a better job of hiding my magic. But you're basically in the crew now, and are quite hilarious to watch, so I'd consider adopting you."

"No thanks. And I still don't know a thing about your magic."

"You say that now, but wait until you get even a little more experience and miss the thrill of making shit up. You'll definitely want to be my partner to keep things interesting. And you know plenty about my magic. We train together, for feck's sake. You're just slow at piecing things together."

"How am I slow?" I asked, outraged. "I know next

to nothing about the magical world, and while you tell me plenty about your magical issues, none of you have told me squat about your actual magic. Or even what sort of magical person you are. Or anything!"

"You'd make a terrible detective."

"You're a terrible…" I grasped for something witty.

"What's that?" she badgered, grinning at me. "Was there a cutdown coming?"

"Shut up," I muttered, looking out the window. My palms itched and a strange expectancy filled me. "Something this way comes."

"What is it?"

"I guess you're not the only one with secrets." I didn't mention that I didn't know the answers to my own hazy, vague premonitions. She'd just have more ammo to make fun of me. "What's the end game here, anyway? What happens when I learn to use my magic effectively?"

"I have no idea. The big-picture stuff is Darius's department. For the short term, I think we're just training you up until the Guild comes for you, then we'll band together to wipe them out. Ain't none of that welcome in *my* town. Hell no. Any organization that allows innocents to be skinned to call demons needs to be ripped out at the root. I'll make them rue the day they decided to come here looking for you."

Reagan was referring to the case I'd helped them

with in Seattle a couple months or so after the storming of the Guild compound. The mages in question had been skinning people alive to call demons into the world. It was disgusting and completely wrong, but the Guild was capable of so much worse, including killing their own members and hiding the evidence.

"So I'm stuck with you for days on end until the Guild organizes enough to kill me," I said dismally, watching the run-down neighborhood roll by.

"They won't kill you, no. They'll capture you. They'll trap you in their facility, torture you into compliance, and then slowly indoctrinate you to support their sick agenda for power and dominance. Sounds like a hoot!" We turned the corner onto our street. A moment later, Reagan tapped the brake. "Ah crap."

She pulled over to the side of the road, down the street from her house. The man I'd met the night before, No Good Mikey, sat on some steps, watching us pull in.

"What's the matter?" I asked, ripping my eyes forward but not seeing anything other than the large, beat-up van parked in front of us.

"I should've answered that call." Reagan fished her phone out of her fanny pack before getting out of the car. I followed suit, clueless about what was happening. All I knew was that if Reagan was nervous, I'd better get ready to run.

"You gotta stop bringing that car around here," Mikey said as Reagan walked over to him. "It's drawing too much attention."

"Yeah, I know." Reagan studied her phone. "I just like driving it."

"No shit, but unless you move to a different spot, that thing does not fit in."

I finally got a glimpse down the street, but nothing appeared to be out of place. Until I scanned the parked cars.

"Crap." I ducked into the shadows next to some random person's stairs. "Why are they here?"

Reagan had the phone to her ear. "Callie wanted to check on us. When I wouldn't call her back, she said she was coming over."

"Oh yeah, that ol' broad came over, all right," Mikey said, grimacing. "She was all up in my face about where the fuck you were. I said I didn't know. That didn't go well. I had to get out."

"It's fine." Reagan shrugged. "We can say we went out to eat."

Mikey turned to look at me. "She looks a mess."

I patted my hair and palmed my clothes. "Why? What's wrong with me?"

"You look like you've been through hell and need to find a darkened closet, a bottle of wine, and some alone time, that's what you look like. Had a rough night?"

"I mean…" I shrugged, straightening my top. "Just running for my life, is all."

He grunted and nodded. Apparently that squared with his impression.

"Good point." Reagan tapped on the banister. "I'll say I took her to the warehouse to train. Or to a park. Or something."

"Might as well just come clean. It's always worse when they catch you lying." Mikey sucked his teeth. "And she'll catch you, mark my words. She'll keep picking until you'll want to pull your fucking eyes out of their sockets."

"Gracious," I muttered. This guy was really colorful.

Reagan blew out a breath. "We need to face the music. Come on, Penny, let's get in the car. And put your battle face on. You look like you're about to get a whipping."

"You better hope that's all you get from that broad." Mikey shook his head. "She's crazy."

"She hasn't given a blood offering to the ward," I said with a sinking stomach as I sat into the car. "She will have had to stand around outside. She hates that."

"I realize that," Reagan said. "There's nothing for it, though. The longer we put it off, the worse it's going to be."

She revved the engine as she prepared to pull into

her spot in front of her house. There stood Callie and Dizzy, right by the steps, arguing about something. Probably how to find us, kill us, and feed us to snakes or something.

As Reagan pulled in, electricity sizzled up my arms before sinking into my body, an energizing, delicious hum that immediately stabilized the magic zinging through me.

I sucked in a startled breath, eyes wide, knowing exactly when I'd last felt that way.

"What's wrong?" Reagan said, parking but not turning off the car. Or unlocking it.

Callie and Dizzy were looking in at us, one with thunder clouds rolling across her face, and the other with a brow furrowed with concern, probably at the tongue lashing we were about to get.

On the other side of the steps, standing in the shadows with his hands in his pockets, was the man who had walked away. Who'd told me to move on.

He'd come back.

"Who's that beyond my stairs?" Reagan asked. "He's a big dude. He can handle himself in a fight, I can tell." A surge of her magic filled the car.

"Emery," I whispered. "The Rogue Natural."

She gave a long, low whistle. "Are you sure he's not a vampire?"

"Of course I'm sure. Why?"

"Because he is a *looker*. Am I going to like him or hate him?"

"I don't care."

She flinched away from me with a giant smile. "Oooh, he's good for you. I suspect I'm going to like him. Come on, let's go meet Romeo."

"Where the hell have you been?" Callie demanded as soon as Reagan half stepped out of the car. "I have been waiting here for nearly an hour, worried sick. Do you not know how to use your phone? Are those your battle leathers? Reagan Somerset, you had better start explaining yourself, or I'm going to rip your magic away and beat you with it."

"That's not even possible. Did you make sure you weren't followed?"

Callie pointed at Emery. "With his help, yes. Very helpful, trained naturals."

Reagan walked around to my side and tapped on my window. "Out ye git."

My eyes were locked on Emery's, and I delighted in the power surging between us, open and raw and wild. This was how I'd felt with those witches, only a hundred times more powerful and thrilling. It occurred to me that while he'd been trained the traditional way, he'd never acted covetous of his power or magical knowledge. He'd figured out almost immediately that I liked to share, and he'd allowed me to do just that. He'd never once shut me out, and when he had been teaching me, he'd never done so at a distance.

If it hadn't been for him, I wouldn't have known what properly working magic felt like for me. I would've tried to adapt to Callie and Dizzy's way of things. He'd made it so I didn't have to.

I owed him so much.

And now he was here.

Reagan knocked on my window again. "Your social awkwardness is really pushing the limits right now."

Emery shifted a little, his big shoulders coming around so that he was facing the others. His deep voice rumbled through me, though the words didn't take any shape.

"Nonsense. She's just worried about what I'm going to do to her," Callie said, snatching the keys out of Reagan's hand and bending to the door. "Where are the locks? What car doesn't have locks? There is nothing super about a car with no locks."

"Just get the key fob close and it opens for you. How old is that Merc of yours?" Reagan asked.

"I drive a sensible car. With locks." Callie did as Reagan said before pulling open the door. "Get out this instant, young lady. I do not know what that vampire was thinking, pairing you with this lunatic." She hooked a finger at Reagan. "And I *certainly* don't know what that lunatic was doing out at odd hours in the night, bringing an untrained—"

"Let's do this inside, hon. You'll wake all the neighbors." Dizzy tried to shepherd her toward the stairs. "This neighborhood is probably armed."

I clasped my hands in front of me and walked toward the stairs slowly, wanting to run to Emery and throw my arms around his neck. Wanting him to kiss me and hold me and tell me about his adventures.

Another part of me wanted to cry, to sob like a wreck and feel his arms wrap around me, for him to promise that everything would be okay.

Still another part wanted to punch him right in the face, wiping away that blank expression and eliciting some sort of emotion, even if it was anger or annoyance.

"And why did you lock me out of this house?" Callie demanded, standing at the top of the stairs with her hand held out, ready for the blood offering. "Is this your life now? No physical locks on anything?"

Reagan laughed as she climbed the stairs after Callie, pulling her sword.

"Oh now, Reagan, that's a little much for a tiny drop of blood, don't you think?" Dizzy asked, shrinking away from her.

"Let her try to lop off my hand. See what happens to her." Callie lifted her chin, her hand still out.

I drifted toward the middle at the bottom of the

stairs and waited, glancing Emery's way. As if on cue, he stepped out and joined me. The air between our bodies heated with electricity.

"Hi, Turdswallop," he said softly.

CHAPTER 29

MY HEART EXPANDED to ten times its normal size at the sound of that ridiculous nickname. I couldn't help huffing out a laugh, expelling some of my pent-up energy. "Hi. You look good. Fresh."

"Darius's people cleaned me up and dressed me. Like last time."

I nodded, waiting for Reagan to put away her sword and take out a dagger. She was like a weapons store when she went out to battle.

"Marie bought me a bunch of new clothes," I said. "One ugly dress and suddenly I'm a pity case."

He laughed and his body shifted, his chest pointed a little more in my direction. He leaned a little closer. I felt his desire to be near, and wanted to answer it with my own.

The pull of him washed over me, begging me to close the distance between us. Emery felt like a lifeboat in the midst of a storm. A place where I could safely unburden myself. He wouldn't judge me or tell me I'll get used to it—he'd just listen, and hold me, and make it more bearable.

Unless I was completely misreading him…

"Turn on the light so I can see what you're doing," Dizzy said, squinting at the dagger in Reagan's hand.

"This ward is…" Emery scanned the house. So much magic pulsed in the ward that it was visible. The light flicked on, illuminating his face. His gaze came to rest on mine, and I drank in his beautiful blue eyes, so unique, with a ring of gold encircling the pupil, and from that, light blue streaking and webbing over darker blue until it all ended in a circle of smoky blue. It was like looking at the Milky Way on a clear night. "The best I have ever seen, Penny Bristol."

"Thanks," I muttered, my face heating with pride. Coming from him, that was an enormous compliment. "Reagan helped."

"But I was told Reagan is not a mage."

"No, she's…" Reagan stopped what she was doing, the dagger suspended over Callie's finger, and lifted her eyebrows at me expectantly. "She's an asshole."

"I've trained her well," Reagan said.

"No, she's just stating the obvious." Callie sighed and reached for the dagger. "Penny, get up here and take over. Reagan is stalling."

"I'm not stalling. I'm giving them a chance to catch up while you are distracted." She nicked Callie's finger. "Though she does need to do a little magic."

Callie winced but didn't pull back her hand. "Should he see this spell?" She nodded toward Emery.

"He'll improve upon it." Without batting an eye, I chose from the magic I had on standby in the cloud above me, and effortlessly re-created the weave. Reagan had been right: practicing over and over had given me magical muscle memory, and now, with the distraction of Emery standing next to me, looking at me, I just let it fly without having to think.

"Impressive," Emery murmured, his eyes on my hands. "Is that your spell, or from a book?"

"Was that condescending?" Reagan put up her finger and tilted her head. "Judges' ruling?"

"It would only be condescending if you were saying it," Dizzy said with a smile, and patted Reagan on the shoulder. He stepped up to get his finger nicked.

"It originated from a book." I waited for Dizzy's welling of blood. "I changed it a little as our paranoia about the Guild increased, and then altered it when Reagan found holes or issues."

"So you are a mage, then?" Emery asked Reagan. His gaze had turned analytical, even shrewd. He would soon learn that there would always be one very troubling unknown in this neighborhood. Her name was Reagan, and she delighted in being mysterious.

"Nope. An asshole, remember?" She tucked her dagger into its holster on her thigh.

Emery's eyes narrowed, but he didn't push.

"You still didn't tell us what you were doing." Callie waited for me to open the door and step aside before she filed into the house, Dizzy falling in behind her.

Reagan stopped next to me, her back to Emery, who still hadn't moved up the stairs. "I'll keep them busy yelling at me. You know, if you want to bump uglies with Mr. Hot Pants. But if he plans on staying, we're going to need to make some changes. I trust you. I don't know him, which means I don't trust him. No offense. Stranger danger, you see what I'm saying?"

While I was still trying to sort through all of that, wondering which part to respond to first, she strode through the door.

Emery looked out over the street, then up at me from under his eyelashes. I could tell he was uncomfortable, which made me nervous for how this conversation would go.

"You can come in." I gestured at the door. "I just need some blood. Or…if you're worried about knives, I can bring you through by touching you."

He ran his fingers through his hair. "I hadn't planned on intruding. I don't want to mess up what you have going here. I just—" He slipped his hands into his pockets again, and my stomach knotted. "I still get forewarnings when you're in danger. From what I can gather, I saw them when you were in Darius's house."

"Oh." The breath exited my mouth in a rush. "Yeah. That was a dinner gone wrong."

"And again earlier tonight. It looked like you were running on grass?"

"Ah. Um…" I glanced through the opened door, wondering if I should go warn Reagan that the Bankses were armed with knowledge.

A shape materialized from the entrance to the cemetery across the street, Smokey drifting through the shadows. If I hadn't known he was for sure human, I'd definitely wonder.

Emery turned nearly immediately, eyeing the creepy guy as he loitered near the wall. Magic streamed up from over a dozen places near us.

"No, no!" I hurried down the steps and put my hand on Emery's arm. A surge of electricity zapped into my hand from the contact, traveling up my arm and then through my body before exiting through my feet. My teeth clamped shut and my toes curled as my blood felt like it was flash-boiling. The breath exited Emery's mouth in a gush.

A moment later, shaking in the aftermath, I yanked my hand away. "Sorry. Don't worry about Smokey. That's Smokey, by the way. Don't worry about him—"

"This guy dangerous?" Mikey sauntered up the sidewalk, eyeing Emery. His gaze hit me next. "And you know what I mean, right? I can see this fool is dangerous. I'd want my sidearm when dealing with him. That I can handle. Is he *dangerous*?"

"He means magical," I whispered to Emery.

"I don't mean shit." Mikey crossed into the street, going all the way around the cars in order to reach his house on the other side. According to Reagan, he wouldn't hesitate to bump chests with wicked-looking thugs, but Mikey clearly wanted absolutely nothing to do with magic. "You know what I mean."

"Yes, he is *dangerous*, but not to you," I said, my hand hovering over Emery's forearm now.

"All right. Just as long as we know what's up." Mikey climbed his stairs.

"Look." My hand lowered a fraction, nearly touching Emery but not quite. I was honestly worried about that electricity again. I'd forgotten how much it hurt. When it hurt. Unlike when it didn't. Which was…

My mind was buzzing, but for a different reason than when I forgot spells.

I cleared my throat, and Emery's gaze came to rest on mine.

"Would you mind…" I thumbed the direction of the door. "Do you want to go in? This neighborhood is colorful. It's best if we get off the street."

That uncomfortable expression crossed his face again. "Listen, Penny, like I said, I don't want to intrude. I just came to check in. To make sure you were okay. I'm fine to leave. You can go on with your life, conscience clear."

I frowned at him, having absolutely no clue what he was saying. Just knowing he was trying to weasel away again.

Normal people probably would've let him do it, too. Those self-respecting girls who weren't prone to embarrassing themselves. But if I'd learned one thing in the past twenty-four years, it was that I was anything but normal.

"Look, fine, I get it. What happened between us didn't mean as much to you. It was, like, a blip on the radar. A few days." I shrugged aggressively, because if you were going to make an ass of yourself, you should do it Reagan-style. "Whatever. But the least you can do is come into the damn house and act like a sensible human being. I promise I won't cry over your shoes or anything. And when you leave this time, it will be with my foot up your ass. Because I know how to defend myself now, and I have no problem turning that defense into an attack if you're going to try slinking away in the night again, especially after being super awesome and leaving sweet notes. I don't even care."

I grimaced, because I was pretty sure I'd missed the mark in there somewhere, but at least he knew where I stood. And where he did if he tried to skulk away, sweet notes or no.

A smile flickered across his lips and a sparkle came to his eyes. "Training with Reagan has been good for you. It's given your natural fire a chance to shine." His face dropped again. "I meant what I said, Penny. If you want me to leave so you can get on with your life, I'm good with that. If it wasn't for—"

I punched him in the stomach.

I didn't even mean to! I really didn't. But a surge of emotion came over me, and before I knew it, I was expressing it in anger, fear, and a little desperation.

Emery wheezed and took a step back, bending at the waist.

Smokey started across the street. "Is he bothering you, Penny? Should I get Reagan for you?"

"He's *not* bothering me, actually," I said with my hands on my hips, ready for Emery to protest. I'd punch him again. "He won't just get in the house like a normal human being. And I know that is rich coming from me, but seriously, what the hell? Is he back to see me, or is he back to dick me around? Is he even happy to see me, or—"

Smokey had already stopped, put up his hands in a universal I-don't-want-to-know gesture, and started backing away slowly. I was still watching him when Emery straightened up, grabbed the back of my neck, and pulled me in.

I met him eagerly, wrapping my hands around his

neck and connecting with his soft lips, intense and insistent. I fell into the feeling of him. His touch. The familiarity of his arms. The comfort of his strength and power against my palms.

Everything about him said, *Home.*

Smokey was gone when we resurfaced.

Emery's body was still flush with mine, his lips only an inch away. "I only want what's best for you, Penny," he said, his hand braced against the side of my face and his thumb stroking my lips. "I know that isn't me. I know that I should leave you alone. That I should give you time to find someone worthy. But I can't. I can't stay away from you. I think about you constantly. I pull up memories of your smile. Your laugh. Your eyes…especially when they burn for me, like they're doing now. And I'm not strong enough to ignore your pull. So any time you want, I urge you to push me out of your life and shut the door. To do what's best for you. But until then, I'm at your mercy."

CHAPTER 30

"SO *NOW* WILL you come in the house?" I asked, after stealing another kiss.

His lips curled under mine. "Okay."

"Well, don't let me twist your arm or anything." I stopped by the ward and turned. "Do you have something sharp?"

"Just take me through for now. That way, you can change your mind."

"Do you want a knuckle sandwich?"

His smile boosted his handsomeness to absurd proportions. "No, thank you." He took my hand and the air buzzed around us. "Lead me through, Turdswallop."

"For once, I agree with the vampire on this one," we heard as he closed the door behind him. It was Callie. "Do you know what a sad day it is when I'm forced to side with a vampire?"

"A very sad day," Reagan said. "One for the record books."

"Hurry," I mouthed, pulling Emery behind me. My tiptoeing wasn't as smooth as I would've liked—pulling

Emery anywhere was not an easy task, and my feet thudded through the hallway.

I caught a quick glimpse of Dizzy looking up at me from the kitchen table. Thankfully, I couldn't see Callie, but I hurried faster so as not to press our luck.

"What was that?" Callie asked after Emery went by. "Was that them? Penny, come in here this instant. You've gone off the rail, girl."

I ducked into my room, pulled Emery after me, shut the door, and locked it. "That won't keep Reagan out, but she seems to be on my side on this one, so we're probably good." I released his hand and crossed to the sliding glass door. After opening it, I motioned him on.

"Is this the only way into the backyard?"

I paused on the back porch, waiting for him. "Crap. No. But again, Reagan is on my side…for now…so I think we're good. Oh, wait!" I dodged around him, heading back into my room, and collected the spell books I'd been studying. Back outside, I motioned for him to take a seat in one of the two folding chairs.

"These have seen better days," Emery said, pinching the top of the chair and wiggling it.

"It looks rough, but it'll hold. Here." I handed him the most advanced book. "That one has the ward in it. It's the—Yeah, the bookmarked one."

I settled back, watching him read through the spell. Little streams of magic rose and twirled around him before settling back down—Emery was subconsciously grabbing what he would need to create the weave before releasing it. He closed the book and looked at me, his eyes shadowed by the overhang.

"You've progressed at an unbelievable rate," he finally said.

"I could always read spells pretty well. Including the zombie one, unfortunately."

"This"—he tapped the book—"is not the ward that surrounds this house. It is a pale representation of the weave I see. I can't even call it a ward, because it's so much more than that. If the Guild had knowledge of spells like this and how to make them, we'd be screwed."

I shrugged, trying to hide my delight at his praise. "Reagan helped."

He shifted, leaning forward a little on his chair. "You said that, but you both keep insisting she isn't a mage. I don't understand how she could help with a ward."

"I can't really talk about her magic. It's a secret for some reason, and while I don't know much beyond that, she wants to keep it that way."

Silence lingered for a moment, and then he nodded. "Okay. As long as you are comfortable with her and this setup..."

"She's my best bet. Callie, Dizzy, and Darius all

agree."

"That was before you left your stronghold and got yourself into trouble."

I held up a finger. "To be fair, that wasn't my fault. That was my temperamental third eye. I mean…" I made a wishy-washy motion with my hand. "Getting me there was my temperamental third eye's fault. I felt weird about her leaving alone, so something told me I had to help. Once I was there, running away from Reagan was my bad, sure. But in the—"

"Wait, wait, wait, wait, wait. Wait." He laughed, shaking his head. "This isn't funny—"

"Literally nothing I just said was funny."

"—because the Guild could've made a grab for you tonight—"

"Reagan would've stepped in, I'm pretty sure. She's super fast. She bonded to Darius, did you know that?"

"But…what? Oh, yes, I heard that earlier. It is…surprising information. Darius isn't the type of vampire to bond, even with a prized asset. There must be more to it. Which I will try to figure out on my own." He paused, like he was waiting for my approval.

"When you find out, tell me," I said.

He chuckled again. He never seemed to know when I was being serious. Which, actually, was all the time. I just had the curse of being unintentionally funny, I guess.

"Fair enough. But let's start from the very beginning, shall we? Tell me everything."

"You mean from the part with the witches, or from the banshee?"

His eyes widened and he stiffened. "She let you go after a banshee? Never mind. We'll get there. I meant, start at the beginning. The morning you woke up after I left Seattle."

A rush of warmth ran through me. I hadn't been a woman scorned after all. The idiot had honestly been trying to do what he thought was best for me. Clearly he shouldn't be trusted to make such decisions in the future, because he was really, really bad at it, but the fact that his heart was in the right place eased the tightness in my shoulders.

I led him through the last six months, stopping occasionally to give more information, stopping other times for his misplaced guffaws, and speeding through the bit about Callie and Dizzy's training.

Surprisingly, he didn't ask many questions about the old vampire, Ja. He was on the same page as everyone else—it was a vampire problem. We should steer clear and let Darius figure it out.

"So you felt connected with the witches?" he asked after I talked about my jaunt into the cemetery.

"Yes. Sharing magic with them. It helped me find balance when I was working with Reagan."

"Reagan knows a lot about spells and mages, then, huh?"

I opened my mouth to answer before I caught on. I narrowed my eyes at him and he gave me a guilty smile.

"Sorry," he said. "That was sneaky. Anyway, so you think mages can form circles, like witches?"

I shrugged. "I don't see why not. Maybe at a certain point the power would get too strong, but a few of them should be able to work together."

"If they all trusted each other." He tapped the spell book in his lap. "And that's why you went with Reagan to banish the banshee?"

"Okay, well, no one mentioned the whole banishing part." I told him all that had happened as the night stretched toward the morning.

"You…captured…a banshee," he said, like he was pulling each word out of a trunk and examining it. That was the way he generally processed my oddest magical experiences. "Umhm."

"Yeah. In, like, a magical cage."

"You captured…a banshee—a *banshee*…in a magical cage. Mhm."

"Reagan didn't think it was all that odd."

"Reagan…didn't think—"

I laughed and kicked his chair. "Would you stop? This isn't odd, trust me."

"Using an untrained, unpredictable natural as bait,

then watching a banshee chase her around the lawn, isn't odd? I guess you're going to tell me that it isn't anything special that you *trapped* one of the most fearsome creatures on the death circuit in a type of spell I've never heard of? Oh. Well, now I know."

"Clearly this is why Reagan and I work as a team. Because I don't know any better, and she's cracked."

"I think that is exactly why it works, yes. Can she share magic with you?"

"No, she—" I flung my finger out at him. "Cheater!"

He gave me a delighted laugh and stood. "Come on, Turdswallop. It's late and we have a long few days ahead of us."

"Why is that?" I let him pull me, then pushed my way into his arms.

"Because you've found a new training buddy. And I'm not nearly so naive."

At the time, I thought he was talking about me. I had no idea he planned on setting traps for Reagan in the hopes of solving her riddle.

CHAPTER 31

THE NEXT AFTERNOON, after tossing and turning instead of sleeping, thinking about those large, luminous eyes soaked with feeling for him, Emery stepped out of Reagan's beat-up Honda in front of a warehouse outside of the city. Last night it had been universally agreed upon that he would help train Penny, and partially agreed upon that he'd need to go home with the Bankses. Strangely, it was Dizzy who'd raised the most fuss about Emery and Penny sleeping separately.

Only a fool would think it was for propriety's sake. The Bankses were clearly in the know about Reagan's secret…and Penny was not. She'd been using Reagan's power, and she didn't even understand it.

Emery hated enigmas. They were liable to get people killed. He especially didn't like them in connection to a special girl who held his vitals in her soft, dainty hands.

"I miss the Lamborghini," Reagan said as she got out of the car. "This bucket of tin is *slow…*"

"It'll probably last longer, though," Emery said, walking around the car to help Penny out.

"And back in the poor days, that would've mattered." Reagan opened her trunk and grabbed out a sleek-looking sword, a dagger, a leg brace, and a fanny pack.

"Nineteen-ninety called, they want their fanny pack back," Emery said, grinning at Reagan.

She gave him a blank stare. "Just for that, I'm not going to pull any punches."

"Oh dear, the girl isn't going to pull any punches." He rubbed Penny's back, hoping she knew he was just kidding. Reagan seemed the sort who liked taunting. It would fire her up and, hopefully, help her forget whatever secret she was hiding.

To his surprise, Penny said, "You don't want to rile her up. She's crazier that way."

"Don't ruin the surprise." Reagan smiled and gestured them toward the warehouse. "Shall we?"

"I put a ward up on the Bankses' house this morning," Emery said as he scanned the flatland around the warehouse. The sun was slipping toward the horizon, but the vampires wouldn't be up and moving around for another couple of hours. It was a prime time for enemy mages to gather around. At the moment, his senses didn't detect anything out of place, but that didn't mean they weren't on the way. They'd surely know about this place by now. "It isn't as good as the one Penny and you did, but it'll keep even the best mages at bay for a day or more."

Reagan pulled open the door, which hadn't been locked. She wasn't concerned about intruders. "I'm getting a bad feeling lately. Things have been too quiet."

Cold pooled at the base of Emery's spine as he watched her sweep the open space just as he had done. She seemed to know quite a lot about the constant presence of enemies, though maybe it was nothing more than self-preservation from having bonded an elder vampire.

"How so?" Penny asked, peeled off to the side and hunching. She looked around the murky warehouse, the hard light gleaming in west windows. Her gaze darted to each shadow in turn.

Various items of warfare sat on racks in the back, near a few chairs that had been set up. Another couple of chairs sat in the opposite corner, nothing around them. The rest of the large warehouse was completely bare, swept clean.

Reagan flicked on the light, chasing many of the shadows away.

"Those aren't...power rocks, are they?" Emery asked, pointing to a collection of various-sized rocks along the back wall.

"No." Reagan didn't elaborate, though Emery

couldn't fathom why she'd have large, mundane rocks lying around. "Penny, you've been in town for a few months now. And while the Bankses are known to be a strong dual-mage pair, for all they know, I'm just a retired bounty hunter. No one knows me from Seamus the sheep farmer—"

"I think you spent too much time abroad," Penny mumbled.

"We should've seen, at the very least, people hanging around my neighborhood, trying to learn our habits. But not even Smokey has seen anyone. I mean, you were out the other night with a bunch of witches." Reagan flicked her finger at Penny.

Hunching further, Penny gave Reagan a hard scowl before drifting along the walls, digging her hand into the multi-compartment belt encircling her waist. It was the same belt Clyde had given her in Seattle. Emery needed to get another one.

As Penny started setting power stones around the empty floor, Reagan strapped her arsenal to her person.

"I do not, for one second," Reagan said, "think the mages at the MLE office are all good guys. Maybe they aren't totally bad, yet, but we'd be simpletons to think the Guild isn't paying for information."

"They didn't seem to recognize me," Penny said, holding the second to last rock Emery had sent her. Her gaze switched to Reagan. Then back to him. "Huh."

"What?" Emery asked.

"Best not to try and understand her weird relationship with those rocks," Reagan murmured. "You'll think she's a quack."

"Like you can talk, Fanny Pack," Penny shot back, her scowl back.

More chuckles racked Emery's body. He'd forgotten how Penny could make him laugh.

Penny dropped the rock back into her belt.

"What was it?" Emery asked, trying to force down the laughter.

"Mr. Happy-Go-Lucky power stone doesn't know which of you it would rather catch a ride with." Penny pulled out another stone, this one deep purple.

Reagan caught Emery's eye before making a circle in the air around her temple. *Crazy.*

"It's only been a day since we helped with that banshee," Penny said. "They wouldn't react that quickly. Not in numbers."

"I'm just surprised they haven't shown up yet. Not one creeper in the bushes. Not one sneak attack." Reagan braced her hands on her hips, watching Penny move about the space. "The Guild normally isn't this patient."

"They are amassing," Emery said, the humor draining from him. "They've been following me in increasing numbers. Darius sent me a message when I was in the

Realm—the Mages' Guild has the gate closest to New Orleans blocked off."

"Darius said that?" Reagan's brow furrowed. She waited for confirmation before shaking her head. "I might need to have a word with that secret-keeping SOB. Old habits die hard, my ass." She waved her hand, and while the gesture might have seemed like a dismissal to some, he could see the hard gleam in her eyes. That vampire had bonded his match, Emery could tell. She was more than she seemed. But what, exactly? "Right. C'mon, Penny, let's get cracking."

After placing the last stone—Mr. Happy-Go-Lucky, she'd called it—halfway between Reagan and Emery, Penny skulked out to the center of the warehouse and turned to face Reagan, who was standing a hundred feet away. Penny's expression crumpled into one of wariness. Her stiff frame and a tight jaw said she was entirely too wound up. She worked better loose, letting the magic naturally flow around her.

Emery refrained from saying anything. He wanted to see how this played out.

Reagan brandished her sword, and Penny's wariness turned into confusion. And then Reagan was charging toward her, faster than he would've believed possible, with aggression in spades. She was on Penny in a flash, and literally backhanded her across the face before picking her up and tossing her across the warehouse.

Emery stepped forward, everything in him pushing to run to Penny's side. Power pulsed from somewhere near him. One of the power stones, throbbing.

Penny, lying on her back, thrust her hands into the air.

Power crackled within the warehouse. Energy scraped across Emery's skin, making his eyes water. Magic blasted from her hands, streaming toward Reagan in a thick weave.

He stepped forward again, but this time it wasn't to protect Penny. It was to tell Reagan to get the hell out of the way. That spell, an intricate, artful weave made up of over two dozen components, would fry someone alive.

Reagan thrust her hand into her opened fanny pack, grabbed out what looked like a casing, smashed it against the base of her sword while muttering what sounded like gibberish, and sliced through the spell just in time. The sword splintered the weave, sending it curling to the sides, but didn't unravel it.

"I hate that trick," Reagan said, running toward Penny as the spell tracked her from behind. As she came close, she reached downward, aiming for Penny's chest.

Penny reacted hard and fast, slapping the hand away and punching up into Reagan's face. The blow didn't land. Reagan jerked back a fraction and swung her arm, hitting Penny's forearm with her own. Before the move could be executed, Penny kicked up, hitting Reagan right behind the legs.

"Good move," Reagan said, twisting to drop her knee onto Penny's thigh. "But my balls are figurative."

Streams of magic rolled and boiled above Penny before running through her fingers, faster than thought, and morphing into something Emery, quite frankly, didn't understand. It wasn't a weave so much as a sparkling collection of harmonic elements, fire and ice in perfect balance.

An explosion without sound concussed the air. Reagan flew backward, her arms stitched down to her sides with unseen hands. A smile graced her face and she didn't struggle or even twist. She hit the ground and bounced before jerking free, her sword still in her hand despite the force of the invisible and unexpected blow.

"Sneaky little thief," Reagan said as Penny scrambled to her feet.

"You said we could share," Penny hollered.

Reagan got up slowly and wiped her forearm across her mouth. "You made me drool a little."

Penny started, staring at Reagan with wide eyes. "Oh no."

She didn't reach for her magic. She didn't brace to fight.

She turned tail and ran.

"There's nowhere to run to," Reagan said.

"No!" Penny yelled. "Timeout. Do-over. Uncle!"

Reagan took off after her, a mad smile on her face. "Use your magic, you scaredy cat."

"No killing, remember?" Penny yelled over her shoulder.

"I'm not going to kill you. I'm going to kick you."

Penny pulled elements out of her belt and from the various items in the room, weaving as she sprinted to the corner then pivoted randomly and headed away at an angle.

"I can change direction faster than that banshee," Reagan said. And then cackled.

"Turdswallop apple sauce," Penny said loudly, getting a weave together as Reagan came within striking distance. "No!"

Reagan jumped, launching at Penny with arms wide, sword held out to the side.

Emery braced himself, feeling the power stone pulse with energy, charging up the entire room. Magic came without him consciously pulling it, running in and around his fingers.

Reagan hit Penny from behind. She wrapped her arms around Penny's body, putting the sword at an extremely dangerous angle. Before Emery could voice a protest or they could hit the ground, Reagan twisted in the air, landing so the sword wasn't a problem.

"You're going to poke someone's gizzard out with that thing," Penny said, struggling against Reagan's hold.

"As long as it isn't mine, I'm good." Reagan released her hold long enough to pepper punches into Penny's back.

Penny grunted, and the weave of magic she'd been making, even while being tackled to the ground, drifted into the sky before floating above them.

"What fecking spell is that?" Reagan said. She didn't look up at it, but she clearly knew it was there.

How in the hell…

"Surprise!" Penny paused for a fraction of a second and received a couple more punches because of it. "Eventually. Surprise eventually." She twisted and jabbed back with her elbow, connecting with Reagan's sternum.

"I could kill you right now," Reagan said, holding tighter.

"Fine. You win. Let me up."

"No way. That thing you're making is nasty. Send Emery away."

"You send Emery away!"

Reagan glanced back at him. He started, realizing he'd drifted forward, ready to intervene without consciously thinking of it. Her shift in focus had Penny twisting again, trying to get an elbow into her ribs. "He's two seconds from rescuing you," Reagan said.

"You send him away. He won't listen to me."

"No. You will take my surprise!"

"This is why men try to keep women dumb. They are much less dangerous to the power structure that way." Reagan stared up vaguely at the cloud of magic drifting over them.

"What are you even talking about?"

Reagan didn't answer. She rolled to the side, hopped up with a grace nearly equal to that of a vampire, and sprinted across the warehouse with a speed nearly equal to that of an elder.

"Are you non-human?" Emery asked.

"A little busy right now," she replied.

She was right. The spell took after her like a shot, seemingly an intelligent entity.

"We need to get you on some nicer spells," he heard Reagan mutter, glancing at him for a moment before digging into her fanny pack and pulling out a casing.

He could've sworn that casing had already been used.

She smashed it to the base of her sword, like she'd done before, and—again—he could see no magic transferred. More gibberish and then she was pivoting and running at the spell, sword up and snarl ready.

It split before she got to it, and he could more clearly see the weave. Wild and raw and fizzing with power, the fine strands creating it nearly sparkled with pent-up energy.

"So this is what I can look forward to, is it?" Reagan said, a knot of concentration between her brows. She swung her sword at one of the misshapen clouds, releasing her hand from the hilt of the sword as it cut through and fried the spell. The free hand swung behind her, and though he was at a bad angle, he could swear the same sort of frying effect happened to the second cloud without anything actually touching it.

She spun, slicing her magical sword—which, again, didn't have any magic he could see—through the second cloud. She was working through them in short order.

Something was definitely off.

But Penny had already moved on to something else. Her fingers palpitated in a sort of rhythm. Eyes glistening and face smooth, she was clearly in her element. She'd found her balance rooted in nature.

Emery stepped closer, wanting to get inside her bubble of magic so he could better see and feel what she was concocting. So he could help and lend his touch. From the distance, he was missing components of what she was doing.

Penny shot the spell off as Reagan turned toward her.

"Clever," Reagan muttered with a smile. "There are holes, though." Her knees bent and her eyes glazed over for a moment, her concentration so intense that it seemed like she was blocking out the world around her.

"Little pockets of deadness. Patch that up, and I'd need to resort to drastic measures to get out from under it."

She didn't bother with the casing this time. She charged, hacking and ripping at the spell with her sword and a clawed hand, fracturing the weave instead of unraveling, dissipating, or countering it. A black spot appeared on Reagan's upper arm and she flinched away. Another on her forearm.

"Ouch." She cut the reaching arms of the spell as Penny created yet another. By the time Reagan made it through the black-spot spell, Penny was ready with another.

Emery watched in fascination as the two engaged in a rare dance. Whatever magic Reagan had, it could counter Penny's extremely inventive, tightly woven spells. And each time she did so, she described what Penny could have done better.

They were a team unlike any he'd ever seen.

Without any outward communication, they stopped nearly at the same time, both of them panting and fatigued.

Reagan nodded. "Good. You're getting better. You didn't take nearly as long to get in the zone. Was it him?" She pointed at Emery.

Penny bowed with exhaustion. "Yeah. He's never guarded with his magic. I tapped into it and…it calmed me. Helped me find balance."

"You embodied his magic, though. Like you do

mine. I could tell because it was so much more interesting than your peaceful, lovey-dovey bullshit."

"Wow." Penny shook her head. "No wonder you love a vampire. You two have the same emotional landscape."

"Yeah. A bit slow of you to just pick up on that now."

Penny walked to Emery and, without a word, wrapped her arms around his middle and leaned into him. She wasn't worried in the least about showing her affection or being rebuffed. She was completely open and honest. It comforted yet humbled him. "Sorry I'm sweaty," she mumbled.

He wrapped his arms around her, supporting her. "I am going to steal your spells so hard, it's not even funny."

She laughed into his shirt. "I stole your magic, so I guess that's only fair."

"This stealing of the magic… That's rare, Penny. It's a gift, like my premonition. It must be."

She shrugged. "Maybe everyone could do it if they'd open up more."

He shook his head, not so sure.

"Ew. You guys are gross." Reagan crouched and leaned her forearms on her thighs. "All right, Romeo. Let's see what you're made of."

CHAPTER 32

I STEPPED AWAY with a groan as Emery accepted Reagan's passive challenge. Passive, because Reagan didn't just run at him and kick him in the face. She was clearly tired.

As I sagged into the chair in the corner, I smiled to myself. I'd made her winded a few times in the past, but this was maybe the first time I'd seen her this tired after a training session. She usually bounced back almost immediately.

It meant I was getting better.

"How does this work?" Emery asked, squaring up with Reagan, completely at ease.

The worst thing you could do was underestimate that woman. She'd shove it in your face and make you eat it. I nearly warned him, too, but didn't want to ruin the surprise.

"You try to down me, and I try to down you," Reagan said, holding her sword at her side with one hand and digging around in her fanny pack with the other.

“How intense do we get?”

“You can see the spells as they’re formed, right? Because you’re a natural?” She pulled out an intact casing and frowned at it. “Huh. I didn’t realize I had another one of these left. That might be fun.”

“I can, yes.”

She slipped the casing into her pocket before going back to the digging expedition. “And did you see what Penny was throwing at me?”

Emery shifted from one side to the other, something he did when he was unsure. “I work differently than Penny. I’ve had a lot more experience. We should probably establish some ground rules.”

A smile worked up her face and her eyes sparkled. “You think you’re going to be too much for me, huh?” She pulled out another intact casing. Her eyes went vague for a moment before she gave Emery an assessing look.

“No.” I shook my head. “Nope. Not on your first time fighting him.”

Her look held all kinds of false innocence. “What?”

“No.” I shook my head again, ignoring Emery’s raised eyebrows. “I know that look. You can try it out next time. Or if we’re working together.”

“Fine.” She sighed and dropped the casing into her fanny pack. “He could’ve probably handled it, though.”

“You can feel the magic?” Emery’s eyes narrowed.

"Like Penny can?"

A wary look crossed Reagan's face. "No." She pointed at her fanny pack. "It was color-coded. Darius is good about organizing."

She was lying, and if Emery's face said anything, it was that he expected as much.

"What about close combat—am I allowed to hit a girl?" he asked.

Reagan's smile was feral. "If you think you're fast enough, sure." She dug out another casing from her fanny pack, holding it in her palm. Her knees bent slightly. She was ready to go.

Emery watched her for a moment before looking around the spacious warehouse. His gaze hit the doorway and then my belt. "Penny, can you empty those compartments on the ground? Preferably closer?"

I jumped up and did as he asked. "How about the power stones? Do they need to be moved?"

"You tell me. They're your friends, not mine." He grinned.

"Leave 'em, Penny." All of the humor and lightness dripped off Reagan's face. "He needs to fight his own battles."

Emery barely cocked his head, but I could tell he heard the challenge. It was meant to rile him up. I couldn't tell if he was rising to the bait.

Reagan worked the casing from her palm to her fingertips before pinching it and smashing it against the base of her sword. I couldn't be sure, but it seemed to squish too easily, as if this one had already been opened. Her lips moved and I heard soft muttering, but no magic climbed the metal of her sword.

"Latin?" Emery asked.

Reagan finished whatever she was saying before tossing the empty casing behind her. "I'm fancy."

"We've already established that I'm a natural who can see magic."

"Thanks for the summary."

"So is what you just did supposed to fool me?" Emery's face was perfectly straight. "Or Penny?" He didn't seem to be joking.

"Yeah," Reagan responded. "Did it?"

A whirl of magic exploded from the items I'd littered around the room, rushing toward Emery furiously. He lifted his hands in front of him, his fingers moving.

Reagan launched forward, sprinting at him.

Not four steps in and his first spell was already jetting through the air, rough and wild, glowing blue.

"Holy shit stains, Batman. That was fast." Reagan cleaved through the spell, leaving a line of charred magical ends in the sword's wake. The spell dissipated into the air. She barely lost speed.

Another spell was zipping at her a moment later,

reddish, tightly woven, and throbbing with power. Its intent was to blister her skin, but it was volatile and off-kilter. She sliced through it without effort.

Emery's eyebrows pinched, and I knew he was problem-solving. It had taken her a while to get through mine. His, though equally powerful, were not keeping her at bay. I knew him—he would adjust accordingly.

He shot off another spell, wove a fourth, and shot that off right after it. Back in the Mages' Guild, I'd had to use casings between my created spells to match his pace.

"Quick Draw McGraw over here," Reagan said with a grunt, slicing through the latest of his spells. She was twenty feet from him now, jogging forward before stopping to deal with a spell. She was working for it, but she was making progress. "These won't get the job done. They're well executed, even though you rushed, and packing power, but they're…meh."

"Meh?" Emery ripped off another, the intent to distract her. As soon as her sword hit the magic, it spiraled out into three whorls of color and light before zinging back at her, crackling the air.

"What the…" She batted the air with her hand and hacked with her sword, like swatting flies. A wisp from the spell strafed across her upper arm, searing it. She didn't flinch. "Even that one. You're on the right track, but it's missing something. Countering those spells is easy. Any gobshite with a lick of sense will have no problem tearing you down."

"It seems I haven't met a gobshite with a lick of sense yet, then."

"I mean…hello? Who am I?" Reagan jogged a few more steps before the next spell zipped through the air, similar to the distracting one, though this one was meant to scald. It broke apart as the other had done, but she was ready for it. She sliced it down quickly, turning her back on Emery at one point to do so.

"Tackle her," I shouted, unable to help it. "Tackle her from behind. She's—" I cut off as she turned around. "Missed it, Emery." I shook my head.

His chest shook, and I knew he was chuckling at me.

"I wasn't kidding," I muttered.

"That's what makes it so funny, Turdswallop," he said, creating a nastier spell between his two palms. More complex, with a weave twice as large, this one should take her back a pace.

"Should've listened to her. *Here's* Johnny!" She sprinted at him in the lull between spells.

He took two quick steps back, not worried about losing ground in order to buy time. Five feet away from him, Reagan bent her knees, preparing to launch.

He thrust his hands forward and the spell rushed at her, a cloud of magic rolling and tumbling through the air.

Unexpectedly, she went down into a slide, like trying to steal second base. The spell drifted over her and she popped up, jumping into the air a moment later. She kicked out. Her foot smacked against Emery's forearm, which hadn't come up to block her in time. He punched his own face.

Reagan punched him in the stomach and the upper leg, then bent and swept her leg behind his, knocking his legs out from under him. He landed hard on his butt and rolled away. In that time, a blast of fire took out the drifting spell, lazily headed back in her direction. It was a homing spell like the one I'd used, but he'd missed a few components in his haste.

By the time he was up, the fire was gone, and she was squaring off again.

He blinked half a dozen times, like he'd been completely blindsided, and I couldn't help but laugh.

"Ms. Gobshite, to you," Reagan said, fisting and straightening her hand. "You've got muscle tone, though. I'll give you that. Giving you a charley horse isn't as fun as it should be."

This time, Emery did brace himself. "Fuck it. Again."

A smile took up Reagan's face. "Don't mind if I do."

She ran forward as he was readying a nastier spell, but the sound of plastic clattering against the floor dragged away my focus. My phone was jumping against the back wall where I'd left it earlier.

Skirting along the side of the warehouse so as not to get hit with a rogue foot or spell—you just never knew with Reagan—I grabbed the phone and checked the screen. A number I didn't recognize.

"Hello?" I asked as Reagan punched Emery's face, faster than should have been humanly possible. He jerked out of the way at the last moment and then landed a solid punch into her stomach. His other hand came around for a left hook, but she ducked in time and powered a fist into his ribs.

He tackled her, smashing his large shoulder into her middle and taking her down. His bigger, heavier body fell on top of her, but she didn't lose her breath like any normal person would've. She rolled with impossible strength, curled up to get her feet lined up with his middle, and kicked out. He went tumbling across the floor.

They both scrambled to their feet. Emery already had a spell at the ready. With one hand, he started weaving and rapidly firing lesser spells at her, cringe-worthy confections intent on keeping her busy. With the other hand, he constructed something he'd obviously gotten from me, but with embellishments stemming from his frustration and desire to win.

"Are you creating multiple spells at one time right

now?" Reagan asked as she muscled her sword through one lowball spell after another. "How the hell are you creating multiple spells? That can't be done."

"I thought you said you couldn't feel magic. I think you were lying." His tone said he was teasing, but his face was screwed up in intense concentration.

It occurred to me that Emery had been trained similarly to Callie and Dizzy. Though he was more flexible, Reagan was likely one of the first people who'd made him rethink his usual fighting strategies.

Welcome to Reagan Land, where every day was a new nightmare.

"Hello?" a man said on the other end of the phone.

I'd completely forgotten I'd pushed *TALK*. "Oh sorry, hello?"

"Penny?"

"Yes, who is speaking?"

"This is Red. The shifter from down—"

"Reagan's friend, yeah. Hi."

"I don't know about Reagan's *friend*..." he muttered. "Hey, you got a minute?"

"Uh...yeah. Wait, how did you get my number?"

"I deal in intel."

I waited for more. Silence stretched between us, getting awkward, until he finally said, "Reagan gave it to me in case I needed to talk to you and couldn't get a hold of her. In case there was danger, or something."

"Ah, right. She's right here, if you—"

"No, no. No, that's fine. She's probably busy." I didn't miss the wariness in his voice. "Listen, I thought you should know. There's been a lot of activity in the bars lately. In this whole area, actually. Mostly in the daytime and early evening. People drift away when the sun starts going down, and then it's just the regulars. Now, I don't know what all of them do, you understand. I do my job discreetly. I listen, I don't ask questions."

"Okay…"

Emery loosed the secondary spell he'd been working on, then quickly brought up his hands to weave a more complex spell between his two palms. Reagan chopped and hacked her way through his newest spell, struggling more with this one.

Without warning, weaving all the while, Emery ran forward and kicked her between the legs.

"Oh!" Reagan's knees buckled and she sank to the ground. "You kick much harder than Penny." The spell dove at her. She waved her palm through the air in what I knew was her last-ditch effort. Fire crackled above her, a thin line over her body, catching the spell. Flame dug into his spell and fractured it, like stress cracks. The next moment she was up, walking a little bowlegged, using her sword again and cutting away the rest of the spell.

Erasing one of her most perplexing pieces of magic

from the air.

"What the… You have a big secret, Ms. Gobshite," Emery said with wide eyes.

"I should never have agreed to fight you," she said, launching at him.

"Penny?" Red said.

"Oh, sorry—Reagan is practice-fighting someone right now. I'm a little distracted."

"Good. She'll have less energy to torment me." Red cleared his throat. "About these people—I mean, you know our neck of the woods is heavily populated with tourists. So I see a lot of faces every day—"

"Who is it?" Reagan said, making me jump. Sweat ran down her face and slicked back her hair. Her breath came in deep pants. Emery had finished off what I had started.

"Red."

"What does he want?" she asked, reaching for the phone.

I handed it over without thinking. My magic might've been getting worlds better and stronger, but my ability to resist orders, even silent ones, from headstrong, competent people hadn't gained any ground.

"What's up?" she said into the phone.

"Who's Red?" Emery asked, pulling up the base of his shirt to wipe his sweaty face.

On impulse, I grazed my fingers across his defined stomach before laying my hand flat against his skin. It felt good to touch him again. To feel his heat and solidity.

I still couldn't believe that he'd actually come back. A large part of me had feared he wouldn't. That he'd forget me a little more with each passing month, that he'd decide the connection between us had only stemmed from the heat of the moment. But he was here, now, and it felt like we were picking up exactly where we'd left off, except I was less naïve, less new to this world.

A hum buzzed deep in my core, and I looked up and caught his Milky Way eyes. The sound of Reagan telling Red to get to the point drifted into my consciousness. "Huh?"

A smile flickered across Emery's lips and he knelt, now eye level with me. "I was too far away to see the weaves you did. I couldn't duplicate them."

"Your magic didn't seem totally balanced."

"It wasn't. You weren't close enough." His thumb drifted over my chin, trailing heat in its wake.

"I was. I used you from the distance. You can use me. It's just a matter of reaching out."

He shook his head slowly and his eyes dipped to my lips. "That kind of sharing still isn't second nature to me. Maybe this special ability of yours is like my foresight. A special gift, in additional to being a natural. You can feel and siphon magical ability from those around you. Borrow their abilities and make them your own."

"Or maybe I just like sharing," I said with a small smile, "and willingly opening myself up to experiences."

"Maybe we'll have to practice opening up to experiences."

His voice, deep and low, spoke of a different sort of practice. A more intimate kind of practice that I was desperate to explore with him.

"We gotta go." Reagan snapped the phone shut, making me jump. "Red is mostly talking gibberish, but he knows something. I can tell when he's trying to be invasive."

"Invasive?" Emery's brow furrowed and he glanced at her, equally taken out of the moment.

"Evasive. Whatever." She stalked toward the door, waving her finger at the ground as she did so. "Get these rocks picked up. You might need them."

CHAPTER 33

"WHAT ARE YOU thinking?" Emery asked Reagan as he met her at the car with me in tow. The sun was nearly gone from the sky, leaving long shadows.

"I'm thinking I still miss the Lamborghini." She pulled open the driver's door and sat down behind the wheel.

Emery opened the rear door. "Do you mind if I sit in the front?" he asked me. "I want to get a feel for what she's planning. She doesn't seem like the strategic type, and I—"

"Yes, sit in the front." I dropped onto the seat and pulled in my legs. "You'll be better at steering her than I will."

"Nothing to steer," Reagan said as Emery shut my door and sat in front of me. "We're just going to get some information from my good buddy Red, and then we're going to figure out what to do with that information. I've done this a million times."

"If you're so close to Red, why did he call Penny?" Emery asked.

"Two reasons." Reagan gunned the car down the lane to the highway. "Man, but I do miss that Lamborghini." She turned. "First, Red doesn't understand what friendship means. Sure, I make his life hell, but does he get picked on by anyone else? No, he doesn't."

I could just barely see Emery nodding slowly.

"Second, Penny's special *look* lured him in. He wants to protect her. They all do. It is pretty damn fantastic. I want that talent so bad. Alas, I'll just have to rely on inspiring blind fear."

"Penny's special…look," he said without inflection.

"Yeah. You'll see. She hasn't done it with you yet. It's this sad puppy sort of look. Pure damsel in distress. It seriously works, trust me. All the boys rush to her side to help."

"She's exaggerating," I said, shaking my head and looking out the window. "The incident she's talking about was right after I was basically chased out of Darius's house. I looked like a wet poodle—"

"Wet kitten."

"—and they were trying to help me. Then Reagan showed up and threw people around and basically kicked down the door."

"It wasn't me. Don't let her fool you—she's got hidden powers."

"A lot of them," he said, still without inflection.

We found a spot to park near the patch of scary

men from the last time I'd been in the area. The sinking sun cast deep pools of shadow beneath the trees. Less people were there tonight, and the ones who were didn't bother to glance up when we stepped out of the car and shut the door. All the same, the feeling of watching eyes and hidden magic hung over me.

Anything could be waiting around here, crouched behind a corner or sitting on a balcony, watching those who passed. They'd have the advantage in almost every scenario. If the Guild wanted to come at us, they'd have plenty of opportunities.

"There. See?" Reagan pointed at me as we crossed the street.

I tried to straighten back up while also letting go of my hoodie, which I was clutching against my chest.

"She looks lost and vulnerable." Reagan made a beeline for the shifter bar. "But that's not even the worst of it. Just wait."

"Are you okay?" Emery asked, his posture nothing like mine. His broad shoulders swayed in time with his confident swagger.

"I'm just not good enough to defend against a surprise attack yet," I murmured, trying to look everywhere at once. Something felt different about this area. More dangerous. It was early evening this time, not the dead of night, and I was accompanied by two experienced fighters, but it felt like we were heading into a death zone. I didn't even need my temperamental third eye for this one—I needed to get out of Dodge.

"She's got nothing to worry about," Reagan said, her confident swagger nearly matching Emery's. "If the worst happens, it'll probably be my ass, not yours."

Emery narrowed his eyes at her, and I could tell he'd just picked up another clue. Reagan was a terrible secret keeper, and I was an even worse detective. I'd clearly given her a false sense of security.

Music spilled out of the bars ahead and people littered the sidewalks, some shaking and dancing on their way, holding drinks and laughing. A small crowd crossed the street, guys and girls in their twenties, whooping and hollering at nothing I could see.

"I wish I could've explored this place like everyone else does," I reflected without meaning to. "Without the overhanging fear that seems to follow me around lately."

Emery slipped his hand into mine and entwined our fingers. "We will. Maybe not now, but someday, we'll drink our way through the town like they're doing."

"You'll end up facedown in the gutter, mark my words." Reagan slowed near the corner and gestured us to get in toward the side. She turned so she was mostly hidden from the people gathered in front of the bars down the way.

"What are you doing?" Emery asked, scanning the

surrounding area.

"Red wanted to meet me at the brewery down the way. A place with a lot of human tourists. He knows I can't cause a scene in a place like that. Not without Roger breathing down my neck again, and ain't nobody got time for that."

"Roger… the Alpha of the North American pack?" Emery's eyes widened.

"Yeah. We have a love-hate relationship. Anyway, I just want to make sure Red's gone. If so, then we need to make our way into those bars and see what we can see. If I get close enough, I'll be able to point out the mages."

"Given how they react to me, I'll be able to tell you which mages are friendly and which aren't," Emery said dryly.

Reagan turned slowly with glimmering eyes. A smile curled her lips. "Yes, indeedy. Fantastic." She turned back around. "As soon as we know Red is safely out of the way, we'll go dangle the bait. Roger may want to do things by the book, but why wait for the Guild to start a fight? Let's get them to play their cards."

"Oh good, you're the bait this time. I like that better." I felt an itch between my shoulder blades, like someone was focusing so hard on me that they were poking me in the back.

Emery turned before I could, and looked in the direction of the gaze. A group of laughing people wearing beads and funny glasses sauntered down the sidewalk. A couple crossed the street, a man and woman with a slight limp. There were more the other way, coming around the corner. People were everywhere, in all moods. Hiding here would be a piece of cake.

"If we mask ourselves with a spell," Emery murmured, "we'll give away what we are."

I clutched my hoodie again. "Reagan, get this show on the road. I want to get out of here."

"I'll get the show on the road, but you're not getting out of here." Reagan ducked, bobbed, and weaved, making a fool of herself while trying to scope out the bars. "With Emery here, they'll be pulling all their resources into one place. And with the Guild's money and power, a few of the lug nuts in Callie and Dizzy's groups will be stupid enough to join their forces. Teamed with the creeps who are already loitering around this city, sticking to the outskirts and waiting until the time is right, we'll have a small army on our hands."

"They'll attack during the day so we can't use the vampires," Emery said. "Given that they've seemed to stop caring about keeping their magic under wraps..." He shook his head and scanned the crowd. "I hate to admit it, but you're right. We need to dangle some bait."

"*The* bait. You," I said between clenched teeth, my

body shaking. I knew a battle was coming. I'd known that for months. But the last few days had given me time to relax in relative safety. Time to better hone my craft. Then Emery had shown up and the danger around me had seemed to melt away.

I'd fallen into my own false sense of security.

And it had just been ripped away.

"Perfect. Yes!" Reagan grabbed my arm and dragged me up the street toward the bars. "Keep that mojo going, Penny. Get those shifters eager to help you. That'll at least give us a few more hands on deck."

A big man with a unibrow stood in front of the bar we'd been thrown out of the other night, taking some woman's ID. She laughed and touched her hand to her chest, making a joke about feeling young again. Her comments were met with a hard scowl.

"Jimmy," Reagan said, crossing in front of him and leaning against the wall beside him. I awkwardly stood next to her, since she hadn't let go of my arm. Emery stood on the other side, staring at me with a perplexed expression, as if he still couldn't see me as a damsel in need of rescuing.

Mr. Unibrow, Jimmy, curled his lips and shook his head. "You shouldn't be here. Management ain't impressed with you right now."

"When is management ever impressed with me?" she asked.

He handed the woman's ID back and took one from a man wearing an excited, dopey smile. "Fair point. Red's gone."

"Good. Say, listen, what's the scuttlebutt? What have you got wandering through here?" Reagan pushed me back against the wall so she could look down the sidewalk.

Jimmy handed the ID back and finally looked at us. His eyes snagged on me, and his scowl increased. "What's the deal with her? She need rescuin' from you or what?"

"See?" Reagan shot Emery a glance. "What did I tell you?"

Jimmy followed her glance, keeping his focus on Emery for a few beats longer. When he finally returned his attention to Reagan, there was a wary light in his eyes. "What are you into now?"

"Nothing you need to concern yourself with. I can't use the help of a sea creature shifter, no matter how perplexing and secretive their mating habits..." Reagan waggled her eyebrows at him.

"What kind of sea creature?" I whispered, losing the battle with curiosity.

"Merman. How do they mate? No one knows." Reagan waved that aside. "Doesn't matter. At the moment. Listen, Red was concerned enough about the strangers of this area to call. What have you seen?"

Jimmy stared down someone who had stopped outside the bar and looked in. The poor guy with the strange taste in Hawaiian shirts clearly liked the music and was thinking about a libation, but the intense furrow in Jimmy's bushy unibrow scared him off. He skulked farther on down.

"We got mages." Jimmy spat to the side, nearly hitting Emery's shoe. "Sorry, bro." He curled his lip. "Heard someone talking about some nasty shit. Shit I don't even want to repeat. Got him all sorts of power, la-dee-da. Had to brutally kill someone to get it. Didn't seem to bother him." He shifted to a wide, aggressive stance. His magic, the call of the sea, deep and powerful, washed over me. "I threw his ass out. Said he couldn't be talking about none of that in my bar. Hell no. But he has friends. I know he does. Shifty-eyed, scrawny little hacks coming in here and staring holes in my back. When I look around, they have something else taking up their attention. Driving me crazy. But I don't know no more than that. I don't know enough to start banning people. Hell, I don't even know who to ban."

"Any other bars you've heard about this happening in?" Emery asked.

"A couple. All magical clientele. But again, aside from a few things people have mistakenly overheard, that's all we know. It's bugging me out. At least you can tell when it's a vampire. Hell, even you." He gestured at

Reagan. "You smell different. Do I care why? No, I do not. I know you ain't human, I know to watch my six around you, and that's that. But these fuckers." His lip curled again. "They're dressing like tourists. They're drinking and trying to fit in. I don't know one from the other, but I know they ain't right in the head. I know they don't give two shits about killing people. That's got me jumpy, I don't mind telling you. I do not want that shit in my town, do you hear me?"

"The real question is, does Roger hear you?" Reagan asked, a gleam in her eyes as she surveyed the street in front of her. It was the look that promised action, and I was just thankful not to be on the other end of it.

"Yeah, he knows, but he doesn't know how big the threat is yet. Doesn't know how many people to bring in."

"Tell him the Rogue Natural is on scene. We've got both targets in town, together. It'll draw big numbers."

Two younger girls stopped outside the bar and looked in before shooting furtive glances at Emery. They giggled, and one flicked her hair.

"Hey, you coming in?" Jimmy asked in a rough voice.

The smiles faltered. The one with long blond hair batted her Bambi eyes at Emery. "Well? Are we?"

They both giggled. I wanted to swat her.

"No, no!" Reagan stepped in front of Jimmy and

pointed a finger at the girls. "No way. He's taken." She jabbed a finger at Emery, who cracked a grin. "Don't you be creepin' on my girl's man. He's not for you. I will cut you, do you understand me?" Eyes wide and smiles dipping in confusion, the girls started backing away. "I will cut you if you so much as glance his way. Tell all your friends. He's off the table, bitches."

Faces fallen, the girls hurried off. I couldn't do much more than stare.

"That was a bit much," Jimmy said, putting his hand in front of Reagan without touching her. "Respect, but it was a bit much."

Reagan laughed and stepped back. "I've always wanted to do that. I could get down with having a girlfriend to defend."

"You don't need more reasons to fight."

"What a horrible thing to say to me." She cracked her knuckles. "Speaking of starting fights, let's see who's in the bar today. If Red comes back, don't let him in. He'll just tell Roger on me."

Jimmy shrugged. "Back corner. Glasses," he said, waving her in. "Give him hell. We need to clean up this town."

Reagan stopped me before entering the doorway. "Give me a moment. Then drift off to the right and try to find a corner. Emery, head to the nearest end of the bar. We're splitting up."

“That’s not a good idea,” he said, his hand firm on my back.

“I need Penny to draw on heartstrings, and she’ll do that better alone in a corner. As for you, I want to see who recognizes you. That’ll be telling.”

“And you?” he asked quietly.

“Why, I’ll raise hell, of course. Smacking down mages in bars seems to be a specialty of mine.”

CHAPTER 34

EMERY TOOK MY hand as Reagan drifted into the bar, her posture a little hunched and her head pointed down a bit. It was her version of skulking, even though she still looked like she was about to kill everyone in the place. Electricity sizzled up my arm and fizzled through the air, crackling with static.

"Whoa, shit." Jimmy stepped away from us. "You guys are packing some heat, huh? Don't blow this place up. I need this job."

"Hey," Emery whispered into my ear, his chest against my arm. The chill on the air caressed my skin and the breeze flicked my hair. "I'll make sure nothing happens to you, okay? You don't have to be scared."

"It's okay," I said, closing my eyes as the throb and wobble of the world around me simmered down into a steady hum. The feel of Jimmy's magic drifted over me like sea foam, soft and salty, lightly scratching. For a moment, the call of the blue depths of the ocean tugged at my heart, begging me to return and drift among its currents. Promising to protect me.

Other magic pushed at me from all directions. Spicy, sweet, gritty, thick—the patrons of this bar represented a cross-section of the magical community, I could feel it. Though I didn't know what they were, the shape of their magic was taking form for me as it played, pushed, or messed with mine.

"Step back. They're going through something, here," I heard Jimmy say, his magic vibrating around me, wanting to lead me to his home. To the place he felt the most comfortable. The most powerful. So he could help.

"Keep your eyes out—that is help enough," I murmured, concentrating on the magical bubble that sprang up so easily whenever Emery was around. "The balance is so easy with you," I whispered.

"I'll make sure no harm comes to you," Emery said.

"It's okay," I repeated. "I'm used to being scared in this town. It's a normal state of affairs. If I start running, look around for danger."

I fluttered my eyes open and walked forward, wondering if I'd be able to hold the balance as his body drifted away from mine. He'd been right. This mutual sharing brought a different feeling than simply reaching out and using his magic. It was a calm, peaceful place that made it easier for me—and him, I sensed—to properly feel the world around me.

I wondered if I could bring Reagan into it.

I wondered if I'd be able to do magic comfortably without it, now that I'd experienced its comforting embrace.

I wondered why the heck I was suddenly the center of attention.

Almost every eye in the bar had turned to me. I'd stopped just inside the doorway, my hands at my sides and my body straight and tall.

Hunch, you idiot! You're Captain Skulks-a-Lot, not a super fighter like Reagan or Emery. Own your mantle.

I bowed my back, but it was too late. Two guys had turned toward me with lopsided grins and puffed-out chests. Farther down, a woman had narrowed her eyes at me, and it clearly wasn't because of the two non-magical tourists with too much alcohol in their system. A pair of middle-aged men met my eyes with sparkles of menace before slowly turning around to their drinks, not saying a word or looking at each other.

The Guild was in this bar. But they were far from the only magical people present. A row of rough-and-tumble men and women had bristled into a state of readiness.

Ready to help me, I gathered.

I could feel it like I had with Jimmy. Their power surged up around them, stuffing the air with territorialism and vicious intent. They felt threatened by the mages, and planned to do anything in their power to extinguish that threat.

I was the thing that could help them, and whatever magical feelers I'd put out had them convinced I could help them.

Which was good, because there was no way I could make a stand alone, but I was also attracting way too much attention.

Beside the table in the corner was a small hollow, visually cut off from the live band on the other side, which was why it was empty, even though the table a few paces from it was full of people.

As I made my way to the empty table, a man I didn't know with dirty-blond hair falling to his shoulders in a wave nodded at me, his eyes glimmering with violence and kindness at the same time. He didn't mean me harm. His companions had already looked away, studying their drinks.

Across the bar, Reagan was sitting next to a youngish guy with a goofy grin. She cradled a tumbler half-full of brown liquid, probably whiskey. Apparently she was the type to drink on the job. The bartender, Trixie from the other night, took Reagan's money with a flat expression and headed to the till. Her posture screamed *wary*. She was uncomfortable with something in the bar, and based on how she'd handled Reagan's violence the other night, it wasn't her.

Guild.

Anger wobbled my balanced bubble, but Emery strutted into the bar behind me, his posture loose and relaxed, confident and in charge. He surveyed the crowd, letting his gaze linger on a few of the male patrons, probably magical people, before drifting out of my view, toward the area of the bar nearest the band. He'd go deaf on this stakeout.

In the far corner, Reagan glanced up at me before shifting her attention back to the crowd in the bar. I couldn't tell who interested her most, because one of the lopsided grinners from the bar cut off my view, his lean pronounced and his eyes slightly glazed.

The dirty-blond man who'd nodded at me stood up, pushing his chair back as he did so. Just over six feet tall with a powerful frame, he turned toward the bar with a loose body that almost looked like it was lounging. Like he was getting in a good stretch before he attacked.

"What do you want?" he growled out to Drunk Guy, and a spicy elixir tickled my magic, like a wind-swept prairie in the hot moonlight.

"I got no beef with you, bro," Drunk Guy said, the words slurring and jumbled together. "I'm just heading over there." He pointed in my direction, and I shrank back without meaning to.

The shifter stepped into the path between me and Drunk Guy. "Does she look like a ringmaster, mate?" he asked.

Drunk Guy frowned and swayed. Confusion turned to anger, and alcohol erased the desire for self-preservation. He bristled and stepped toward the shifter. "Why don't you get out of the way, bro."

"I said, does she look like a ringmaster?" the shifter said, not moving. The change in his body was slight, but I could feel raw power and brutal grace exude from him. "Because if not, she has no need of clowns."

"Get him out of here, Steve," Trixie yelled across the bar. "He's had enough."

"With pleasure, love." Steve, the shifter, grabbed the man by the shirt with both hands, lifted him without effort, and muscled him toward the door.

As soon as they left, I caught another glimpse of Reagan, downing her whiskey and staring toward the corner that Jimmy had pointed out.

She nodded to Trixie and slapped another five on the bar, now staring straight ahead.

Steve wandered back in, seemingly without a care in the world. He nodded at me as he passed, then shrugged at my muttered thanks. He took his seat without a word, and the others around him shifted and adjusted their positions. Certain figures stilled, their hands in front of them, close together. Others straightened up, ready for action. Still more shifted and fidgeted, looking around uncomfortably. It felt like we were all in a pressure cooker, waiting for something to blow.

My attention was drawn to one of the middle booths in the bar. The occupants were studying each other intently, silent communication in their eyes.

I edged farther out of my nook so I could see better.

Magic wisps rose feebly from the hands of the man nearest the bar, his hands clasped next to his empty glass. Another mage had her hands below the table, magic rolling into a messy sort of weave intended for destruction.

"This is about to kick off," I told Steve absently, edging still farther out.

"It was about to kick off when these maggots wandered into the wrong part of town. We're just waiting for the go-ahead."

"No, I mean, it is about to kick off *right now.* They are creating shitty spells that will get Reagan riled up, which will get Emery riled up, which will make me do something stupid. You might want to walk out now."

"What? And miss the fireworks?" He laughed and turned in his chair. I got the impression he was preparing to surge up and out. The people around him pushed their chairs back a little, too, also in anticipation.

"You don't know what you're messing with," I said through clenched teeth.

"They don't scare us, love," Steve insisted. "Just lead the charge. We're right behind you."

"I meant, you don't know what is going to come at

you, probably accidentally. I have no idea what I'm doing!"

Steve looked at me in confusion, but it was too late to explain.

A man with wire-rimmed glasses and a comb-over popped out of the corner booth. *Glasses.* A gush of magic ballooned up in front of him, intending to melt the face off someone. The weave was loose but orderly, and he'd called it up quickly. And it was directed at Reagan.

Magic twisted through my fingers without my prompting it. As I rocketed off a spell, I saw streams of magic rushing at Emery. We'd all joined the fight.

Reagan stood gracefully from her stool and reached for her sword, but something held her back. She probably felt my spell. "Wearing glasses doesn't make you smart, four eyes," Reagan said with a laugh, leaning back against the bar to watch.

My spell slammed into his, eating it away while ingesting its power and forcing it to change direction. Changing it so it grew larger but less heinous. Forcing it back on him, and whoever was with him.

Emery shot his spell off next, hitting one of the middle-aged guys at the bar who'd looked at me for just a moment when I walked in. He cried out and fell off his stool, landing on his back and shaking.

The guys at the back table grabbed at their pockets,

trying to get more ingredients for their spells. Those in the middle booth all shifted, probably arming themselves with ingredients.

CHAPTER 35

"STEVE!" I POINTED at the table.

Steve and his friends were up in a flash as Reagan launched forward, grabbing the woman from the corner booth, who'd (smartly) jumped off her stool and run for the back exit. Screaming from the corner booth drowned out the squawking of frightened tourists.

Steve grabbed the guy across the table with one hand before dragging him over the bar. The mage got off his spell, which threatened to blast Steve's face with something frozen.

I ran at them while creating a weave, but Emery dodged in front of me, faster and more efficient. He got his spell off, hitting the mage in the dead center of his forehead. A crack said the force had snapped his neck.

"Cleanup on aisle five," Trixie yelled, jumping over the bar. "Get them out of here, Jimmy."

Jimmy rushed in and started grabbing non-magical tourists. "For your own safety," he said as he wrestled them out. "Come back tomorrow for free drinks on us.

So sorry. These things happen."

Trixie followed him out, marshaling other non-magical tourists with no such explanation or offer.

A surge of intent rose from the corner where Emery had been stationed. I stepped out with my spell still building between my fingers, then stopped dead.

Mary Bell. Callie and Dizzy's acquaintance.

A glimmer came to her eyes when she saw me. "You found your knight, I see." The spell she'd been weaving dissipated between her hands, and she slid off her stool. "Don't mind that." She nodded at the magic fading into the world around her and dropped her hands, walking toward me. "I just wanted your attention."

She stopped in front of the door, five feet from me, no hostile magical intent sullying the air. "I have a message for you."

"Does Callie know you hang out here?" I asked, confused. Emery hadn't done anything to her, so he clearly hadn't thought she was a threat. But the spell she'd been creating was horribly vicious and gruesome. It would mangle bodies and render the victims almost unrecognizable.

I didn't even know if she had enough power to finish the weave. But maybe back in the day, before she'd lost her dual-mage partner, it had been her go-to. She certainly seemed familiar with the somewhat complex weave.

"The line between good and evil is horribly blurred," she said. "Good people sometimes do horrible things. Bad people occasionally do good. So trust in the person who shows their good intentions. Do not listen to their words. Watch their intentions." She held up her finger as the commotion around the bar began to slow. "But be slow to trust, if you have to at all."

"Uh-oh, you shouldn't be in here," Jimmy said, rushing in and putting his arms out to direct Mary Bell out of the bar. He didn't recognize her as a mage.

But she'd been in the bar. Alone. With a lot of (almost certainly) Guild members.

"Most importantly, young Penny. Stay true to yourself. Magic works best when we are who we were meant to be." She gave me a knowing smile before letting the large doorman usher her out.

Could I hope she was just spying for Callie and Dizzy? She'd be the right person to do that. She was familiar with the morally corrupt side of magic. I couldn't believe she would turn now, after all these years, and after having already tread the wrong path—and lost everything for it.

"Penny," Emery said, walking over with sure steps, not even winded. Reagan stalked over from the back hallway, dragging an unconscious woman. She glanced at the back booth. I could see limbs hanging off the seat and table, but the mages weren't dead. Not unless my spell had gone wrong.

"You okay?" Emery asked, running his hand across my lower back. He stared down anxiously into my face.

"Yeah. Did you see Mary Bell?"

His eyes went distant for a second and his brows lowered. "I don't remember that name."

"The little old woman in that corner." I pointed.

His brow furrow increased and his head tilted. "Now that you mention it, she looked vaguely familiar, though I can't say where I've seen her before. She wasn't doing any magic."

"She did after you left. Well…" I saw Reagan talking to Steve as the rest of the shifters started tying up rogue mages and moving them to the back. "She started a dark spell, but let it go once she saw me." I shook my head. "She doesn't make sense to me."

Emery looked out the door. "Should we go after her?"

"No." I patted the compartments on my utility belt, only belatedly realizing how stupid I probably looked. Although Reagan had her fanny pack on, so in the absurd wardrobe contest, I would come in second. "We'll let Callie and Dizzy handle it."

"Okay." Reagan clapped once, stepping over a prone body and stopping when she reached us. "Here's the situation. You guys make these things a lot more civilized, and I'm not sure I like that."

"I like it," Trixie said, walking back behind the bar. "I'd like it even better if you'd hurry up taking out the trash. My salary is in tips. No customers, no tips."

Reagan spread her hands. "I'm the muscle, not the cleanup crew."

"Me too." Steve lounged against the bar, watching us with an easygoing expression. Now that the threat was gone, he seemed like a pretty laid-back guy. I wondered what animal he turned into.

Reagan glanced at the bar clock. "We've got about an hour or so before the vampires wake up. I want to clear it with Roger, but I think it would be best to deliver these mages into the vampires' possession."

Steve grimaced. "I'm not so sure he'll be into that idea, love. Roger isn't so friendly with vampires." It was clear Steve had no idea who Reagan was, and how closely she was connected with both camps.

Reagan turned and stared at him for a second.

"Hello, beautiful," he replied. Trixie started laughing.

Reagan turned back to us. "I'm going to stay here with the mages and get this sorted out. Darius will want information about their rank and ability, so I'll probably head over to see him after this."

"Roger certainly won't want an elder sticking its fingers into all of this," Steve said.

Reagan cocked her head in annoyance and stuck up

a finger. "I didn't get to bust many heads in here today. Given how much I ardently hate the Guild, that upsets me. You do not want to tumble with me right now."

"*Au contraire*, a tumble sounds like exactly the thing to clear some pent-up aggression." A smile slowly slid up his face.

Trixie laughed again and shook her head, clearing off the bar. "I say you take him up on that, Reagan. If he wants to blindly go where no sane *man* would go before him, who's to say boo?"

"That would go over well with Roger, sure," Reagan said dryly. "Killing one of his prized nitwits."

"Ah, now." Steve touched his palm to his chest. "That's hurtful."

Reagan sprouted a grin. "Anyway." She motioned toward the closed door before tossing Emery the keys. "You guys go straight to the car and head home. Now is not the time to be the bait. Wait behind the ward until I can assess the extent of their host."

"This crew won't know all the details, even if you question every last one," Emery said, tucking his thumb in my butt pocket. I got the distinct impression he thought I was a flight risk.

"I'm not even sure they'd send sheriffs into the bars," Emery said, "and sheriffs would only know enough to carry out whatever jobs they were given. If the Guild hopes to get Penny and me out of here, or kill me and get Penny out, they'll have sent more than a few sheriffs. They wouldn't want to waste any of them on a possible bar fight."

"You know an awful lot about how the Mages' Guild works, mate," Steve said, his slight shift speaking volumes. Or maybe it was the sudden powerful surge of primal magic that clued me in. "That rings an alarm bell or two."

Reagan laughed and headed to the bar. "For being at the heart of a messy game, you don't know much about the players. He's the Rogue Natural. If you don't know who that is, ask someone who has even an inkling of knowledge of the magical world." Reagan pushed another five across the bar before turning to him. "Or do you just really enjoy being the butt of blond jokes?"

His eyes sparkled. "You sure you don't want that tumble? It would be a wild ride."

"For you, surely." Reagan grabbed the whiskey Trixie had just poured. To us, she said, "Get gone. Darius won't want you around if he needs to come down here."

A chill of fear worked down my back. "Why? Is he still pissed at me for wrecking his house?" I did not want to be on his shit list.

The smile dropped off Steve's face as he noticed my change in demeanor.

"There it is. Teach me how to camouflage myself like that." Trixie laughed as she poured a beer.

"It's not you, it's his recovering roommate." Reagan took another sip of her whiskey. "That old vamp is not just healing; Darius thinks she's headed back into the thick of vampire politics, and based on what he's read about her—what he thinks is her, anyway, which is what he's pieced together from myths, legends, and so forth—she was a doozie of a player back in the day. Something he *should* have figured out *before* plying her for information and getting buddy-buddy with her. He claims he couldn't have known it was her in those myths and legends because he'd never seen that side of her." She made a face. "I'm not sure if I believe him. He hates being wrong. And now look what he's done."

"Created an enemy?" Steve asked.

"No. Woken up a vicious mastermind who orchestrated as well as fought in several history-changing cultural movements. He thinks that old broad was a chief instigator in the witch burnings, which took out a lot of her competitors."

"What does that have to do with me?" I clutched my hoodie, my legs trembling as I thought about Ja, how she'd stalked to the top of the stairs after getting through my magic and two powerful vampires.

"In the future?" Reagan sipped her whiskey. "Nothing at all. She will be Darius's problem. Well, Darius, Vlad, and all the other powerful elders. She won't trouble the minions directly. But a vampire who's been woken up is similar to a newbie. She needs lots of blood and can go a little crazy. He doesn't want her crazy igniting your crazy and destroying the whole town. We've got enough issues. So, for right now, you two need to stay in your respective corners until you level out."

"Roger won't like that much at all, either." Steve narrowed his eyes at Reagan, albeit playfully. "You sure know a lot about vampires."

"And you are sure slow to pick up on what everyone else already knows." Reagan nodded toward the door. "Get gone, you two."

"This is why I don't like dealing with you," Red said loudly to Reagan as he skulked into the bar, his fists balled. "We are *supposed* to be watching and waiting. Not shaking up the whole town!"

"*You* are supposed to be waiting and watching," Reagan said, sitting on a stool. "I'm supposed to cause trouble. And look, we each carried out our duties. Cheers to us. Want a drink? I'm buying."

"I don't drink, you know that." Red pulled out his cell phone.

"He's going to tell on you." Steve laughed and paid for his beer.

"What else is new?" Reagan watched Red walk to the back. "He probably won't give me the credit for telling him about one of the super elders being back in action, either." She shook her head. "Ungrateful."

"Yeah, he did stand there and soak that right up." Steve nodded, unconcerned. "I best not tell him any of my secrets."

"Let's go," Emery said, steering me toward the door.

"Why did we agree to come here?" I asked quietly.

"Hindsight," he answered as we pushed open the door and stepped out into the evening air.

CHAPTER 36

EMERY MONITORED THEIR surroundings as best he could, keeping his hand on the small of Penny's back. She was fucking amazing in the heat of battle, and in the future she'd be unstoppable, but right now she was extremely unpredictable.

Thankfully, Darius had showed his genius in pairing Penny with Reagan. Reagan was just crazy enough to make the situation work. She didn't seem to want, or need, any sort of plan. She was fast on her feet and could handle close combat like a champ. She also didn't need to own the show. When Penny had reacted in the bar, Reagan had held back and allowed her to handle it. That spoke of trust and teamwork.

He scanned the way ahead, ignoring the seemingly chaotic but actually quite organized cloud of magic hovering above them—something Penny seemed to collect and hold whenever she got into a situation that made her nervous—and headed toward a grassy area between the split in the road. People loitered in groups, standing and sitting, nowhere to go or maybe just in no hurry to get there. As far as he could tell, they didn't present a problem to them.

Though…the surroundings looked familiar for some reason.

Adrenaline rolled through him when he spotted the tree from one of his visions about Penny. A patch of weeds rested under the hanging branches, blanketed in shadows.

Not just any foretelling. He'd sensed someone sitting under this tree, waiting for her—to take her back to the Mages' Guild's headquarters, probably—not a physical death sentence, but one that would crush her spirit. Based on what he'd heard from Callie, Dizzy, and Reagan, "proper" training would likely do that to her. And the Guild would do a lot more than "properly" train her.

They'd break her.

Was this a base camp of sorts? Close to the bars where magical people hung out, and tucked into a place where vagabonds loitered. It would be the perfect setup for someone who wanted to watch without getting noticed.

"Don't come this way anymore," Emery said with a rougher voice than he'd intended. It was his survival voice, the one he used when he was in the wilds, dealing with people who would skin him alive for his possessions if he so much as turned his back.

As he probably should've expected, she looked up at him with those huge blue eyes, widened in fear. An aura of her survival magic rose around her, the crystal white shrouding her like an angel. It was the most beautiful, pure, perplexing sight he'd probably ever seen. He'd never seen survival magic do that—wrap around the body and emit a vibe that would help keep the person safe.

The effect showcased her vulnerability and her desire to be protected—the reason the shifters were willing to take on Reagan and the mages for her. With the vampires, it probably did the opposite, pumping out a sort of challenge and authority to scare off newbies. Well…scare off the newbies and enrage ancient elders.

It was clear she had no idea she was doing it. Her subconscious and her magic were working together, responding to the situation how they deemed fit.

"What would happen if none of us had been trained in the current methods, Penny Bristol?" he asked, rubbing her back. "How many different ways of working magic would there be?"

"What do you mean?"

"Growing up as mages, we're taught specific ways of doing things from an age when we don't know how to think for ourselves. By the time we have the power to experiment with magic, we're already entrenched in the supposedly 'right' way of doing things. I've learned a great many things out in the wilds by myself, things that have forced me to think outside of my teachings. It has given me an incredible edge over my peers. Made me the undisputed best. But I've still played by the rules, more or less. Bending them and breaking them occasionally, but always keeping them in mind. You…" He shook his head and glanced down the street, checking for followers. "You aren't even using the same playbook."

"When you first met me, you said that I just needed to will it, and it would be so. Or something like that."

"Yes, I did. I remember that. I didn't know you were a natural, then."

"What's the difference?"

He blew out a breath and shrugged, looking for the car. "I mean…there shouldn't be a difference. I will things into existence all the time, after working out the recipe, as you call it. But if I'd known you were a natural, and not a witch with very little power, I would've told you to get those spells into your head. Learn the guidelines so you didn't hurt yourself or someone else. Study, study, study."

"But after you figured out I was a natural, you still didn't say that."

"By then we didn't have time. You had to learn as quickly as possible, so there was no time for the standard approach. Maybe we got lucky in how it worked out."

Emery stopped in the place they'd left the car. The red Toyota was still there, but the white sedan was missing. Instead of Reagan's car, pushed back a little too close to the Toyota, there was a brown station wagon taking up what could've been two spots. "Wasn't it here, or am I remembering incorrectly?"

Penny pointed at the Toyota before looking beyond and then behind her. "It was here. I remember getting out and seeing from this angle. So yeah, it definitely had to be here."

He laughed. Didn't do a thing to calm his growing anxiety, but it tickled him that she even had a unique way of remembering where a car was parked.

"Crap," he said, his smile dropping away.

"Hondas go for a lot of money at chop shops," Penny said. Her face fell as she eyed a Honda up the street, in better condition, and then another across the street. Her face fell. "Granted, they typically boost them in groups."

"Do you know that from TV?"

"No. Veronica had a Honda once. It disappeared when all the others in the neighborhood did. The police said that's what happens sometimes." She pointed at the Toyota. Then a Mercedes up the street. "If you were going to steal a car, there are much better options." After a pause, she said, "Let's go. Now."

"Good idea." He grabbed her arm, silently keeping her at his pace. He should've remembered her speed. Soon she was yanking at *him*, wanting to go faster.

A backward glance didn't tell him much. People ambled along the sidewalks and streets, ready to enjoy the night. No one looked their way, and certainly nobody stared. But then, anyone watching them wouldn't want to be obvious about it. A glance every now and then would be enough.

Regardless, no one had randomly stolen Reagan's broken-down car, which bore its fair share of bad paint and dents. They needed to get to shelter, *now*.

"What's the situation with Darius?" he asked. "Do you trust what Reagan is telling you?"

"She's a terrible liar, so yes. She didn't need to say a word, though. We do not want to mess with the extreme elder staying with him. Trust me. Her and I don't seem to play nice together. But Reagan seemed more worried about us staying in the bar. Maybe Darius's house is safe?"

Emery licked his lips, glancing behind them again. Nothing had changed, and he didn't see anyone he'd noticed on his first sweep, which meant very little. "Maybe. Or maybe getting us out of the bar was just a precaution. We could chance going back."

She clenched her jaw and said something under her breath that sounded like "nuck fuggets." "The car getting stolen right now is fiercely bad timing."

Bad timing for us, great timing for the Guild. They'd clearly taken advantage of the situation.

"You got that right." He pulled her to cross the street. "I know you are more knowledgeable now, and can do things on your own, but—"

"It's fine," she cut in, looking away right before they continued on down the sidewalk. Houses rose on either side and pedestrian traffic reduced a little. "I don't mind being manhandled as long as the person doing the manhandling is someone I trust that also has an idea of what to do in the given moment."

"That makes things easy," he said, teasing but also meaning it.

"It seems my mother's training has really come in handy. I keep getting thrown in with headstrong jerks. My complacency melds just fine."

"That's not very nice," he said with a grin, clutching the back of her shirt. He had no idea what might pop out at them. At all costs, they needed to stick together. Since his first reaction to danger was to do a spell, and hers was (usually) to run like hell, keeping contact was necessary.

"At least you won't beat me up," she muttered, bringing out her phone. "Do you have a plan, or does it just seem like you do?"

"It just seems like I do. Though going back to the

bar is our smartest bet. If Darius is bringing his new friend to keep an eye on her, they probably haven't shown up yet."

"You don't think so?"

He gritted his teeth, uncertainty rising through him. It was a shifter bar, which gave jurisdiction to Roger. If Darius waited too long, he might lose his chance to interrogate the mages and gain firsthand knowledge of the situation. Emery doubted Darius would take the risk.

Of course, it also seemed implausible that Darius would bring a dangerous elder out in public with him, but that possibility was dangerous to Penny. More so than Emery would like to risk.

"*Damn it.* We need a plan B." He wanted to break something in frustration. Instead, he took a deep breath. Best not to panic Penny. Then she'd *really* be unpredictable, and that might be lethal in their current situation. "We can't walk to Reagan's place from here, even if that wasn't a horribly bad idea. I'm not great at stealing cars, even if *that* wasn't a horribly bad idea."

"Right. Does your phone work?"

"Yes, why?"

"Do you have a rideshare service on it, like Uber or Lyft?"

He patted the phone in his pocket for no particular reason. "No. It only has the apps that came with it."

"One of us needs to be the designated tech-savvy one. I'd hoped that would be you."

"Hope dashed."

"Not at all. You just need to learn. I'm pretty sure you can. You're smart," she said, utterly serious. He couldn't help chuckling despite the situation. "You should set Lyft up on your phone really quick and call for a ride."

"Except I don't have an account to download apps. Or a credit card to set up an account...to download apps."

"In the house that Jack built," she said randomly before exhaling. "Okay, plan C. Do you have any cash? Or wait, what am I thinking? We can see if Callie and Dizzy are—"

She spun, ramming his arm with her elbow and knocking it away from her. Her hands pulled up to her chest and magic pulled from her cloud and into a tight, focused weave three inches thick. A moment later, he knew why.

A bright red blast, full of dazzling elements, flew at them from behind. Sophisticated, practiced, and somewhat powerful, the spell had clearly been created by an advanced user.

Penny's spell blasted out toward it, wrapping it up easily before turning end over end, eating through it.

Shapes slipped behind the corner a block down, the

attacking mages taking cover. Emery and Penny were wide open.

"Let's go," she said, grabbing his arm and yanking him forward. "There are two more grisly spells in the making. I don't know how many more of them are around, but it's safe to say we're outnumbered, and this isn't a good place to fight."

"If we don't take them out, they'll just—" Her spell, having successfully consumed the other, grew in power and continued on its way. "It is headed back to the user."

"I hope so. I don't honestly know if it'll work. We made No Good Mikey use a casing to attack me, but my spell didn't reach him in the end. He'd already scrambled over the fence, into his yard, and shut himself into his house before my spell started pursuing him. He was not impressed with Reagan tricking him into using magic. Or being a magical target."

Emery didn't have time to laugh at her antics. Black fog clouded his vision and he saw the way ahead, teeming with bodies and flashing magical spells.

"We can't go straight. We need to turn up here. Pick up the pace." He started to jog. "They're here in numbers. Our stint in the bar must've given them time to organize."

"There are a great many ways out of here," she said, yanking him right at the next corner and then down another street. A group of girls yelled and jeered at a group of guys on the other side of the street. One of the guys was showing his man-boobs and shaking his rather large belly. "We can walk quickly down the middle of Bourbon Street and blend into the crowd. You'll have to take off your shirt, though."

"You first."

"I'd rather be the one jeering and whooping." She laughed, strangely not a forced sound, given the situation, and shoved him left at the next corner.

With the next turn, the black fog rushed into his vision, only to clear immediately when Penny pulled him around the corner. "One back there."

A jet of magic roared behind them, the power blistering as it passed by.

"They're either packing serious power, or they're constructing spells together," Emery said, breathing heavily now.

"I thought mages didn't work together."

"Not in the way you're thinking. Not like witches. Remember when we made that spell in Darius's warehouse? We each created half of it, then merged it together? Mages work that way when confronting a larger power source. Or else naturals would go unchallenged."

"Like building a Lego village with someone." She nodded, like that made sense, and pointed in front of them. Beyond a roadblock cutting off traffic, people meandered up the middle of the street. Neon light glowed and spilled across the cement, sliding over the passersby. Music pulsed and people moved, lifting their plastic cups and cheering for no reason other than the fun of a constant party.

"We'll walk down there for a ways." She grabbed his hand and they veered right, around the roadblock and into the crowd. The crowd wasn't as dense as it would be for a festival or Mardi Gras, but there was ample opportunity to hide. "Stay to the middle," she said. "Keep with the crowd. When we can, let's break away and run again. We need to get away from the mages."

"I agree. The chase is on. If we can get them to follow us instead of surround us, we'll be fine." He clutched her hand, smiling for show and even moving a little to the pounding music blasting out of a nearby bar, fitting in with the group of people in front of them.

"You can dance." She shook her hand loose before slipping her arm around his middle. His gut tightened in a way that wasn't appropriate for the situation, and he exhaled at the warm feeling unfolding in his chest. He let his arm fall around her shoulders as she said, "I've always liked to dance."

"I don't know about dancing, but I can jive to rhythm well enough."

"Jive?" She smiled at him, and the world around

them started to dim. Her effect on him was not helping him focus. "Next you'll tell me you have fancy feet."

She chuckled and scanned the area around them. Her hand gripped his waist a little tighter and her face dropped, now looking through her eyelashes.

He followed her gaze. A scarred-faced man stood at the side of the street with cunning eyes and a naturally downturned mouth. He wore scraped-up leather pants, a worse-for-wear leather duster, and a black shirt.

"Someone must've told him you were dangerous," she whispered.

Emery laughed. "Or tricked him into thinking it was a costume party." He looked away, scanning the other side of the street, then above them, just in case someone hanging out on one of the balconies looked out of place. "He's a mercenary. They aren't clever in their fashion choices. The Guild is outsourcing. Unless he's working for someone else."

"Is he magical?"

"Maybe. Or else he's just a thug. He either doesn't know what he's up against, or knows exactly what he's up against. The choice of outfit would be the same for either situation. We're hoping for the former, obviously."

"They want us really bad," she said, that halo of survival light covering her body. This time, it expanded to cover him as well.

Unbelievably, his survival magic kicked in, too, welling up from deep inside of him and rippling into hers like a new current in a tranquil pond. The colors swirled and mixed until they blended, pumping with power and turning a hazy gray.

"Sorry," he said, spotting a plain woman with a tight bun and a purple sash around her neck. The color signified power level, he remembered, though he didn't know which tier that specific color was.

"For what?" Penny's nails dug into his sides. Beyond the woman, who was obviously with the Guild and showing her higher status, leaned another mercenary, this one in somewhat newer leathers. Either that meant he made a good living, or he was a greenie.

Emery hoped for the latter.

"I made your snow-white halo a muddy gray," he said, not liking the numbers stacked against them.

She shrugged. "You turned me from the color of a blank slate into a drab color. At least I have a *little* color now."

He laughed despite himself, remembering their conversation in Seattle about her white survival magic versus his black. He'd always seen his magic as a reflection of his soul—black—but she'd flipped the script, saying she had no color because they'd all fled, but he was full of them.

A crowd of guys stood to the side, looking up at two

girls dancing on a balcony, ready to flash their goods.

"Here we go." Emery pushed Penny in front of him and shoved his way into the group of guys, lifting his hand and pumping his fist. "Take. It. Off," he chanted. "Take. It. Off."

Penny lifted her fist and joined in.

The guys weren't long in jumping on board, and the combined chant drew more onlookers. One of the girls lifted her shirt and the guys jumped and threw up their hands, splashing beer down and dousing the sleeve of Emery's hoodie. He jumped with them, his hands on Penny's shoulders to keep her close.

She threaded between the bodies, dragging him with her, until they were at the edge of the group. After taking a quick look around, she led him away from the others. A moment later and they were in a group of ladies staggering down the sidewalk.

"Did you see that guy flash his dick?" Penny asked the girl next to them.

"Oh my gawd." The girl swerved at Penny, ducking her head into Penny's face with wide eyes and a gaping mouth. She was clearly drunk off her ass and having a hard time navigating her high heels. "*No!* Where? Was he packing?"

"Up there. He was *really* hot." Penny nudged the girl next to her. "So was his friend. Shirtless."

"Who?" the other woman said, blinking at Penny.

"No, you guys." Penny pointed across the street before grabbing the girls to either side of her and pulling them with her. "Over here. Free beer and super-hot guys."

"I'm…getting married," one of the leaders of the dozen said with serious attitude. She didn't follow.

"No, they're gay," Penny insisted, stalling on the street so they didn't spread too far out. "They're just good to look at. Hello? Free beer." Her attitude rivaled the bride's.

"Wait, who are you?" The girl next to Emery looked at him in confusion, and then a smile slid across her face and her eyes half drifted shut. "Hi."

"He's one of the dancers! You guys, come on." Penny motioned everyone forward.

"I'll buy the first round." Emery held out his arms for them to grab as they cheered. A girl on either side took hold, and one grabbed his shoulders from behind.

"I want in," someone said as the others chatted and laughed, following in a tight pack.

Penny worked her new friends to the back, making Emery's part of the group take the lead. As he neared the next corner, he spotted a man tucked into an alcove on the other side of the street, scanning those who passed. From his vantage point, the man had a view of their street and the one beyond it, not nearly as busy as Bourbon Street, but still going strong as the evening rushed on.

The man's gaze followed a couple entwined in each other's arms. Emery ducked down enough to let the heeled height of the women provide him with cover. A moment later, the man was scanning the large group, lingering on exposed skin more than checking out faces. After finishing his halfhearted perusal, he shifted his gaze to another couple heading his way on his side of the street.

"Just up here, ladies," Emery said, getting them to cross kitty-corner. He met Penny's eye, and she jerked her head to the right; he nodded. "Okay, have a good night."

"Wait, what?" One of the girls scowled at him as he disentangled himself.

"No, wait," another said.

Still another didn't bother protesting. She just lunged for the goods. "Yes, *puh*-lease," she purred with a dopey smile.

He un-cupped a hand from an area it didn't belong. "Not cool, ladies," he muttered, slapping another hand away.

"Run," Penny said urgently, looking back the way they'd come.

He took off at her side, running straight for a space between two houses. Murky brown light filled the gap, only about five feet long before a fence halted their progress.

"Okay," she said, panting. Her halo dissolved, and his with it. "Do you think there's any chance we'll run across a natural?"

He thought it over, guessing what she was thinking—they needed a spell to conceal them, *now*—and starting the weave. "Doubtful. They won't have her running around the streets like a footman."

A few people glanced at Emery and Penny as they passed, stalling and looking at Emery's hands. They probably thought he was rolling a joint or something.

"Hurry, help," he said, trying to work as fast as he could.

She closed her eyes, and the electricity he'd grown to expect from working with her sparked across his body. Ducking her head, she began weaving a concealment spell completely different to the one she'd created on the fly in the Guild compound in Seattle.

"Stop," she said, her fingers stilling and her weave dissipating as she did so. "Start again."

He followed her direction, immediately seeing what she was doing.

Filling in the holes.

His weave was tight, organized, and uniform, but she worked more magic in between the fibers, creating a beautiful tapestry humming with power. She started messing with his weave as it was rolling out of his fingers, no longer filling in the holes, but working with him to make it stronger.

"A Lego house," she muttered. "It's easier to start from the ground up than it is to put a Lego in the hole after the house is built. You'd have to smash it first, and that would make the whole thing less structured."

The spell draped in front of them, creating a stationary wall and magically sheltering them from the curious eyes on the street. Giving them time to catch their breath.

"And now for one that'll move with us." She closed her eyes, magic drifting to her fingertips.

"This isn't how Guild members create a spell," he whispered, seeing her patterns and tweaking his to meld better.

The usual hum of their energy bubble intensified, and their joint spell fluxed and pulsed, morphing into something almost alive. The colors wound around and within each other in a breathtaking way, the patterns and textures not something even the finest artist could duplicate. Power vibrated along the weave and around them.

That wasn't what made him suck in a breath and blink his eyes open to stare at her in surprise.

The still air hung heavy around them, kissing his skin. The rough walls rose on either side of them, sending out a strange sort of pulse that didn't feel alive, but felt…*there*. Like he'd sense them even with his eyes closed. The blackened sky looked down on them, nearly ready to reveal the twinkling stars within. Over all of this, a sweet, intoxicating song drifted between and around them, pulling them together and connecting them in a way he'd never experienced before. It felt deep and complex and solid.

His heart swelled, and the ever-waging war within him, fueled by the pain, solitude, and death he'd experienced…calmed.

The corners of her mouth lifted. "This," she said, riding a sigh. "This feels exactly right. This is what I need. It feels so much better than when I worked with the witches in the cemetery." Her eyes drifted open, revealing her beautiful blue irises. "I've found my other half. My polar opposite." Her smile drifted higher. "My true balance."

"It feels…" He couldn't find the words. Didn't know if there even were any to describe the completeness he felt in that moment. The *one*ness.

Her gaze delved into him. In the past, he might've flinched away from that searching gaze. Closed himself off. Run. Instead, he wanted to reciprocate…wanted to look down all the way to her soul.

"This is what I feel like when I'm with you," she said softly, full of feeling. "This is why, no matter how long you stay away, I'll never forget how good it feels when you're around."

CHAPTER 37

THE SPELL DRIFTED around us, hugging us in its perfectly balanced hold, in time for his lips to crash down onto mine. For his arms to wrap around me tightly, squeezing me into his hard, warm body.

It wasn't the time. Not even remotely. And no matter how much I wanted to keep at this until our bodies were as intertwined as our magic, we needed to get out of this part of the city before the enemy finally surrounded us.

I loosened my grip on his waist, wondering if I'd have to zap him to get him to back up—if I'd have to zap myself first to make sure I followed through.

But before I could muster the resolve, he backed off, his palms sliding down my back.

"Sorry. Impulse control," he said, our breath mingling, heating the air between our lips.

"We need to go," I said softly, focused on those soft lips.

"I know."

"We need to get home safely." My gaze shifted back,

taking in the whole of his handsome face.

"I know." The weight of his hands felt too good on my hips.

My eyes met his. "So we can get to a bed and do this right."

His fingers dug in and his whole body stiffened. "That isn't helping, Turdswallop," he said through clenched teeth.

I chuckled. I couldn't help it.

I slapped a palm to his pec before roughly pushing him away. His eyes burned down into mine and he sucked air through his teeth. "That is also not helping," he said with a rough voice.

"Sorry. Impulse control." I forced myself to turn away, my body painfully wound up, and looked out at the street before us. The air shimmered with a soft violet, and I knew that was the spell working. "Okay, here's the plan. We can't hail a cab when invisible, and we can't step out of invisibility lest they see us. So basically, we need to get to a place they don't expect us to go, then call a cab to come to us."

I turned back to make sure he was on the same page.

He stood with his hand on the wall, bent slightly at the waist and leaning forward as if in horrible pain.

He gave me a thumbs-up. "Yup. Good. Just need one moment."

I shook my head, heat throbbing. “Men. So weak.”

“We just aren’t equipped to take on intoxicating women. Nature made sure you hold the ultimate power.”

“What a poor excuse for your insistence on thinking with your dick.”

He spat out a laugh before straightening up. “Are we running or walking?”

“Don’t know. It depends if any mage worth their salt is out here.” I held out my hand, and he took it. “Ready?”

“I wish we had a different life together.” His voice was dripping with regret and sadness. He obviously meant it.

But if this wasn’t the time to strip down and make this pounding ache go away, it certainly wasn’t the time for us to feel bad for ourselves.

“Then how would we have met? Chin up; let’s go.”

We stalked out of the gap between the houses—well, he stalked, I scooted.

Night swept down from the sky and dusted the sidewalk. The first bold star twinkled above, leading the way for the others. Someone screamed down the way, the sound quickly turning into peals of laughter. A woman chased a man across the street before stopping and turning back the way she’d come, bowing over with laughter.

"This way." I headed left, dodging and weaving between people coming our way. When the magic slid over their bodies, they frowned and looked around in confusion, some rubbing their arms and others shivering.

"I heard this place was full of ghosts," one of the people we passed said as she continued down the street.

"Let's pick up the pace," Emery whispered.

"Do you hear something?" a guy said, looking around.

Apparently the spell didn't suppress sound as thoroughly as I had hoped.

A woman wearing an orange sash around her neck stood at the next corner, scanning the way. A cord dropped from her ear and into her shirt. They weren't doing a great job of hiding what they were, let alone their rank.

Thinking on it, though, I'd only seen a couple of sashes. I wondered if that meant they'd hired out for most of their people.

Cold licked at my spine as I remembered Mary Bell at the bar earlier. How many others in Callie's camp hung out at bars stuffed with Guild members? How many had accepted promises?

I turned, forgetting to tell Emery. Since he was way heavier, the spell yanked me back toward him and I bounced off him. "Sorry. I wanted to go that way." I pointed.

"Where are we going?" Emery asked before jolting.

I felt it a second later. A searching-type spell had ballooned over the street before dropping on us like rain.

He swore and zipped off a spell, but it only blew a hole through a small part of the searching spell. The rest didn't fizzle away, only curled back a little, landing on the edge of our bubble and burning bright red.

"What are the odds that they won't see that?" I asked as a shock of fear coursed through me.

"Run, Penny! Run!"

With the soundtrack from *Forrest Gump* rolling through my head, we took off. The Guild woman slapped a hand to her ear and yelled something into her other wrist. People startled and pointed at the flare of red zipping at them, seemingly disconnected to anything else. Some hurried out of the way, and others watched with wide eyes until it washed over their bodies with a ghostlike zing of energy.

A busy street lay up ahead, two lanes of cars in each direction flying past. Beyond it was a green area with looming trees and wild bushes. An old cemetery, a tourist attraction, was down that way, leading into a rougher part of town.

It was probably safer than where we were.

"Hit that park. Let's lose them in the night." Emery

didn't turn left or right to look for a crosswalk. With a firm hold on my wrist, he stopped for a moment to survey the cars, then pulled me forward.

"Wha—eeiiii?" I let out a squeal, panic stealing my motor skills, and was half dragged across the pavement. A car zipped past our backs, swerving away from the splash of red on our bubble, which was now dying down. Another almost hit us in a head-on collision before Emery yanked me forward, pulling me onto the concrete divider in the middle of the street.

"Are you insane?" I asked through the fear chattering my teeth.

"That's how you cross the street in a great many third-world countries," he said without apology.

"They're all on the same page in those countries. Cars can see you in those countries. You're going to get us—No!"

He yanked me out again, stopping a little beyond the white line, somehow knowing the car would see the fading red light, swerve, and bump the curb before correcting too much and nearly catching us. The car in the other lane swerved the other way, reacting to the first car.

Before I could yell a profanity that was sorely deserved, he'd yanked us across and was running, towing me like a boat on a trailer.

"You're out of your mind," I said, barely keeping up

with the adrenaline trying to lock my knees. "We're in a fight right now. I know you're just back, and this should be the honeymoon period or whatever, but we're fighting."

"Thanks for the warning." He pulled us onto a wooded path and then into the trees as a spell streamed past us. It hit a bush and blasted outward in a rainbow of color, very pretty, given that it could have put a hole in our backs. "Hurry."

Shouts sounded from all around us. I looked back to find more than a dozen people trying to get across the street, half of them running for the crosswalk. A stray brown dog had joined in the melee, scampering across the street with the first group of mages.

Honks drowned out the dog's playful bark. Drivers yelled out their windows at the mages forcing their way across the street.

Bushes stole my view and I blinked in confusion.

My brain had gone offline.

"Okay. No biggie. We're alive." I wrestled past the fear and pushed forward, easing my tense grip on Emery's arm.

Trap. Maim.

Someone was in the overgrown, wild park with us, waiting idly with a spell nearly at the ready. I'd felt the same thing in the Quarter. They used the ingredients to call the spell to life over and over again, letting it dissipate at the last moment. Ready to fling should they see us.

Why not just put the spells in casings?

Like I'd done in the Quarter, I pulled Emery away from the feeling, not even seeing the mage this time, but knowing they were somewhere in that mess of foliage off to the right.

After a short jog, he slowed and shook his head, pulling me a different direction. His breathing quickened as he slowed again, looking back the way we'd just come. "What was wrong back there?"

"A mage lying in wait," I said.

I could barely see the troubled expression cross his face in the soft moonlight. "We can't go these other ways," he whispered. "They have something like wards set up. I don't understand why we can't fight through them—I just know we won't. One of us, in each scenario, will die." He shook his head. "I didn't get any flashes the other way. Maybe that was because you steered us away, but we should try—"

Find.

Magic ballooned into the sky before raining down again. I weaved a spell, working within my desire to keep us hidden. Emery shot off a different spell, then another, burning bigger holes in our concealment spell each time.

I let mine loose, rising to meet the spell falling

down. When they touched, a smear of blue blazed above us. Our concealment spell disintegrated.

"Crap," I whispered. "That didn't work."

Emery grabbed my hand. "Come on—"

He barely made it two steps. Shouts and yells preceded a dozen people crashing out of the dark foliage looming around us. Someone hopped up onto the lip of a dry fountain, ingredients in his or her hands. At the distance and in the oily darkness, all I could see was a shape.

"Call Darius," Emery said, turning his back to me. "Quickly."

"Come out, come out, where ever you are," the person on the fountain said in a scratchy voice. "Or is it 'ready or not, here I come'? Either way, your hiding is at an end."

I navigated my crappy phone with a shaking hand. If we made it out of this alive, I was definitely going to cave and get a smart phone. This was the last straw.

"After the call, get ready to throw out the nastiest spells you have, Penny," Emery said in a low tone, viciousness ringing in his voice. "We have the power scale on our side."

"I'm not at all sure that is true, especially considering how many casings we have at our disposal," Scratchy Voice said. "And don't trouble yourself with your vampire friends. We've made a few vampire friends of our own. They think working *with* the Guild is a better business arrangement than working *against* us. They want a piece of Seattle, you see. And Durant holds the monopoly. Through us, they can turn the tide of power. With them, we can rid ourselves of the shifters, and have a monopoly of our own. You see? A smart alliance will yield the greatest results."

Ten of them, tightening their circle around us. All held ingredients in their hands and had magic writhing in their grasp.

"Unless you have Vlad on your side, and I doubt he would openly go against Durant, you lot are the biggest group of idiots I've ever encountered," Emery said, his tone much lighter than the situation seemed to warrant. "And I have encountered a *lot* of idiots."

The brown dog skittered out from a bush and turned to the side, staring at us as though wondering what we were doing. The thing had a terrible understanding of impending danger, hanging around here.

"There isn't even a voicemail box," I said, checking to make sure I'd dialed the correct number.

A huge well of magic rose up around us.

We could build a Lego house, but they were constructing a village. Several pieces of an enormous whole were about to come together.

With the intent to lock us in the middle.

"Give them everything you have, Penny," Emery

said, and I could hear the worry in his voice.

Without help, he didn't think we could make it out of here.

CHAPTER 38

I DROPPED THE phone, no time to spare. The little dog scattered, finally, and I wished I could go with him.

In hurried movements, I dug out the power stones and tossed them on the ground as streams of magic rose from all around us, zooming toward Emery. My collection of raw power hovered above me, as usual when I was upset or in the midst of a battle, and I tore the elements down in harried clumps, thinking of the poor dummy in Reagan's yard, which had taken so much abuse these last few days.

As if on cue, the spells we'd practiced rolled through my memory—the feeling of them, the intent behind them, and a new way to balance them. Not thinking, just reacting, I focused on what needed to be done, trusting in Emery, our balanced bubble, and my knowledge to have my back.

A spell blasted out from him, smacking one of the mages. She screamed, a high-pitched sound, and dropped to the ground, clawing at her chest. I let loose one of the nastier spells the poor dummy had suffered, feeding it power as it rose into a whirlwind before darting forward and slapping the mage directly in front of me with a series of magical razor blades.

Three people ran in from the messy park path, all mages with satchels open and casings in their hands.

"Faster, Penny," Emery said, zipping off another spell.

Breathing deeply, I pulled power from Mr. Happy-Go-Lucky, weaving and mixing in jerky movements, trying to work faster.

Emery let off a spell, which hit its target, but two more mages ran in to take the place of the fallen.

Another weave was ready, this one downright vicious, and I flung it out, waving my hands through the air as I did so, remembering the underlined directions in the spell book.

The magic wrapped around the three intended mages before invisible spikes punched holes in their bodies. Screams turned to gurgles as they sank to the ground.

I worked on another, not pausing, as still more people crowded into the clearing, one wearing a leather duster and stupid hat. A mercenary.

Emery fired off spells faster now, sacrificing complexity for speed. Mages fell, and the looming spell around us wobbled before stabilizing, more hands present to keep it alive. To finish it…

A spell from a casing streamed toward me. I caught and countered it easily, but it cost me the spell I'd been making.

Mr. Happy-Go-Lucky pulsed in impatience. The other rocks added their chorus, but I found it very strange that Mr. Happy-Go-Lucky, usually such a happy fellow, should start a mutiny. When I got out of this mess, I was going to send it on a ride with the safest person I could find. That would piss it off.

Mages stood in a zigzagging line in front of us. One took a step forward, trying to find his way into the haphazard circle around us. Most of them stood ten feet away, working their magic. No one charged. No one had to fight from over their shoulders. No one had a weapon besides magic.

Briefly, an image of Reagan popped into my head. It seemed like a lifetime ago, but she'd brought a gun to a magic fight in that decrepit old stone church.

Still not thinking (Reagan's training had finally seeped in), I was running at them with bared teeth and a very human and probably stupid growl.

"Penny!" I heard Emery yell.

The mage in front of me froze, his eyes wide, his spell dissipating on his fingers. Then I was on him, punching him in the face then pulling up my foot and slamming it into the side of his knee. Cartilage cracked and he screamed before I moved on to the next mage.

It took a special person to do magic while they were being throttled. Or so Reagan had said. Hopefully she'd been right and I was just as abnormal in this as I was everywhere else in my life.

I flung a grisly spell over my shoulder, one I'd used on her dozens of times. Unlike Reagan, the mage didn't unravel the weave before the spell struck. It splashed him with skin-eating magic, ripping out lumps in his face and tearing through clothes and skin on his body.

I didn't have time for a gurgling stomach. Upchucking at how gross it was would have to wait.

The next mage got a boot to the face, not fast enough to block my attack. Emery downed another mage, and my next spell took out two more. But more kept coming. We were kicking ass, but their overall numbers had barely dwindled. And most likely *would* barely dwindle until we were captured. They'd known where we were, and they'd been prepared.

"We need a Hail Mary," I yelled, jabbing my fingers in the next mage's eye. "Or to run."

Emery countered a spell from a casing before firing off one of his own. Another spell came at us, then another. He countered one, threw up a screen made with his survival magic to stop another, and surged forward. His fist smashed into the nearest mage's face, doing damage much more quickly than if I'd made the hit. He executed a perfect side kick Reagan would be proud of, dropping another mage like a stone before darting between two more and blasting them at close range with a spell.

My heart dropped when two more mages ran down the path, followed by another from the other direction.

There were just too many.

"We have to run," I yelled, hitting two with another nasty spell. I didn't worry about balancing my weaves. About finessing them. There wasn't time. I zipped them off as soon as they were done. Thankfully, my power was so much stronger than most of these mages that it was enough to hold them off.

Lord help me if they brought in powerful mages.

"Emery, we have to run!" I repeated. He wasn't answering me, and I suddenly realized why. He'd seen it earlier. There was nowhere to go. They'd completely rigged this area with traps and used themselves as bait. They must've had people stationed around the various exit points of the Quarter at the ready, just like the ones stationed inside the Quarter itself, their spells at the ready. That larger spell split into perfect little pieces.

The Guild had figured out how to combat the unpredictable.

"You run, Penny," I barely heard as Emery threw a smaller man into a larger. They both went down. "You run. Back the way we came. Call for help. Come for me, if you can."

My heart tore a hole in my chest. It lodged into my throat and choked me.

I'd only just gotten him back. Was I going to lose him again so soon?

"No," I said, the next spell ripping through someone's middle. "No!"

"Penny—" Emery started, intent on talking sense—even though we both knew he was bound to fail miserably—but a deep, earthshaking roar drowned him out.

The sound worked through my middle and froze my blood, the fear it caused primal and ancient. My movements slowed and my eyes widened. I couldn't help but look for the source of the sound. Only Emery kept working, firing off spells as fast as ever, taking advantage of everyone else's distraction.

Another roar, this time closer, made my teeth chatter. I backed up without being able to help it, envisioning a huge, lethal predator tearing through the bushes with its mouth gaping and teeth bared.

A moment later, that was exactly what happened.

A giant lion, larger than the ones that roamed the modern plains of Africa, surged into the scene with feline grace. It gave a loud grunt, blowing out of its nostrils, before pausing to stare at the mostly immobile group before it. Its huge, shaggy head swept from one side to the other, taking everything in.

The little dog from before scurried out from behind

the great lion and headed off to the side, pausing to take everything in.

A few of the mages stepped away, unsure. Still more stood and stared with open mouths, like I was doing, taken aback by the sight of a big jungle cat within the city limits.

My brain shuddered to a start.

Big cat.

Shifter.

"Help!" I called into the uneasy silence, not at all embarrassed about freaking out.

Like a starter gun had been fired, the scene burst with activity again. Mages cracked casings and shot them at Emery, me, or the lion.

Wolves burst out of the foliage around us, synchronized and deadly as they began their attack. Vicious growls cut through the shouts and screaming. Wolf bodies slammed into mages. Teeth found jugulars.

Another roar, deep and powerful, and a large shape emerged from behind the fountain and lumbered into the mix, a giant bear.

"Work, Penny," Emery shouted, grabbing a mage who had come out of his stupor and tried to run for it. "If they get away, they'll try again another day."

"Why are you rhyming at a time like this?" I blasted a mage making a run for it. He lost use of his legs…because I'd made him leave them behind.

Gagging, I used my rodent zapper on another, and a half-assed spell on one more, trying to get the spells out faster again.

The lion burst into the remaining mages. It swept a large paw across human bodies, opening gashes through their middles. He clamped his teeth on a mage's shoulder and the side of her throat before ripping her head off, ending the haggard screaming.

The bear roared and stood on its back legs, swiping its claw as someone readied a spell.

The mages broke, sprinting for cover. The wolves were on it. Faster on four legs, and with the added benefit of improved sight in the darkness, they jumped onto the retreating figures, forcing them to the ground and ripping at their vital organs. Screaming and groaning mixed in with the growls and roars. Limbs flailed. Chaos reigned.

I danced from side to side, ready to help. Ready to shoot off another spell. But furry bodies kept obscuring my view. Then, in a matter of minutes, it was all over. The noise died down. The movement slowed.

My panting was unnaturally loud as I stood next to Emery, in the center of a disastrous circle filled with blood, bodies, and keyed-up animals.

My stomach finally gave out and I heaved. It wasn't the most professional thing to do, admittedly, but I could no longer help it.

"Penny." Emery wrapped his arms around me rather than holding my hair back, as befitted the situation. "Are you okay?"

"I'm okay." I wiped my mouth and pushed him so we could back away. "You?"

His breath dusted my face. "Yeah. Got a couple scrapes and bruises, but yeah."

Waves of magic pushed at me, and I knew by feel that it was the shifters' magic I was feeling. The space was no longer occupied by a bunch of downed mages and animals. Now it held mages and naked people.

"Uh-huh." I dropped my forehead to Emery's shoulder. At least I wasn't the only one stuck looking unprofessional after a battle.

Someone grunted, and I couldn't help but look. Steve, previously the lion, stretched in the moonlight before scratching his chest and dropping his hands to his sides in fatigue. "Two back-to-back changes will really take it out of you. Least you could've done was leave a few more for us."

Emery pulled one of his arms from around me and stepped forward, dragging me with him. He reached out to shake. "Thanks a million. We were getting buried. You turned the tide."

Steve, completely unconcerned with his lack of cover, thrust his hand into Emery's. "Not at all, mate. We would've been here sooner, but we ran into some sort of magical wall. Lost one of ours trying to get through it."

"Oh no, I'm so sorry!" I said.

"Nah." Steve waved my sentiments away. "He was an asshole. A real know-it-all. That's why I sent him first. Don't tell Trixie, though. She didn't like him much, either, but he was good in bed, apparently."

I was pretty sure my face was frozen in a very strange look. I didn't know where to go from there.

"Anyway." Steve glanced around the ground and clucked his tongue as more men and women, all equally as unworried about the state of their undress, slowly made their way in our direction. "Red said they stole Reagan's car and chased you two to this area."

"How would Red know all of that?" I asked suspiciously.

Steve gestured toward the dog still off to the side, watching from a distance. "He followed you. He might only be a dog, but it gives him the ability to make more changes than the normal shifter without depleting his energy level."

"But…we were invisible." I remembered how the shifters outside the bar had sniffed me out the other night. "Ah. He followed our scent trail. But how'd he let you know?"

"Right? I told him, he needs to carry a little doggy fanny pack for a cell phone. He could be Reagan's sidekick." Steve boomed out laughter. Red lowered his head and snarled. "Yeah," Steve said, "he didn't think that was funny. But he's got phones stashed around the city. Following and reporting is his job. He has to have a way to report. So when he saw what was going on here, he called me up."

"And Reagan?"

"Is busy with the vampire. She's apparently got a thing going with that elder." Steve wiped his lip with his thumb and shook his head. "I didn't expect that, I'm not going to lie. No one tells me anything. I mean, I get the sex appeal, but he's a vampire. You should never trust vampires." Emery and I nodded knowingly. "They're questioning the mages. The vampire took all the live ones before Roger could get back to us."

"They didn't think this was more important?"

"We don't work with vampires, love. They do their thing, we do ours."

"They didn't tell Reagan," Emery said softly, his tone even. I couldn't tell if he was making a judgment or not.

"Didn't need to, did we?" Steve smiled. "Don't get me wrong, if she wasn't with that elder, we surely would've let her in on the fun. But as it was…" He spread his hands. "Roger sends his regards. He was happy to help, and he hopes you keep this situation in mind should we ever need something."

"Ah. A forced trade." I rubbed my eyes, not really

able to deal with this right now. "And how are the vampires so different from the shifters?"

Emery huffed out a humorless laugh as Steve said, "That's not very nice. For one, we're cuddly when we change. Much furrier and nicer to look at."

"That's true, though I doubt you smell any better when you get wet," I said.

Emery choked on his laugh this time, half turning away to wheeze out more guffaws.

A flare of green followed by a wave of shifter magic, weak in power, preceded the dog's alteration into a thin, lanky Red. He stood and quickly cupped his privates, thankfully worried about propriety. "I told him not telling Reagan was a mistake," Red said with a know-it-all air. "She's going to be pissed."

"Women are always pissed about something." Steve glanced down, and I followed his gaze before I could stop myself, only to instantly shift it when I got an eyeful. "I better get going. The cold isn't kind to my bells and tackle."

"She's not an ordinary woman," Red muttered. "I'm not going to take the fall for this. I'm going to tell her it was your call."

Steve hooked a thumb Red's way, his smile almost infectious. "He's awfully jittery, isn't he?"

A younger guy wearing basketball sweats with buttons down the pant leg for easy removal jogged over and handed Steve a pile of sweats.

"Hey, is anyone driving?" Emery asked, looking around.

"Yeah, you need a lift?" Steve rolled back on his bare heels as he shook out the hoodie. "Of course you need a lift, what am I saying. Sorry about that. I'm always a little slow after fast changes. Come on, we'll get you wherever you need to go."

"But what about..." I pointed at the fallout of the battle.

"We'll get someone on that," Steve said. "We'll use a cleanup service and bill the vampires." Steve laughed again, though I didn't get the joke.

Fatigue dragged at me after I collected my stones and phone. Emery slipped his hand into mine. Softly, he asked, "Can I stay with you tonight?"

I leaned against his arm. "Yes. Reagan can deal. We need to stick together."

"I agree. This was only the force they had stationed in this part of New Orleans. We'd be naive to think they aren't gathering in a temporary headquarters somewhere. They'll have more. The question is, how many more?"

Red drifted in next to us. "That's what I would have told Reagan if she hadn't stood me up. In addition to calling in big numbers, I've heard that they are hiring anyone willing to work for them." He glanced around warily. "If you ask me, they know what they're up against, and they're rising to the challenge. You might be more powerful, but they have the numbers."

CHAPTER 39

After one of the shifters dropped us off at Reagan's house and we took a slow, touchy-feely shower, Emery and I sat at the kitchen table, staring at my phone.

I'd called my mother. She hadn't answered, but a reckoning was coming.

Up until that point, she'd assumed everything was fine. That I was busy training, we hadn't seen hide nor hair of the Guild (which had been mostly true up until recently), and life was bumping along. I wasn't a good liar, but luckily, Veronica, Callie, and Dizzy were excellent. When I accidentally set off alarm bells, they covered for me beautifully.

Well, I was about to ring the alarm gong. We needed help that only my mother could (hopefully) provide.

She was going to be so pissed.

My phone vibrated against the table.

I glanced up at the clock on the oven. Eight-oh-three. Fifteen minutes after I'd called. Fifteen minutes before she had to get her popcorn and TV ready for her favorite show.

Hopefully, she hadn't figured out how to work the DVR, and the conversation had an expiration date.

Emery nodded slowly, offering support. I could see my wariness mirrored in his eyes. He'd met my mother. He knew the score.

I picked up the phone with chin held high and pursed my lips, ignoring my shaking hand. I opened it, then wiped away the dirt that showered the table top.

"Hello?" I asked in a calm, steady voice.

"No, you may not marry that boy. I don't care that he came back; you barely know him. And while we're on the subject, no, you may not *live* with that boy. He is to stay in his own residence until you have *dated* him for at least a year, do you understand me? Are you practicing safe sex? You're not stupid, so I assume you are. But do you remember the talk we had? Sex is not the same thing as porn. Those are different. You need to show him what—"

"Mother, Mother, *Mother*!" I leaned back in my chair, immediately rattled. "Would you stop? What are you—How—"

I had to stop and regroup. All I'd been through, and this woman could shake me up like a canned soda.

"I know he is back. Is he sitting there with you? Don't get me wrong, he's a nice boy, but Penny, he is much more experienced than you. You need to—"

“Mother! That is not why I’m calling.”

“It might not be why you’re calling, but it is certainly an issue. Let me talk to him.”

“No. No! Listen…” I put my hand up to stall her, as though she were in the room. “Listen. I’m in a bit of a pickle, and we need some advice.”

Silence filled the line briefly. “Fine. We’ll table that discussion for now. What’s up?”

I took a deep breath, not really sure where to start. “I’m going to put you on speaker. Can you be normal for just a few minutes?”

“Penelope Bristol, I am your mother. You should know that I do not have an ounce of *normal* in my body.”

Why did she make things so very difficult?

“Fine.” I pushed the speaker button and put the phone in between Emery and me. “I’m here with Emery.”

Silence.

That was better than talking.

“We are sitting within an extremely thorough ward that not even a large force can break through,” I started. “But it isn’t at the Bankses’ house.”

I grimaced, waiting for the other shoe to drop.

Still silence.

That was no longer better than talking. It meant she was saving up her aggression for a big blow.

"I've been staying with Reagan, who is extremely knowledgeable and powerful." I waited for something. Nothing came. "Callie and Dizzy's training wasn't working, so Darius took over. Not the training, but the managing of it. He hasn't really organized any details yet because there was an issue with some vampires at his house and he's a bit tied up. So I'm kind of stuck with Reagan, although she has proved an excellent teacher. I've come very far. I'm not fast enough yet, especially in a battle, but I'm much better. Control-wise, anyway. I'm really coming along."

The silence stretched.

This was really not good.

"And, through a spur-of-the-moment accidental marooning in the French Quarter, we *may* have, accidentally, taken out a favor with the shifters to avoid getting captured by the Mages' Guild."

More silence.

"And so…I called you," I finished lamely.

"I see," she said after another pause. "Anything else?"

"Oh! I kind of went against Callie and Dizzy's wishes and chased down, then captured, a banshee. I was only in danger for a very brief period of time, so I really think that's a non-issue." I swallowed audibly. "In the grand scheme of things, I mean."

"I see," she said much more slowly. "And does that

boy have anything to say for himself?"

Emery cleared his throat and leaned forward a little. "I accept whatever punishment you choose to level on me, but I love your daughter. I'm just trying to do right by her in any way I can."

Adrenaline washed through my body, sending jitters and tingles and cold and hot racing through me all at once. I gripped his arm and turned toward him, tears fogging my eyes and heat soaking my heart. I'd opened my mouth to tell him how I felt—even more deeply than when I'd first told him—when the front door crashed open.

Metal squealed as it tore from the frame. Screws flew, hit the ground, and rolled away. The wood crashed against the wall before tumbling into the entryway.

"What was that?" my mother yelled.

Emery was already up on his feet with a spell in front of him, ready to throw.

I stayed in my seat, knowing that it was best to give Reagan a lot of room when her dander was up.

"What the fuck are you doing?" I heard Reagan ask, her heavy boots treading over the door she had just kicked in. Her own door. But not the original door, oh no. It had been replaced a time or two before this, if Mikey next door could be believed. He'd proved surprisingly chatty after our not-so-great first meeting.

Fire exploded between Emery's hands, wiping out

his spell. He back-pedaled, his eyes wide.

"Don't bother," I told Emery, turning back toward the phone. "You won't win. Best case, you'll get a kick in the face and a *move*."

"She would know," Reagan said in a rough voice filled with anger. "Why in the holy fuck didn't you—"

"Do you live in a barn?" my mother hollered through the phone.

Reagan paused with a confused expression, standing in the archway of the kitchen.

"This has gotten out of hand," my mother continued into the silence, taking control via the phone despite sitting half a country away. It was her superpower. "Sit down, all of you. How many are there, just the three, now? Or is that accursed vampire hanging around in the background as well?"

Reagan cocked her head, then lifted her eyebrows at us. Emery and I stared at her silently, waiting for her to answer my mother's question. We both knew there was no sense trying to play mediator. She'd just tell us to shut it so Reagan could answer.

"Darius is at his house in the Quarter," she said, stepping closer and looking down at the phone. "He is dealing with some issues there."

"Is one of them answering his phone?" I muttered.

"Penelope Bristol, if you have something to say, you say it so everyone can hear it," my mother badgered.

I picked at my nail as Reagan cocked her head the other way, taking another step closer. It was like she was hearing a dog whistle.

"It's just, we were in trouble, and I couldn't even leave a voicemail for him," I said, trying not to be sulky, and failing. Old habits, as they said.

"We'll get to that," my mother said. "Reagan, honey, have a seat and let's talk about this sensibly."

Reagan, who usually hated terms of endearment from strangers, moved as though in a trance to an open seat, looking mildly confused and a little delighted.

"Emery, you might…close the door," I said, glancing back at the entryway where part of it was in view, splayed on the ground. "Or maybe just prop it up so the whole neighborhood isn't peeking in."

"While he does that," my mother said, not asking about it, as though propping up kicked-in doors was a normal occurrence, "let's go over this again, shall we? Let's start with the change in your training."

A half-hour later, after helping walk my mom through setting up the DVR, which really shouldn't have been so hard, she was mostly caught up on the broad strokes of the situation, plus a few details. Other details she'd already known from randomly using her various *Seer* abilities to check on me.

Turned out she'd known all along about the larger milestones of my journey in New Orleans, but in an effort to stay true to her word, she had stayed out of it, letting me get a grip on my own. I was, quite frankly, gobsmacked by her self-restraint.

Gobsmacked.

"So you are now in league with vampires and shifters," my mother said in a disapproving voice.

"Join the club," Reagan muttered.

"Young lady, if you have something to say, say it loud enough for us all to hear."

Reagan frowned at the phone and, amazingly, entwined her fingers in front of her and hunched forward a little. "Darius's phone disappeared earlier this evening, right about the time Penny must have called. He already has a new one. It seemed like a minor issue until he learned of the…coincidence in timing."

"Only dimwitted fools believe in coincidences," my mother said.

"Right." Reagan nodded. "I would not have thought it possible, but clearly they have someone on the inside. Vampires. It seems the Mages' Guild has made alliances of their own, and they are, in essence, taking on Darius. For him not to have seen this before now… It's surprising. He's really slipping."

Rustling filled the phone, probably the sound of my mother shifting. "Even elders can get complacent as time progresses. Things go moderately smoothly for a few hundred years, and they get into a rhythm. This little shake-up will be good for him. It'll sharpen his edges. We need that going forward. I hate to say it, but he's a strong ally. It'd be better to have him with us than against us."

"He'll stay with me, and I'll stay with Penny. That's a certainty," Reagan said with a gravity to her words that squished my heart. She wasn't in league with many people. That she would cast her lot with me, when I was at the heart of a boatload of danger, really spoke volumes about her loyalty.

I smiled at her and touched her forearm.

"No." She shook me off. "Don't get weepy. It's gross."

We dealt with touching moments in different ways.

"Fine," my mother said. "The question we need answered is what to do now." Movement sounded in the background.

"Darius thinks—"

Emery held up his hand to stall Reagan. He shook his head. "She is one of the most gifted *Seers* I've ever come across. Wait to hear what she has to say. She was integral in keeping us alive in Seattle."

Reagan's lips downturned and she pulled her chair closer. "Really? Neat. I've only come across a few decent tarot readers. All assholes. So this fits."

I stared at the phone wide-eyed, wondering if my mom would retort. When she didn't, I let out a breath. I really didn't want to see the two butt heads. That would probably make my life hell.

"Did you get anything much out of the mages?" I asked quietly, not wanting to disturb whatever my mother was doing.

Reagan pulled her gaze up from the phone. "Sadly, no. A couple were hired from different areas of the country. They answered an ad, of all things. I also talked to Red. Well..." She put her elbows on the table. "I kicked him around the place, actually, when I found out he knew you were in trouble and didn't tell me." Her jaw clenched. "We're having a rift in our friendship, he and I."

"That's probably better for him," I said. She gave me a blank stare. "That you stay away, I mean. You scare him, I think."

Emery chuckled helplessly, bending over his clasped hands, his body shaking. The guy could find a joke in anything.

Reagan's smile gave me nervous shivers. "No. It is not better for him."

"What he said about the Guild bringing in people was true, then?" Emery asked with a lopsided smile.

Reagan blew out a breath and sat back. "They know what they're up against. And I'm not talking about two powerful naturals. I'm talking about a rogue mage with no friends, a newbie with no clue, an easily infiltrated ragtag crew of New Orleans magical social drinkers, vampires that can't help in the daytime, and shifters that aren't totally sure they want to fully engage in a full-out magical battle. We're all over the place. Our side is a mess. We—and I really mean you two—stirred up the hornets' nest without any plan. And yes, sure, we thought the New Orleans contingent was a decrepit, disorganized faction, fat and happy. But *surprise*, they're not. So now we have to figure out how to bail ourselves out. Do we go guerilla and plan lots of little, stealthy attacks? Do we…" She rubbed her hands over her face. "That's actually all I have. I don't even know what we do. And given how much Darius has screwed up lately, I don't trust anything he said. So forget that I was going to offer advice."

I stared at my empty hands and thought about getting a drink, but then thought better of it when I remembered the excessively strong drinks Reagan would likely force on us.

Through the crappy phone speaker, in a slightly tinny, haunted voice, my mother said:

"Her path has been set. Her journey is in motion. He will complete the pyramid of power. The curse breaker will join the oath takers and forge a bond in blood. It is in this union that the way forward shall be writ. That they shall learn their highest level of power, and hold the kingdom from falling."

CHAPTER 40

I LOOKED BETWEEN Reagan and Emery. Emery studied me. Reagan cocked her head, staring at the phone.

"Right, but what *is* a curse breaker? I mean, besides it being me," Reagan said. "No one seems to know."

"Do you know what it means?" I asked her.

"No. That's the thing with *Seer* types. They give you all these windy answers that could mean eight different things. Then some traumatic thing happens that you wish you could've gotten a heads up on, and the *Seer* says, 'See? I told you that would happen.' It's annoying. Too bad your mom is no different."

"I beg your pardon?" My mother's voice was weak.

"While I don't totally disagree," Emery said softly, "Ms. Bristol is the genuine article. I imagine we are meant to be together—"

"Well la-dee-dah," Reagan said, getting up and heading to the cabinet that held the whiskey. Something was clearly troubling her.

"—and that foretelling was hinting at future events."

"What'd I say?" my mother asked. I could hear distinct clicking and figured she must've brought out the tape recorder, something she'd done in the past when she hadn't had (or hadn't trusted) her audience.

"I work alone," Reagan said.

"I think we could tell that by the fix my daughter and her male *friend* got up to this evening, yes. So much for you sticking with Penny through thick and thin." My mother's voice sounded on the tape recorder and we heard the message again. "Huh."

"See?" Reagan pointed at the phone.

"No, that doesn't help you now. That bears some reflection. Important, though. Let me reduce my scope, see if it gets us more information." My mother sighed. "Back to the grindstone."

Reagan unscrewed the cap. "Penny? Drink?"

"Water. Without the tequila or lime."

Reagan frowned at me. "I don't carry that."

"I'll get it." Emery rose from the chair.

"And by the way, we're not in a kingdom right now." Reagan pointed at the floor. "We're in the Brink. There are two other kingdoms, and I won't be helping you keep either of them from falling."

Emery startled and stared pointedly at Reagan.

Once again, my mother's haunted and distant voice came through the speaker. "The bonds of sisterhood have formed. Your unique circle has been set. Now you must harness the power of the underworld."

"Come *on*." Reagan braced against the counter and sagged, dropping her head. "Why did I have to get involved? *Why?*"

Emery was still studying her. "'You need the boss of the boss. He'll connect you to the highest level of power in the underworld.'" His eyes met mine. "Isn't that the text your mother sent that one time? In Seattle? Remember, when we were trying to connect with Clyde in the hotel? We needed to get to Darius, instead. Clyde's boss. Because Darius…is connected to Reagan."

"Snitches get stitches," Reagan said, wild-eyed. "I don't care how old she is."

"I'm old enough to ring your bell," my mother said.

"Mother, would you relax?" I rolled my eyes.

"That boy has a dynamite memory, I'll say that much," my mother said. "He is still not moving in with you, Penelope Bristol."

If only I could hang up on her.

"It can't be," Emery whispered. He leaned against the counter, bending a little to try and see Reagan's face. "A few months back, I heard there was a disturbance of some kind in the underworld. There was a rumor of a mage and a vampire down there. Word is Lucifer himself plans to look into it. It wasn't a mage at all, was it?"

"You should stop gossiping around the water cooler," Reagan said, not looking at him.

"What did she say?" My mother's voice was muffled.

"Those weren't rumors." Emery crossed his arms over his chest, shaking his head. Awe crossed his expression.

"What's happening?" my mother asked.

"Mother, would you stop?"

"But what's happening?"

"Emery is piecing together a secret that could get him killed in the next three seconds." Reagan still didn't straighten, but her body had gone a worrying sort of relaxed. Not resting relaxed, crouching-tiger-hidden-knife relaxed.

"Why does it matter, though?" I asked, completely dumbfounded. "We know she has a ton of power. What changes?"

"Yeah, Emery?" Reagan said in a dangerous voice. "What changes?"

He stared at her for a long moment. Pressure filled the room.

"I feel cheated," he murmured, scratching his chin. Reagan's head snapped up. I could tell she was as confused as I was. "I could've figured that out on my own. I had all the clues. They were all right in front of me. Even your magic. Penny stole it when you were practicing in the warehouse, right? *Incendium* and *glaciem* magic—fire and ice. I've seen each of those used before. With a little downtime, I would've figured it out sooner, I know I would've. I haven't seen both of those powers used together before, of course—that's something only Lucifer and his heirs can do, or so the legends go. I would've realized that, too." He shook his head, narrowing his eyes at Reagan. "I definitely would've figured out your secret on my own. I was cheated the opportunity." He clucked his tongue, as if it were her fault, and turned back to the cabinet.

And just like that, the bubble of expectation popped. A breath I didn't know I'd been holding released.

"Both of you are crazy," Reagan said, now watching him.

"In answer to your question"—Emery took down two glasses—"aside from a question/answer segment, nothing changes. Who would I tell? I'm in exile. I have no friends, other than Penny and a couple of shifters that want no business with politics, and apparently we have a foretelling pinned to our collective heads. Penny and I could use the help, quite frankly."

"I still don't understand what's happening," I admitted, feeling even more dunce-like and out of touch than usual. Could Emery really be saying Reagan was an heir to *Lucifer*?

Emery filled the glasses with water and headed back

to the table, glancing at Reagan as he passed her. He sat down next to me. "We have an ace in the hole, that's what's happening. And if I'm reading the situation right, and if the rumors are true—which I had scarcely believed, because they were *so* far-fetched and told to me by gamblers and thieves in the Realm—if she helps us, we can't let anyone get away to share the tale." He placed a glass of water in front of me, looking at Reagan. "You really went down there?"

She poured herself a generous helping of whiskey. "Yes. And while this was probably inevitable, it's not sitting well that another person is in on this secret."

"Tell me." Emery leaned forward. "Were there dragons?"

Her lips didn't move, but her eyes glimmered. "I'm not telling. You'll have to go down and see for yourself."

"I can't. I don't have any demon in me." He sipped his water, his eyes hungry.

Now a smile did break through. "Darius knows you well, I'll give him that. What mischief-maker wouldn't want to tour a place he isn't supposed to go?" She shook her head with a sly smile. "You'd better be careful. He thinks you're integral to getting his people in."

"Me?" Surprise flitted through his eyes.

"You and your brother played that trick in the Realm, right? Pissed off the elves with your illusion?" He nodded slowly, pain sparking in his eyes at the mention of his brother. Reagan nodded. "Then yes, you. There's a wall set up down there. That's what keeps people out. Take down the wall, and in ye git."

Emery blew out a breath and his gaze fell on me. His eyes softened. "Probably a challenge for a different life."

"Yeah, right." Reagan took another sip of her whiskey. "Point Penny in the right direction, tell her it'll be fine, and let her bumble around until the whole place is in an uproar. She'll do great."

"I've gotten better," I mumbled, shaking my head. "So…you have power from the underworld?"

"Yes," she said. "A lot of it. And I can do things neither of you can even imagine."

"And *that* is what you need to take to this fight," my mother chimed in, amazingly silent up until this point. "The three of you will need to solve this problem. I see no other way. And I agree with Emery. Leave no witnesses. The cards are very clear on that. Also, when you talk about important secrets that mean your life and death, you should probably make sure the phone isn't on speaker. Just for future reference. You don't have to worry about me, but just for the sake of pointing out what should've been obvious, you'd do best to remember that."

Reagan stared at the phone with a gaping mouth. My mother did have a point…

"So what is it we're going to do?" I asked.

"We're going to let them think they're surrounding us, and then we're going to show them who they are really messing with."

AN HOUR LATER, after coming up with a horribly loose plan that involved very little planning at all, something that Emery seemed to have no problem with, I said goodbye to my mother and decided to turn in for the night.

"Three is a crowd for a house this size," Reagan said as we left the kitchen. "Extort Darius to get you a place of your own. Better yet, I just found a secret bank account of his. Let's go on a spending spree and see how long it takes him to realize the money is gone."

"I cannot believe..." Emery shook his head as he followed me into my room. I closed and locked the door for the first time since moving there. Nervousness hatched butterflies in my stomach. "She is truly one of a kind. Naturals are rare, but there are a few of us. She's in a league of her own."

"It doesn't change anything major, though, right?" I asked.

He shrugged as I wrapped my arms around his middle, his eyes softening and his breath dusting my face. "Not your friendship, anyway. Or her annoyance of another person in her house." He smiled. "As for our lives down the road, who's to say? I thought my life would be over by now. And yet…" He bent to kiss me, running his lips across mine.

"I love you too," I said against his lips, and my stomach flipped over. "It's deep, it's constant, and it will never go away. I can feel that as strongly as I feel the nature around me. It's a certainty. I don't know that I believe in fate, or soul mates, but…"

"I do." His lips curved. "Or, I should say, I do now." He went in for another kiss.

The pounding ache was back, deep in my middle, and then lower and lower. Heat unfurled within my body as our kiss deepened. I pulled him by the neck toward the bed before settling on it. He lay on top of me, the weight of his body pushing me into the soft mattress.

"Will you make love to me, Emery?" I asked, my voice filled with lust and longing. I couldn't hide the quiver of doubt, though. The fear of what was to come. Of how this might change things.

"Are you sure?" he asked softly, his hips pushing forward, applying pressure where I needed it most.

My body responded eagerly, desperate and needy. A glorious fever broke across my skin, and suddenly I'd never been so sure of anything in my entire life.

"Yes." It was spoken on a sigh, and he didn't hold back any more. He pulled up the bottom of my shirt before tugging it over my head. My bra went next before he fastened his hot mouth on my budded nipple.

His fingers worked at my pants and I struggled with his belt, ripping it open before sliding his pants down. He yanked his shirt away and I marveled at his hard chest, corded with defined muscle. Power and strength in a gorgeous package.

Skin on skin, frenzied kissing. Then his frame went taut, signaling a struggle for control. No, I wouldn't let him hold back now. I took hold of his face, kissing him more deeply, my heart pounding as hard as my core.

"No, wait," he said, out of breath. "Wait." He leaned his forehead against mine. "Are you still…" He licked his lips. "Will I be your first?"

"Yes." I stroked the side of his cheek.

He shuddered softly. "I love you." He captured my lips before backing off again, his body tensing. "I need to be completely in control for your first time. I'm scared I'm going to hurt you."

"That's kind of how it goes, isn't it?" I said, my voice breathy. "You can't really get around that."

"I know, but…"

I felt his heat against me. Yearning made me reach out for him.

And then my mother's obnoxious voice sounded in my ear.

"Hold on," I said, and he practically jumped off me.

"It's okay. We can wait. I know this is a huge decision—"

"Would you relax?" I laughed, letting out a little pent-up nervousness, and dug through my nightstand drawer. I checked the date on the foil packet before handing it over with a burning face. "I thought you'd be back sooner. But they last a while, so we're good."

His eyes, so deep, so full of emotion, watched me settle back onto the bed. He ran a hand up my thigh, over my belly, beside my breast, and up to my chin before lowering himself over me. Softly, he touched his lips to mine.

"You are a dream come true in a life full of nightmares." His lips traced my jaw. "You're my savior, Penny, and I'm honored you have chosen me. That you had enough faith in us—in *me*—to wait for me. I am completely undeserving, but I know how lucky I am to have found you."

He drifted down my body then, stalling in various places before gliding his lips to my apex. I arched and gasped, relishing in the tremors the warm pressure of his mouth sent through my body. My knees drifted wider and I clutched at the pillow, soaking it in. My loud moan saw him headed back up, his kisses soft but urgent. Needy.

"Here we go," he said under his breath, and I heard the foil crinkle.

His body was shaking, and it wasn't from pent-up

need.

I smiled as he took my hands and lifted them above my head, entwining our fingers. Crinkles of skin folded at the corners of his eyes.

When I smiled, he shuddered out a laugh. "I'm really nervous," he said.

"I'm not." My smile melted away as a strong, deep feeling took over me. "I'm not even remotely nervous. I've been waiting for this moment. For you. For this *life*. I was always going to end up here. My path was full of zigzags, but there's no one else I could've ended up with. Or you. The proof is all around us." I let my head fall to the side, and his gaze followed.

Magic jumped and danced within the room, all different colors and patterns. Swirls and mini-explosions, it was beauty in movement. I felt his body against mine, the silk at my back, the heated air between us and the chill beyond. I felt connected, utterly. Balanced, completely. At one with him and my surroundings.

"Look at me, Penny," he commanded softly.

Our eyes met, and he thrust.

CHAPTER 41

A BANG SOUNDED at the door and Emery awoke immediately, lifting his hand to weave a spell.

"No, no, no," Penny said sleepily, pulling down his hand and wrapping it back around her.

"What the hell?" Reagan shouted through the door. "You get a boyfriend and suddenly I can't kick open your door without breaking shit? That ain't right, Penny. That ain't right. Wake up! It's time to kick some ass."

A glance at the clock said it was ten a.m. Light glowed around the curtains in the room.

Emery dropped his hand to Penny's bare shoulder and turned his head so he could breathe in the fragrance of her hair. His heart swelled and he closed his eyes, soaking in the feeling of her body curled around his and her leg splayed across his thigh.

A fierce protectiveness surged through him, followed by a sense of humbled honor.

How the hell had he gotten so lucky? What trick of the universe had landed him here, with her? Lying with her like this, after the experience he'd shared with her last night…he never wanted to leave her ever again. Not for a moment. She was his, and every fiber of his being was absolutely hers.

But then, he always had been hers. He knew that now. He'd just been fighting it.

She stirred and pulled back enough to peel open a blue eye before offering him a sleepy smile and settling back onto his chest. "Morning."

Another thud on the door. "Get up," Reagan called. "They have to repair the front door anyway. What's one more door? That's a warning. Heed it."

"She's not kidding. She *will* come in here." Penny rolled to her back, grimacing. "Ow."

"Are you okay?"

"Yeah. Sore. It sucks that women have all this drama with losing our virginity. Kind of a dick move on the creator's part. No pun intended."

He turned and propped up on an elbow, watching her slowly wake up. "Regrets?"

She rubbed her eyes, blinked another few times, and met his gaze. Her eyes sparkled with emotion and a smile tugged at her lips. "Obviously no regrets, but with all the hubbub the world makes about losing your virginity, you'd think there would be balloons and dancing monkeys or something. But nope, just some pain, eventually followed by soreness."

"So I was terrible?"

She laughed and snuggled into him. "I think you know better. Those sounds weren't made by a bored or unhappy woman."

He kissed her shoulder. "I'd say you could've been faking it, but I do know better. If you hadn't been into it, you probably would have told me."

"Last warning, you filthy buggers," Reagan called through the door. "I imagine by now that the Guild has gotten a tip about what we're doing today. I told Callie to mention it to her people in passing. Someone is bound to have leaked it. The Guild is surely readying for an attack as we speak."

The moment faded away as reality seeped into Emery. He softly rubbed her back. "I only have a vague knowledge of what Reagan's magic should be able to do. Very vague. This sounds like a suicide mission."

"Yes, it does." Penny sighed, patted his side, and rolled away. "But that's kind of how she rolls. Besides, my mother said this was the way. We know to listen to my mother. Man, did you just hear what I said? And to think, I thought one day I wouldn't have to. Congratulations, universe, you win."

He laughed and pulled the sheets away, climbing from the bed. His clothes lay on the floor where he'd left them, dirty from the day before. "I don't suppose we can go to the Bankses and get another change of clothing before we storm the castle?"

"Doubtful. Reagan's will probably be dirty—"

"Five, four…"

"Hurry up," Penny said, pulling on her shirt.

"Three, two…"

"Go, go, go—" Penny reached the door, threw the lock, and opened it in harried, panic-stricken movements.

Reagan paused with her foot in the air and her hands balanced to the sides, ready to kick. A smile graced her face and she lowered her foot. "Barely. Just barely."

Penny huffed at her and turned back to finish getting dressed.

"Hurry up," Reagan said. "I want to get the show on the road."

"Have you told Darius about this?" Penny asked.

"No." Reagan filled the doorway, wearing her standard uniform of leather pants, a tank top, and her hair in a ponytail. "Let's see how he likes secrets. And it's day, so when the shenanigans wake him up, he'll be half panicked, knowing I did something stupid."

"You two have such a strange relationship." Penny pulled on a sweater before bending to her utility belt. She slowed, then cocked her head. A moment later, she stood up slowly, her eyes on me and her brow furrowed. "We do need to go to the Bankses' house. There is something there we need."

"I don't need to—"

She held her hand up. "No, it's..." Her eyes went distant. Then she shrugged. "Something has arrived. We need to pick it up. I feel it. It's important, whatever it is."

Reagan cocked her hip. "I didn't think you had any of your mom's talents."

"I don't really." Penny bent to the collection of stones, loading some into her utility belt. "Not where it is actually useful. I only get vague inklings every now and again, and plenty of questionable intuition."

"Well, super. In that case, sure. To the Bankses' we will go," Reagan said sarcastically.

Despite her tone, she hadn't been lying. To the Bankses they did go. Penny dashed out of the vehicle (a new loaner from Darius—a Mercedes SUV), rang the bell, hugged her friend from Seattle, and brought back a plain brown package that looked awfully familiar.

"I sent that," Emery said, something in him clicking in a hollow, strange way. Like Fate's hand had reached through time, pushing him to take the risk to collect that stone and send it so that it would be back in time for this very fight. He knew it was a coincidence. It had to be. But...

Only dimwitted fools believe in coincidences.

Oh great, now he had Ms. Bristol's voice in his head.

That couldn't be good.

"Here." She handed up the package from the back seat.

"We stopped here to get a rock?" Reagan said, backing out of the driveway as Callie came to the door with a frown. They hadn't filled Callie and Dizzy in on what we were doing, knowing they'd insist on coming.

"Yeah." Penny didn't elaborate.

Emery tried to hand it back. "I sent this for you. I hadn't realized I would be coming back myself when I mailed it. Or that it would take so long to get here. The mail is really slow overseas."

"Open it. It'll be faster." She waggled her finger at him.

"Right." He shook his head as he took down the layered spell and then handed the package back.

She tore through the paper, a hungry gleam in her eyes. Clearly she liked presents. He had to remember that. After opening the package, she stared down into the box for a second, a blank look on her face. She cocked her head. Then handed the package back.

"I know it's not the best looker of the ones I sent," he started.

"No, it is not," Reagan said after catching a glance.

"You must've known you were coming back on some level," Penny said. "It's not interested in me. It's interested in you." A line formed between her brows and she put her palm on one of the compartments on her utility belt. "And Mr. Happy-Go-Lucky wants to tango with it. Seriously, Mr. Happy-Go-Lucky is high-maintenance. Thank you for the gift, but I'm not so sure I'm liking it."

"Holy crap are you weird," Reagan said.

Penny's brow furrowed as she harrumphed and looked out the window. Emery laughed at their antics while taking the rock out of the package. It felt good to have it back. He felt its pulse vibrate through his hand and then burrow deeper, into his body. It echoed outward, joining the bubble of magic within the car, and reacting to the connection he felt with Penny with a fizzing sensation. As soon as he got out of the car, he had a feeling his connection with the natural world would be enhanced too.

"I really did send this back for you," he said in a wispy voice as they exited the highway.

"Or maybe for my safekeeping," Penny said, unperturbed.

"Okay." Reagan turned off the radio. "We're getting close to the warehouse now. Here's the situation. It's a day like any other. As far as they know, we're going to the warehouse to train. Of course, what we're really going to do is load up with some spells. I have a bunch of herbs and crap out there, plus color-coded casings. I don't care what spell goes in what color. I won't be using them. You do what you want. Don't use all your energy. Oh, and we should set up some wards and tripwires or something, I don't know. We'll play that by ear—"

"Play that by ear?" Penny leaned around the seat in an effort to see Reagan's face. "Are you kidding? That's one of the first things we have to do if we're going to do it. Not to mention we'll have to make sure they didn't beat us there and set traps of their own."

"Yeah, I know. So when we get there, we should have a think. Then we do the spells, and eventually they'll feel like they're ready to make their attack, and the show will begin."

"What—" Penny fell back against the seat. "I don't think there is a worse planner in all the world. I really don't. Why turn off the music for that? You're basically saying we should get out and wander around like dopes."

"Yes. Perfect. I'm in," Reagan said. "Let's get there, get out, wander around like dopes, and see what grabs us."

"Unreal," Penny muttered from the backseat.

Laughter bubbled up through Emery, light and joyous, which was very strange, because the three of them were about to challenge an entire host. They were basically going up against all the king's horses and all the king's men, and trying not to end up like Humpty

Dumpty. It was madness. All of this was madness. Their probability of success had to be so low it was negligible. And yet…

He blew out a breath and looked out at the slightly overcast day. Up ahead on his side stood the warehouse, waiting for them like a great, empty beast. "Madness," he murmured, the first traces of uncertainty worming through his gut.

"That's how you know you're doing the right thing. When the odds are severely stacked against you," Reagan said, turning into the small lane leading up to the warehouse.

"I think you've got the wrong idea about how math works," Penny muttered from the back.

"Did you talk to Red this morning?" Emery asked as they parked, trying to hunt out any glimmering spells around the area. Nothing jumped out, but wards without additional spell work woven in would be invisible.

"Yeah, that good-for-nothing dog turd." Reagan parked and pushed the door open. "He's thinking the mage count must be in the eighties."

Emery's joints stiffened and fear bled through him. Suddenly, he couldn't seem to force himself to open the door. He had his hand on the handle, but it refused to move.

"Are you okay?" Penny asked softly.

"What are we doing, Penny?" he whispered, his body starting to shake. *Eighty?* That was madness. Madness! Last night he and Penny couldn't defeat a comparatively tiny host.

Eighty? It was impossible. They would never make it out.

She would never make it out.

After his parents had died, he'd loved exactly three people in his life. Real, honest-to-God love. One as a brother, one as a surrogate son, and now Penny.

He'd lost his brother. He'd helped kill his surrogate father after the man betrayed them.

He could not lose Penny. He couldn't send her in there to die. It wasn't in him.

"We need to leave now," he said, taking his hand away from the handle. "We need to run."

CHAPTER 42

I STILLED IN the back seat, never having seen Emery like this. Even in the dire situations, when all hope was lost, he hadn't once panicked.

For some reason, that calmed me. Chased away my own panic.

"What's up?" I asked, reaching forward to lay my hand on his shoulder.

"Even with Reagan, we don't have the power to go up against eighty people. It's impossible."

"It could only be fifty. Red must have been guessing."

"Or it could be a hundred."

I squeezed his shoulder. "My mother is backing this idea. That means there is a real chance we'll come out ahead. And your foresight didn't go off—Wait, did your foresight go off?" He shook his head, his face pale. "Right. There you go. It does sound impossible, that's true. But look, you have your new power stone, and it has faith in you. And a lot of power, actually. We have Reagan. She's incredible, she really is. And we can get hundreds of casings stored up. She brought a bunch with her from her secret stash at home, remember? Some are probably even ours. She stole them from the vampires."

"Why are you going along with this?"

"Because…well, because everyone around me is pushy, and you all seem to think this is the right way to do things. But if you think about it, all these people are in town for us, and they were going to come for us sometime. At least this is on our terms."

He deflated and shook his head.

"Come on." I patted his shoulder. "Buck up. We can do this. We have a future. I mean, my mother basically foretold it. It was gibberish and only made a mild amount of sense, but it was a future involving Reagan's…secret. We should trust in that."

"I foretell futures all the time. It's how I avoid them."

I didn't have an answer for that one, so I said, "Sure, yeah," and got out of the car.

"There was a tripwire over here," Reagan said, standing off to the side next to a few trees. "It ran over there." She pointed across the small parking lot. "We drove through it. I took it down, but it's too late. Someone with midrange power knows we're here."

"Think they'll drive in?" I asked, walking around the car to get Emery.

"Well, they certainly aren't going to take camels."

"Right." I rolled my eyes and knocked on Emery's window. "Come on. The first step is the hardest."

"Your turn to play strongman, huh?" Reagan wrinkled her nose and put up her hands. "There is something else out that way. Do you see it?"

"What do you mean, my turn to play strongman?" I waited by his door.

"Dual-mages." She waggled her finger in our direction. "You switch off the different hats, right?"

"We're not a dual-mage."

She put up her hand to block the sun. "Not yet, but something changed after you left the bar. You're acting like the Bankses. I can see it. Hell, I can feel constant shifting between you. It's pleasant. I like when your rage shifts around. That's the most fun."

"But we didn't do anything different." I remembered the feeling when we'd created the concealment spell together in the gap between the houses in the French Quarter. We'd blended our weaves into and through each other to make the kind of comprehensive, tightly packed spell I'd never achieved on my own.

We'd merged, in a way. The balance I'd always felt with him had become more grounded. Our roots had dug deeply into the ground, entwining as they did so, and our energy had reached into the sky. Oneness.

I wondered if the dual-mage situation would boost

that effect again, as it boosted the magic of Callie and Dizzy.

"You've got all the essentials lined up," Reagan said, walking toward the warehouse with her hands out. "Becoming a dual-mage pair would be a natural next step. Of course, that means forever. Scary stuff."

Biting my lip, I knocked on Emery's window. "Get out." I rapped harder.

"See? Right now you're wearing the bullying hat. Callie wears that most of the time. After this, though, I bet Emery will wear that hat, if he can learn how to say no to you. Or…I guess guys get to be called commanding. Women always get the short end of the stick. But clearly you need to wear it right now, because he turned chicken." She made sounds like a chicken, loud enough that I knew he heard.

I couldn't help laughing. "We're about to be killed. Do you take nothing seriously?"

"Oh, honey," she said with attitude. She was probably mimicking someone, but I didn't know who. "We're not going to be killed. Let's get these tattletale spells down, and I'll tell you exactly what we're going to do."

It took me a few moments to get Emery out of the car, plus a whopping ten minutes to get him into the warehouse. I finally ended up punching him in the face. I'd tried everything else, and Reagan had advised me to jar him out of it, so I did.

I was pretty sure he could've easily dodged or blocked my punch. My heart wasn't really in it. But he'd let it hit. Probably so I'd hurt my hand.

Which I did. He had some sharp cheekbones, and I had some (evidently) weak knuckles.

A moment later, his eyes had changed and fierce determination had taken over. In other words, the normal, confident problem-solver Emery. I got to go back to coasting. Which gave me a stronger appreciation for Dizzy's near-constant state of happiness.

Now we stood at the back area of the warehouse beside a long table with a plethora of ingredients organized across its surface. It reminded me of Darius's warehouse in Seattle, where we'd done a few spells to sell to him.

"When did you set this up?" I asked, looking over everything. The collection of power stones was a little lacking, but I had a pretty good collection with me.

"I called it in last night while I was waiting for Darius," Reagan said. "I figured we could all work together on some really tight spells, like that ward, and then create an arsenal of casings to keep at the house. We'll have to raincheck that, of course. We need quick, nitty-gritty spells. Also…" She put her hands on her hips as she examined the various baskets of casings collected at the end of the table. "We might need to special order some larger, more durable casings in the future. I have a feeling these won't be enough for what I am thinking."

"We put a powerful spell into two casings," I said, remembering working with Emery in Seattle.

Reagan turned on me, and anger crossed her face. "That secret-keeping jerk. You see? Every time I think we're being open with each other, that elder has something up his sleeve. He implied Emery did that spell. He didn't mention you at all. Which I find a little suspicious, since, you know, I knew you first." She frowned, pausing for another beat, before wiping it away with her hand. "Whatever. That doesn't matter right now. He's got plans. Fine. So do I. I don't understand those plans, because your mother is like all other *Seers*, but I have them. And I won't be spilling. He can suck it."

"A very odd relationship," I muttered.

Reagan ignored my remark. "That spell you two did was in two casings. An even more complex spell might take three or four. How the hell can you quickly grab out four casings from among many, sort through them for the order, and then release them all while in the heat of battle? No, that's not going to work. Well, for now, it probably has to. Okay, here's what we need..."

Reagan spent the next few minutes listing off the types of spells we'd ideally have ready for the battle ahead. Everything from attack to defense to marvels of nature. Then she described the more important and pressing matter of creating gigantic walls to keep onlookers from seeing the massive battle. We were supposed to create a Not-So-Great Wall of China to basically run along the outskirts of the land surrounding the warehouse, though she wouldn't say why it needed to be so massive.

Then we needed to wander through the fields and make sure there weren't any traps and magical pitfalls that had been planted prior to our arrival.

As she was winding down, her phone rang.

"Red." She tapped the face of the phone and put it to her ear. "Hello?"

Emery plucked at my sleeve before looking over the organic offerings. "Let's focus on those walls first. They'll need to be strong and magical, and they'll need to be in casings. We don't want them to know we're essentially trying to lock them in...until we lock them in."

"Locking in eighty people to our three." A tremor rolled through my body, begging me to do what he'd suggested in the beginning. Run!

TWO HOURS LATER, I was jarred out of my extreme focus. A warning shook my bones. My teeth rattled.

I backed away from the elaborate spell I was working on, letting it dissipate and drift into space. Emery straightened up next to me, his body going taut. The magic around us instantly changed from busied loops of beautiful designs, to rolling, boiling bubbles of pure magic and energy.

Reagan glanced over from what she was doing on the other side of the warehouse. Magic draped across the walls in patterns that barely made sense to my eye. A little blurry, sometimes glowing and glittering in places, the weaves seemed to shift into tangible things—walls and chairs and draping vines—made up of moving, surging, and pulsing colors. A high gloss covered the whole thing, and the intent felt *majestic*.

It was the first time I'd ever seen actual weaves with her magic.

"What's the matter?" she asked.

"Tripwire three was set off," Emery said, back to working on his spell.

"Five for me," I said, refocusing.

In two hours, we'd created a small pile of spells tucked into casings, some of which would soon be used to create the sight-blocking, sound-deadening walls. We also had a half-dozen magical tripwires placed around the fields surrounding the warehouse. In addition to alerting us of intruders, the tripwires would give a little tag to the first ten people who passed through them. Then, when we released certain casings, they'd get a nasty surprise.

This was assuming they didn't find and tear down the spells immediately, of course.

Reagan looked back at her spell. “Okay, let’s pack it in. Get some water and a rest. That means they are crawling into position, the snakes.”

“Two hours is a long time,” I said, picking up my power stones. “If this were a normal practice, we’d probably be done by now.”

“We’d be getting ready to go to the car.” Reagan left her spell, but it didn’t fold back into the universe. It stayed where it was, a strange sort of hall of magic within the warehouse. “Either they’re planning to surprise us as we leave, or they’re slow to get organized.” She stopped by the door and put her palm on the wood. “I wish we had a spell for seeing through solid material.”

“Humans came up with that one. It’s called glass.” Emery grabbed his basket of spells and walked it back to the table.

Reagan turned and stared at him, before glancing up at the various windows high in the walls. “This is true.”

A tingling sensation crawled up my spine. Mr. Happy-Go-Lucky awoke from a bored stupor and sent out a pulse of power.

Emery, now stalking across the room toward Reagan, stalled and glanced back at the stone. “Did you feel that?” he asked me.

“Yes.”

He nodded and resumed his walk. "That's what drew me to it in the first place. That pulse. A moment later, I was ambushed by goblins."

CHAPTER 43

"AMBUSHED..." IT TOOK a moment for that word, and its implications, to set in. Adrenaline raged through me, erasing all fatigue. "How can you be so blasé?"

I snatched up my basket with suddenly shaking hands. Two casings jumped out and rolled away. After collecting them again, I hurried them to the table and went back for my stones, collecting them and putting them in their various compartments. Except for Mr. Happy-Go-Lucky, Emery's Plain Jane, and my chunk of Red Beryl, pumping fiery power into the air. It was trying to keep pace with the other two, which would hopefully help boost its power.

"Calm, Penny," Reagan said in a firm tone, nothing like her usual flippant attitude in the face of danger.

"How can you tell me to stay calm when you sound like that?" I blew out a breath, my legs shaking.

"We're prepared. We're ready." Reagan shot Emery a confused and distracted look when he stopped beside her. "What do you want?"

"I'm your ladder. Stand on my shoulders so you can see."

A half grin flitted across her face. "No, you wouldn't have figured out my secret on your own. You were told, and you still have no idea what I can do."

His expression closed down—which was replaced by wide-eyed shock when Reagan rose into the sky, floating or levitating or flying, I didn't know, but she left the ground and floated up like a freaking genie.

Up until then, I'd had no idea how much she was holding back.

"You win." I palmed my heart, in complete awe. "Hands down, you win the contest for the coolest magic. No question."

Emery nodded mutely.

Reagan stopped her ascent at the side of the window and looked out.

A swear word drifted across the warehouse.

I danced from side to side, my flight reflex in overdrive. Mr. Happy-Go-Lucky started pounding with power, thrusting it into the air like a drumbeat. The Red Beryl fizzed and sparkled, something I had never seen it do.

Plain Jane stayed true to its look. No excitement at all. Cool as a cucumber.

"That's why you're Emery's. Right there, that's why. Stone matches master." I blew out a breath and jogged in a small circle. I had to do something; I could feel the presence of magic now—sharp, dull, ragged, smooth, all pumping into the warehouse. Collecting in a huge pool of magical intent.

"Oh gobbledygook twatwallop. Butt crack solstice alert. Flubber fart bugger balls."

"What is she saying?" Reagan said in exasperation.

"I think she has abandoned her usual recipe for slant-swearing in panic." Emery watched Reagan float to another window. He cocked his head. "Another two tripwires."

I rose my hand, jogging in place. It felt like my spine was wiggling as people tramped across my tripwires. "Tripwires. Tripwires."

"We're surrounded," Reagan said, lowering. "They must've collected out of sight and marched at us in synchronicity. They had information on us. They've been watching."

"What's the plan?" I asked, wringing my hands.

Trap. Kill. Trap. Kill.

It felt like a *huge* magical net rose around the warehouse. Some of us would be preserved. Some killed.

I would live.

Reagan would surely die.

I wasn't sure about Emery.

"Oh bull cocks. Fuckity shit stains."

"Whoa." Reagan laughed.

"Penny Bristol, I am telling your mother." Emery laughed and stuffed ingredients into his pockets. "I should've gotten a new utility belt."

"Here." Reagan unslung her fanny pack from around her waist. "Use this. I won't need it now that I'm not pretending."

He paused, looking unsure.

Reagan shook it. "Hurry."

He didn't step forward.

"What's the matter?" she asked impatiently.

"I made it through my youth without ever succumbing to that trend, only to do so in my twenties?" He shook his head.

"If you call it a fanny pack one more time, I'm going to break your face. It is a *pouch*! Now put it on, Mr. Fashion." She zipped it up and chucked it at him.

Reagan paused in front of her magical spectacle. If I didn't know better, and maybe I didn't, she was unsure. That was not good.

As if hearing my thoughts, she said, "I really hope this works."

"Oh good, yeah. Yes, let's hope it works. Yup." I jogged in another circle like a hyperactive dog. "But let's not say what *it* is, exactly."

"It is my father's legacy, and it is about time I learn to use it." She blew out a deep breath, turning to watch Emery adjust the fanny pack to fit around his much larger waist. He shook his head as he clipped it on.

"We are in a very bad situation, about to get worse, but it would be remiss if I didn't mention that someone should get a picture of him wearing that." I pointed at him as I attempted a sort of tap dance across the floor.

"What in the holy hell are you doing, Penny?" Reagan demanded. But she did raise her phone and snap off a picture of Emery. Before filming me.

It would've looked better if I'd taken even one tap dance lesson in my life.

Emery pulled out handfuls of empty casings. "Are you a hoarder? What is all this?"

"It's for show. Let's go, Emery. Your lady love is about to lose it."

"Oh, I've lost it. It's gone. Long gone. And you know what?" I clapped and danced back toward them. "There isn't one closet in this whole godforsaken warehouse. Not one. Not even a freaking nook or cranny. There is nowhere to hide. I've gotten myself into a pickle this time. Did you know they are basically chanting *kill, kill, kill* out there? Yeah. Magically chanting it. Do you know who they want to kill?" I pointed at Reagan. I pointed at Emery. "Maybe. I don't know. But definitely—" I pointed at her again.

"It makes it more fun when they mean business." Reagan watched as Emery finished shoving ingredients and casings into the fanny pack. "We ready?"

I jumped in place, the throbbing of magic outside the warehouse at a fever pitch. Spells would come soon. Huge, powerful spells intent to tear the warehouse from its very foundation. They'd been preparing, all right. All these months, they'd been preparing. Collecting magic, building spells, assembling a freaking army.

All to combat three people.

We had no chance in hell.

CHAPTER 44

"PARLAY," I YELLED as a mighty spell bore down on the warehouse. "Parlay!"

"We're not pirates," Reagan said, pulling her hands up from her sides. "And they can't hear us in here."

"A spell is coming right at us!" I ran at Emery, grabbed his arm, and tore his survival magic from within his body. I had no idea how, but I didn't care. I smooshed it with mine, and yanked at the three throbbing power stones, releasing as I did so.

A concussion of magic rocked out from my body, stopping in the middle of the warehouse before exploding outward without sound, a gray mass heading for the walls.

At the same time, Reagan grunted and shoved her hands outward.

The four walls of the warehouse bowed in the middle before ripping outward. The roof flew off as though from an explosion, ripping from the ends of the walls. Metal screamed. Glass shattered. Emery threw his body over mine.

The magic I'd thrown flew beyond the mess of broken walls and roof, expanding outward. The incoming spell hit it with a flurry of sparks, stopping its progress. Shimmery green warred with gray. Magic zipped away in all directions, hitting the ground and pooling acid.

Emery pulled off me and worked a spell. Without thinking, I added my weave to it, fortifying his efforts before weaving my own spell to blast out a wave of intense heat all around the warehouse, hopefully taking out their first line of attack.

Emery released his spell, aiming beneath the two warring spells, counteracting the potentially dangerous-to-us fallout. Without pausing, he bent to me, now working within my spell as I'd worked within his. If we each did separate spells, we'd get them out faster, but that would be for the heat of the battle. Now we needed a few larger waves of power to keep them from rushing in and immediately overcoming us.

I shoved the spell into existence and looked up.

And froze.

Twisted metal lay to each side of where we stood. Beyond, stretched around the warehouse in a large circle, the mages slowly walked forward.

There had been more than eighty.

At least double.

Their spells zipping off to try and counter the large bubble of our combined survival magic. Satchels hung to one side of their bodies, unless they were wearing the dusters and stupid hats, and small sacks to the other. I'd bet those were full of casings.

My newest spell rolled outward, making it past our bubble of survival magic and immediately encountering rapid-fire spells. Flame and color burst out of it, but magic continued to slam into it from all sides. My spell was strong, but it couldn't hold. Not with that much opposition tearing it down.

"They're spread out," Emery said, yanking me to standing. "That's good for us. This was a good location. Perfect."

He had some strange ideas about perfection.

"Get those magical perimeter walls out in the fields," Reagan yelled, standing in front of her magical spectacle again. It was still there, now standing on its own.

Thankful for some direction so I didn't start panicking—again—I turned and snatched the casings off the table. Emery didn't follow suit. He jogged to the center of the warehouse and started a new spell.

"No, it's okay. I've got it," I said sarcastically, running to the firing point we'd agreed upon earlier and cracking the first casing.

The bubble of survival magic started to disintegrate under the continued barrage of the green spell and the mages' casings.

"Hurry!" Reagan yelled.

A pulse of power blasted out of the casing, whooshing by me and out of the quickly dissipating bubble. A few planes of vibrant, revolving color sprang up in front of some of the mages before the attack spell attached to the wall spell washed over them, taking a couple to the ground, eliciting a few screams, and leaving the rest unharmed. No one stayed down, though some had a harder time crawling to their feet.

I made it to the next spot, and Emery met me there, grabbing a casing from me and running.

I cracked the next wall casing, then sprinted to the final location.

The last of our survival bubble washed away, pulling at my energy reserves as it did so.

I cracked the final wall casing before pulling out my power stones and throwing them across the ground.

"Here we go," I heard Reagan yell as *stun* spun toward me from somewhere to my right.

I turned and fired, hitting it with my rodent zapper, then following up with a spell to unravel the intent. All around us, the mages advanced.

Emery might not have meant it at the time, but his advice to focus on my will was the most important advice he ever could've given me.

"The tripwire spell," Emery yelled above a rushing of power. My ears popped as I ran for the table, already on it.

Energy pushed and pulled at me, hot and cold, churning my stomach before soaking into my body. That complex feeling of Reagan's magic infused my being, my magic, as I grabbed the casings in question, cracked them, and began to throw them rapid-fire.

The day blinked.

I blinked with it, shielding my eyes from the sudden darkness.

The day blinked again.

"What's happening?" I heard Emery say as the spells zipping at us slowed.

I didn't slow. Not like when that lion had come. This time, I knew better.

I cracked spells and squinted through the strange blurring of the world around me. It looked as if someone had come through with an eraser and rubbed at all the lines, shapes, and colors.

My stomach rolled again, like I was on a roller coaster. Perspective distorted.

I pushed through it and grabbed the casings from Emery's hands, cracking them quickly.

Magic flew out, bending and twisting through the air, zooming toward the unseen victims. No screams reached my ears, not with the *whup, whup, whup* of power wobbling around me.

I grabbed my basket of spells and turned toward the

middle of the warehouse before noticing Emery was staring at Reagan with his hand to his forehead, blocking out the glare from the occasional flashes of sunlight.

"Come on," I yelled, but my voice got lost. As soon as it left my mouth, it was sucked up into the strange vortex of power pounding around us. So I kicked him in the shin.

He started, saw what I wanted, and nodded.

There was no time to marvel at the crazy chick who had a *lot* more power than anticipated. Even knowing what she was, I was awe-struck. It was time to catch these mages with their pants down.

At the center of the warehouse, I staggered when the magic flashed above and around the field like lightning. A sudden tangerine sky faded slowly into blood red before settling into a very dark crimson, almost black. It appeared to touch down to a distant horizon hundreds of miles away. White-gray clouds slowly stretched and drifted across the sky before shrinking until they spread out along a rippling surface of deep blue, nearly black water at the horizon, giving the scene an incredible amount of depth. Rocks sprang up in the distance, but the rippling water didn't splash or move against them. The visual effect messed with my head and gave me the jitters.

"I don't like this," I said, my limbs shaking. I should've been firing off the casings. I should've been doing battle, especially since I knew this was some sort of trick. Instead, it was taking everything I could muster not to unravel Reagan's false reality. "What's happening?"

I'd never liked it when the Muppet Babies disappeared into an imagined reality on their cartoon show, and I didn't like this, either. Drugs weren't for me, magical or otherwise.

At least I wasn't alone. Emery was in here with me. He looked behind us and started.

Everyone else had disappeared. Including Reagan.

We seemed to be marooned by ourselves in this strange, altered reality.

Off to the left, in the sea of blackened water, rose a white-gray pole, shaded with black. It looked like a celebration of Emery's and my smooshed survival magic. It grew taller and taller, filling out as it did so.

"A tree trunk," I said, closing my eyes as vicious intent rang out from somewhere near me. Aimed at me. "Wait." I peeled an eye open, looking in that direction.

Emery startled again. He was getting a premonition.

"This is an illusion," I reminded myself. I cracked a casing right before Emery shoved me so hard that my neck cracked. He dove the other way and a jet of blazing purple roared past me.

"Oh, it's on!" I hopped to my feet and started rapidly firing again, closing my eyes now, not trusting what they were telling me.

"Look!"

The scene had changed again. The tree trunk had grown into a large tree, its leaves white, black, and gray.

"I'm not doing that, right?" I asked in confusion. "Somehow?"

"No. Over here." Emery turned me in the other direction.

Mages came into view now, standing shin-deep in the fake water. The water didn't interact with their bodies, and no wetness soaked their clothes.

Stars blossomed in the sky. Little pricks at first, but they enlarged as we watched them.

"What is the point of all this?" I yelled over the rushing of power.

"It's Reagan. She's messing with their perspective…and ours. But we're probably supposed to do more than stand around and watch it happen." He plucked at my sleeve. "Let's do our part."

"We don't even know what our part is!" I stuffed my casings anywhere they would fit before taking off running at his side.

Flatten.

"Watch out!" I cracked a casing on impulse, then jumped to the side, hitting debris and falling, turning it into a roll.

"We're at the warehouse line where the wall used to

be," Emery yelled as more people came into view behind us, like a screen was being pulled away to reveal what had always been there.

I cracked another casing and the magic sped out before me, spreading as it went. It smacked into five mages, churning through them. A woman's face screwed up in pain and she grabbed at her chest. A man clutched at his privates. It was clear to see what was the most important among the various mages, since the spell was uniform.

All five went down, their screams never reaching my ears.

Emery hit a line of eight mages with a simple yet brutal spell, just powerful enough to bring them to their knees. He tried to run forward, but tripped and fell at an angle, floating in the air.

"The warehouse wall. Or roof." He tried to climb off, but a spell jetted toward him. He rolled over, barely dodging it in time, and sent off a retaliatory shot.

I cracked casing after casing, cutting huge holes in the line. Thankfully, they weren't being replaced, but a quick look behind us revealed the mages were over the crazy spectacle. They were making their way toward us quickly, intent on trapping us.

Always with the trapping. But this time we didn't have any shifters to help.

"She has to do something other than make illusions!" I yelled.

That was when I noticed what the stars were morphing into.

CHAPTER 45

"WATCH OUT!" EMERY slammed into me as I looked up, trying to place that strange thrumming sound.

Large beasts, like elephants with wings, thundered down from the sky. They opened smallish mouths with large teeth.

"But it's only an illusion. She won't actually kill anyone with those," I said, staggering back toward the corner of the invisible warehouse wall.

A female mage with a purple robe, a higher-tiered Guild member, staggered as she looked up, probably in awe. Or confusion, because those flying animals were whack. Reagan had a very strange imagination. Weirder, even, than mine.

I barreled into the mage, jabbing her in the eye before elbowing her in the face, and took her to the ground. I kicked out at someone else, my boot connecting with his jaw and knocking him backward. I called up a fast weave of moderate power to take a third mage before he could reach for his smaller pack of spells.

A huge roar quaked my heart and shook my bones.

I ducked instinctively and looked up. Amazingly, like with the lion incident, Emery didn't. So I grabbed him and yanked him lower.

The winged elephant thing swooped down. From its little mouth belched a thick stream of fire. Blistering heat washed over me and I shrank back, throwing up my arms. Emery threw a shield of black survival magic over both of us, keeping some of the heat back before it dissolved.

"Maybe we weren't supposed to run out here after all." He struggled back toward the warehouse, dragging me with him.

"This is why we should have discussed the plan more!" I tripped over that blasted invisible warehouse wall or roof, falling to my hands and knees. Emery helped me up again and we scrambled forward.

A mage stood before us with an orange sash. I couldn't remember what level that made him, but the last casing in my pocket assured me it didn't matter. My spell spread across him and bent him backward.

The *crack* made me gag.

A roar preceded a blast of heat and pressure, knocking us forward. Wings beat at us overhead, the flapping elephant things sailing by before swooping low on the other side of the warehouse and belching fire.

My foot hit a lip of something and I tripped forward. Emery did the same a second later, splaying out right next to me on the smooth warehouse floor.

Sear.

"Move!" I rolled to my back, pulled down magic, and threw it into a hasty weave right as the incoming spell reached me. I raked the spell, countering it before scrambling backward so it didn't reach me before it dissipated.

Emery flung a spell ahead of him from his belly, opening slashes across three mages approaching the lip of the warehouse.

"I think we were supposed to keep mages from reaching the warehouse," I said, flipping over and pushing to my feet.

"My bad," he said with a grunt. Standing now, he flung spells in rapid-fire toward mages standing in a cluster, looking upward.

Above the hubbub, floating in the air like a goddess, with hair whipping in the wind, hovered Reagan. Power ripped from her like lightning as the flapping elephant things swooped and rolled, spewing fire on those not fast enough to get out of their paths.

"We were definitely supposed to cover her back." Emery took off running, and I paused only long enough for an *I told you so* about our failure at interpersonal communication.

I mean, how much more proof did a person need?

A weave in progress but not quite ready, I ran with my hands in front of me and rammed my shoulder into the back of a mage who'd been seconds away from firing a spell at Reagan. He fell forward and I finished the weave, turning and firing it out. It opened up across the warehouse floor turned weird, swampy pond, rolling and tumbling toward a line of mages who'd made it past the Dumbos-from-another-mother.

My spell caught them at the knees and legs, crushing through bone and tissue.

"Oh, gross. Emery, switch." I spun away, my stomach rolling, seeing a few mages tripping over the far corner of the warehouse. I took a few steps forward, feeling Reagan's pulsing magic, diminishing in power. She was expending more than she needed to with this weird false reality, and it wasn't long from running out.

"We need to speed this up," I yelled.

I rodent-zapped those mages, punching holes in parts of their bodies. The ball of heat I'd sent out continued to roll, capturing two more would-be escapees before running out of power. Emery fired off one spell while building another, fired off a third, and kept building the second.

"He's always a step ahead." I dug in my pockets for more casings, but came up empty. Just me and my imagination.

A mage staggered up, half burned. Another was basically crawling. Emery took out one and I sent a simple spell of magical spikes to deal with the other. Elephant things flickered above us. Then the whole false reality flickered, bright sunlight blasting down, blinding me. Darkness resumed, and now I couldn't see a thing. Blinding sunlight again.

"This is the worst," I yelled at Reagan, who was lowering from the sky.

The day resumed, bright and full of color. The green of the grasses and trees rushed back in.

Bodies lay strewn in the fields, blackened and burned. A wildfire was smoldering near our protective walls. A smattering of mages had survived the onslaught by hanging toward the back. They'd obviously done so to protect themselves from the elephant things and our flying capsules.

"It's the last stand," I heard Reagan say. She was on her knees to my right.

Emery looked from her to me, and I knew we were thinking the same thing.

She was done. We had to end this.

Without a word, we were running in opposite directions, charging toward the remaining mages and mercenaries.

Pulling at everything I had left, I yanked energy up from my toes, still feeling the balanced bubble connecting my magic to Emery's despite the fact that we were getting farther and farther apart. I mixed two vicious spells together and stopped short, remembering the balloon searching spell that attached to us last night.

I started to back up, which caught the attention of the three mages left in my vicinity.

They paused their weaving for a second, staring at me. It was that pause which sealed their fate.

I closed my eyes for a moment, pulling the wildness and rage of Emery's magic and the complex mixture of fire and ice of Reagan's powers into my spell. I sent that up into the air. Instead of ballooning, it merely opened up like a parachute before drifting down.

The three mages went back to work, but I had already turned away and was running toward an injured mage attempting to escape. A quick spell to his middle ended that right quick, and I lost some of my breakfast.

Screams reached my ears now that the false reality had completely faded. I turned back in time to see the three mages' throats exploding, and realized I'd confused the weaves. I hadn't intended it to be so violent.

I lost the rest of my breakfast.

Someone on the periphery ran for it.

And maybe that was the reason for the false reality. Since Reagan had helped us create the spells for the protective walls—she had *actually* trapped them in instead of just keeping outside eyes and ears from seeing what went on inside. She'd forced them to remain. Forced them to keep her secret.

With her magic gone, that was no longer the case.

I took off in hot pursuit, pulling together my pumping arms to get a weave going. Then I realized I could do a one-handed weave *with* the pumping arm. So I lessened the complexity of the spell and gained on the cowardly man in the stupid hat. In a hundred more feet, I let the spell loose. My spell dragged him to the ground and started to shred through him.

I spun, breathing heavily, and my stomach rolled again. I needed less heinous spells. Killing someone didn't have to be so colorful. There was no point to it besides being gruesome for gruesome's sake.

Jogging back, I saw a line of fire in the distance, beyond the warehouse, spreading in front of someone attempting an escape. It grew, now chasing that person back toward Emery. He shot off a spell, knocking the enemy to the ground.

My boots made crunching noises on the burned ground. The breeze whipped at my hair. My breath sounded loud in my ears.

But that was because all the other sounds had died down. Quiet rang as loudly as the battle had minutes before.

I swept my gaze around the area, searching for anyone left standing. Debris and bodies were littered all through the field, unmoving. Three people were still on their feet.

A sob choked me and tears of unbelievable relief rolled down my hot face. I couldn't believe it.

Reagan and Emery were two of the three. I was the last.

We'd done it.

The three of us had gone up against a host of nearly two hundred or so mages and mercenaries, and somehow, we'd survived.

As I continued toward the ruined warehouse, I caught sight of Reagan swaying on her feet. She pulled down the lingering fire, completely in control of it despite her empty power tanks.

We would've never been able to do this without her. Not with all the vampires, shifters, and mages who were friendly to us in New Orleans. She was our ace in the hole. More powerful than anyone in the Brink, I had no doubt.

And the only way we'd have a prayer of taking down the Mages' Guild permanently.

Emery and I owed her our lives and our freedoms, and if we made it out of the next leg of our battle with the Guild alive, we would be forever indebted to her.

My mother's haunting words came back to me:

Her path has been set. Her journey is in motion. He will complete the pyramid of power. The curse breaker will join the oath takers and forge a bond in blood. It is in this union that the way forward shall be writ. That they shall all learn their highest level of power, and balance the kingdom.

Reagan's was the path that had been set, because it was my journey in motion. Emery completed our pyramid of power.

I stopped and scanned the field littered with enemy bodies.

Emery and I were still learning to work together. We hadn't even boosted our power by officially joining as a dual-mage team. Reagan, too, was still learning, if what she'd said earlier was true. And together we'd downed an army.

Shivers coated my body. Pyramid of power, indeed.

Reagan fell to her hands and knees.

CHAPTER 46

EMERY MADE IT to Reagan at the same time Penny did, so he stepped back, nearly tripping over his own feet in the process. Weariness made weights of his limbs, dragging at him. He could barely keep his spine straight within the bone-weary fatigue.

Penny, not looking nearly as ragged as he felt, knelt next to Reagan and put her hand on the other woman's back. "Are you okay?"

"Tired," Reagan said, her head drooping. "Very tired."

Penny nodded and took a knee, looking out at the deathly still fields around them. It was an eerie comparison to the flurry of activity that had come before.

Emery staggered back another pace and Penny's gaze fell on him. He could tell she was assessing the damage. How she could still function was beyond him. But then, his brother had always said women were stronger in the field, their strength of will hardier than the roots of an oak, pushing them past their own distress to help those around them.

"That's why God gave the gift of birth to woman," his brother always said, "because he could trust in mothers the most."

"Just…so I'm on the same page," Penny said, dropping her other knee and sitting on her heels. "You're the one who created that false reality and those weird elephant creatures, right?"

"Yes," Reagan said. "Neat, huh?"

"No. It was awful. I hated it."

"Never go to the underworld."

"Well, that's the plan." Penny bit her lip. "And you did that…why? I mean, because you probably could've just fire-bombed the whole place."

Reagan sucked in a deep breath before twisting around and sitting hard on her butt. Emery joined them and took a knee, still in absolute shock. His brain had yet to process the strange alternate reality. The battle. The hard-won victory.

"I had a few options," Reagan said, looking out over the field before her gaze landed on the wall of the warehouse, resting haphazardly on the crushed car beneath it. "Darius will never let me near one of his cars again."

Penny followed her gaze. "But, I mean…that's fair, I feel like. You ruin every one of them."

Reagan sighed. "We need to get a cleanup crew out here."

"Yes. But you were saying, about the mind chaos?" Penny said, her voice carrying an edge.

"Mind fuckery, yeah. Well, I could've just stopped at the walls to keep people in, but since they were invisible, people would've tried to get out, run into them, and bounced off. Once they realized it was magic holding them in, they'd work to bring it down. Which would drain my energy and steal my focus."

"Hmm. Mhm." Penny's agreement didn't sound convincing. Emery had a sneaking suspicion she didn't really *want* to understand Reagan's incredible magic, which was so far above and beyond what she was already struggling to understand. Emery honestly didn't blame her. He was more or less used to what magic could throw at him, and yet…Reagan had created an entire alternate reality. And not just an illusion! Those strange flying creatures had come to life. They'd killed and maimed.

"But, with that wall, I could have just fire-blasted everyone, like you said. See what I'm saying?" Reagan said. Penny shook her head, her eyes glazing over. Reagan ignored it. "So that made the wall an attractive option. But there are dried grasses all around us, and I worried the whole place would catch fire. So then I'd need an additional wall to suck out the flames, right before the solid wall. See?"

Penny didn't even bother shaking her head this

time. She just stared blankly.

"That would all have been doable, but let's be honest, I know those parts of my magic pretty well. This was a great opportunity to practice my less-used powers. I figured I'd go for it. Fool the brain with the eyes, further confuse the brain with solid walls they could no longer see, trapping them in, then kill them with the fire dragons—"

"Dragons?" Penny asked, finally coming back alive. "Those were supposed to be dragons?"

"Yeah. I missed the mark a bit there." Reagan climbed to her feet, followed by Penny, ready with a stabilizing hand. "But the rest of it looked pretty cool, didn't it?"

"The water didn't make things wet. It didn't, like, splash." Penny braced her hands on her hips and half bent, finally showing her fatigue. "It didn't account for people walking through it. I couldn't see the ground. No, it wasn't cool. And people disappearing and reappearing and—"

Emery put his hand on her shoulder to keep her from flying off the handle, trying to keep back chuckles as he did so. A lopsided smile crossed Reagan's face.

"Definitely don't go to the underworld, you'd—" Reagan's head jerked around, her eyes narrowing at Penny. "Did you try and cut out the illusion?"

Penny's eyes rounded and she put up her hands.

"No, I swear. Emery, tell her. I thought about it for only a second. But I didn't act on it. I still can't believe you didn't warn me!"

"Hmm." Reagan tapped her mouth as she slowly walked to the edge of the warehouse. "I wonder if you could. We'll have to try."

"No, thank you," Penny said quickly.

Reagan sighed and looked around at the gruesome tableau. "My warehouse is gone." She squinted up at the sky. "Should we check for survivors, or just make sure there aren't any?" She lowered her eyes to Penny and quirked an eyebrow. "Should we show Emery what the people down under can do?"

"What? Australians?" Penny backed up. "I don't know what you're talking about. Don't include me in your crazy."

"Too late. Your mother said I should." Reagan held out her hands, palms up. Floating fire sprang above them, hovering. No magic connected the flame to her palm. No streams of energy flowed through her fingers or from the elements around them. She'd called it up from nowhere.

"Annnndddd…" The flame disappeared. She moved her hands through the air toward the field. Fire sprang up there, growing when she raised her hands, crawling across the already burned ground and over the bodies.

"No, no, no, no." Penny slapped one of Reagan's

hands out of the air. That didn't affect the fire in the least. "No! We need to identify them. Find out if they were Guild, not Guild, where they came from—you can't just destroy evidence. I swear, Darius must want to throttle you at least ten times a day. You and he are nothing alike."

Reagan's smile, which had sprouted when Penny slapped at her hand, grew. "You get me."

"No, I don't."

"You do. You get me."

"I don't even get what you're talking about. I just stated facts. And asked questions."

Without any movement from Reagan, the fire rose off the ground. And so did Penny.

"What the—"

She bumped down a moment later and Reagan shook her head. "I'm too tired. Fine, you win. Let's get cleanup in here. Or get the shifters to section it off until Darius can send in his guys and look everyone up. I'm tired. I need a bath."

"Training is going to get a lot worse now that she can show all her powers," Penny mumbled.

"See?" Reagan took her phone from her back pocket. "This is why I love Penny. I create a huge illusion, with fire-spitting dragons—"

"More like Dumbo's un-talked-about uncle—" Penny mumbled.

"—move fire through the air, lift *her* in the air, and all she can think about is how I'll torment her in training."

"That's a strange reason to love someone." Penny heaved a deep breath. "It's over, then, right? That wasn't just wishful thinking on my part? We won."

Reagan's laugh was low and humorless, and Emery knew exactly what she was going to say. So he did it for her.

"It's far from over," he said, connecting eyes with Penny. "Either we keep running, or we do forcefully what my brother tried to do delicately. Either we spend our life in the wild, or we stand our ground, ask our friends for help, and claim the ultimate vengeance for our loved ones."

"We tear down the Guild," Reagan said with fire in her eyes. "Those filthy bastards."

Penny looked between Emery and Reagan, but her gaze stuck on him. And what she said shocked him.

"It isn't the ultimate vengeance. It's doing the right thing. We have to tear it down, yes, but so it can be rebuilt. We have the power to do it, and the scars to make it personal—those things make it our responsibility." Penny shifted, her stance widening. Magic whispered around them, blending in with the breeze. "This time, they came to us. Next time…"

Reagan smiled.

"We go to them," Emery finished, feeling Penny's infectious fire running through him. "We harvest the spells we planted when we were first in the Guild compound."

That weird brown rock with the stripes of color—Mr. Happy-Go-Lucky, Penny had called it—pulsed from the other side of the ruined warehouse.

"Stupid power stone," Penny muttered.

She was on board. She wasn't even fully trained, but she was ready to storm the Guild again.

But was he?

CHAPTER 47

"WHAT DO WE have to expect from this, Penny?" my mother asked from the small table in Reagan's kitchen.

She'd taken the first flight out of Seattle after speaking to me. When she hadn't found us at Reagan's, she'd gone to the Bankses', where she'd been greeted by Callie and Dizzy's magical group, minus a few players.

A good few.

Those few would never be going back, either, because they had never left the fields around Reagan's destroyed warehouse.

Only two people hadn't been accounted for at the warehouse or the gathering. One of the defectors utterly shocked everyone. High in power, lots of ambition, and so ridiculously entitled that he had probably danced to the Mages' Guild's tune the moment they promised him power and riches, John had disappeared. I was the only one not gobsmacked.

And the other had people clucking their tongues and nodding their heads. Of course she had gone back to the dark magic, they said. Wasn't it what she was used to?

Mary Bell.

Callie had verified that Mary Bell's presence in the bar the day of the first attack was unusual. Paired with her interest over my movements, it indicated she'd up and joined the Guild. The fact that she hadn't returned just cemented it. Though old, she was still a high-powered mage. The Guild could find a use for her. Of that, Emery was certain.

Still, it didn't quite ring true to me. Everything she'd said to me painted a picture of a more rounded individual than the others in the group. A person on a different path, who had learned from her mistakes. Grown from them. I didn't buy that she'd gone back to the Guild.

But she'd certainly gone somewhere. Her rental was vacated and her phone number disconnected.

It wouldn't be the first time I was wrong.

My mother had been staying with the Bankses for the last week. She'd ordered me to join her and leave Emery behind, and for once in my whole life, I'd told her to shove it.

I had literally said, "No. *Shove it.*"

A very tense thirty seconds of silence had ensued, during which everyone present stared at my mother, waiting to see what would happen. But all I got was a "Good girl." Then, to ruin the moment, "Do not get pregnant or I will kill you. With my bare hands."

"We expect to get a very large apology," I said to her now, finally answering her question about what we should expect. I leaned against the counter. "We will trust in the safety of numbers, and leave the house with no extra holes in our bodies." I watched my mother tap the elegant invitation sitting on the tabletop between the wine glasses.

Darius had invited us to dinner.

Needless to say, I was a little nervous.

"Is that old vamp going to be there?"

I knew my mother was talking about the extreme elder. "Yes. She has fully recovered from her injuries, and from centuries of idle nothingness, from which she is extremely relieved to have woken up."

"You created a monster."

"No, Mother. I *woke up* a monster. There is a difference. And it wasn't my fault. It was Darius's fault, which he fully admits to. Which is why he is inviting us to dinner. And now we've come full circle."

"Don't sass me, missy."

I sipped a glass of wine as movement caught my eye.

Emery filled the archway, clothed in a tailored suit that fit his wide shoulders before reducing down to his trim hips. Smart black dress shoes peeked out from his pressed gray slacks. His hair was done up in a messy style, short on the sides and long on top.

He straightened out his arm and adjusted his cufflink with the other hand, very *GQ*. He might've spent the last several years rolling around in the dirt in various parts of the wild, but when he wanted to, he could really clean up.

My heart fluttered and I shrugged for no particular reason.

"Penny Bristol, you look beautiful," he said, his blue eyes soft.

I felt my face flame (my mother looking on with a hard scowl made things awkward) and I shrugged again, still for no particular reason.

"That Marie has good taste for young women." My mother nodded as her gaze slid down the red silk dress that hugged my slight curves and showed a bit more cleavage than was probably prudent. "Why she was trying to dress me, I have no idea. I don't have anyone to impress. Waste of time, in my opinion."

"You have Marie to impress." I smoothed my shimmery dress down my thighs, suddenly shy and embarrassed and acting stupid. I'd been living with Emery for a week, and usually things were easy between us. He handled my crazy with laughter, and I ignored most everything he did unless it pertained directly to me, because I was used to ignoring my mother. But now, when we were dressed up, and he was looking at me like that, and I was remembering the feel of his hands…

"Emery, how do you plan to earn money?" my mother asked, capable of ruining any moment with gusto.

He sauntered toward me with his confident swagger before reaching around me and into the cabinet. When he reached forward for an empty wine glass, his heat fell across me and I shivered. "I've promised my spell-working services solely to Darius. For now. He pays extremely well."

"What sort of harebrained world traveler promises exclusivity to an elder vampire?" my mother asked.

Emery glanced at me before pouring himself a glass of wine. "A desperate world traveler worried about the woman he was leaving behind."

Warmth filled my heart and a smile played with my lips.

My mother huffed. "Well, now you're at his mercy."

He wrapped his lips around the rim of the wine glass, and a different part of me filled with warmth. After he took a sip, he grinned. "That was before he put her in mortal danger, messed up, and made her fend for herself. For now, it's wise to keep the attachment. He's an elder, yes, but he's the best of the lot. He'll give me plenty of wiggle room. In the future, I have an easy out and plenty of room for bartering."

"Worst case, we'll just sic Darius's girlfriend on

him. She'll be more than happy to ruin his life." I edged my hand along the counter like a high school kid on a first date and bumped it off his hip. I was nearly twenty-five, but I was acting like a besotted teenager.

He wasn't. He slid closer and wrapped his arm around my shoulders.

My mother huffed again.

The doorbell rang.

"Reagan is going to meet us there, correct?" my mother asked for what seemed like the eight hundredth time.

"Yes. And Callie and Dizzy. We have lots of backup, Mother, relax. If that old vampire goes crazy, we'll be fine. Which you know, because your cards told you so."

"Those cards aren't always right, you know that."

"They aren't ever right for me. But if they've ever failed you, you've never mentioned it." Suddenly, all those near misses in Seattle were called into question.

"Come on, love," Emery whispered softly, sliding his hand to my back. "We don't want to keep the vampire waiting."

In other words, he wanted to get away from my mother.

A black limo was waiting outside for us. Beyond it, standing next to the opening of the cemetery, stood Smokey, creepy as ever. He nodded to me as we walked down the stairs.

Next door, No Good Mikey stood near his steps, also watching.

"What's going on?" I asked, slowing.

"Nothin'." Mikey shifted so he was leaning against his banister. "Your mother yelled at Smokey for scaring her earlier. I just came out here to see if she'd do it again. Had him scattering like a flock of birds. Ain't never seen him so spooked."

"I did not yell at that man," my mother said, clunking down the stairs behind us in her old boots. Marie was going to hate them. "I simply stated my observation that men who stand on street corners and gawk at women might someday find themselves castrated and thrown down a well."

"Mother, really?" I pushed Emery to the side and made sure she got down the stairs and moved toward the limo before she came out with something else. "He's not even on a street corner."

"He is standing in front of a cemetery. That is worse than standing on a street corner."

"Then why didn't you say that?"

"Because 'street corner' has a certain ring to it." She nodded at the blank-faced, handsome limo driver who was holding the door for her. "Couldn't send a human? They had to send the enemy?"

Mikey cracked a smile, the first I had ever seen from him. "She's a hoot. She has safe passage in this neighborhood."

"No she doesn't." I pointed at him. "Ban her. Seriously. For your own good."

He laughed this time, and sauntered off in the other direction.

"Why does everyone always laugh at me?" I wondered aloud, climbing into the limo.

Darius's front door was fixed. Upon entering the house next to my hard-faced mother, I saw that his entrance way had also been fixed. They'd done unbelievably quick work.

Fragrant flowers lined the stairs like last time, cut from their living plants and on their way to death's door. They really set the right atmosphere, though I still wasn't sure if he was intentionally going for that.

Moss, acting the part of butler, greeted us formally, wearing a tux, as stiff as ever. "Miss Bristol, Ms. Bristol, Mr. Westbrook." Moss offered a slight bow. Very slight. His face could've cut granite. Reagan must've been harassing him already this evening. "Welcome."

"Vampires really know how to host," my mother murmured as we climbed the stairs. "Too bad a body can't relax in their company."

Both dining room doors stood open, and as we approached, I felt the first wave of intensely spicy power, vicious and lethal and smooth as silk. It was much more powerful than Moss's, and it was basically on display, crowding the room and drifting out to catch anyone passing by.

Ja.

"That's not normal for vampires," I said, slowing. Magic curled between Emery and me, sparking and fizzing and then collecting above me. I'd largely tried to stop doing that, since it made it easy for me to go off the deep end at a moment's notice, but amassing elements was my go-to when I sensed even a little danger. It was a hard habit to break. One I wasn't even sure I *wanted* to break.

"Just a moment," Moss said, entering the room.

"Either the vampire doesn't have control, or she is wondering if you do," Emery whispered, studying me. He couldn't feel her magic, but after a week of hardcore training together, not to mention one occasion in which we'd accidentally gotten sucked into (or possibly started, but I really didn't think it was my fault) a bar fight with a few shifters, he was really good at deciphering my reactions.

He still wasn't super at heading them off, though. Not when Reagan was enabling me, at any rate. Hence the bar fight.

The magic pulsed once, a shock wave that blasted into my core and crawled up my spine, dragging out my survival magic. I wrapped it around myself like armor, strong and hot and ready to do battle.

"Nope. Don't do that," Emery said, using his own survival magic to layer mine, calming me down.

It was another thing we'd been practicing: how to use our survival magic in new ways, often together.

"She has to be baiting you," Emery said in a low whisper, making sure the vampires, with their excellent hearing, couldn't catch his words. "Don't give her a reason to react."

"Forcing Penny to take the high road, is that it?" My mother asked, not at all worried about vampires overhearing. That, and she lacked volume control at the best of times. "Weak, that. Very weak."

Moss appeared in the doorway with thinned lips and wary eyes. His bow was furrowed a little deeper, his posture a little stiffer.

Maybe it wasn't Reagan who would cause problems for us tonight.

"Please." Moss held out his hand for us to enter.

"I still think this is a terrible idea," my mother said. "In fact, I ate at a fabulous place in the Garden District the other day. Let's go there. I made friends with the barman. I'm sure we could get a seat."

"Come on, Mother," I said through clenched teeth, *this close* to taking her up on it.

Emery stepped aside so my mother and I could enter first. The table was set with delicate china and crystal. Candles flickered in gilded candleholders down the center of the table and along the walls, a serious fire hazard that probably didn't matter, given that Reagan was on scene.

Darius and Reagan stood from their chairs on one side of the table. The three empty chairs next to them had presumably been left for us. The Bankses sat on the other side, with Marie next to them, and the final member of the group—a familiar woman with a beautiful face, slight frame, dark tan skin, and liquid black, wide-spaced, beguiling eyes that held the wisdom of centuries—sat the farthest from the door, directly across from Darius's seat.

Those dark eyes sparkled as they beheld me, and a tiny pulse of her viciously entrancing magic pushed against my heart, letting me know she was completely in control…and she knew that I was not.

"Hello, everyone," Reagan said with a serene smile, wearing a striking deep blue dress that plunged down her chest and flowed around her legs. She took Darius's hand as they made their way to us, playing the part of host perfectly and surprising the heck out of me.

Darius wore a tux, perfectly molded to his muscular body and probably as expensive as the GDP of a small country. When they stopped in front of us, he bowed deeply. "Thank you for joining us."

"Thank you for having us," Emery said, sticking out his hand to shake Darius's.

We took our seats, the chairs held out by vampire servers who showed up at the exact right moment. After they poured our wine, they zipped out again, faster than a human, but not so fast that it looked strange.

"That dress looks lovely," Marie said to me with a gorgeous smile, her curves showcased in a purple and black lace dress that really got the heart pumping—and I wasn't even into that sort of thing. "And Ms. Bristol, what a lovely…ensemble."

My mother nodded and reached for her wine. "Thank you. It was one of the few I packed, just in case."

Marie's smile tightened, and I knew she was annoyed my mother hadn't accepted her help with fashion.

"Hello," Dizzy said, beaming. Callie nodded in hello as well.

"May I introduce Ja." Darius motioned to the extreme elder before holding the chair for Reagan to sit. "Ja, please meet Penny, Emery, and Penny's mother, Karen."

"Is it Penny, or Penelope?" Ja asked, her voice deep and sultry.

"My real name is Penelope, but people call me Penny," I said, taking the seat next to Reagan that Emery held out for me.

"Penelope suits her better," Marie said.

"It does." Ja nodded minutely. "I shall use that. It is

good to see you again, Penelope. I owe you a debt."

"No," my mother said. She made a slash across her neck as Callie and Dizzy shook their heads. "You don't."

"You do not," Callie mimicked. When the two agreed, people tended to just get out of the way. When they didn't…well, the cops had been called a few times from neighbors worried about domestic violence.

Ja's eyes sparkled, still on mine. "They are wise, not wanting you to have a connection with a vampire." Her gaze slowly made its way to Darius. "I would press the point, but doing so would impose on the merriment of the gathering."

"You are free to speak your mind, I am sure," he said. "They will let you know when they no longer welcome a particular topic." He glanced down at us, and Reagan reached over and took his hand, twining her fingers in his.

In that moment, I saw it. His eyes flicked to her and softened, the deep light of emotion shining within them. A small smile curved her lips. While she always tried to make his life hell, and he tried to manipulate hers, they were doing it out of mutual adoration.

Their relationship was still weird. Strong and deep, sure, but still weird.

"Yes." Ja smiled and followed my eyes, her gaze flicking back and forth between Reagan and Darius. "Quite a surprise, isn't it? An elder with emotion. I would not have believed it if I hadn't witnessed it myself."

"I can scarcely believe it myself, I can assure you." He bowed his head a mere fraction. "As we've discussed."

"Of course." She refocused on me, and I got the impression something had just passed between them in a subtle exchange I'd probably never understand. "Penelope, I would like to apologize for our meeting. I was not in a place to appreciate it. It took me by surprise, I must admit."

"She is truly exceptional, is she not?" Darius asked.

"Truly. One of only a handful I have met throughout my many long years to capture my notice. Capable of great things. And discovered by…"

"Reagan," Darius said.

"I found her in a closet." Reagan took a sip of her wine as servers filed in with the soup course. "She's mine."

I frowned at them and opened my mouth to interject, but Marie flashed me a hard stare and Callie lightly shook her head. Emery took my hand, and I could tell something was at work that I didn't understand.

As usual. I'd be surprised the day I *did* understand everything.

"And Emery," Marie said softly. "It was he who showed her the way, isn't that right, Penelope?"

Callie huffed. I didn't need to ask why—she'd wanted to be the one to take that mantle.

"He was the first to show me what it was to be a mage, yes," I said. "Then Callie and Dizzy showed me what it was to be part of a community."

The dual-mages beamed, and I felt my heart squish. It was true, and I would always value everything they had done for me.

But it was Emery's turn to feel the force of Ja's beguiling stare. Heat kindled deep in her dark eyes. "A handsome young natural. And your choice is made, I see."

"Yes." He squeezed my hand as Reagan bristled. She was still hell-bent on beating people away from Emery for me. Even a passing glance from another woman was enough to set her off. Where was she when I got hit on, though? Laughing and nudging Emery to start a fight, that was where.

"Pity." Ja's smile said she was joking. Or maybe hungry. It was hard to tell. "I sense a natural pairing. How extremely rare. My goodness. If only I had been awake to have discovered you two. The things we could do." She dipped her head and smiled coyly, and I realized I was staring at her in rapture, hanging on her every word. It wasn't even that interesting, what she was saying, but her musical voice lulled me. That was probably part of her magic. She was even more wily and dangerous than Darius. "Forgive me, please," she continued. "How crass of me."

"I'll say," Reagan said in a dry voice, and Dizzy started chuckling.

"Well, Penelope," Ja said, "you have my eternal gratitude. Based on what I have gleaned, we are heading into some turbulent times." Her gaze rooted to Reagan. "This happens in cycles, of course. Powers awaken, or are found…" Reagan's eyes started to burn now, but Ja just smiled. "Stands are made. Agendas pushed. Kingdoms toppled. Darius is amassing some serious players in anticipation of what's to come, as any well-positioned elder ought to. I am late to the game."

A wave of vertigo swept over me and I felt Reagan and Emery stiffen. *Kingdoms toppled.* My mother looked more closely at Ja, then at Darius, her wheels turning.

"I am not interested in the politics of the Realm just yet," Darius said, dipping his spoon elegantly into his soup. I looked down at my own dripping spoon before accidentally clattering it against the bowl.

"I was not talking about the Realm." Ja's eyes sparked, and a pulse of her ancient power cut through my middle.

A blast of magic welled up, filling the room. Hot and cold and climbing the walls…

Reagan was responding to Ja's insinuation, and it

was inviting me to respond with it.

I squeezed Emery's hand as my power surged, out of my control.

"Penelope," Ja said, her face turning away from Reagan's heated gaze. Her magic was torn away, leaving a strange absence. She was intentionally kicking the hornets' nest, that was clear. "I am in your debt, bound by honor. Should you ever need assistance, I am at your disposal. You need but ask."

Callie, Dizzy, and my mother all started shaking their heads. Ja pretended not to notice.

"Now." The extremely old vampire stood, and Darius stood with her. "Darius, thank you for allowing me to intrude on your hospitality. I will leave you. I must reestablish myself within the Lair. I do hope you can understand."

"Of course." Darius bowed.

"Goodbye." She smiled at everyone, but it seemed like it was just for me. Based on Dizzy's preening, however, he clearly thought she had reserved her notice just for him. Everyone probably had the same impression. "It was lovely meeting you all. I'm sure I will see you again."

With that, Ja glided from the room, leaving silence in her wake.

"Stay the hell away from that vampire, Penny," Reagan said. "Far away. She is…something."

"She is a serious power player," Darius said softly, looking after her. "I am owed a debt as well. It is a priceless commodity, I have no doubt." He fell silent for a moment.

"Am I in danger?" I asked.

"No," Darius said. "Not even remotely. You will be forgotten for a time while she reestablishes herself in our hierarchy."

"You won't be," Reagan said to Darius, squeezing his hand tight.

"She will change things, yes. But this won't be the first time our carefully balanced hierarchy has been in turmoil." He leaned forward, and the pressure on the room released. His smile put stars in my mother's eyes before she remembered herself and turned it into a frown. "So, Penny, Emery. I hear you have not yet become a dual-mage pair, yet there is a definite magical balance between you two. I must look into this idea of a natural pairing. I have not heard of it."

"Neither have I," Emery said.

"It's pleasing," Reagan said, "the feel of their magic. Potent and powerful, but in an inviting way."

"Yes." Darius nodded and dabbed at his mouth.

"To be a dual-mage pair, you need to pledge your lives to each other," Callie said, her tone even.

"And you're too young to be doing that," my mother said.

"We were their age, hon." Dizzy looked around at the other bowls, clearly wanting more soup.

"They barely know each other," my mother said.

"Wow. This is seriously awkward." Reagan grinned.

Emery's jaw was clenched and his eyes haunted. And in that moment, I knew—he was fighting the pain from the demise of his brother. In his mind, becoming a dual-mage pair with me would mean replacing what he'd lost, admitting that his brother was gone forever.

He wasn't ready to let go.

I squeezed his hand in support. Time would tell. If it was meant to be, it would be. In the meantime, we had a lot ahead of us.

We needed to take on the Mages' Guild. And this time, we needed to stop them for good.

Made in the USA
Coppell, TX
08 November 2021